The music of desire...

Trent watched Amy's fingers on the keys of the pianoforte. He had heard this piece before, but it had never sounded like this, as though the pianist were giving everything to the music. Each touch, each note said "love." That was absurd. His ward could have no notion of love any more than he could. True love was a myth.

Amy opened her eyes and looked at the keys. She knew that she dared not lift her eyes to glance at Trent. One disapproving look from him and she would stumble. With each touch of her fingers on the keys she imagined herself touching Trent, the nape of his neck, that unruly hair. She wondered what it would be like to kiss him. She had seen couples kissing, and knew there was some importance to it, but they always looked so hungry, it seemed ridiculous. *Somehow,* she thought, *it would work well with Trent. He would know exactly what to do.*

After the Beethoven sonata, she moved on to some Mozart and could hardly keep her mind on the piece. She wondered what it would be like to live with Trent, to taunt him every day in a playful way, to have him finally figure out that she was teasing him. She smiled with satisfaction as she contemplated his eventual realization, that confident smile of his and what form his revenge might take. She pictured his hands about her waist, his arms holding her, his lips pressed to hers. But here she faltered and almost missed a note.

Books by Barbara Miller

Dearest Max
My Phillipe
The Guardian

Published by POCKET BOOKS

THE GUARDIAN

BARBARA MILLER

SONNET BOOKS
New York London Toronto Sydney Singapore

An *Original* Publication of POCKET BOOKS

A Sonnet Book published by
POCKET BOOKS, a division of Simon & Schuster, Inc.
1230 Avenue of the Americas, New York, NY 10020

Copyright © 2001 by Barbara Miller

ISBN: 0-7434-1229-X

First Sonnet Books printing August 2001

10 9 8 7 6 5 4 3 2 1

SONNET BOOKS and colophon are trademarks of Simon & Schuster, Inc.

Front cover illustration by Gregg Gulbronson

Printed in the U.S.A.

for my editor, Caroline Tolley,
whose insightful questions and advice
turn ordinary men into heroes

THE
GUARDIAN

1

❧

Berkshire, England
March 1816

"**D**amnation!" Amy shouted as she crumpled the letter and threw it across the library. The kitchen cat jumped up and shot out of the room as though she had lobbed a rock at it. Lively, the black-and-white spaniel raised its head and whined.

"Of all the stupid men in the world," she said to the dog, "Trent Severn has to be the most dense." Amy got up from the desk and retrieved the letter from near the hearth where a cozy fire burned. "Thankfully, I will have to put up with his interference only another three months."

She sat in one of the pair of wing chairs handy to the fire and pressed the paper flat in her lap, noticing a grass stain on her gray muslin frock. The dog got up and came to lean against the chair, and Amy automatically stroked its head. She glanced up as the setting sun slanted its last fiery rays through the big window that looked out over the stable yard and horse pastures. The mares and foals had all been brought in for the night and Tartar, the old stallion, let out to exercise in their pasture.

She owned Talltrees, a stud farm beginning to make a name for itself because of the quality of its horses, and she was not going to be able to purchase the younger stallion that she so desperately needed. As she bent to read, the sun mocked her with one last beam catching and lighting fire to one of her auburn locks that had escaped the untidy knot at her neck. She tossed the coil of hair back over her shoulder impatiently as she read through the letter again for any crumb of hope it might contain.

> *Miss Amy Conde,*
>
> *Your request for an advance on your allowance for the purpose of buying another horse is inappropriate. You should ride the horses on the estate.*
>
> *Any future correspondence about the estate should be referred to Mr. Fenwick, my agent in Berkshire.*
>
> *As Ever,*
> *Trent Severn*

As Ever, Trent . . . Stupid As Ever Trent. If what she suspected was true, Fenwick was robbing her estate. She had written to Trent about it, but since she did not know what figures Fenwick reported to Trent she could prove nothing. And Severn only replied that it was not her concern. Her guardian was too dense to realize she was being robbed, too stupid to listen to a woman. Much good it would do her to send her letters of complaint about Fenwick to Fenwick himself. When she turned twenty-five in June, Talltrees would be hers absolutely and Trent Severn could no longer throw these obstacles in her way. She wondered what *As Ever Trent* would say when he discovered she had made a success of the stud farm. He probably never bothered to check the books himself.

But writing to him was clearly as fruitless as it had always been. She wondered what he was like and pictured the dark, somber boy who had attended her father's funeral fifteen years before having turned into a mirthless, spectacled lawyer. Was he in law or did he just run the law office? And did he run the shipping business where their fathers had also been partners, and the foundry? She would have thought him very stuffy, but that was not what the London newspapers said of him. One affair after another was reported in the gossip columns, and with his own clients. Amy slumped in the chair.

Perhaps she should be glad *As Ever Trent* had never come to Talltrees while she was home, and glad also that he left her to her own devices as much as he had all these years. Beyond sending Fenwick for the books each quarter and sending her a draft for her allowance, she had no contact with him other than what she initiated, and she could see that was useless. Most likely the man would not know a stallion from a hobbyhorse.

She went back toward the large desk where she was copying over her ledgers for the quarter. Fenwick would be coming soon and he never returned the small notebooks of income and expenses she handed over to him. So she always made a copy for herself. And she could make the income and expenses cancel each other out almost to the penny, so as not to put any more cash into the man's hands. Firing him in three months' time would be one of the greatest pleasures of her life.

She was contemplating just what she would say when she discharged Fenwick, as Minton brought in her dinner tray with that perpetual curl of disapproval to his lip. But she saw no point in eating in solitary state in the dining room. That would only remind her that she was alone. She had not, in fact, taken a meal there since her elderly aunt had died two years before. She preferred to eat in the library surrounded by the studbook and breeding charts, her books and journals, and with Lively lounging on the hearth. Of that, too, Minton disapproved.

As she ate she brooded on Trent's neglect of her estate and his failure in her eyes to act as a proper guardian. When she had completed all her entries she got out the breeding charts, trying to figure out a program for this year, when the current stallion was related to half the mares on the place. If she could not get a new stud she would have to sell some mares, and since she could not get a good price locally, that might mean a trip to London or York. Lord Covington had a young stud he wanted to sell, but she could not meet his price, so the animal would go to the York sales this week. But she wasn't even sure she liked the look of the beast. If she had to go to London or York anyway to sell mares, it would be far better to make that trip to buy a stallion and bring new blood into the line. She had to do something soon if she meant to breed the mares this spring. As it stood she was going to lose a whole year. She pushed the papers away impatiently. Running Talltrees would be a joy if only she were not doing it on a shoestring. Sometimes she felt like giving up, but that would mean selling all the stock and putting men out of work. Once it had been set in motion and she had taken control of it, she could not end the business, could not bear to admit defeat and quit. There must be a quick way to sell some colts.

A rattle of wheels on the drive roused her to walk to the window. But it was nearly dark now and she could not imagine who would be arriving at this hour. Fenwick came in daylight even on those occasions when he had pressed his unwanted marriage proposals on her. If this was Fenwick she would know how to deal with him.

Amy resisted the urge to go to the front door, but walked to the mirror over the mantel to practice her most menacing gaze, the one that sent the stable lads hopping about their duties.

After a few minutes she heard the scuff of booted feet in the hallway and the solemn tones of the butler, then a low, slurred and careless voice—not Fenwick's nasal whine.

"Oh, is she still up? Damn! I had rather not see her," the man said in the hall without regard to the possibility of her hearing him. More snatches came to her. "Don't disturb her. Only mean t' stay the night. On my way to Portsmouth."

Amy jumped when she remembered that Portsmouth was where Trent's ships docked and that he had a house there. She flushed with anger and took a step toward the door but stopped herself. She did not suffer fools patiently and had been known to demolish a man with a sentence. If she lost her temper with Severn . . . but this was an opportunity to confront him that she might not have again. When it sounded as though he meant to go on upstairs without so much as greeting her, she went to the library door and yanked it open.

Minton jerked guiltily, and the man who was carefully removing his driving gloves cocked his head at her as though to see her better.

"Please come in . . . Trent," she said in her sternest voice. When she turned and walked toward the fireplace she wondered why she had called him Trent. Perhaps it had been the confused look he had given her, or that he had not looked nearly as old as she had expected him to. There was, after all, only five years between them. It was the worst of bad luck that both partners in Severn and Conde had died, leaving Trent in charge of her affairs until she turned twenty-five. Trent and Amy were not related, the closest tie being that Trent's parents had been her godparents, a connection his mother ignored except when she wanted to be annoying.

Amy tried to be displeased with Trent, but the man who confronted her was neither humorless nor spectacled; he was quite handsome and he had a teasing set to his mouth.

"Amy Conde?" Trent asked as he swayed against a chair and tried to focus his green eyes on her. She remembered those eyes. The color had made him seem cold and distant that last time she had seen him, at her father's funeral. But just now they made him look vulnerable, as though he were in pain. His short black hair was wind-whipped and his face looked weary as though he had come a long way.

"Must apol'gize," he said as he blundered toward her. "Got a trifle foxed en route, 'm afraid." He reached for Amy's hand and missed. She held it out to him and it seemed to stabilize him, for he was able to bring it to his lips and stare up at her as though he could not quite believe what he was seeing.

Amy gazed at him in wide-eyed amazement, for the brandy fumes emanating from Trent indicated he was quite drunk. "Perhaps you should sit down," she suggested.

She had to move quickly to rescue a vase on the small table he bumped as he lounged into one of the chairs by the fire. She placed the vase on the desk and said, "Would you like some coffee . . . Trent?"

"Coffee?" he mumbled, noticing the dog and holding out his hand to it.

Amy nodded at Minton and he went out, leaving the door scrupulously open.

Amy watched Lively grovel toward Trent, wagging her tail as though he were her long-lost master. She shook her head at the weakness of some females.

He twisted in the chair to stare at her, but the rapid movement must have upset his equilibrium, for he held a hand to his forehead as though trying to steady himself. When he focused his eyes on her again, she gave him that stern glare she had been preparing. If Trent Severn made a habit of getting dead drunk, possibly he was mishandling her affairs as badly as Fenwick. But in his weakened condition she might be able to push forward her case for the advance on her allowance.

A spate of throat-clearing at the door was followed by the reappearance of Minton. "Cook is brewing some coffee and tea, sir, and warming some dinner for you."

Trent stared at the man as though he had sprung from the woodwork.

Minton hesitated. "If you would wish to retire to the dining room . . ." Minton took two steps toward the open door, like an eager puppy, trying to hint his master into a walk.

"Dinner is the last thing I want," Trent said, straightening himself in the chair.

"Perhaps Miss Conde would like her dinner then," Minton insisted.

Amy recognized this as her cue. She was being rescued and ordinarily she would have swept out of the room, but since Trent was perhaps not thinking quite as clearly as he normally did, she decided to dig in her heels and press her suit about the money.

"Have you forgotten? I already dined, Minton," she said, glancing at the tray of dishes and giving her voice a definite tone of dismissal.

"Yes, miss," he replied as he rolled his eyes at her and walked out, carefully leaving the door ajar.

Amy almost immediately regretted her decision, for Trent was looking her over in a very disturbing way as she stood clutching her hands in front of her, trying to cover the grass stain on her dress.

Trent squeezed his eyes shut, then squinted to focus on her. "You have grown." He directed his bleary gaze toward the fire then and used one thumb and forefinger to massage his temples.

"It has been fifteen years since you last saw me. Of course I have grown up. I am almost twenty-five and your guardianship of me is nearly at an end."

Trent reached down to pet the dog again and Amy began to suspect that he was not listening to her. She retreated behind the desk and sat down. Vacantly she wondered if Trent would even remember any promise he might make while in such a condition, but she had to try. "In consideration of that, might you think again about my request for a loan for the new stallion?"

"What?" He sat up and stared at her, bringing his booted feet to rest on the floor as though he meant to get up.

This time she felt a flush creep into her cheeks. Why should she be embarrassed? Trent was the one who was drunk. "I wrote asking for an advance on my allowance so that I might buy a new stud."

"But you are a young lady. Why do you have to concern yourself with stallions?"

"I have been running the breeding program here since I was seventeen."

"That cannot be," he insisted, scrambling out of the chair and leaning on it again as he regarded her. "There is a head groom here. Masters. I was sure he was in charge of the horses."

"I assure you I am old enough to manage Talltrees. But it is imperative that I get the new stallion immediately. Otherwise I lose a whole year of breeding."

"An advance on your allowance? But do you know what such horses cost?" Trent asked, making his way to the window and leaning his head on one of the cool panes of glass.

"Of course I know," she snapped. "I am painfully aware of what everything costs, down to the last oat."

Trent turned to stare at her. "So, you've a temper to match that hair."

Minton wheeled in a tray with cups and saucers, and both a coffeepot and a teapot on it. Amy got up and poured a cup of strong coffee for Trent, stirring in a great dollop of cream. "Drink this. You will feel better."

"Somehow, I doubt it," he said as he took the cup and downed a swallow of it.

Minton offered a plate of cake and got a blank look for his pains, so he retreated again.

"My hair is not red." She pulled one of the locks around to regard it in the firelight. "It is auburn."

Trent looked up at this and gave her a weak smile. "Perhaps it is not as carroty as before, but I am afraid it would still be described as red in London."

"What does it matter what color my hair is? No one ever sees me. I am alone here and I like it that way."

Trent stared at her in disbelief. "Don't ever say you like being alone," he replied harshly. "For one day you may wake up and find that you are, indeed, alone." He looked out the dark window again.

Amy stared at him, unable to fathom what he was talking about. "It is not my fault I am alone," she replied truthfully, wondering if Trent were talking about her loneliness or his.

"Must you shout?" Trent asked in a strangled voice.

"But you are expressly trying to provoke me. You are just as maddening in person as you are in your letters, *As Ever Trent*."

"What did you call me?" He stared at her as though she had sworn at him.

Amy unfolded the crumpled letter and held it out to him. "You always sign yourself *As Ever*. See?"

Trent looked at the paper as though he had never seen it before. "As Ever, Trent?"

Amy had a sudden glimpse of a different man than the cold and menacing rake she had been prepared to meet. This one was tired, lonely, and in pain.

"I do sign my name that way now and again. I have never had anyone take exception to it before."

"I take exception to your ignorance of my affairs. Hopefully that will be the last such letter I get from you."

"Oh, I did not write this. Lester must have answered for me." He tossed the paper back onto the desk.

"Your secretary?" she asked. "So he is the one who has been saying no to me all these years?"

"The ever reliable Mr. Lester. He usually does consult with me."

"Oh, so you did say no but could not be bothered to do it yourself. Why did you even stop here? Was it just to annoy me?"

"I left town late, too late to get to Portsmouth. I just need to rest my horses overnight."

He finished the coffee and poured another cup for himself with studied care. This he sipped black. "I shall be gone in the morning," he said slowly as though he were counting each word. "I just forgot how old you are. I didn't even think I would see you. Last time I happened to arrive for an overnight stay your dragon of an aunt would not even let me set foot in the house. Where is she, by the way?"

She stared at him for a moment, then looked down at her paperwork. He could not have said a more hurtful thing if he had tried. But he was not trying to hurt her. Her aunt had said that when a man was drunk he said exactly what he thought. She mattered so little to Trent that he had forgotten all about her. "My aunt died two years ago," Amy said quietly.

"She died?" Trent stared at her in shock. "Why did no one tell me?" He put the cup down and staggered back to the chair to sit and lean his head back.

Amy shook her head. "I wrote to you. Have you no memory of it?"

"No. Someone should have informed me you were without a relative here."

"But I am quite well able to take care of myself."

He glanced up at her, his brows furrowed over those troubled green eyes. "Perhaps Lester did say something at the time," Trent conceded. "Was it the beginning of March, 1814?"

"Yes, but what has that to do with anything?"

"Just after the Battle of Orthez. I remember now. I wasn't in the country. I meant to come. I hope Mother took care of everything. Who is here with you now? Your governess?"

"I have not needed a governess for many years."

"But you should not be living here alone, unprotected."

His concern seemed so genuine, if belated, that Amy hastened to say, "I am not without protection. I have a cook and a butler. And I imagine even now she and Minton are hatching some plan to rescue me from your clutches."

"Clutches?" Trent asked in confusion.

Just then Minton came to the open door to fetch away the tea cart and her supper tray. He busied himself tending the fire, then came and asked if she were not tired.

"Tired?" Amy repeated. She considered teasing Minton a little longer, but his haggard old face held true concern. "Yes, I think I shall go to my room now." She handed her cup and saucer to Minton as she gathered up her books and papers.

Trent left off watching Minton tidy the tea cart. "Wait, explain what you meant by—"

She turned in the doorway. "Perhaps tomorrow, Trent, when you are more capable of understanding an explanation."

"More capable?" he asked of the closed door. But she was gone. Trent felt somehow that he had lost a match, but he could not exactly grasp how, or even what had been at stake. He only knew the room was less interesting without Amy in it, which was an odd observation for him to make, drunk or sober. He had still been thinking her a child, had assumed she would be in bed when he arrived at Talltrees, if he thought about her at all. Lester did frequently bother him with some missive from Amy, but how could so much time have passed without him realizing Amy Conde was now very much a woman? Perhaps she possessed even more poise than most women had. There was something else. Oh, her bosom had developed, though she was still very thin for her height. Not a scarecrow by any means, but . . . He stopped himself from further evaluating her in this way. She was not some society miss to be stared at and wagered about. She was the child her father had entrusted to his care. Not his care, but his parents, her godparents. And he was responsible for her now.

"But when did all this happen?" he asked the dog. The creature sighed and rolled over at his feet. As Trent reached down to scratch her he tried to remember the last time he had been at Talltrees. That had been last year to look for horses for the desperate Belgium campaign, and the pickings had been slim. Amy had not been home then, but off visiting a neighbor. He had been so preoccupied with supplying the army with cannon and shot for the war in the Peninsula and then Belgium that he had only bothered with Talltrees when his friend Draco Melling needed horses, and usually he sent the grooms for those. Draco was in the 1st Royal Dragoons and, since he was a big man, favored the sturdy stock from Talltrees.

Thoughts of Draco reminded him of their first encounter at Cambridge when Draco had sided with him in a fight with half a dozen upperclassmen. How had so much time passed? The answer was simple. They had been at war for nearly a decade and he should not have assumed the rest of the world would stand still while he did his part shipping cannon, uniforms and food to the troops. And here Amy was, adult enough to rip up at him for his forgetfulness. The next thing he knew she would be blaming him for her being left alone.

His disordered mind tripped over the last time a woman had taken him to task—his recent rejection by Draco's sister Diana—and he realized that he would never be able to visit the Mellings again, not without a great deal of awkwardness. He had known Diana forever, had felt it was time he married, and she had been flirting with him for years. But clearly he should have made sure Diana was in accord before plunging ahead, for her refusal had been passionate. He pictured Diana's dark hair and eyes, so like Draco's and her mother's.

Lady Melling had often stood in Trent's estimation as the ideal mother. He had worshiped her as a boy, but here was the upshot. He had assumed that the daughter would be as agreeable, as patient and as kind, that she would age into the same comfortable sort of woman that her mother was. It just showed the imprudence of trying to marry into a family, rather than focusing on the woman herself. All Diana's childhood tantrums now came back to Trent with vivid clarity. She had gotten over none of her foibles while he and Draco had been growing up at school together and had not lost her selfishness while Draco suffered the privations of the army.

Trent had left London directly after her passionate refusal, not taking time to even pack a bag. After several
hours' drinking at an inn near Guildford he had decided
that he had made a complete fool of himself. And he was
still alone.

Diana Melling. Trent tried to picture her glorious dark
hair and flashing brown eyes, but a red-haired chit with a
punishing glare kept intruding on his mind. Now who?
Oh, yes, Amy. The girl suddenly grown to womanhood.

And it *was* his fault she had grown up alone. Some-
time in the last fifteen years he should have found an hour
to arrange for her to have some company. A lively girl
like Amy needed a companion, or better yet, a husband.

He leaned his aching head back and closed his eyes,
trying to make himself realize that the little girl he remembered sniffing back her tears by her father's grave
was now a woman. It made him feel damned old. He supposed he would have to set matters right here before he
could continue to Portsmouth. Otherwise his conscience
would never let him rest.

2

He dreamed of death, cold and white, with snow falling on a coffin, and an open grave. He saw a red-haired girl in a thin black pelisse, trying not to weep for fear her tears would freeze. He saw himself standing apart from his parents. He was cold, but not letting it show, the way he had never let anything show. With their constant arguing they had made him miserable, but he was too proud to let them know.

He looked across the grave at the girl and knew the foreign impulse to go to her and put an arm about her. He who had never been hugged, and never known any sign of affection from his mother. But he did not know how to go about it, so he stayed where he was.

Amy's father dead, and his to follow in eight years, crushed by one of his own cannon as it fell from the winch at the foundry. Trent had been the one to find him, alive still, but pinned and dying by inches. He had been trying to talk, to tell Trent something. But it made no sense. A warning to be careful of *her son*, he had said over and over. His dying father had not even recognized him, had regarded him always as his wife's son. And at

the end he had the distinct feeling that his father had
thought he had loosed the cannon. Trent could almost feel
the weight on his own legs. He tried to move, could not,
and sat bolt upright with a groan that frightened the dog
off the bed.

Trent fell back in a cold sweat, but when Lively came
to lick his hand he caressed her ears. He was always good
with animals because they never rejected you—they were
more honest than people. They never betrayed, never lied,
never talked about you behind your back. And most of all
they never argued with you like a red-haired termagant.

The aroma of coffee pulled Trent out of bed. He found
hot water for shaving, an unfamiliar razor and shaving
brush, and a cup of coffee left for him by someone who
must be very soft-footed. His own valet would have
dashed the draperies open to awaken him.

As he sipped the coffee his stomach protested with a
lurch and a growl. He realized he had not eaten since
breakfast the day before. He also remembered, as he
poured hot water into the washbasin and looked at himself in the mirror, that he could not drink brandy. But yesterday he had not much cared what happened to him.
Fortunately he'd had his groom, Jessup, with him to drive
the team when he was no longer able.

As he washed and shaved he wondered why his
mother had not supplied Amy with a suitable companion.
She had designated herself in charge of Amy's education
and had found her a governess. It seemed a sad lapse on
her part to leave the girl alone here for two years. But perhaps she visited often enough to assure herself of Amy's
well-being. Certainly his mother traveled from her house
in Bath to London often enough. He had never found time
to think of it before but the girl should have been presented at court, had a regular come-out. His hand hesi-

tated as he took the last swipe of whiskers and lather away. No need to ask his mother why that had not happened. His reputation must have been the bar to that. Launch an innocent girl into society from Severn House, where he had kept a mistress?

He splashed the lukewarm water on his face, trying to obliterate the guilt that rode his brow. But when he looked into the mirror, it was still there. Now that the war was over, now that he was no longer essential to the supply chain that had contributed so much to vanquishing Napoleon, what was he good for?

He stared at himself for a moment, and taken by surprise, he realized he did not look like anyone he knew. He would in fact pass such a fellow on the street, putting him down as a young jackanapes, ripe for trouble. He did not look like the hardened rake society had branded him since his youth, nor an arms dealer, or even a man of the law. He was a man without a mission. He had work to do, to be sure, legal and investment matters to attend to, but what was the point of it all?

Now that Napoleon had been defeated and the war was finally over, he had nothing of real importance to do, except perhaps make up for lost time by making proper provisions for Amy. God, what she must think of him! He had been almost incoherent last night. And his denseness had provoked her into revealing that she was a spirited young woman with a competence for running a business and considerable strength of will. He was not sure how to make it up to her or how to face her except to offer his belated help. And an apology. He did owe her that.

He plunged his face into the warm water, then dried it. If Amy was fifteen years older, then so was he. Thirty now, and with a reputation that kept decent women at arm's length. That had been Diana's reason for refusing his marriage proposal, that no decent woman would have such a man. How had she put it? No fortune, however large, could compensate for having to endure the stares of the ton. And she had no doubt he would continue his profligate ways after they were married.

He put on his wrinkled shirt from the previous day and was just wondering if he could do anything with his crushed neckcloth when the scream of a stallion rent the air, immediately followed by the angry voice of Amy Conde. *Oh, no, what now?*

He threw up the window and poked his head out in time to see two grooms, each wrestling with a lead line as a lathered stallion between them tried to escape their control. Amy dashed out of a barn and toward the flailing front hooves to snatch at the halter. She was going to get herself killed. He bolted from the room and raced down the stairs. By the time he got to the stable yard he saw only the rump of the horse disappear into the open door of the breeding barn. No sign of Amy's crumpled body. He crossed the intervening lawn and cobbled yard at a dead run to discover the girl standing alone with the stallion's rope as she led him up to a tethered mare.

"Are you insane?" he demanded, more of the half-dozen grooms in the barn than of the girl. He leaped in front of the horse, pushed Amy aside and grabbed the animal's halter. It reared with an angry bellow, lashing out with a front hoof that shredded his shirt to the waist. The horse lifted him off his feet and tossed him aside as though he weighed nothing.

Trent crashed into a post with his shoulder and could not suppress a grunt of pain. To his amazement Amy was back on her feet shouting at the pawing stallion in a hard low voice at odd variance with her size or strength. She stamped her foot at the horse and the beast actually flinched.

"Now see what you have done with your impatience, Tartar. Settle down and focus on that mare. That is your job."

Trent struggled to his feet with the help of Masters, the head groom. He was ready to leap back between the horse and Amy, for she had hold of the lead rope again, but Masters held him back, and the stallion dipped his head and snorted. The beast shook himself, then lifted his nose and curled his lip, trying to scent the mare. Apparently she was in season, for his shaft descended rapidly. Under Amy's guidance and with her urging the stallion came up over the back of the mare and found his mark with absolute surety.

The mare turned her tail out of the way and whinnied a little as Tartar braced himself with a foreleg on each side of her, his teeth clutching her mane for stability. It was an amazing sight and it was over in less than a minute. Trent was so impressed that he did not think to protest that Amy was not only a witness but a participant, perhaps even the instigator of the process. The stallion backed off, still sweating.

"See," Amy said to the horse as she patted his neck and slipped a bite of carrot into his mouth. "Good boy. You need not have made such a fuss." She turned to Masters. "He'll be fine now. Have them cool him well."

The sight of his ward giving the stallion a treat as a reward for performing sexually was bizarre and shocking, but it was also funny. Trent turned to Masters with a limp smile. "Am I to understand that this is a normal morning event at Talltrees?"

"Well, sir, this is a breeding farm," the middle-aged groom said with a grin.

"It is easier for me to handle Tartar than any of the lads," Amy said, walking up to Trent.

"How could that be? You are so light."

"The same reason Lively fawns at your feet. We are of opposite sexes. Do you know you are bleeding?"

"What?" Trent followed the stare she was directing at his chest to discover the horse had scraped him down his ribs. "That is nothing." He pulled the tatters of his shirt over his bare chest as he began to walk back toward the house, strangely reluctant to let her see the wound.

"But it should be dressed," Amy insisted from his elbow. "A horses' feet are not clean."

"Do you realize you could have been killed?" he asked.

"Certainly not. Tartar would never hurt me."

Trent had gained the terrace by the back door. "Perhaps not intentionally, but if none of the grooms can handle him he is not safe. You will not always be around to control him."

"It is not his fault he sometimes has trouble performing," Amy insisted. "He is getting on in years. Now come down to the kitchen and let Cook see to your wound."

For some reason Trent did not resist her hands tugging on his arm as she led him the few steps down into Cook's sanctuary.

"Bandages, Mrs. Harris, and some of your own salve," Amy ordered. "Oh, Minton, can you lend Trent a shirt?"

"You've let Tartar get at him," Minton concluded as he went up the back stairs.

Mrs. Harris merely clucked her distress as she pulled a small jar off a kitchen shelf and bent over him like a mother hen. Trent could not understand why he was letting Amy gently work his shirt off. She should not see him half naked. But he felt as though he had been plunged into a household where all the rules were different and nothing he knew was of any use at all.

"So Tartar has injured someone before?" he asked before his breath hissed in at the touch of the cold salve on the inflamed scrape.

"He stepped on Masters's foot and broke it, but it was not the horse's fault," Amy said. "Tartar gets frustrated when he is incapable. And I did ask you for a younger stallion."

Trent stared at her but said nothing more as Mrs. Harris produced some clean linen and proceeded to bind up the wound.

"So that is your wound from the duel?" Amy said.

"Hush," Mrs. Harris warned.

"How do you know about that?" Trent asked.

"Oh, I know a lot about you."

Trent left off looking skeptically at the bandages and turned to stare at the girl. But Minton returned with a scrupulously pressed white lawn shirt and Trent's coat. Trent donned the garments rather than resisting, though it was not his ribs that were the problem, but a throbbing shoulder. Some wounds never healed.

"Is there any of that coffee left?" he asked.

Mrs. Harris lifted the pot and looked about to serve him a cup in the kitchen, but Minton took it from her and informed them that breakfast would be served in the dining room in five minutes.

Amy let Trent seat her as though he did not have a raking brush burn on his side, and a bruised shoulder into the bargain. "Did you want to speak to me about something?"

"Your . . . occupation," he replied darkly as he took a seat across from her.

"I already explained that. Would you let any of your people do something you were afraid to tackle yourself?"

That stopped him and must have called up some awful

memories, for he shook his head and stared at her in a menacing way.

"We were speaking of your stupidity, not mine."

"Then advance me the money to buy a new stallion and we will give Tartar a nice long rest."

Minton entered with a laden tray and they waited until he had delivered to Trent a cup of coffee and set before them platters of eggs, ham, and biscuits. After pouring Amy's tea he bowed. "I shall have your shirt mended unless you would wish to wait for your valet—"

"He is not coming. My valet quit," Trent said. "I would appreciate you taking care of that. And Minton . . ."

"Yes, sir?"

"Thank you for the loan of the shirt."

Minton nodded and left.

That was better, Amy thought. *If he could speak civilly to Minton, he could not be in such a very bad mood.* But the flashing green eyes that turned to her held no promise of understanding. She slid an egg onto her plate and reached for a biscuit. "Your breakfast is getting cold."

Trent said nothing, but he did eat. An egg and some ham, plus three or four biscuits. She refilled his coffee cup.

He stared at her sharply. "What did you mean when you said, 'I know a lot about you'? How could you have known about that duel?"

"I read the *Morning Post.* If I surmise aright, you got the wound last year in that duel with Lord Vox. Then I realized you had been shot by a jealous husband and you did not want to talk about it in front of Mrs. Harris."

"It was your tender ears I was keeping the tale from."

"But I know all about you. I have been following your career."

"My career? If half the things they printed were true—"

"You would have to be a much older man, for one

thing." Amy realized this was not the best remark and occupied herself spreading jam on a biscuit.

"Leave my age out of it. If I agree to purchase a younger stallion, will you promise to assign his management to someone else?"

"Then you are going to lend me the money?" Amy asked, careful not to commit herself.

"The purchase of breeding stock is a capital expense."

"You mean I do not have to pay you back?"

"No, of course not." Trent leaned back in his chair and studied her. "It is all your money anyway. I do not know where you got the idea it should come out of your allowance. But I do not want you to buy another such murderous beast."

"I will find a gentle one." *There, that was a promise she could keep.* "Young studs are easily satisfied and easily tired," she teased.

"Will you stop speaking about this breeding business in such a matter-of-fact way? If anyone were to hear you they would consider you the veriest trollop."

"Why? Breeding horses is a business and one I am good at. It has nothing to say to my character."

"It is not a business typically practiced by young ladies. I appreciate the fact that you have made a success of it, but to speak of it in these terms makes you singular."

"It is fortunate that I learned all I could, for you have surely neglected it."

"I had the law firm, the shipping business, and the foundry to run," Trent growled. "I had assumed Masters could handle such a simple thing."

"He can, in the ordinary way," Amy said. She risked a glance at him, but calculated that the breakfast had made him sluggish. "But not with a broken foot."

Trent nodded. "We are where we are with it."

"And since I have been running it all these years, for me to pretend ignorance of it would be stupid in the extreme."

"But what will other people think of you?"

"What other people?" Amy asked.

"And that, too, is my fault." Trent blew out a tired breath. "I am sorry I neglected you all these years. But I thought Mother was looking out for you."

"I had rather she did not. She never comes here that she does not set up the servants' backs. And all she ever does is criticize and bring me improving volumes, some of them in French."

Trent choked out a laugh. "You too? Perhaps you are better off without her, then, but that does not excuse my ignorance of your situation."

"No, not when I wrote apprising you of my difficulties," Amy replied.

"I am trying to apologize. I realize my fault is extreme and that you have every right to be impatient with me—"

"Oh, very well. Go ahead, then." Amy folded her hands and waited patiently, drawing a rueful look from Trent.

"You do not make this any easier. I am sorry I had no time for your problems and I will focus on them now. So please forgive me for . . . fifteen long years of neglect."

"Well said. But the only problem I have at the moment is the stallion. So if you could just leave me with a check I shall make all the arrangements."

"Just a moment. There must be other things you need." He reached across the table and touched the frayed cuff of her riding habit. "Won't you let me really help?"

She drew her arm back, not ashamed of her worn coat, but touched that he noticed. "I suppose I could show you around the place. But you have been hurt."

"It is only my right side. I can ride left-handed."

3

⚜

"H ere are the yearlings and two-year-old colts," Amy said as she walked with him to the first pasture. "We actually do a good bit of halter and leading work with them. We catch them first thing after they come to eat breakfast. Then we work with the older horses. The grooms are all riding exercises at the bigger training field with the older colts."

Trent only glanced at the half-dozen younger horses being led by the smaller stable boys or ground driven with long reins. "So you breed carriage horses here, as well."

"We ground train all of them. If we cannot sell them for hunters or hacks, we can usually sell them for carriage work. We have to teach them to prance a little more, but that is usually no problem."

When they got to the training field Trent counted five grooms besides his own and no less than eight horses ranging in age from three to five. Where the devil had these been last March when he was recruiting so desperately for mounts for Draco and a few others of his acquaintance?

"You hid them," he concluded, speaking the accusation out loud before he could stop himself.

"Of course I hid them," Amy said, her cheeks turning

pink. "You stole my best horses four years running. I was not about to let that happen again."

"I did not steal them," Trent said in confusion. "The estate was paid for them."

"I did not see any of the money," Amy replied. "And I did need it."

Trent shook his head. "That too is my fault. We will have to sit down and discuss finances later."

"Do you still want to ride?"

"What about that tall one?" Trent asked. "He does not have the look of the rest of your horses."

"That is High Flyer, a five-year-old, and a little gangly," Amy replied. "I hold out the hope that he will grow into those legs."

"Is he by Tartar?" Trent asked of the black colt. "He does not have the look of him."

"No, Tartar throws mostly blood chestnuts. Flyer came free inside a new mare I got at a sale. The owner claimed she has some Darly Arab in her. He must not have known she was caught. She's given us a good foal every year since then. In fact, she's ready to foal any day now."

"His chest is wide enough," Trent stood back and eyed the colt, who seemed to realize he was being scrutinized and danced about, dragging a groom almost off his feet.

Amy bit her lip and stared at Trent. He suspected she did not think he could handle the animal.

"If you want to try a hunter, I would suggest Cullen or Hannibal," Amy said, pointing to a matched pair of chestnuts. "They are from the same mare, a year apart, and are very keen at fences, natural jumpers."

Trent saw his groom Jessup watching the others take the four- and five-year-olds over the low jumps in the fenced paddock and motioned the man over. "What do you think?"

"These were not all here last spring," Jessup said.

"I know. Saddle that one for me. The one called High Flyer."

"Yes, sir."

Amy cast Trent a puzzled look. "He is not one of our best. Why do you want to ride him?"

"I think he has an eager look to him. If I were looking for a war horse I would pick him."

"But you are not buying war horses anymore. Oh, very well. Masters, have them put my sidesaddle on Hannibal."

"Where did you hide them?" Trent asked as the grooms readied the mounts. Amy did not duck her head shyly but looked him in the eye with a challenge, her pretty lips compressed with determination.

"I merely took the oldest and best for a very long ride."

Trent nodded. "You could not have done all that alone. Did Masters know what you had planned?"

"He counseled me against it. Do not ask who helped me to save my horses. You would probably discharge him."

"I wish you had not done it," Trent said, thinking back over their desperate straits a year ago. Napoleon had escaped Elba and the renewed war had sapped the resources of a country already tired of war. He had thought of enlisting himself until he had been wounded by Vox. But that was all past. He was going to have to put it behind him and focus on the future.

"My reputation was beginning to suffer," Amy said. "I was supposed to be able to supply strong hunters and I had been selling the second best for years."

Trent looked as though he were going to say more, but Flyer distracted him. The horse kept jiggling the bit in his mouth, so Trent stepped up to him and ran his hands smoothly and quietly over the horse's nose and face, talk-

ing to him gently, the way he would like to talk to his
ward, if the past did not keep getting in the way.

Amy could not hear what Trent was saying to the animal, but she could see what he was doing. Everyone else
tried to hop onto the beast as quickly as possible so as not
to get dumped. But Trent was doing some sort of calming
ritual. He ran his hands all along the horse's body and
down its legs, picking each foot up as he got to the hoof.
To Amy's amazement, Flyer quieted under Trent's touch
as he never had done before, not even for her.

When he was ready Trent took an iron grip on the
reins, spoke a few words to the horse and mounted. Trent
eased the reins and at the first sign of bit jiggling, ran his
hands along the animal's neck and spoke to it. Flyer
flicked back his ears and listened.

When Amy looked at the grooms they were all staring
open-mouthed at this performance. So she mounted Han
without any assistance. Perhaps there was more to As
Ever Trent than met the eye. But they would see what
stuff he was made of at the first jump. Amy kneed Hannibal and started out of the yard at a smart trot.

Since the horses were already warmed up Amy
thought nothing of jumping the gate leading out of the
field, and Hannibal obeyed with eagerness, carrying her
over the four-foot obstruction and landing solidly on the
other side. She brought Han from a canter back to a trot
so she could see Trent get dumped. If he were smart he
would give Flyer a test pass to look the gate over, then
circle for a longer approach. But he urged the youngster
smartly forward, pressing him, correcting his pace, slow-
ing him, so that he could see the gate. He had the horse
almost to a stop when they reached the gait and Flyer
leaped it nearly from a standstill.

Together they looked so beautiful it gave her chills. Whatever happened with the other horses, Trent must have Flyer. No one else had ever been able to ride him like that, not even her. Where had that come from, that charitable impulse? From her sense of justice, she supposed. If Trent was the only one who could handle the horse, it was better off with him than someone who would try to break its spirit. It was not because she felt sorry for Trent or found herself liking him in spite of all his past faults.

Trent actually laughed as he drew abreast of her.

"Where's the challenge?" she asked. "That horse could have stepped over the gate."

Amy brought Han to a circumspect walk for the wooden bridge across the deep stream that bisected her property. Trent would have to dismount and lead Flyer across the wooden span. She paused on the other side to witness his comeuppance. Flyer started his bit jiggling again, his signal he was unhappy with something, but Trent leaned so far forward over the horse's neck, Amy thought he would surely fall off. Flyer took a step, then another, then rattled the rest of the way across, rolling his eyes as if demons were on his heels.

Amy nodded her approval and Trent grinned at her. As Ever Trent actually had a wonderful smile. Too bad he saved all his smiles and gentleness for horses and dogs.

The next jump was a hedge that shut off the view of the other side. Han took it willingly enough, the new leaves brushing his belly. Just when Amy thought they had better turn back and look for Trent's body, Flyer burst over the hedge without letting it touch him. He landed in front of her and gave a little cavort of sheer joy, as Trent rode around her, laughing. Flyer had never jumped that hedge before, and Amy had no idea how Trent had persuaded him to do so now.

"I think Flyer likes to lead," Trent said as he rode past her.

"But you do not know the way," Amy protested.

"That will make it exciting." He glanced back over his shoulder as he urged the colt on.

Amy followed in their wake, hoping no one would be hurt too seriously. Flyer thundered up to the water jump and took it so long he did not even get wet, where Han splashed in the shallows. And that was the last she saw of them as they entered the woods and cantered along the well-beaten trails, though she could hear them ahead of her. Amy loved the sounds of riding through the tall stands of oak trees that gave the farm its name. She enjoyed the squeak of leather and jingle of the bits reverberating crisply in the cold morning air as she rounded a loop of the trail. She gloried in the spark of recognition Han conveyed as he saw the next downed log and measured the distance to it, then took it as though this were a game.

Amy had often wondered about the usefulness of breeding horses for the monied rich to play at fox hunting or rabbit coursing, when they really just wanted a good romp with a horse. But she would not have traded this feeling for the world.

Trent was waiting for her at the top of the hill, riding Flyer in alternate left and right circles and making the animal change leads as though it were something the creature did every day.

"Where to now?" he asked.

"The closest village is that way, or we could ride down the hill toward Biddenham. There are shops there in case you would need to buy anything."

"Such as a shirt? Let us go to Biddenham, then." Trent leaped Flyer over the low wall and let him have his head galloping down the hill. Amy was hard-pressed to keep up with him on Han even though her mount was carrying less weight. She began to think that Trent would have made an excellent cavalry officer, for he had no notion of fear when it came to horses. And then she remembered what had happened to many of those men and felt thankful he had not thrown his life away. There she was, liking him again, but when he smiled at her she could not help herself.

He was waiting for her at the bottom of the hill and she led the horses in a walk till they approached the stone wall that separated Gaskill's property from hers. Then she took Han to a canter and leaped the four-foot obstruction, looking back to see Trent following.

She waved at Gaskill's ploughman as they rode through the fields toward the river. That brought a puzzled look to Trent's face.

"Should we perhaps stop and say hello to your neighbor?" Trent asked as they trotted past a neat brick house.

"Ordinarily yes, but Mr. Gaskill is in London this time of year."

"His fields look very wet," Trent said as he pulled Flyer to a halt to regard the river, which must be one of the upper reaches of the Thames.

"Yes, he has the most flooding of anyone in the area," Amy agreed. "If we had come down the other slope of the hill we would have ended up at Fallowfield where we get our mail. If we go upriver until we strike the road, it leads us straight to that village if we go left, and to Biddenham if we go right."

Trent nodded and made Flyer walk along the towpath abreast of Han.

"Trent, I have been wondering since last night exactly how many of my letters you do remember."

"You mean, did I ignore them all or actually read some of them myself?" Trent quipped.

"Yes, because I do have another major concern other than the stallion."

"Assume the worst, that I either never read or have forgotten most of what you wrote."

"Or belittled it, telling me not to worry about financial matters when they most definitely are my concern."

"I shall have to have a talk with Mr. Lester. He seems to have taken a great deal of license with my name. Out with it. What else have I neglected?"

"I suspect Fenwick has been cheating me. You said the money you were paid for my horses should have gone into the Talltrees account, but so far as I know it never did. Fenwick never lets me see those accounts. If we did not raise our own grain and shoe our own horses we would be in the suds. I cannot get him to pay for so much as a bridle."

"What? Does he think you deal only with the household accounts?"

"There is no household money either. There is only my allowance."

"Nonsense. I pay the servants wages and a generous amount for food. I'm sure there must be money set aside for the upkeep of the estate. Masters must have charge of it."

Amy stared at him for a moment, almost forgetting to steer Han. "What are you talking about? I pay the servants wages out of my allowance."

"Since when?"

"Since I turned eighteen and you increased my allowance. Mr. Fenwick said it was because I was to pay the wages now. But the increase in no way covered—"

"I shall kill him," Trent said quietly.

Amy turned to see that Trent had halted Flyer and that

his face was set into grim lines of disapproval. She was glad the flinty green glare was not directed at her.

"So, you had no suspicion."

"And what is worse, Mr. Lester ignored your warnings. I can scarcely wait for an interview with Fenwick."

"He will be here Thursday for quarter day."

"He will come when I say."

"He does live in Biddenham," Amy hinted.

"We will stop and command his presence tomorrow."

Trent gave a bark of laughter as he guided the now jumpy Flyer past the bridgehead. "Easy boy, we are not crossing this one. Something to anticipate, then."

Amy smiled at his wicked grin. "Do you care for another canter before Flyer jumps out of his skin?"

"Yes. I shall try not to leave you in the dust."

But Flyer did run off from her, and she expected not to see Trent again until she reached the town. It was a fine day and she enjoyed her solitary canter along the shaded road, thinking she could like every day to be like this one if Trent rode with her and was so agreeable. It was flattering to have his attention for a little while, even though nothing would come of it. Oh, he might buy her the stallion and rid her of Fenwick, but then he would go away and she would probably not see him again for years. This guilt he felt over his neglect of her could not last.

Trent was an intriguing character. Every once in a while he dropped his guard as he had just now and she would catch a glimpse of someone else entirely, buried deep inside Trent. Not a businessman, nor a sensible guardian, but a white knight of sorts. And then he would slam the door shut again and ride off like a skittish horse, afraid that once you got a halter on him, you would never grant him any freedom.

She brought Han down to a walk a half mile from the

town, then saw Trent was walking Flyer back up the road
to meet her, looking a little abashed. Perhaps he was feeling guilty that he had ridden off and left her.

"What is the matter?" she asked.

"They may think it odd if we arrive separately."

"But I arrive separately here every time I come and no
one ever says anything. To be sure they would think nothing of it."

"Do you not even take a groom with you?" he asked.

"Yes, if we are on a training ride. None of them will
ride sidesaddle, so I'm the one who trains the mares. Then
there are four or five grooms with me, but we usually do
not run into the town then. It can create too much havoc."

"Four or five?" he almost squeaked.

"If one groom lends respectability, I should think four
would be even better."

"Well, it is not," he insisted.

"Why not?"

"If you do not even know, there is no point in explaining it to you."

"You had no answer," she accused. "So you cut at me
to keep me from realizing it. Well, it will not work. Besides, I already said we do not take training rides into
town anymore so there is no reason to upbraid me."

He cast her a calculating look. "So you can tell when I
am bluffing."

"Yes," Amy answered cautiously.

"Oh, well, see that you do not give me away," Trent
said as he pulled Flyer up in front of the most expensive
shop in town and dismounted.

Amy ignored the fact that she usually slid off her
horse unassisted and set her hands on his shoulders as he
lifted her to the ground. Those green eyes were confused
and her immediate response was to help him.

"What is it?" she asked.

"Nothing. Something about riding Flyer makes me feel . . . odd, as though I weigh nothing."

"Happy?" Amy asked. "Because he so obviously is." She gave Trent no chance to deny it but walked ahead of him into the shop picking up the skirts of her riding dress as they came to the muddy entryway. "Do you realize how rare it is for a horse to actually like to cavort all over the country with a man on his back?"

"Yes, I do," Trent said as he paid a boy to hold their horses.

His demands for ready-made shirts raised an eyebrow but the shopkeeper and his wife supplied these articles and a half dozen neckcloths that passed his approval. As he dickered with the merchant Amy checked various bolts of cloth, spending a good deal of time stroking a green velvet.

"An excellent choice for your new riding habit," Trent said and made her jump.

"Oh, no, I could never afford it."

"Of course you can. At a hundred pounds a quarter for seven years I make out that Mr. Fenwick owes you almost three thousand pounds."

"Trent, do you really think I can recover that money?"

"Oh, we will, or he will go to prison."

"Before or after you kill him?" she asked, smiling at his idle threat.

He pulled the bolt down from the wall. "I shall play that by ear. Forest green suits you. It brings out the color of your hair—no, your eyes."

She smiled at his slip and was amazed that she could find him so charming now, when she had always thought him her nemesis. He also helped Amy select material for an evening dress and insisted on picking out the lace and trimmings, paying for it, too. Amy noticed that he disliked the knowing looks that passed between the merchant and his wife. He made a point of asking when his *ward's* dresses would be ready, but she did not think they believed the relationship. It had been something about the way he chose the lace, as though he were picturing her putting the dress on that had changed their opinion.

Their condescension made Trent stiffen, and it gave her an odd feeling to have them assume she was "kept" by him. She might not have minded if they had thought her his wife, but the sidelong looks implied mistress and she hated them for judging her. Hated even worse them thinking that she would let a man take care of her when she was quite capable herself. Trent should have known it would be improper for him to buy her things, even though she had not.

They stopped at Fenwick's house but he was not in, so Trent left explicit instructions with the housekeeper that Fenwick was to come to Talltrees tomorrow afternoon. On the ride home they went by way of the roads rather than the fields and she lost herself in wondering what it would be like to be Trent's wife, to catch him at his little tricks, to accept his generosity, to chide him for his mistakes. She shook herself mentally. She should not read anything into his kindness beyond what it was, an apology for his years of stupidity about her affairs. And she should not forget all the work and pain he had cost her just because he could be charming when he chose to be. She suspected he could be cold and vindictive when the need arose. She might even get to see that side of him tomorrow.

They rode up the drive to Talltrees in midafternoon and she took him to the library and showed him her books, and after explaining her accounting system left him alone as she went to check on the mare who had not yet foaled.

4

When he returned to his room after a long afternoon in the library, part of it spent dead asleep at the desk, Trent found a new shirt laid out on his bed and a freshly pressed neckcloth. As he washed and gingerly changed his shirt, leaving the bandages in place, he admitted to himself that Amy displayed her father's zeal for business. There was not a groat spent without a necessity. She had managed to keep the place up and make a success of it under the most trying of circumstances. He wondered if he would have done so well in her place.

She was not what he was used to in a woman. She did not fawn on him or stroke his ego, and she was witty enough to get the best of him. But would she be able to take care of herself when she came into her entire property or would she be snapped up by some fortune hunter? He made a mental note to warn her about such men, but that lecture coming from a rake such as himself was like to be met with one of her impatient smiles, that tilt of her head that said, yes, she knew all about that and a reminder of some other fault of his. He smiled in anticipation of having her chide him in her matter-of-fact way and felt a strange melancholy overtake him. He had been missing this all these years, cheating himself out of her company when it would have meant so much to both of them to know each other. They would not have felt so alone. They might have—

No. Amy was not for him. He must never think of himself as fit company for her. It would have meant much to him to have her friendship. Nothing more. He must never think of her in any way but as his ward.

When he presented himself in the dining room he found Amy there with her nose in a newspaper and a crumpled letter lying by her plate. She had changed from her outmoded blue riding habit into an equally worn brown gown. She looked up, a bit surprised. He wiped the scowl from his face over the gown and sat down.

"One of the lads picked up the mail and papers while he was on an errand in Fallowfield. Do you want the *Times?*" she asked.

"I would prefer it over that gossipy rag," he said nodding at the *Morning Post.*

She carefully folded the paper she had been reading and handed it to him as she opened the *Post*. "Let us see if they have any idea where you have disappeared to," she teased.

Trent waited for an uncomfortable minute while he tried to focus on the market news. Prices were up, no one had any money to buy food, the members of Parliament were making fools of themselves again, and the world in general was going to hell. But he did not care what happened. Nothing seemed of any importance right now except mending his fences with Amy. He reminded himself that after ignoring her for fifteen years he could hardly expect to earn her respect in a day or two, but he must do something if she had been as badly treated by Fenwick as he suspected.

"Well?" he demanded impatiently.

"Oh, nothing about you, I'm afraid." She folded the newspaper and laid it beside her plate. "When I read about your duel, they said they did not look for you to live. I did not know for many weeks if you had died or not." She looked up at him, her beautiful mouth slightly parted over delicate teeth. And her warm hazel eyes looked concerned. Actually they were more the color of fall honey, rich and amber, promising sweetness where he had no right to expect to find any.

He tore his gaze away and back to the paper. "Good Lord. You did not look for my obituary in the *Post,* did you?"

"No, in the *Times.* You are a public figure no matter how much you wreck your private life."

"You know nothing about it," he said, giving an inward shudder at the wreck of his life. Five affairs in ten years. He might not be the blackest man in London, but he was running in the forefront.

She opened the crumpled letter again and reread it. He was relieved to observe that it did not come from his secretary.

"Bad news?" Trent finally demanded.

"Fenwick has invited himself to dinner on quarter day. You know what that means?"

"Enlighten me."

"Another unwelcome marriage proposal."

"Not, I think, after the message I left for him today. I shall take care of Mr. Fenwick when he comes tomorrow. You should have told me he was pestering you." Trent folded the paper with finality.

Amy smiled with satisfaction. "An inadequate defense, since you do not know if I already complained of that or not."

"I wondered if you would realize that and call my bluff," he said as he watched her lively countenance.

"Ordinarily it might work on people when you sound puffy with indignation like that. Do you really speak in court or do you hire someone to do that for you?" She was sitting regarding him with her chin propped on her hands as he had seen an appellant court judge do just before dismissing his case.

"What brought that up? I employ a staff to argue cases. My capacity is now advisory in the law firm. My skills are in investment, not oration."

"Good."

He was prevented from snapping a question back at her since Minton wheeled in a cart with the first course of dishes on it. Trent was certain that the lad serving as a footman was one of the grooms who had not been able to control Tartar that morning.

When they had served the fish, vegetables, small hen, and then left, Trent stared at her. "I pay the wages of a footman."

"Roddy serves in the house after his chores are done." Her honey-colored eyes lit with awareness. "Oh, no, do you mean Fenwick is not just robbing me, but overcharging you as well?"

"Yes, I gave them all a raise in salary two years ago."

"And he kept it for himself, no doubt. Well, I will see that they get it if I recover my money."

"Fenwick has more turns than a screw." Trent took a sip of wine. "But I will deal with him later. Why did you ask about the law business?"

"Just curious." Amy waited for him to carve the hen as she helped herself to the other dishes.

"My training is in business law. I employ a corps of solicitors to handle my clients' cases. They also find barristers willing to represent my clients." He passed her a breast of the fowl.

"I have always wondered if it is not a conflict of interest to have your firm represent someone who . . ."

She looked uncertain how to proceed so he prompted, "A woman, you mean?"

"Yes, a woman for whom you . . . have developed an attachment."

"But I do not represent them, at least not at the same time. Such attachments are never of any length and the courts move so slowly that by the time a case such as a divorce comes up, we are no more than passing acquaintances again."

Amy nodded slowly as she chewed a bite. "I see, so you do have your standards."

"Why am I explaining this to you? My *affairs* are none of your concern. You should never have been reading about them."

"But is it not a perception in the ton that you may, shall we say, precipitate the end of some marriages, where your firm later represents the female party?"

"That is the perception." He sliced himself a bite of chicken and chewed methodically, wondering how to end this discussion.

"And you are not going to defend yourself?" She pushed her vegetables about her plate as though they displeased her.

"I never dignify gossip with a reply."

"That is a good answer." Amy nodded again. "I shall have to remember that one."

"You had better never find occasion to use it in front of me. Tell me the truth." He pointed his fork at her. "In what light are you regarded locally? I will find out if you mislead me."

"Why should I? I am quite proud of myself. I am considered a great gun with horse training, a capital rider after hounds, and no man's fool. I know how to drive a bargain—"

"I thought so. In fact, it is worse than I feared. You are an eccentric."

"What?" Amy demanded. "Because I am better at certain things than other women?"

"Because you are obtrusive. I had assumed you to be living in seclusion."

"And I had assumed you to have more sense than to treat me like one of your mistresses."

"What are you talking about?" He had a notion what was coming and took a large drink of the claret to fortify himself against the tirade he now expected.

"You jab at me about doing training rides with grooms, or going for the post alone, and then you pick out clothes for me as though you did it all the time. Well, I suppose you do for other women. I know what those people in the shop thought of me and it was damned uncomfortable. I shall never go back there again."

Trent looked at his plate and pushed it aside. "I admit that was an error on my part. But I cannot help what people think and if they are going to be small-minded about it, they will gossip about you for living alone, too."

"Small solace for me. You will be gone in a day or two. I have to live here for the rest of my life."

Trent looked up and smiled at her. "Well, no, you don't. You can travel, with the proper chaperon, of course. You may wish to marry. I was meaning to warn you."

"What now?" she demanded.

"You are something of an heiress. In point of fact, our fathers jointly owned the legal firm, the shipping business and the foundry, and left them to us in equal shares. So you should be careful what sort of men sidle up to you."

"*I* should be careful? Shouldn't it have been your job to keep ineligible men like Fenwick away from me?"

"Yes, and I have already owned to my error in that regard. I will deal with Fenwick tomorrow. But Talltrees is only the smallest part of what you stand to inherit. You don't want to take up with some bounder."

Amy got up and stood behind her chair, her knuckles clenched whitely on the back of it. "If I am an heiress I have seen little evidence of it. I scrimp and save trying to make a success of Talltrees, believing my whole life depends on it, and you tell me it does not matter? How do you think that makes me feel?"

With that, she left him. It was as though he had been slapped, and without considering the consequences he dumped the contents of his wineglass down his throat. Damn her. He had never met a woman so determined to have the last word about everything. The hell of it was that she was right. Telling her this late in the game to be careful of men was useless. Her own good sense had kept her safe from them.

And offering her fortune as the magic solution to all her troubles had cheapened all her hard work. He knew that feeling. Would he never be done apologizing to her?

Amy stalked toward the library in a fit of rage. Why had she let him provoke her? She mended the fire and threw the poker into the rack so violently even Lively left the room, probably to fawn at Trent's feet, disloyal beast.

When she could force herself to think calmly again she realized that she had let her curiosity about him prompt her to bait him. She herself had set their feet on the road to an argument. And she had thought she was being so careful. Why did she let him bring out the worst in her?

No help for it now. She went to the desk to put her ledgers away and found that Trent had made one or two corrections to her figures. This set her to working the sums again to make sure he was right and, damn him, he was both times. But he was finding pence. If he had just been over these ledgers, then he knew her true state of affairs and the extent of Fenwick's fraud. Why would he make her feel as though her struggle had been without need? From his point of view he would always be there to bail her out, but he had not been until now. And she had not known he could so easily help her when she faced all those ends of quarters with so little money left.

It suddenly hit Amy that she did not want Trent's help. Certainly she did not want him lecturing her on whom she should marry. She had no intention of marrying anyone. Yet, if she could choose a husband it would be someone who enjoyed horses, someone with a natural bent for bringing out the best in them. Trent, in other words. How could he be so adept with animals and so doggedly clumsy with women? No wonder he ran through mistresses faster than a ram through a flock of ewes.

She closed the ledgers and paced to the window. She did not care if she was an heiress. All she cared about was Talltrees. And Trent in his position with full power of attorney could make her life miserable these next few months if she annoyed him too much. So, the wisest position would have to be to irritate Trent as little as possible while he still had any power over her. If he got rid of Fenwick and gave her the money for the stallion, that is all she would ask of him. Every day that passed without him interfering meant a day closer to freedom. So she would bide her time and count the days until she could be rid of As Ever Trent.

She went to bed with the aim of being coolly polite to Trent for the balance of his visit. When she heard him come up the stairs a few hours later he was talking to someone, and after straining her ears for another voice, she realized it was Lively the spaniel who was the recipient of his confidences. *Poor man,* she thought, before she could help herself. If he was alone it was probably because he drove everyone away with his stupid advice.

5

The sound of sleet hitting the window pulled Trent to consciousness. But this was March. Must have been dreaming. He dismissed the noise and lay in a half-doze, the warm spaniel curled at his feet. Strange that Lively would fasten onto him.

Trent heard a thump and it jolted him awake. He never slept well in a strange house. He lay still, listening for a moment, and heard the distinct sounds of someone tiptoeing past his room. Probably going to use the necessary at the end of the hall. But the footsteps were going the wrong way and Lively raised her head and gave a faint whine. The dog looked at him as if to say, "Do something."

Trent got up and crossed the room, massaging his sore shoulder. He cracked open the door and looked down the stairs just in time to see the outside door close. He went to his window and saw through the early morning fog a cloaked figure making its way toward the stable. It was Amy, damn her. As he pulled on his riding breeches and boots he wondered if she was ignoring his warning that she not handle the stallion.

Trent swore under his breath when he could not find a

shirt, but he was not about to delay to light a candle. He threw on his coat and made his way down the stairs, careful not to raise the house. He would have words for whatever misbegotten grooms were letting Amy do their job of controlling Tartar.

He strode down the walk toward the stable bay and saw lantern light through a crack in the door to the breeding barn. He wrenched one of the large end doors open to discover half a dozen grooms and Masters besides. Amy detached herself from the group and came to him, smiling as though she were about to offer him a high treat.

"I did not know if I should wake you or not," she said, taking his arm and drawing him toward the lantern. "Have you ever seen a foal born?"

"No, never," he gasped as waves of embarrassment flooded over him. He looked over Masters's shoulder to watch a gray mare lying on her side, grunting. She raised her head to look around at her huge belly in an accusing way. Suddenly Trent felt overwhelmed, incompetent and incapable. He had never felt so helpless since he had found his father dying.

"Is she going to die?" he asked, wishing there was something he could do to help.

"Oh, no," Masters answered. "Gay always lies down like that."

The mare heaved herself to her feet and circled the large birthing stall. She paused when she came to Amy and the girl slipped inside the ring of men and began a slow massage of the horse's sides and stomach. Masters went to the other side of the mare and likewise stroked her. Trent wished that it had occurred to him to massage the horse as Amy was doing. Anything would be better than inaction at a time like this.

"She is going down again," Amy warned and stepped

back. A gush of fluid spurted from the back end of the mare, followed by something white. Trent had the most awful feeling she was going to lose something vital, but had this been a loop of intestine it would be pink, would it not?

His fear must have shone on his face for Amy said, "That is the placenta and it is a head presentation. We will not interfere unless she takes too long. But Gay never has a problem."

Finally the white shroud tore asunder as the long legs and head of a foal appeared a little more with each contraction. It was wet and black, or nearly so.

Trent felt a sudden bubble of joy rise up in him, the way he felt when he was riding. He wanted to go to the mare and reassure her.

"She's getting up," Amy warned. "Hold her head, someone."

As the mare swung around, Trent grabbed her halter and began his calming talk, what he would use on the most terrified horse. He heard a plop from the back of the stall and smelled the hot fecund scent of the birth as though it were something he was remembering from a past life.

He dared to look and Amy was on her knees in the straw pulling away the membrane and rubbing the foal with handfuls of straw. The little head thrashed and with her bare hands Amy cleared the mucus from its nose and mouth. One of the youngest grooms turned pale and scrambled out of the stall. Trent focused on calming the mother and finally let her turn slowly to examine her young. The mare bent her head and sniffed, then began a thorough wash job on the foal, which lay in a confused jumble of limbs. Masters efficiently tied off the cord in two places and cut it close to the foal.

Trent looked back and the afterbirth still trailed. Amy

got up, wiping her hands on the straw. "Gay is very good at this and is always a good mother."

"What about that?" Trent asked, feeling stupid since he seemed unable to say the word.

"It is better to let her deliver the afterbirth naturally than to pull on it. If she retains any of it she will die of the infection." Amy went to a bucket that was sitting by and washed her hands. She looked at him and smiled. Trent became conscious of his state of undress and buttoned his coat over his bare chest.

"What is it?" he asked, not knowing what else to say.

"Another filly. That is the problem. Tartar is so old he throws mostly fillies now and they are not in demand as much as colts. She will be a nice one, though. She is black now, but she may turn gray like her mother, or stay black like Flyer." Amy was drying her hands on a piece of toweling. "We shall need a name for her. Would you like to choose it?"

"I would not know what to call her. Odd how something that has nothing to do with me can make me feel . . . that there is hope in the world. I am not used to it."

"I am glad you woke up, then. Most men would not be at all interested."

"Who could not feel this . . . gladness, like a laugh about to burst from you?"

After several attempts the foal thrashed and popped up onto her feet, looking amazed to be standing. She wove unsteadily and nearly tumbled forward but managed to collect her legs under her.

"You can imagine what Flyer looked like when he popped out," Amy said. "He was all leg."

"So this little lady is normal-looking?"

"Yes, they all look disproportionate at first. Lady?" Amy nodded. "Good name."

The foal wobbled toward the back of the mare who was enjoying a bran mash.

"She looks like she's trying to crawl back inside," Trent said.

"I think that is why the teats are at the back. The foals can find them better."

The mare swung her head around to lick the foal's rump and it started to nurse. Gay expelled a snort of relief to have the foal begin to drain her full udders. A general murmur of approval went up from the men and boys.

"We should get to bed," Amy said, reaching for her cloak.

Trent took it and placed it around her shoulders as they walked out into the foggy morning. The dew was dropping off the trees in a gentle intimate rain that they would have missed had they not been awake at this ungodly hour. "I can see why you love this place," he said.

She stopped and turned to him. "Then you understand what it means to me." Her voice was a soft whisper carried on the mist. The dew glistened on her eyelashes and beaded her cloak like fairy dust.

"Yes, but you should not be here alone."

"But I have stayed here alone, as you put it, successfully for years."

"That is my fault, but you should not have to be alone forever."

She sighed, her breath eddying visibly in the damp air. "What if I prefer my independence?"

"You should have someone to share such joys with you." He nodded toward the barn.

"Most men do not appreciate being awakened in the middle of the night to watch any kind of baby being born, let alone a horse. You are a puzzle, Trent."

"Why?"

"City-raised and yet you ride as though you were born on a horse."

He smiled. "I had not much of a home life myself. When I was sent away to school I met Draco Melling, and he used to invite me home for the holidays. The Mellings have an estate in Northampton, Marsh Court. I was enthralled with anything that had to do with the place, and lacking a willing pupil in Draco, Lord Marsh mentored me instead of his own son."

"What a shame that your friend did not appreciate his father."

"Still does not. I do not see why I got along with Lord Marsh better than Draco, except that I was rather estranged from my own father."

"Makes you wonder if the medieval custom of fostering out did not have some merit."

Trent smiled sadly. "That is the sort of remark that would point you up as a singularity in London."

She smiled and tucked a wisp of hair under her hood. "I suppose I would never be able to say anything about birthing foals?" she teased.

"Worse," he said with a laugh, as he put a companionable arm around her.

"Then it is a good thing I am not going there or I would be left with no conversation."

She looked up at him expectantly as they began to walk toward the house and realizing what he had done, he let his arm drop as though it were broken. She walked away from him and he stared after her, bracing himself for that jolt of loneliness he always felt when she left him, but what he felt was a sort of peace he had never known before. For he knew he would see her again in a few hours.

Of all the women he had ever met, Amy was the only

one who seemed to have everything sorted out right. There was many a man who was less capable and clear-sighted. So why did he want to change things for her? Perhaps because her reactions were not feminine at all, at least not in his experience. She was like some creature in between two worlds who had been pressed to fill both roles and stood now independent of her sex, neither asking for a man's help, nor welcoming it.

He told himself he wanted the best for her, a good husband, children of her own. But why was that? What if she truly did not want a family? Of course, she had no experience of family, so she was no judge.

As he looked about him in the growing light he dug around in his conscience and found one other possibility. Because he would not have any. Was that it? He would never have any heirs, so he wanted Amy to have some children to pass things on to. He looked into the future and saw himself as some sort of devoted and amusing uncle. Well, there were worse motives.

He stood alone for a time on the stone walk as the swirls of mist created fantastic shapes out of the shrubbery and the trees, showing their tops up as though floating on some Oriental sea. The fog was beginning to lift and he watched raptly, calling back Amy's soft words to keep him company. Strangely he felt that he dare not go inside now or he would miss something important.

A breeze kicked up and blew down the hill from the north, pushing the mist back toward the river. He leaned his head back and realized the stars had burst through like diamonds in dark velvet. He felt wealthy, full, content for no reason he could think of. He stood looking up in amazement. Why had he never noticed the night sky before?

He gave as his excuse that the war had kept his head

on his shoulders and him hard at work. But he knew that was not so. He had known that if he let himself feel any joy, the whiplash of sadness that would follow would be too much to bear. And he had not anyone he could explain this to. Amy? Before her, most of all, he must not drop his guard.

He had done a hellish thing by not providing some kind of family life for her, but what could he, a bachelor, have done other than ruin her reputation? They were far too close in age for anyone to think his interest in her innocent, even though he felt a hundred years older. He had just given her an impulsive hug, and though she had accepted it with her usual grace, it had startled him. He liked her more than any woman he had ever met. What was more, he admired her. But no matter how much he enjoyed her wit, her beauty or her unique view of the world, he must not think of her as a woman he could have.

As Amy undressed and crawled into bed she thought about Trent. He had seemed so loose, so human tonight. And he had embraced her and joked about her social deficiencies. In spite of his good humor, she had left him when he had started talking about London again. Why could he not understand that she did not want what other women wanted? She did not even know what other women held dear. But if she were to say this to him, he would argue that she could not then know she did not want it.

He was a cunning man and she was determined not to fall into any more of his traps. Above all she must remember that there was more danger about him when those eyes were soft and joyful than when they were cold and shuttered. He had a trick of making you care about him just before he crushed your hopes. She would not let that happen again.

But she could not banish Trent from her thoughts altogether. He was an enigma, sad except when he was surprised out of his gloom. Horses and dogs seemed to have a way of drawing Trent out, but his joy never lasted long. He was punishing himself for something and she doubted that he even realized it.

She carried his images to sleep with her, of Trent throwing the barn door open and looking surprised, Trent with his coat half-open, and that seductive dark track of hair down his chest. He had buttoned his coat when he had seen her looking at his chest, as though he were modest. That did not seem like the actions of a rake. But perhaps he behaved differently around her. She almost wished he did not make an exception for her. Then he might not seem so shuttered.

She had seen other men stripped to the waist on those occasions when they had to pull a foal. But those were mostly skinny lads. There was nothing small about Trent. She wondered how a man who surely must spend most of his days behind a desk could have developed such musculature. Another mystery to solve.

6

Trent awoke to a rumble of voices from belowstairs and something familiar about the tone of the deeper voice sent him to the window. A groom was walking Draco's bony gelding toward the stable block. Now the urgency to get downstairs overrode Trent's care in dressing. If he knew Draco, he would invite himself to breakfast, if his host or hostess were there or not. And most servants were so enchanted with the soldier they brought him the best of everything.

Trent tramped down the stairs a few minutes later—without a headache, to his amazement. Minton reported the arrival of a Captain Melling and Trent wondered if Draco's sudden appearance would upset Amy. But Amy was nowhere in evidence when he strolled into the dining room. Draco was just unfolding his napkin and by the expectant smile on his face Trent guessed he was hungry. Even though the last battle of the war had been fought nine months before, the soldier still wore his scarlet Dragoon jacket with the gold braid of his captain's rank. Draco arranged his silverware and looked up at Trent with a crooked smile.

Trent poured himself coffee, and did no more than glance at the eggs, before helping himself to bread and ham. "How did you find me?"

"Well, you headed west out of London and you never got to Portsmouth."

"You rode the whole way to Portsmouth and back?" Trent sat down.

"I guessed you didn't stop to pack so I had your butler gather up some clothes for you. Do you realize your valet has quit? Anyway, the housekeeper at your Portsmouth house reminded me of this place, so here I am."

"What are they saying about me in town?"

"Nothing yet, but that kind of thing has a way of getting out." Without taking a bite of food, Draco downed his first cup of coffee in one gulp and went to the sideboard to pour himself another. "Real cream. We would have killed for this in Spain."

Trent looked up and nodded sadly, watching Draco arrange ham and biscuits on his plate and seat himself again. Draco was looking better, not as thin as he had been when shipped home from Belgium last year. His long brown hair still fell in his eyes, but he was sporting a mustache and a goatee now to cover a scar on his chin. And his dark eyes had lost that hunted edge. Trent felt a sudden overwhelming closeness to Draco. His best friend was now a hardened soldier, but they had grown up together at school. He had helped Draco through his exams and Draco had kept the bullies from killing the slighter Trent.

When Andrew Severn had died in 1808, Trent had been prevented from enlisting in the army by having the whole of the businesses owned by Amy's father and his father dumped on him. So when Draco threatened to enlist as a common soldier, Trent had bought his friend the commission he had wanted for himself. This had made Draco extremely happy, but alienated the Mellings from Trent for many years.

Now that Draco was safely home, they had forgiven Trent for helping Draco fly against his parents' wishes. That was why the idea of marriage to Diana had seemed possible.

"What is it?" his friend asked.

"What is what?" Trent cut away at his ham and brought a forkful to his mouth, chewing slowly as he considered possibilities.

"That look. The one that would usually get us called up before the headmaster."

"I was just thinking. Did your parents broach the subject of your own marriage to you last week?"

"My God, Trent. They have made a list." Draco hunched over his coffee cup as though he were discussing battle plans. "They do not think I can do anything for myself, not even pick out a wife. I thought eight years in the army would have changed something. But I will tell you this. Just because I am to inherit the title someday does not mean they have any say about who I marry or when, or even *if* I marry."

"Precisely." Trent nodded his approval of this stand.

"Precisely what?" Draco asked suspiciously, his dark eyebrows bristling over this troubled brown eyes. "I never could read your mind, you know."

"You need to find a wife on your own."

"But I do not want a wife at all."

"I agree you do not want one of those spoiled London misses, who will make each season a living hell. You want a quiet girl who will be content to live in the country and take care of your estate, perhaps one who shares your love of horses."

Draco looked up at this last remark. "What are you talking about?"

"I have a ward, Amy Conde, who is nearly of age. I do not want her to fall into the hands of some fortune hunter."

"Is this the daughter of your father's partner? But I have never even met her." Draco stared morosely into his coffee.

"You are a veteran. I assure you she will look upon you with the utmost admiration. You have only to spend a few days getting to know her, pop the question, bring your mother up to meet her, then spirit her off to your father's estate in Northampton for a visit before you take up residence here."

Draco narrowed his eyes and stared at him. "Are you mad? I just told you I do not want to marry anyone."

"She is an heiress," Trent promised with a lift to his eyebrow that indicated just how much of a fortune Amy was going to inherit.

"As though that would weigh with me. So are all the others."

"But Amy is a quiet girl, used to being alone. She would never expect much of you. Just sit for a moment and compare her to all the ladies on your father's list. Think of the innumerable dinners with those chits and their families."

Draco gave a profound shudder and opened his eyes. "No, Trent. Abandon this notion. I have had it with marriage." Draco leaned back in his chair, making it creak, and regarded his friend with a troubled expression. "Why not marry her yourself?" he finally asked.

"Oh, no." Trent shook his head. "She is too innocent by far."

"And that would last, what? One night?"

Trent looked miserably out the window toward the stable, trying to wish away the brutal truth of Draco's remark. "There is a certain freshness, a naïveté that lasts a lifetime. And Amy has that. I wish her to be married to someone who will not crush that in her, who will not carry her into society to make her live down his reputation, and who will not ignore her."

Draco stared at him and shook his head. "You're waxing poetic. You have got it bad."

The front door banged and someone ran up the stairs, then back down again. The door to the dining room opened and Amy stood on the threshold in her same worn blue riding habit, with an inquiring look on her face. She clutched a whip and gloves in one hand.

"Come and breakfast with us," Trent said gently.

"I breakfasted hours ago, but I will join you for tea." Amy put down the whip and gloves, and went to claim a seat as she stared at Draco.

"Let me present Captain Draco Melling, Lord Marsh's son," Trent said. "This is my ward, Miss Amy Conde."

"My pleasure," Draco said, rising momentarily as he bowed before seating her.

"You have been down looking at the new foal," Trent guessed.

"Yes, it is remarkable. We usually keep the newborns inside for a day, but she was racing around her stall so we let Gay and Lady out with the other mares and foals."

"When did this all happen?" Draco asked.

"Last night," Trent said. "It was the most amazing sight."

"You got up in the middle of the night to watch a horse birthing?" Draco chided.

"I am afraid Masters must have awakened Trent by throwing pebbles against my window." Amy turned to Trent with a smile. "And you must have thought the very worst."

Trent choked on his coffee.

"That is why you threw on your clothes so quickly," Amy continued.

"The worst?" Draco prompted with an amused look.

"Trent must have thought one of the horses was down with colic," Amy continued.

"Precisely," Trent replied, blotting his mouth on his napkin.

Amy swallowed her bite of muffin. "I must tell you that we have almost no colic here. I think it is because we pasture the horses so much and do not keep them shut up in their stalls more than we have to."

"That is a relief," Trent said.

"Is that your gelding in the loose box?" Amy asked Draco without ceremony.

"Yes," Draco agreed. "Titan is finally getting some flesh back on him. He is all I have left from the war."

Amy cocked an eyebrow at Draco. "Were you looking to buy a new horse? We have three or four that would be up to your weight."

Draco laughed. "You think so? And just what is my weight?"

"Close to thirteen stone when you are higher in the flesh than now. Are you looking for a hunter or a hack?"

Draco nodded his agreement of her assessment and sent Trent an amused look.

Trent put down his coffee cup and watched as Amy poured herself some tea and stirred cream into it.

"I have several good prospects you might consider. I can show them to you after breakfast, if you like."

She smiled at Draco as she had never smiled at Trent and his friend returned the smile wistfully as though puzzled at her friendliness. *He should not be,* Trent thought. Women always fell for Draco. It was those soulful brown eyes of his.

"I should like to see your horses," Draco said.

"They have all been bred here at Talltrees and are out of Tartar, except for Flyer. We're not sure of his parentage."

"Tartar?" Draco asked, staring intently at Amy. "He is known for breeding high-couraged colts. I would dearly love to have one or two of his get."

"You have heard of our horses?"

"I have ridden them," he said.

When Amy sent him a confused look he said, "In the Peninsula and Belgium."

"Oh," Amy said, dropping her gaze to her cup. "I see. Trent acquired them for you." She picked up her teacup and took a sip.

"Yes," Trent agreed. "I did get Draco several colts from here."

"If you are finished then, shall we go look at your horses?" Draco asked. He rose with the precision and smartness his red uniform decreed and pulled out Amy's chair for her. She turned to smile at Draco, and Trent wondered if she was not all that different from other women. They all fell in love with Draco. Perhaps it was not only those brooding brown eyes. It might also be that long hair that brushed his forehead when he bowed over their hands, or the broad shoulders.

Trent sighed and got to his feet, leaving his breakfast unfinished. "Yes, let us see them by all means."

Draco took Amy's arm and led her out the door, making small talk about the fineness of the weather for riding.

"I think we should try one or two of the older colts this morning," Amy replied.

Trent noted that she did not say two or three of the colts. Did she think he was hung over and unable to ride? As they walked through the first bay of the stable block, Amy pulled a carrot from her pocket and handed it to Tartar, who took the whole thing into his mouth before crunching it down. He accepted her petting and scratching, casting no more than a wary glance in Trent's direction. Draco managed to stroke the arched neck without mishap, though Tartar pawed at the wooden floor impatiently. Amy handed a second carrot to Draco, who fed the treat to the horse expertly, careful to not get a finger in the way of those powerful teeth.

"Very touching," Trent said dryly.

Amy cast him a tolerant stare as she walked through the stable yard toward the pastures. "The mares and foals are turned out here, closest to the stable in the daytime, with the colts in the other field when they are not being worked. I doubt that any of the mares would do for you, though Trent might find one the right size for him."

Draco chuckled and Trent sent him a measured scowl as they made their way past the yearlings and two-year-olds being trained. Finally they came to the training field with the older colts.

"Cullen and Hannibal are both strong and heavy," Amy said. "Which would you like to try first, Captain Melling?"

"I think Cullen has an eager look to him."

"Very well. Masters. Have them saddle Cullen for the captain and send one of the boys for my sidesaddle for Hannibal."

"Masters," Trent said, "tell Jessup I shall ride Flyer again."

"I wish I'd had a few of these beauties last year in Belgium," Draco said.

"Oh?" Amy asked weakly.

Before Draco could answer Trent spoke up. "Do you realize that those horses you hid from me could have saved men's lives?" he asked, proud of the puzzled frown that now marred Amy's brow.

"I had not thought of it that way." She glanced in Draco's direction, then cast her eyes down.

Trent was pleased that she did not know what to say during the awkward pause he had deliberately created.

"Do not listen to him, Miss Conde," Draco said, as the grooms led the three horses over. "A few horses more or less would have made no difference. I am glad you hid them, for they are alive now."

Trent decided he had contrived that rather well. Draco, in his knightly way, had been so courageous in removing the sting from Trent's comment, that any woman would fall for him. If Amy could like Draco, his problem might be solved. And he would have done his friend a favor.

Even as Captain Melling lifted her into the saddle, Amy realized that his remark about the war had been a lie. He had tried to spare her feelings. As the soldier mounted, Amy glanced at Trent trying to get on the dancing Flyer. She knew from that moment that she would rather hear the most horrible truth from Trent than all the sweet lies Captain Melling could tell her. She did not want to be protected, no matter what a man's motive. She wanted to meet life head on as she had always done. If she had erred by withholding her horses, then she would have to own up to that.

She took them over the same course as the day before with Cullen jumping the gate with little assistance from Captain Melling. Trent did not have to work quite so hard to get Flyer across the bridge. After they took the woods trail successfully and gathered at the top of the hill, Amy said, "If you do not mind we will cut across the hill and through Squire Duncan's sheep pastures, which he allows us to hunt. Then we could go into Fallowfield for the mail and newspapers."

"Very well," Trent said.

Amy pointed Han at the low wall that marked the border with the squire's land and jumped it, looking back to see Captain Melling just make it over. He had interfered with Cullen, but the horse had managed to correct itself enough not to come to grief. She supposed being in the cavalry did not necessarily mean you were the best rider, even though you did it often. Flyer sprang over it like a gazelle, then tossed his head as he cantered up. He had a different look about him today. The horse did not look ungainly with Trent on his back and she decided it was in the way Trent collected Flyer, pulling in all that length of leg and those big feet to make them do the job they were meant for.

"I suggest we trot and walk them the rest of the way to the village or we'll scare the sheep," she said.

Captain Melling forged ahead of them, seeing the path across the corner of the field to the road.

Amy glanced across at Trent and decided to apologize before he got ahead of her. "I did know what you wanted with the horses," she said. "So there was no excuse for me to be so disobliging as to refuse them for the army. And if I had known they were for Captain Melling . . ." She looked at the back of the soldier's red uniform as he set Cullen up to jump the coppiced hedge bordering the road.

"I believe you mean it," Trent said with some surprise.

"Yes." Amy held her breath but once again Cullen corrected his approach to the hedge unerringly and carried Captain Melling over. "For me the war had no face before. I knew no one involved except you, and I did not really know you."

"But I had no part in it."

She smiled sadly at him. "Oh, your foundry made no guns or cannon? Your ships carried no ammunition? I am not stupid, Trent."

"I did what I could, though it was little enough."

"Is Captain Melling badly affected by the war?"

Trent's head snapped around to regard her. "I believe so, but he does not like to let anyone know that it has changed him."

"How has it changed him?"

She asked it, not knowing what answer to expect, but he stared at her as though he were measuring her.

"He is quieter, more thoughtful, less likely to laugh. I bought him his commission. Whatever has happened to him these last eight years is my fault."

Amy heard herself gasp a little. What a cross for Trent to lay on himself. Compared to this his neglect of her was nothing. "Why did he come to you for a commission?"

"His mother was adamantly against him going, and his father—Draco is an only son. How could he let him go? I sent him because I wanted to go and was too stupid to realize how dangerous it would be, how long it would take, or what it would cost." Trent closed his eyes for a moment as though he were shutting out some horrible image.

Amy nodded as she made the impatient Han walk toward the hedge. "And you are still friends. Have his parents forgiven you?"

"More or less. Well, not his sister. Her opinion of me I cannot even quote to you. And why am I telling you all this?"

"I strikes me that you do not have anyone else you could tell. I am in much that state myself."

"That, too, as we both know, is my fault. Come, we have tarried long enough. If we do not catch up to Draco he will be sitting at an alehouse in the village and half-sprung by the time we get there."

"One more question," Amy said "How could Lord Marsh have taught you to ride so well and Captain Melling so indifferently?"

"But Draco is an excellent rider, a cavalryman."

"No, he rides any horse as though it were the same horse. You ride a horse as though it were the only horse in the world."

Trent stared at her for a moment, looking thoughtful. "Draco cannot afford to fall in love with his beasts, since he so often loses them." Trent kneed Flyer into a canter as they approached the hedge and the horse lifted him over without brushing a tendril of greenery.

Han took the tree row without any wasted effort, having surmised how little of it was solid. They cantered toward Fallowfield then, and when they arrived found a boy walking Captain Melling's mount outside the only inn.

"I knew it," Trent said as he dismounted and tossed his reins to the boy. He came around to help Amy down and she was surprised by the warmth of his hands, the gentleness with which he lifted her. She stood looking up into his smiling face and became conscious that his hands had not left her waist and that Trent was staring at her in a puzzled way. Suddenly some barrier came down and Trent frowned. His hands fell away and he took the reins from her and handed them to another ostler who had come to help.

"You may want to order them unsaddled and lunch here," Amy said as she removed her gloves.

"Why?" Trent pressed a coin in the palm of each boy.

"Cook makes only breakfast and dinner, unless you gave orders otherwise. Captain Melling will get nothing to eat until five o'clock."

"Hmm. I could do without, but Draco might perish. Very well. Unsaddle and walk them," he called after the ostlers. "Water them after they are cool, but no grain."

She preceded him into the coaching inn, which was also the receiving office, and asked for her mail at the desk.

* * *

Trent scanned the tap room and found Draco with his feet propped up enjoying a large ale. "Come, we dine here."

"Do you want me to bespeak a private parlor?" Draco stood up slowly.

"Considering Amy is with us, I think we should eat in the common dining area."

As they walked back across the hall they discovered Amy was already sitting at a table.

"Who wants the *Times* and who the *Morning Post?*" She held the two newspapers out to them and Trent snatched the *Times* from her. Draco put down his glass of ale and languidly opened the *Morning Post,* peering at it as though the print were too small. Trent interrogated the landlord on the fare for the day and ordered the soup, a roast chicken, bread, cheese, fruit and tea.

He noticed that Amy had been watching him and lifted an eyebrow to ask if he had made some error. "Do you not approve?"

"I have never dined here before, so I do not know. She used the table knife to open the single letter she had received. A little "Damn," escaped her and Trent looked up, though Draco merely turned a page.

"I feel it my duty to mention that such language is not becoming in a lady," Trent said absently, hoping not to irritate her again by commenting on propriety.

Amy looked sharply at him. "You would swear, too, if you had just gotten a letter from your mother."

"Mother?" Trent asked absently. "What does she want?"

"She means to come for a visit. She wants to make sure I will be home in two weeks' time. She has a *delightful* surprise for me."

"That sends a cold chill down one's spine," Trent said. "But perhaps she has found a suitable companion for you."

Amy gave him a pathetic look. "Her surprises are never delightful."

"Why, what has she done to you?"

"Sent me Miss Forney for a governess, for one thing."

"And what was wrong with her?"

"Other than her drinking problem and teaching me French hazard, nothing."

"She taught you to dice?" Draco asked.

"Cards as well, though I think silver loo and speculation are respectable games. At least Fenwick's fraud gave me an excuse to get rid of her." Amy crumpled the letter and tossed it into the fireplace.

Trent stared at her. "If you were married, Mother would not be able to intrude on you in this way."

"Am I to marry simply to keep your mother at bay?"

"Just a suggestion." He folded the *Times* and laid it aside. Even when she was berating him, Trent found Amy fascinating.

Amy's eyes narrowed as she stared at Trent. "Now that I come to wonder about it, how do you keep her out of *your* house?"

Draco coughed.

"In my case my unsavory reputation compels her to stay at a hotel when she is in London."

"Oh, I had forgotten. You usually have a mistress in residence at your house."

Trent opened his mouth to protest.

"Uh-oh," Draco said, then took a quick drink to try to cover the sound.

"Spit it out," Trent demanded. "What are they saying of me?"

"Nothing much. Ten to one no one will even guess they are talking about you."

Trent snatched the paper out of Draco's hands and left him reading thin air. "Where is it?"

"The society column, fourth paragraph." Draco sent Amy a resigned look as he drained the contents of his tankard.

" 'The interested reader may try to guess what *cit,* so recently welcomed back into Lord M———'s house, was refused by that notable's daughter. Apparently no fortune, however vast, can compel some ladies to marry. The rejected suitor is reportedly on his way to his residence in Portsmouth to lick his wounded pride—' What rot!"

"Easy, Trent. They did not name you, though Father will be mad as fire, about that Lord M——— bit."

"What is so very bad about that, Trent?" Amy asked. "They have said much worse things of you in the past."

Trent glanced sharply at her. "Just how long have you been following my . . . *career?*"

"Aunt read the *Morning Post* religiously. I suppose I should have canceled it when she died, but it made me feel closer to her to have it coming. And it does have some useful information: who is selling his string, whose horse is winning at the races . . ."

Trent directed his menacing glare back to the paper. "I think I will buy this damned rag and run it out of business."

Draco chuckled and cuffed Trent playfully on the shoulder. "Forget it. Everyone else will have done so by the time we get back to London."

"I can, at least, make liars of them. This *cit* is not going to Portsmouth."

"Because of a few lines in the paper?" Draco asked.

"Why not?" Amy asked.

The food arrived just then and Trent neglected to answer her. He had told her too much of his private affairs already. Why he had confided in her he did not know. It seemed to be such an easy thing to do when he was on the back of that silly horse. Now he wondered if he had said anything shocking to her. He had a way of doing that, blurting out the truth and getting a shocked look from a lady. But Amy never looked shocked even when she should be. That was probably due to her upbringing. And that, most certainly, was his fault.

"You never used to be so touchy," Draco said with a mouthful of bread. "Forget that affair with Diana."

Trent could see Amy looking from Draco to him expectantly. "It was not an affair. I asked Draco's sister to marry me and she turned me down. It was a simple matter."

"But she need not have shouted down the house," Draco said. "Ten to one some footman or maid sold the item to the *Post*. Why did Diana get so angry?"

"How should I know? I do not think like a woman." He cast an accusing glance at Amy.

"She may have taken exception to something you said, Trent."

Trent glared at her.

"It's possible," she said with forged innocence.

"I never talk down to Diana just because she is a woman," Trent said. "I merely recommended that since the war is now over and Draco is safe at home, I thought it was time we got on with our lives. And since we had known each other forever, would she like to marry?"

Amy's eyes grew round and she glanced at Draco, who guffawed.

"What?" Trent demanded innocently.

"I'm surprised you did not ask her to clap hands on it or sign a contract," Draco said with a snigger.

"It seemed a reasonable offer," Trent replied. He caught the innkeeper's eye and mouthed the word "brandy."

"What about it, Miss Conde?" Draco teased. "Would you consider such an offer?"

"Well, it would not make me angry, but then I think I am not like most women. There is more business to me than romance. If I were an ordinary girl, I do not think I would like to hear that the war and Draco were more important than I, or that you were only asking me because I was the only girl you knew well, or that—"

"Enough!" Trent shouted. The innkeeper brought the brandy and Trent downed a swallow of it, hoping once again to numb the pain of his recent rejection. He only succeeded in burning his throat and giving his stomach an uncomfortable jolt.

"And what should he have said?" Draco persisted, leaning back in his chair to regard her with amusement.

Amy looked up, her delicate lips smiling fondly as though she were conjuring up a pleasant daydream. "That he had loved her for an age, but felt unworthy; that he could no longer live without her; that if she refused him he did not know what he would do; that he might put a period to his—"

Trent choked on another swallow of brandy. "But none of that is true."

"Oh," Amy said with mock surprise. "You do *not* love her."

"Of course, I do not love her. I do not love anyone. Marriage is not based on love."

"What then?" Amy asked, and waited expectantly.

"Property, like a treaty between two countries. I worked very hard on those marriage settlements and she would not even look at them."

Trent could see that Amy and Draco were trading dubious looks and wondered how this conspiracy between them had started and how he had come to be discussing his private affairs in the public room of a common coaching house.

"Then it is probably good that she refused you," Amy concluded, taking up her teacup again.

"Of course it is fortunate," Trent almost shouted. "I go on quite well without Diana, and I now think it would have been a monstrous mistake if I had married her."

"Then, when you return to town, you will not be wearing a hangdog face, but your usual confident expression," Amy predicted. "You will make light of the tale. You did offer for her, after all, for Draco's sake, because you are so much a part of the Melling family. You might have thought that she was in expectation of an offer from you. You are relieved to find out otherwise, that she has not been breaking her heart over you. You have both decided you would not suit, which is so much less scandalous than a broken engagement or a ruinous marriage."

Trent realized he had been staring at Amy raptly as she concocted this tale, gazing at some imaginary scene in which he figured as a normal person, rather than a bumbling oaf. He gave his head a shake. "But none of that is true, either."

"I am not saying that you have to say it. But if you go back to town with a smile on your face, rather than your usual scowl, that is what people will think."

"There may be something in what you say." He pushed his drink aside and looked once again at the *Morning Post* before he folded it up and tossed it onto the fire.

"Glad to see that you are not stupid, either." Amy finished her tea.

Trent shook his head and found himself smiling at her quite against his nature. No, he was not stupid and he knew she had just talked him out of getting drunk and falling into a towering rage, but he was not quite sure how she had done it. Even the best of women seemed to harp on and on about a topic until they drove him to drink or anger. Amy was like a splash of cold water in the face, a bit of a surprise at first, but all things considered, a welcome change.

7

━━◆◆◆━━

They had finished and called for the horses to be saddled again. Trent, for one, was leaving the place with relief, when a foppish gentleman in a greatcoat wandered in and nodded in their direction. Trent's eyes traveled instinctively to Amy, before snapping back toward a man who had every reason to damage Trent if he could. He had been Trent's rival for Diana's hand.

Draco glanced up and said. "Shelby Wraxton, is it not?" before Trent delivered a warning kick under the table.

"At your service, but do not let me interrupt your party. Lost a wheel off my phaeton and had to walk these last three miles."

"We are just waiting for our horses to be saddled," Draco said, rubbing his shin and glaring at Trent. "Come and say hello to Severn."

"How goes it, Wraxton?" Trent asked, rising and taking the offered hand.

"Things have been better. Worst of all, it is a new carriage, just delivered yesterday," he said as he drew off his gloves. "What a charming companion, gentlemen. Am I not to be introduced?"

"This is Miss Conde . . . my ward," Trent said reluctantly.

"Your ward? I had no idea you were such a sober old dog as to have a ward, Severn. I picture you as still tearing up the town, cutting men out with their intended."

"I have little time for that anymore. Too bad about your carriage, but we must be getting back. They are bringing our horses around now."

"Nice to make your acquaintance, Miss . . . Conde. I must say, if I had such a charming companion as you, I would spend a good deal more time in the country than Severn does."

After they had mounted and ridden out of the village, Draco glanced at Trent. "He was wrangling for an invitation to stay at Talltrees."

"I know that," Trent said. "Did you know he had applied to your father for Diana's hand?"

"Oops, no. Father does not confide in me much."

"His clothes were rather odd," Amy said, "and I found myself unable to like him on such short acquaintance. Was it encroaching of him to thrust himself on us?"

They both stared at her.

"Your instincts do not betray you," Trent said. "Wraxton is not the sort of man you want to know, or like."

"What sort of man is he?" she persisted, the hint of a dimple suggesting she was baiting him again.

Trent furrowed his brow, trying to form a reply fit for her ears.

"A bad man . . . an evil man!" Draco said theatrically as though he were talking to a child.

Amy burst into laughter and even Trent grinned at his friend.

"Suffice it to say that you should avoid his company,"

Trent added. "If I could have denied him an introduction to you I would have done so."

"He trapped you into it, so he is also a manipulative man," Amy concluded.

"Do not let him worry you," Trent said. "You will not encounter him again."

"Oh, I am not afraid of him. I simply do not like him. If the need arose, I could get rid of him."

"What is that supposed to mean? Have you had occasion to . . ."

"Depress pretensions?" she supplied.

"A genteel way of putting it," Trent remarked.

"One or two of my customers were after more than horses, so I made them pay through the nose for the stock they bought. And your own agent is forever importuning me to marry him. I wish you would—"

"Then it is just as I feared. You running this business is very bad for your reputation. It will not do."

"Oh, Masters handles most of the sales. We have been working together so long that we have a system."

"A what?" Trent stared at her in confusion.

"I name a price, a high price. Masters in confidence lets the man know what I would be willing to take—"

Draco burst out laughing. "Which is still higher than your bottom price."

Trent let out a gasp of exasperation. "You have been running a rig, the two of you. I shall have words for Masters."

"And if you lose me the best head lad in two counties I shall have words for you."

"I could discharge him if I wanted to," Trent threatened playfully.

"Oh, that would make you popular with the rest of them. And I could hire Masters back in three months."

Amy flicked her whip and got Han into a gallop, leaving the two men in her dust.

"She has you there," Draco said.

"You are supposed to be helping me. Are you sure you do not want to court her?"

"I think I shall have more fun watching the two of you argue."

They returned midafternoon to find Fenwick's whiskey in the stable yard and his pathetic horse being led in for a feed.

"Damn," Amy said. "He is probably in the library enjoying a sherry."

"I would appreciate it if the two of you could amuse yourselves for the next half-hour. I have a bone to pick with Mr. Fenwick, a whole carcass, in fact."

"But I want to be there," Amy pleaded. "I want to fire him myself."

"I have a list of his crimes. Check it over for me just to make sure I have not missed anything, Amy."

She snatched the list and read over it, whistling at the total. "Yes, the household money we never saw. You have it all."

Trent took the list back and put it into his coat pocket. "Now amuse yourselves for a while. I have a man to demolish and it will not be pretty."

"But I want to come and watch you kill him," Amy said so sincerely Captain Melling glanced at her uncertainly.

"I think there should be no witnesses. I can always say he slipped and plunged out the window of his own accord."

Amy laughed as Trent strode toward the house. "Let us go check on Lady's progress."

Melling nodded and they walked to the mares' pasture to see Lady running circles around her mother. The foal had got two of the older foals to play chase with her. But she far outsped them, tearing on a vast arc of speed around the field until Gay was pressed to neigh at her and bring her in for a feeding.

"She makes me feel giddy just watching her," Amy said.

Captain Melling leaned on the fence and watched the horses at play with a vague smile. "Trent is an amusing fellow, isn't he?"

"What he said today about not loving anyone. What did he mean by that? If he never loved anyone, why then, did he have so many affairs? By my calculations he has taken a new mistress at least every other year."

"He has a penchant for rescuing women."

"What do you mean?"

"He takes them under his protection."

"That is a rather medieval way of saying it."

"No, I mean it. He has only had two real affairs that I know of, the first ten years ago and this last thing with Vox's wife last year. The rest were women making use of him. The affairs were knitted by the gossipmongers."

"Then perhaps the *Morning Post* is less reliable on these matters than my aunt led me to believe."

"No doubt."

"Come, let us go sit where we can see the library window, just in case."

Captain Melling chuckled and took her arm to escort her to the garden behind the library. They sat on the sun-warmed stone bench in front of the ornamental pond.

"The gardens here are lovely," he said, scrutinizing a bed of jonquils. "Do you have the ordering of them?"

"Yes, I spend all winter planning them."

"We have extensive gardens at Marsh Hall, my father's estate. It is too bad Trent never had a chance to take you there. You and Mother would get along famously."

Amy looked up at him and smiled. Perhaps he had made up his mind about the horses already. "What do you think?" she asked. "Will you make me an offer?"

Captain Melling looked dumbfounded and spun toward her so violently he almost fell backward into the pond. "An offer, after only one day?"

Amy noticed he was sweating though the day was rather chill. "Well, I have a particular reason for wanting to complete the arrangement quickly."

He cleared his throat nervously. "And what would that be?"

She hesitated as they heard shouting and angry voices coming from the library. Amy looked hopefully at the window, then back to Captain Melling. If she confided to him that she wanted to buy her stallion herself, he might let it slip to Trent. "I cannot tell you. Most men can make up their minds about such things in an hour."

"Who told you that? Trent?"

"Of course not. What would he know about it?"

The soldier seemed distracted by the argument going on in the house, but they could not make out actual words. "He is the one who suggested the match."

"Match? I suppose Han and Cullen are a matched pair. What do you say to two hundred and fifty pounds each?"

"What?" The captain twitched his head to the side as though he had no idea what she was talking about.

"For Cullen and Han. I do not offer Flyer, since I think Trent wants him."

"Oh," Captain Melling said slowly as though a light were dawning. "Well, yes, I like them fine. Yes, of course, I shall meet your price on the horses."

"Indeed? But we have not even haggled yet. I did tell you about my methods. I mean to play fair with you."

The soldier mopped his brow. "No, they are worth every penny."

A door slammed then and Fenwick scrabbled down the walk toward the stable, his elbows and knees jabbing out of his ill-fitting suit. His normally pinched face was even more ugly when suffused with rage and the shock of gray hair on his forehead was standing straight up until he jammed his hat on his head. He paused once to glare at her, shake his fist and say something she could not catch. It was odd. She had never been afraid of him before, but seeing him so angry made her glad she was sitting with a soldier.

"How prosaic," she finally said. "He left the normal way."

"Believe me, Amy. There is nothing normal about this household."

Amy stood up. "We have a deal then?" She held out her small hand.

Melling grasped it and shook it. "That we do. I shall go inside and write you a draft from my bank."

"And I had better go see if there is any blood on the carpet." Amy strode up the walk to the back door.

Trent stepped away from the window, feeling both puzzled and disturbed at the same time. They had been sitting in intimate conversation in the garden the whole time he had been abusing Fenwick and it ended with a handshake? What was he to make of that? Did they have an understanding? If so, why did she leave Draco standing there with such a confused look on his face?

But that was not what disturbed Trent the most. Even though he had set Draco on to Amy, the sight of another man courting her caused some demon to rise up in him, prompting him to want to stride down the walk and take Amy away in a protective embrace. He tried to tell himself that his paternal feelings had finally been aroused, that all he wanted to do was keep her safe from all possible hurt, from all men.

He backed away from the window with the growing realization that it went deeper than that. He heard her run lightly up the stairs, a familiar sound now. Amy never walked upstairs. He smiled sadly, realizing how much he was going to miss her when they went their separate ways. But part they must, before he made a complete fool of himself. And whatever dog-in-manger feelings he had about her, he had better be able to conceal them from Draco if the two had reached an understanding. Marriage to him was her best option.

8

When it was time for dinner Amy dressed herself in her best gown, the green merino, and wrestled her unruly hair into a knot of curls at the back of her head. She thought she did not look so ill by candlelight, though she would never compare to the London beauties. Why did it matter? Nothing would come of it. Trent only thought of her as a responsibility, not a woman.

As Amy entered the room she noticed Lively, her spaniel, under the table at Trent's feet. Trent looked at her dress then pointedly ignored it and smiled at her. Captain Melling got up to push her chair in for her. Trent ran an impatient hand through his dark hair, leaving one lock askew over his forehead. Amy stared at him, running imaginary hands through his close-cropped curls. How wonderful to be a man and have the freedom of short hair.

"Captain Melling is buying Han and Cullen," Amy announced.

Trent opened his mouth to say something, then something registered in his mind and she could have sworn a look of relief passed over his face, closely followed to her surprise by a flush of embarrassment.

The soldier cleared his throat, nervously arranging his place setting and staring at the wine Minton was pouring with some concern.

"I thought you preferred Flyer to the other two, Trent," Amy said.

"Yes, I shall pay whatever exorbitant price you ask for him, Amy. He is a unique animal."

They were interrupted by the arrival of a brisket of beef, a whole salmon and an array of spring vegetables.

"So, you two were discussing horses?" Trent asked as he sawed at his portion of beef and took a large bite, his jaws working as he carefully chewed it and swallowed.

The soldier laughed at Trent's petulant look and brought his friend's frosty glare to bear on himself. Then he nervously gulped his entire glass of wine and arranged the goblet carefully at the tip of his knife.

"Yes, what else would we be talking about?" Amy asked, tasting her portion of salmon.

Trent's eyebrows furrowed in concentration, giving him a menacing expression. Amy had leisure to study his face again. The intense green eyes told her nothing. But that expressive mouth, with the full lower lip and the impatient little indentations at the corners, that was what she could use to judge his moods.

"I had expected you might get beyond horses."

Melling cleared his throat again. "We were somewhat distracted by the altercation in the library."

"You seemed to have dispatched Fenwick without my aid," Amy said. "I still think you might have let me watch. I have been looking forward to his dismissal so much longer than you."

Trent stopped chewing and stared at Amy, his lips compressed in thought. "He turned ugly as I expected and made a lot of idle threats. I did not want you exposed to that."

"What could he threaten us with? He is in the wrong and it is provable," she said as she looked up at him with a smile.

Trent took a gulp of wine. "He seems to think it inappropriate for us to be staying in your house with no chaperon."

"And yet he never thought it inappropriate when he visited and inflicted himself on me for dinner. Well, it does not matter. We have Captain Melling here now."

This surprised a grunt of laughter from Trent, and the soldier shook his head.

Trent dropped another bite of beef to Lively in a bored fashion that clearly disgusted Minton. Normally the dog was permitted in the library, but never in the dining room or withdrawing room. And normally the dog was devoted to her, but today it merely whimpered apologetically in her direction and worshiped at Trent's feet. Somehow Amy did not think the roast beef was the only reason.

She glanced at Captain Melling and was startled to see just such a worshipful look in his eyes. Amy wondered what Trent could do to inspire such devotion. She vowed then never to become one of Trent's court for, from her scant experience of him, he could be quite careless of other people's feelings. She did own to some sympathy for his loneliness; she was lonely herself. But she must never let him know that he was more interesting to her than someone amusing to talk to, that he was a much bigger part of her life than she was of his.

Melling interrupted her reverie to ask, "Do we ride again tomorrow?"

"Yes, if the rain holds off. When do you have to leave for London again?"

The captain was opening his mouth to answer her when Trent interrupted. "Where is this stallion you want to purchase? Perhaps we should ride over and look at him."

"Not if you are going to gainsay me. As you know from the studbook, Tartar comes from the Godolphin line of Arabs. Lord Covington over by Biddenham has a young stud from the Byerly line. I must send one of the grooms over with a message at any rate. I promised to give him an answer by midweek, for he means to send all his excess stock to the York sales."

"Send your note in the morning," Trent said. "Let him know we mean to look at the animal."

They spent the remainder of the meal discussing the rival merits of the three foundation sires and their progeny, with Melling holding his own, but Trent displaying a more keen knowledge of horses than Amy had expected. He finally agreed with her plan to bring in a different strain and she sighed with relief.

"Having settled that, how shall we pass the rest of the evening?" Captain Melling asked.

"I could play the pianoforte for you."

Trent stood up when she rose. "Ah, so your governess did teach you something."

"Any skill I possess along that line we can lay at my aunt's door. While you have your port I will go to the drawing room and look for my music."

Trent persuaded Draco to skip the port, and did not even let his friend light one of his cigars. They carried their glasses and the bottle with the remains of the dinner claret into the room and took two comfortable high-backed chairs. Amy glanced up at them over the top of the music stand as she arranged the sheets.

Trent wondered if she realized how much he cared for

her and how relieved he was that Draco had made no marriage overtures. He knew in his heart that would be the best thing he could offer her—his friend. But he could not help wanting Amy for himself.

The music rolled over him and he stopped thinking about marriage or anything at all as the lively notes rose and fell like the words of a language he did not have the cipher for. He felt shut out of whatever world Amy had entered, as though he were standing outside a drawing room and looking in on a happy scene, a foreign scene. It was the way he sometimes felt about the Melling household, that he was merely an observer.

He ripped his mind away from thoughts of family, Draco's or anyone else's. He and Amy did share that particular pain, he reminded himself, that they had no real family. His mother did not count. The guilt he had been trying to assuage by buying Amy things washed over him now as her fingers lightly told a tale of courage, of daring, and of hope.

He pushed away the cause of her need for courage, his mismanagement, and tried to focus on something joyful. Flyer. Had he actually laughed while schooling that high-strung colt? Amy's fingers on the keys played on and on, and she no longer looked at the music. She had her eyes closed as though she were blind and feeling her way. She must have played this piece often. And she must feel a little blind in trying to deal with him. He did not think he would like to have to do business with himself.

Trent had heard the piece before, often enough to anticipate the next section, but it had never sounded like this, never, as though the pianist were giving everything to the music. Each touch, each note said "love." That was absurd. His ward could have no notion of love any more than he could. True love was a myth.

*   *   *

Amy opened her eyes and looked at the keys. She knew that she dared not lift her eyes to glance at Trent. One disapproving look from him and she would stumble. With each touch of her fingers on the keys she imagined herself touching Trent, the nape of his neck, that unruly hair. She wondered what it would be like to kiss him. She had seen couples kissing, and knew there was some importance to it, but they always looked so hungry, it seemed ridiculous. *Somehow,* she thought, *it would work well with Trent. He would know exactly what to do.*

After the Beethoven sonata, she moved on to some Mozart and could hardly keep her mind on the piece. She wondered what it would be like to live with Trent, to taunt him every day in a playful way, to have him finally figure out that she was teasing him. She smiled with satisfaction when she contemplated his eventual realization, that confident smile of his and what form his revenge might take. She pictured his hands about her waist, his arms holding her, his lips pressed to hers. But here she faltered and almost missed a note.

She had the theory of it down, knew certainly what people looked like while kissing. But they complicated it by moving their mouths around and she had a feeling it would take a great deal of experience to master the skill. She realized she had come to the end of the piece and that Trent was staring at her. What had she been thinking? Kissing Trent? He was beyond her reach and she must never forget that. She looked up at him with a challenge as though she had done all she could to prove she was competent at more than horse training and double-entry bookkeeping. His gaze was soft and yielding, but sad, terribly sad. How awful to have such regrets that even music could not take you away from them for a while.

"You are amazing," Captain Melling said. "She is good enough to play in London, is she not, Trent?"

"High praise," said Trent, "but well deserved. What other talents have you hidden from us?"

Amy came around the instrument to sit across from them. "You must understand my studies have been conducted somewhat independently." She cleared her throat. "Miss Forney being so often under the weather. I know French, of course, and Latin—"

"Latin? Why Latin?" Trent asked with an amused look. "Only men in law, medicine or the Church need know it."

"Why only men?" Amy countered. "Latin is the root language of many English words. I should think everyone needs it."

"Yes, why only men?" Melling asked, with the corner of his mouth twitching.

Trent looked up at his friend with a twisted grin. "As you never bothered to learn it, you may never know. What else have you learned?"

Amy stared at Trent. If he did not know the answer to something, he hid the failing by asking another question. This was valuable information. "History, map-reading, and mathematics."

Trent scowled at her, traded a suspicious look with his friend, then asked, "What did you do to amuse yourselves in the evening, you, your aunt, and Miss Forney?" Trent got up and wandered over to the fire to give the logs a halfhearted kick.

"Read, or discuss the news in the papers."

"Good Lord," said Trent, drawing back as though she had some horrible disease. "You are not bookish, are you?"

Captain Melling laughed at the gasp of outrage from Amy.

"If I am, it is not my fault. What was I supposed to do with my evenings?"

Trent leaned his arm along the mantel and observed her closely, plainly enjoying the flush of anger that had crept into her cheeks.

"Well, really now," she said, taking up the train of their conversation. "Next you will be telling me I need not have learned all that horrible law!"

"Law?" Melling gasped.

"No need whatsoever," Trent said.

"What possible use will that be to you?" the soldier asked.

"Well, I do not know." Amy glanced from one to the other of them and suddenly her eyes narrowed as she realized how much Trent was enjoying baiting her in front of Captain Melling.

She turned on his friend in her outrage. "I am surprised you did not go into law, *Draco*. Your name means lawgiver."

"Well, I was supposed to, but it is the dullest thing imaginable. If not for Trent I would have washed out the first year. It has always been the army for me. Now ask me to lead a charge or storm a fortification and I'm your man."

"When exactly did you wash out, Captain Melling?" Amy taunted.

"Oh, you may as well call me Draco, now that you have rung a peal over my head. And I did not get sent down," he protested. "I left school to join the army . . . just a moment. We were discussing *your* education."

Amy folded her hands in her lap. "I think I did an admirable job, considering I had no direction whatsoever." She stared at Trent as though to say the ball was in his court.

"You may have overstepped what was expected,"

Trent said, "but so long as you do not go telling people what you know, I fancy no permanent harm has been done." Trent wandered across the room to the pianoforte and touched one key softly.

That's when she knew that he envied her that skill, and his lack of it drew her to him. So he did not have everything he wanted. And if he ever married perhaps he would look for a woman who had the power to make him sad or happy with her fingers moving over the keys.

She knew that she wanted to be that woman, but nothing she had learned had prepared her for Trent. She might make him laugh for a moment, but how could she make such an unhappy man content forever? And yet she would have accepted the challenge of it if he had asked her to. But he would never ask and she would never know if she were equal to the task. The idea drained away like the dying vibration of a musical note.

The door opened and Minton announced Sir Shelby Wraxton. Trent looked as though he were going to explode.

He turned to Amy and said, "I wish you would go to your room now."

Wraxton was in the room before she could reply, effusing his greetings everywhere and kissing her on the hand in a mushy way. She did not like Wraxton but she resented being sent to her room by Trent in her own house as though she were a scrubby schoolgirl.

"Who ever heard of such a thing, not able to fix my wheel until tomorrow?" Wraxton asked.

"Perhaps Trent should send Jessup over to help," Amy suggested.

"Do not trouble yourself over it, Amy. I believe you were speaking about retiring," Trent said firmly.

"Retiring?" Wraxton asked, his sandy eyebrows

raised, giving his brown eyes a beady look. "The evening has only begun."

"She has a headache," Trent explained.

"Headache?" Amy asked, giving Wraxton her most dazzling smile just to spite Trent.

"Yes," Trent enunciated. "The one that has been splitting your head these past two hours."

"Oh, *that* headache," Amy responded. "It has gone away." She thought she could almost see steam rising from Trent as she asked Wraxton if he had missed dinner.

"Oh, I have already dined, but I will sit with you. Perhaps a glass of that wine. I must say this is cozy, the three of you here, all alone?" Wraxton ended the statement as though it were a question.

"Except for Mrs. Harris, of course, and all the other servants," Amy replied.

"Mrs. Harris?"

"My housekeeper."

Trent was staring at her and she had a feeling it had to do with more than Cook's sudden promotion to housekeeper.

"What is the news from town?" Draco asked.

"Frankly it has all to do with Severn here and your sister."

"Diana?" Draco asked. "What has she done now?"

"Turned Severn down, for one thing, though now I think I see that I might have been misled in that. Did you ask Miss Welling for her hand, Severn?"

"Of course, as a matter of form," Trent said, flicking a piece of lint from his sleeve. "I have run tame in the house for years."

"Because of his friendship with me," Draco supplied.

"I feared—thought Diana might be in expectation of an offer from me," Trent explained.

"But you found it to be no such thing?" Amy asked in-

nocently, promulgating the story she had made up for
Trent and proud that he had decided to use it.

"No, she was not," Trent said, his eyes raking Amy in a
menacing way, but the corners of his mouth twitching. "She
catalogued out the many points upon which we would not
suit each other. In the end we were agreed not to marry."

"Ah, but London runs on gossip, such as the rumor
that I had applied for her hand, as well."

"Did you?" Draco asked.

"I got no farther than Lord Marsh's interview," he
drawled, making Amy raise her eyebrows.

Trent glared at Wraxton as though he would like to
strangle him.

"I just thought of something," Amy volunteered.
"Since there are four of us we could play cards much easier than with three. Is that not a wonderful idea?"

"Delightful," Trent said acidly.

"Just the diversion I need," Wraxton agreed.

Amy left the men to arrange their chairs at the small
table as she hunted out the cards. Wraxton was not a big
man by any means, and he did not look nearly so dangerous as Draco and Trent seemed to imply. If she won
money tonight and added that to Draco's payment, she
would be assured of having enough for her stallion even
if Trent did not like it.

She talked them into playing loo since she knew that
best. Initially most of the coins on the table were silver.
Whenever she won the pot she raked it into her sewing
basket.

Wraxton persuaded them to sample a bottle of burgundy from the wine laid down by Amy's father and then
a bottle of brandy. Amy saw no harm in a glass or two
served in the library as a way to close a deal so long as
Masters was present and Minton was about. But she

would probably never tell Trent that she had relied on the extensive cellar at Talltrees to loosen up many gentlemen buyers.

She noticed that each time they filled Draco's glass he tossed it off like water. The more the men drank the more the depth of play frightened her, since she more than once staked all her winnings. She disliked the hiss of displeasure from Trent when she did that, but she won those hands and won often enough to believe she was fleecing the men, all of them, while they were in their cups. None of the three was counting his cards very well, Draco throwing good money after bad on the most forlorn hands, Wraxton driving the stakes higher and higher, while Trent came up to any challenge no matter what cards he was holding. Was this some sort of ego match? If it was, she was like to be the only one to benefit. By her count there was nearly five hundred pounds on the table now, mostly in gold coin.

All eyes turned to Trent as he drained his wineglass and began to scribble an IOU to cover his call.

"Come now, Trent, put up your watch or something," Wraxton said.

Trent searched his pockets and finally produced a small case from his coat pocket. When it landed in the pile of money, Wraxton reached for it, but Trent grasped his wrist.

"The contents are worth far more than what is already staked. You have my word on that."

"The word of a gentleman is always acceptable," Wraxton said, withdrawing his hand.

"What is that supposed to mean?" Trent growled.

"Are we going to play or talk?" Amy demanded, almost jumping out of her skin at the suspense.

Draco threw his hand down and pushed his empty glass away. Wraxton displayed cards only slightly better than the ones Trent laid down. Before Wraxton could move again Amy spread out the winning hand.

"Damn!" Wraxton said. "How does she do that? I have never seen a woman with such a run of luck."

"Luck?" she asked as she gathered up her winnings. "I do not believe in luck. I trust to mathematics."

"Ah, you have a system." Wraxton leaned back and regarded her with a wicked smile.

"I know how to count the cards, sir." Amy raked the pile of guineas into her sewing basket along with Trent's mysterious box. "I really should not have played with you all while you were in your cups."

Wraxton sighed. "I assure you I am not drunk, if that is what you are thinking."

"Oh, well, that is all right then. I think I *will* retire now."

"Stay yet." Wraxton grasped her hand. "I am used to getting something for my money. At least some conversation."

Trent grasped Wraxton's wrist in such a way that the man flinched. "I think you forget yourself."

"Come now, Severn. All in a friendly way."

"Amy, I do wish you would go to bed . . . now!" Trent ordered.

"I am going, but not because you told me to." She ran from the room and went lightly up the stairs. When she got to her room she locked her door and spread her winnings out on the bed. Five hundred and sixty pounds and change. Plus there was Trent's box. She thought about giving it back to him. She probably would not need it with Draco's draft in her pocket. She slowly sealed the money into small separate packets and put them away, not all in the same place.

Well, if she were going to give it back to him, then there was no reason not to see what it was. She opened it and a ring glittered warmly in the candlelight. A sigh of sheer pleasure escaped her. A diamond set in a circle of smaller stones. It must be worth a fortune. Of course she would never keep it. Or at the very least she would let him redeem it for what he owed the pot. She slid the ring onto her finger and it settled there as though it had always belonged to her. Just like Trent had settled into her house and into her heart.

She could conjure him up in her imagination now as though she were seeing him, that glorious dark hair, with the one lock that curled seductively over his brow, those glittering green eyes, and that mouth. He always looked as though he were ready to disapprove of something, but she was mastering the trick of making him smile. *What would it be like to kiss Trent,* she wondered again? There was a flutter of expectation in her stomach at the mere thought.

She remembered what his chest looked like, the planes hard with muscle and brown as though he had often gone bare-chested. It made no sense. Nothing about Trent added up. He was both charming and infuriating, kind and cruel. He could be generous and yet had ignored her all these years. And the ring—he could not have meant it as a surprise for her. There had been no time.

Suddenly she realized it had not been meant for her at all. This was Diana's ring, and she had almost exposed his hurt in front of Wraxton. Amy removed the jewel and placed it back into the case. Perhaps he could return it.

She went to sleep trying to imagine how a woman could be so stupid as to refuse Trent even with all his inconsistencies and flaws. The puzzlement of him could make life interesting for a lifetime.

A key grated in her lock and Amy sat up in bed, wondering what Mrs. Harris could want at such an hour, but it was Wraxton, looking rather disheveled by the light of the candle he was carrying.

"What are you doing here?" she demanded. "And where did you get a key to my room?"

"There is a row of them in the butler's pantry." He leaned unsteadily against the door, managed to relock it, and slid the key into the pocket of his dressing gown. He put his finger to his lips in an exaggerated manner. "Quiet, now. I can see you want me." He staggered a little as he approached the bed and Amy instinctively reached for the candle. Like a fool he handed it to her and she promptly directed the flame at the back of his hand.

"Arrgh! You little fiend!" he shouted to the darkened room. Amy slid from the bed but dared not get close enough to try for the key. Instead she made for the window and wrestled it open. She had only a slight amount of trouble swinging herself over the sill and onto the trellis in her nightgown. Actually it was a safer climb in her bare feet than if she had been wearing shoes. Wraxton leaned out, grabbing her by the nightgown.

"Come in here! Headache, indeed. I know a tasty morsel when I see one. You are no more Severn's ward than I am. You are his latest light skirt."

"No!" She struggled in his grasp but succeeded only in tearing her nightgown. She shouted for Trent, then, as loud as she could. She heard a door bang and someone pounding on her bedroom door.

"Amy, what is it? Open up."

"It's Wraxton," she called, hitting at the drunken man's probing hands.

"Damn you, Wraxton. I shall kill you for this."

She heard two heaves and then the door shuddering open. To her surprise Wraxton sailed out the window in his nightgown and landed in a holly bush where he lay quietly moaning.

"Serves you right," she said, looking down at him.

Trent's hand reached down to grasp her by the arm and he pulled her up onto the sill as though she weighed nothing, then whisked her inside.

He hugged her to him for a moment. "Are you all right? He did not hurt you?"

"No, he did not have time." She was rather touched Trent did care, when taken by surprise, anyway. She savored the all-embracing warmth and safety of his arms and was glad that he seemed reluctant to let her go. She buried her face against his warm chest as the sounds of the waking house floated up to them, Draco thundering down the stairs, Minton and the others opening their doors and asking each other what was happening.

"What the devil?" Draco said from the yard. "Must have been drunk enough to fall out the window."

Trent's chuckle vibrated against her cheek, and when he released her, she shivered a little, but not from the cold.

"A little frightened, are you?" He held her to his chest again and splayed his hands out over her back to warm her. She snuggled against him, listening to his heartbeat settle from excitement to its strong steady throb. It touched something in her, and she felt suddenly alive in a way she had not before. She was only one layer of cloth away from his bare skin and she wanted so to touch him.

Amy gave a shuddering sigh and Trent suspected she was crying. Even an enterprising woman could be frightened and the temptation to kiss her fears away was overwhelming. If he was not careful he might do something as unconscionable as what Wraxton had been planning. He slowly slid his hands up to embrace her shoulders and pulled her back from him to try to see her face in the dark. This matter of hugging someone was not so hard after all. He thought he had managed it rather well. He brought his fingers up to trace her cheeks but they were dry. Her eyes were wide and rapt with excitement. "Not crying?" he whispered.

"Oh, no. I never cry." Amy held the torn sleeve of her nightgown together. He felt that familiar pull of longing, but it was beyond something sexual. He wanted her and the bright future she could have. Yet to so much as touch her again would contaminate her.

He moved as though in a trance, bent to her as though he were bewitched, and kissed her, his mouth slanting over her, his tongue nudging her ripe lips open. His arms were around her again as though they could think for themselves and her hands . . . what were her hands doing stroking his back? Her tongue met his shyly at first, and she tasted of strawberries. He wanted to lose himself in the taste, the scent of her. She slid her tongue alongside his and pressed herself to him. He imagined being in bed with her and slid one hand to her rounded buttocks. She gasped a little then, and the spell was broken.

He dropped his arms and stared at his hands as though they were foreign things that had betrayed him. Amy stared at him, her suffused lips parted, her eyes wide with surprise, and her head cocked to one side as though she meant to ask him something.

"Oh, my God! What have I done? I am so sorry."

"I am not," she whispered.

"Never tell anyone what I did. You must try to forget it. I had far too much to drink."

"I am all right, but we had better see how Wraxton is. We might have a problem, if you have killed him."

"You stay here. I mean it. If I do lose my temper and kill him I do not want you to see."

By the time he had gotten downstairs Draco had pulled Wraxton out of the holly, and none too gently.

When Trent emerged from the house he strode purposefully toward Wraxton and grabbed him by the throat, backing him up against the wall of the house.

"Don't hurt me," the man choked out.

"Hurt you? I shall do more than hurt you if any whisper against my ward is ever heard in London. I shall find a higher window next time and they will be scraping your miserable guts off the cobbles."

Trent ordered out the antiquated traveling carriage Amy's aunt had used, and had Wraxton tossed into it in his nightshirt with his baggage. He then told Jessup to take the man to the doctor's at Biddenham.

An hour later Trent was lying in bed wide awake with his bad shoulder thumping dully. He had opened the window a crack to let in some cool air to clear his head. What was he thinking, to be seducing his ward? That was his problem; he had not been thinking. In the excitement of the moment he had forgotten she was not just any woman. He was in a position of trust, not a position of his own making, but the world had certain expectations of a man in charge of an innocent young woman. He had to remember his life was always under scrutiny. If he betrayed the slightest hint of romantic interest in his ward her reputation would be ruined.

Why had she gone so still in his arms, like a captive bird, playing dead in the hope that it can escape? He could never remember feeling so betrayed by his own body before. He wanted to protect her, to make her life better, and he had only made it worse.

There had been some darker feeling, indefinable, like

a shadow in a cave. He had never felt before that he was a threat to women. Various of them had done unscrupulous things to him with impunity. He did not expect them to be other than petty and scheming. But Amy, with less reason to trust him than any of them, had turned to him in her hour of need. And he had taken advantage of that. He must see her married to someone else to protect her from the one man who was the most danger to her. Trent Severn.

9

~ಿ~

The sound of a spade rasping against earth gave Trent the illusion someone was digging a grave in the dark. For Amy's father or for his? Or perhaps his own grave. The spade struck a rock and Trent opened his eyes. It was no dream, for the scrape of metal against earth continued as he stilled his pounding heart. But there was no snow. Through the slightly open window a warm breeze drifted, smelling of freshly turned earth and all its possibilities. Bright sunshine creeping in through the window hangings drew him out of bed. From his room Trent could see all of the stables but only part of the gardens. His head ached from the wine last night, but that was the least of his worries. How was he going to face Amy this morning?

As he shaved and dressed that dark sad thing stirred in him again and he recognized it as guilt. He had felt it when his father had lain dying at his feet. If only he had gone to the foundry that day. He had spent enough afternoons there against his mother's wishes and without his father's consent. But he arrived too late and regarded his father's death as his fault. Just as Amy's solitude was his fault. But in her case it was not too late to make amends.

As he left his room he went to her door and knocked. It swung open on its hinges, the splinteded frame unable to hold it shut and giving stark evidence of his desperation to get to her the previous night.

It was a Spartan room, more like a boy's than a girl's. On impulse he went to her armoire and opened it. There were no more than a dozen dresses, mostly well-worn and nothing presentable for evening wear. The bottom of the wardrobe was not full of pretty slippers as it should be, but several pairs of sturdy riding boots, a set of spurs, two crops and a pair of gloves. He closed it and went downstairs thinking about the barrenness of her life.

From this day forward he must never let her know that he felt anything except the most benign interest in her. And he had offered her to Draco just because she was an inconvenience to him. He felt badly about that now. He should have discussed it with her first. Still it would be better if she married Draco than a stranger. He tried to picture Amy and Draco married and once again had to shake his head, for the image would not come. It would be best not to picture Amy in bed with anyone. He tried instead to picture Amy playing the pianoforte for a worshipful Draco, and he was surprised to feel a spark of something he had never felt for his friend before . . . jealousy.

When he got to the dining room he realized how early it was and went out to see who was making such a racket. When he came around the corner of the house there was Amy in sturdy shoes and a worn skirt, spading one of the flower beds. Amy looked up when she saw him, her cheeks pink with exertion and her unruly hair curling around her neck. He read uncertainty in her face as his dragging steps took him toward her. She was expecting a rebuff.

He cleared his throat. "I pay for a gardener as well."

"So do I," she replied, turning over another spadeful of earth. "But I like digging the beds. Besides, Pellow is so old he cannot do it."

"Let me help."

"You are helping. You freed me of the dreaded Fenwick."

"But I exposed you to Wraxton." He took off his coat and took the spade from her. "I mean, let me help now."

She surrendered the tool to him and folded his coat over her arm. He bent to the work as though he were not a gentleman, and the task was not foreign to him. In fact he enjoyed spading since you could see the results.

"You are a mystery, Trent. It occurs to me that in spite of the *Post* I really know nothing about you."

"There is not much to know."

"But you are obviously used to this kind of work."

"With the war I turned my hands to a great many tasks that might not otherwise have come my way. Digging fortifications was one of them."

"So you were there some of the time?"

"Someone had to go get Draco when he was wounded."

"I wish I'd had, when I was growing up, just one friend as close to me as Draco is to you."

He stopped and looked at her. "That should have been me. I do not know why Mother wanted us raised apart, but she seemed determined that we would never be in the same household together."

Amy laughed. "I just had a thought. Perhaps she intended for us to marry someday. So she would not have wanted us to think of each other as siblings."

She looked at him expectantly but with a little fear, he thought, lest he crush this idea of hers like a clod of earth. It came back to him what she had said last night. That she was not sorry he had kissed her. But it was probably the first kiss she had ever received. Trent wet his lips. "I had not thought of that. Do you see her as a matchmaker, that she would care about happiness for either of us?" Trent stopped and leaned on the handle of the spade.

"Well, no, but she might not want my fortune to be bestowed on a stranger. She might think it convenient to keep the businesses, the partnership together."

"That is true. When you marry, if you are not careful about the marriage contract, your husband might get everything."

"How is it left? Not to me when I marry, but to me unconditionally?"

"Yes, when you are twenty-five you are free to follow your head or your heart as you choose."

She stroked his coat as it lay over her arm and he could almost feel the caress of her fingers.

"Perhaps I will find a way to do both. Look, you have finished."

"Yes, it is a relief to find I am competent at something. You had better go and change if we are to have any breakfast before we go to view this paragon of a horse you've picked out."

Amy came to hand him his coat and she was entranced with the maleness of him, the strength of his back and arms. There was so much power rolled up in Trent, and he was giving her some of that. Of course, it was only a horse after all, but he was not failing her this time. He was really going to do what she wanted.

As she walked back to the house a happy bubble of excitement rose up inside her. She felt pretty, as she changed into her riding habit. Even though it was the same dull riding costume she had worn yesterday, she made sure she set her hat at a becoming angle and tied up her ragged curls so that they did not show so much. She thought she looked different somehow, desirable. That kiss. That kiss meant everything to her.

Trent had looked bewitched, intoxicated by her. Her heart gave a flutter of joy and she felt a deep warmth spread up her thighs and center between her legs. It was wondrous to want something so much that you lost your reason.

She pulled on her riding jacket and picked up her whip. It would be best to make no reference to the kiss. She felt closer to Trent for having a secret to keep for him, something to hold in her heart, where there had never been anything before.

What had changed was that she was in love with Trent Severn, but she pulled up short on the threshold of her room when a disagreeable thought penetrated through the happy haze of her love. Just because Trent wanted her, did not mean that he loved her or even that he could love her. She must not forget that she might have a long pursuit ahead if she meant to have Trent.

As the axis of her world shifted she tried to formulate her next move. Getting Trent to marry her seemed like such a great thing she thought she would have to inch up on this goal. One kiss had been progress, but as Draco said, men did not like to be hurried or anticipated.

And she had to remember that Trent was perverse. She had to arrange it that marrying her was his idea. And for that to happen she must keep him at Talltrees. If ever he left he would be beyond her reach. And to think that two days ago she wanted rid of him.

He was an intelligent man, as was Draco, yet they never bothered to look at the world from her point of view, or to consider that she might think differently from men. That put them at a disadvantage. So her tactics would be to keep Trent here as long as possible and to learn as much about him from Draco as she could. That would be the best means to get inside Trent's defenses.

"So, Wraxton is not dead," Amy said to Draco as they breakfasted while Trent washed up.

"No, more's the pity." Draco spread jam on his toast. "I knew he had been hanging about my sister, but I had no idea he had applied for her hand."

"So you have that against him, too. Still, I would not have wanted him to die. At least not here."

Draco looked up at her. "He does have a badly scorched hand, which will be a little hard for him to explain."

Amy looked stricken. "It was an impulse. I am sorry, but I could not think how else to get away from him."

"Too bad we had so much to drink or we would have heard your screams immediately."

"I did not want to raise the house and make a scandal, but when he grabbed me I had no choice."

Draco laughed and poured himself more coffee. "Well, a scandal is what we may have all the same. Trent warned him what will happen if he speaks of this incident, but I place no reliance on Wraxton's promise."

"I am sorry." Amy picked at her toast, unable to focus on food when she was hungry in another way.

"It is our fault. We should never have let him stay. But I think Trent was trying to convince him that our visit here was innocent."

"No, it is my fault. I should have gone upstairs when Trent ordered me to." Of course then she would not have found out about Trent's attraction to her. "I should have trusted his judgment."

"He may be autocratic, but his judgment is always . . . usually sound."

"When is it not so?" Amy stared at him, hoping for some revelation about Trent.

"When it touches on his own health or happiness." Draco looked away. "There, he seems to err quite abominably."

"By proposing to your sister?"

"Good example."

"Or getting himself shot over Lady Vox."

"I was in Paris in the spring of '14 with the army of occupation."

"Did Trent really have an affair with her, as her husband suspected?"

"That is his business. I would say you should ask him, except that you probably would."

"Trent's firm handled Lady Vox's case when her husband divorced her."

"Yes, I know. It was highly irregular. He had trouble finding a barrister to plead the case."

"I think it was very heroic of him."

Draco stared at her. "Heroic? Not a madman, falling on a sword?"

"Not much of a difference. You, of all people, should realize that."

They broke off talking when Trent finally came down the stairs. But he had only just sat down with a cup of coffee when a thunder of hooves and pounding on the door brought Minton up from the kitchen.

He came into the dining room carrying a large package. "An express rider," he said as he handed Trent the bulging packet. "The rider will wait for your reply," Minton said skeptically as he eyed the bundle.

Trent pushed his coffee aside. "It looks as though Lester has found me."

"Must you deal with that today?" Draco asked. "We will be late."

Trent used his bread knife to open the packet. "I had better at least see what awaits me. Why don't you and Amy have a ride while I go through this?"

"But Trent," Amy pleaded. "What about the stallion? If we do not buy him today he will be on his way to York."

"An hour, no more. When you return, we shall take the curricle to Biddenham. My team needs to stretch their legs. Now leave me to this."

"Very well, we shall come back for you in an hour," Draco said.

After forty minutes Trent was able to dispatch the rider with replies on the more pressing matters, but it was clear that Lester was hard-pressed to make some of the business decisions that Trent should be making. Yet he found himself strangely reluctant to post off to London. Amy had become such a part of his days, and now his nights, that he was having trouble imagining life without her. He considered having a horse saddled and catching up with Draco and Amy, but finally decided just to take the spaniel for a tramp and work out the kinks in his shoulder. They had gotten no farther than the gardens when he saw Amy galloping down the far pasture slope alone. What's more, she was riding High Flyer astride, so that her habit was rucked up above her high boot tops. She cleared the tall gate on the far side of the pasture. Trent waved at her and shouted, but unheeding, or unhearing, she jumped the near gate and disappeared into the stable block. Trent was striding to the stable on a fast boil when he was almost run down by one of the grooms riding out at the gallop. He had no more finished cursing at him than Amy ploughed into him on foot.

"Trent!"

"Amy! What is the matter?"

"Draco's had a fall, and he was barely conscious when I left him. I sent for the doctor and asked them to hitch up the hay wagon. Is that the best thing to carry him in?"

"I suppose." He followed her back to the stable yard. "Where is he? Can we drive to him?"

"Almost. He's by way of Squire's lane. He tried to jump that untrimmed hedge and got caught and pulled off. I did not want him to take Flyer, but he seemed so sure of himself." Amy watched Masters loading a pile of blankets, some flat boards and long rolls of linen they normally used for wrapping the horses' legs.

"But what the devil are you doing on this horse?" Trent demanded, wresting Flyer's reins away from a frightened undergroom.

"I left the mare I was riding in the field. I had to go out in the lane to catch Flyer anyway, so I rode him in."

"And risked breaking your own neck. I thought you said you had never ridden him before."

"I never said that. I said he will not tolerate a sidesaddle," Amy admitted.

Trent shook his head as he digested this information. "Get into the wagon," was all he said. As Trent mounted Flyer, Jessup crawled up on the wagon with her. Amy hoped his presence would prevent Trent ripping up at her, but it did not seem to matter to Trent who heard him.

"So Flyer would never tolerate a sidesaddle. You rode him astride?"

"There was no one else able to ride him and he had to be trained."

"Then Flyer is *your* horse," Trent concluded.

Jessup sent her a look of surprise, admiration almost, but Trent looked as though he were going to throttle her.

Trent stared at Jessup and Amy thought the groom was in trouble, too, but Trent said nothing to him.

"I see you have done very much as you have pleased all these years and made fools of all the servants."

"It is not their fault. Why would they even guess I could ride Flyer?"

"But what you do is dangerous. You could have been killed."

With that final retort Trent rode off to look for Draco. When they arrived twenty minutes later the soldier was sitting up, leaning against Trent, and apologizing for all the bother he had caused. Only then did Trent relax his face into a derisive expression and joke with him until he and Jessup had helped him onto the wagon. Amy sat on the hay and held onto Draco, for he was light-headed and dizzy. Trent and Jessup had to help him into the house.

Amy waited for Trent in the library, pacing as the doctor tended to Draco. She was sure Trent did not know about Draco's vision problem. And this fall might make it worse. She suspected the soldier could not see out of one eye, or only imperfectly. That might be why he misjudged fences and was so obsessive about arranging his place setting. Much as she sympathized with Draco not wanting it known, she now realized his secret was dangerous.

Trent came in finally, the lines about his mouth grim and strained.

"Do not keep it from me," Amy pleaded. "How is he?"

"We will not know for a few days if he has taken any permanent harm. He keeps falling asleep." Trent walked to the window and looked out.

"I will sit with him."

"No," Trent said tiredly. "He is my friend. I will stay with him." Trent's mouth turned even grimmer. "I should never have put work ahead of our plans. If I had been with you he would not have taken Flyer."

"But he might have fallen off of Cullen or Han. You must not blame yourself."

Trent rubbed his left hand tiredly over his eyes. "You do not understand. I bought him the commission. All his other injuries were my fault. I was so relieved when he came back from the war. To have him almost die again is more than I can stand."

Amy could feel Trent slipping into despair and wanted to reach out a hand to stop him, but she was not sure how he felt about her at the moment. If anyone was to blame for Draco's fall it was she.

"I excuse your riding Flyer to inform us about Draco. But all those other risks you take are not excusable or explainable in any way. What amazes me is not that you do it. I begin to believe there is nothing you are not capable of. But that you were never discovered?"

"I ride early before anyone is about. Anyone seeing me would only have thought it was one of the lads."

"You dressed in boy's clothes? That is why you were never caught out."

"You said in your letter to ride the horses on the estate."

Trent looked bewildered and did not even argue about what he had said. "But I did not expect you to throw your leg across the most dangerous animal on the place short of the stallion."

"I am sorry I worried you," Amy said tentatively, "but I think you overstate the risks. If Draco had been more used to Flyer, it would not have happened."

Trent rested his hand on the windowsill. "I cannot think what to do at the moment, but I have to take Draco back to London and I cannot be worrying about you at the same time. I want your word that you will keep away from all the horses until I can return. I mean I want you to stay in the house."

"But the horses are all I have," Amy pleaded. "It is like asking me to stop breathing."

"I won't be gone above a week. But I cannot leave with a quiet mind unless you promise me."

After an immense struggle, during which she stared hard out the window, Amy finally said, "I cannot promise. I will not lie to you, and I am sure I will not be able to keep away from them. They are my only friends, you see."

Trent stared at her, amazed. Any other woman would have lied to him and done as she pleased. He felt himself blinking with the effort to comprehend her, not that she would defy him, but that she had no friends. When he thought about it, there had been no visitors to the house. She spoke of no one outside the servants and the tradespeople. That, too, was his fault, he supposed. He was so angry with himself he did not know what to say to her. "I cannot just leave you here. I have to know you are safe."

"What is so different now? A few days ago you scarcely remembered I existed."

"I am here now!" he said desperately.

"Well, it is too late." Amy gripped her hands together till the knuckles shone white. "I have grown up quite without your help and I do not know how to take you now."

He stared out the window for a moment, the one he had threatened to throw Fenwick from, then looked back at her, having come to a decision.

"I have not told you everything. Before Fenwick left he made some threats."

"Oh, what could he do? Ruin my reputation? Well, I do not care a farthing for my reputation. Anyone who knows me will never believe him."

"But he also made threats against you, against your person. I cannot leave you here unprotected."

"Then take me with you." Amy took an uncertain step toward him, then halted. "I can help take care of Draco."

Trent wanted to reach out his arms to her, wanted to hold her and protect her from all harm, but he compressed his mouth and looked away. "And you would stay where? At my house? I shall think of something."

Amy blew out an impatient breath. "What could Fenwick do?"

"He could kill you, as you ride at training exercises or walk your dog. Do not underestimate how evil someone can be just because you hold him in contempt. As for Draco, I begin to think he has taken too many head injuries. I wonder if he should be riding at all."

"But what else is there for a cavalry officer?" Amy pleaded.

"He will have to find some other occupation."

"But it was my fault," Amy blurted out.

"What do you mean?" Trent asked quietly.

Amy talked so fast she almost stuttered. "I lost my nerve and hesitated at the hedge. He had to pull up or override me. That is why he fell."

"You?" Trent scoffed. "I wager you have never hesitated in your life."

"Nevertheless, I did this time."

Trent felt his face turn ashen and he closed his eyes for a moment. There was nothing she could have said that would have caused him more pain. He was having a hard time choosing between his duty to his friend and his responsibility for his ward. That she caused the accident should make no difference. It could have happened at any time. Draco was not safe, would never be safe. And he could not protect Amy, either. For a man married to control, it was a bitter realization. Not trusting his voice, Trent went to the door and let himself out.

When Trent closed the door, there was dead silence from the other side of the panel for a moment, then Amy heard his footsteps as he strode away. She wished now she had not told that lie. It would keep Trent from finding out about Draco's vision problem, but had she really done Draco a favor? What if Trent let Draco ride Flyer again and Draco did get killed on the horse?

And she had hurt Trent, by making him have to choose between her and a lifelong friend. Now that she had come to his notice, she was making his life chaotic, and he was not used to it. Once again she felt sorry for him, for his need to control everything and make it safe. Didn't he understand that control was an illusion, that how safe you were had little to do with how careful you were?

But she would never get to tell him these things for he was now unreachable. There was no point in waltzing with the notion of marrying him someday. He must hate her for causing the accident to Draco. It would be best if she put him out of her mind and focused on Talltrees. How odd that the object of her whole life's ambition could be pushed out of her mind by one tight-lipped, guilt-ridden man.

10

It was well past midnight and Trent still sat by Draco's bed. His friend was asleep and breathing easily. Perhaps there was no permanent harm done. Why then had he been so cold to Amy? She had made a novice's mistake and had owned up to it. That had taken a good deal of courage. And she had not given him a false promise, one she knew she might be tempted to break. Not to mention her clear thinking in getting help for Draco. He should have managed the interview without telling her about Fenwick's threats. He could leave Jessup here to look out for her until he returned. Or have him take her someplace safe, out of Fenwick's area.

What a damn shame. He had wanted to spend time with her, learning about Talltrees, perhaps teaching her a thing or two about . . . what could he teach her? That the world was never as fair to women as to men? That she would not have as many choices because she was a woman? That was the very thing he had always hated about his society.

It had shocked him to realize that she had no friends, that she was indeed a prisoner here at Talltrees. Perhaps that was not entirely his fault, but he certainly was not blameless. And was it so extraordinary that an inventive girl would find a way to occupy herself by training horses? If he were dealing with a boy he might be merely amused that the lad had ridden Flyer as well as all the others. He might, in fact, have encouraged such boldness in a boy.

But what to do with Amy he had no idea. It was no longer possible just to find a competent companion for her. Because of Fenwick she now needed a protector. If only his mother had taken her in hand.

Why not now? Amy was no longer a child. That had been his mother's main objection to housing her, as he recalled. He thought of his mother's town house in Bath. It was like a citadel. No one was admitted without good reason. And she had just written to Amy, so his mother must be home. He would send Amy to stay with his mother in Bath until he could come back and deal with Fenwick. He found writing materials at the small desk in Draco's room and began a letter to his mother, concentrating on the advantages of her keeping Amy for a few weeks or even several months.

What then? Perhaps he should think beyond her coming of age. If he waited until Amy could do as she pleased, what would society think if she then chose him? It did not matter, for they need not live in London. Talltrees was close enough. It was too tempting for him to think of Amy as his. He pushed the thought away and finished the letter.

Draco stirred and fought the covers. Trent went to speak to him and restrain him.

"Wickham?" Draco mumbled.

"No, it is Trent," he whispered, taking Draco's hand in both of his. "Wickham was one of your lieutenants. Remember. He is dead."

"Wickham, dead?" Draco asked, his gaze confused

and bright with fever. "I saw him just the other day. What of the others?" The names spilled from his lips frantically of men he had fought beside; some Trent knew to be dead; some alive still or maimed. He gripped Trent's hand so hard it was painful.

"Halsey was just a boy." Draco fell back exhausted into an uneasy sleep. Trent kept Draco's hand locked tightly between his own hands, as though he could pull his friend back from whatever black abyss he faced in his nightmares.

"Draco, I thought you have not been hurt, but I think I have killed you, if this is what you face each night. No wonder you drink."

Trent sat like that for hours, torn between his guilt over Amy and his need to take care of Draco. When it was safe to take Draco back to London he would have to tell Lord Marsh about these nightmares. It had cost Trent much to alienate Lord Marsh by siding with Draco about the commission. This might ruin his welcome for good and all. If Amy would not have him, he would be alone. The thought had never bothered him overmuch until now, for there had been nothing to lose. Now there was Amy and he may already have lost her.

When Amy awoke she hurried into her clothes and went straight to Draco's room. To her delight and surprise he was scowling at a breakfast tray that contained only some porridge and tea.

"You are awake," she said.

"I am famished. Be a good girl, Amy, and see if you can get me something to eat."

"It is better when you have a fever to eat lightly." She came to rest her hand on his forehead.

"See, no fever. Ask Trent."

Amy jumped as Trent came in through the open door.

"No, but Mrs. Harris is insistent that the invalid not have either eggs or meat. She did, however, send you this toasted bread."

"Anything," Draco said, grabbing the plate and dunking one of the pieces into his tea.

"If you are feeling as hungry when we reach Oakingham, I shall buy you breakfast there."

"You are going today?" Amy asked in disappointment. "Would it not be better to wait a day or two?"

"No," Trent said in a clipped voice. "For you are departing for Bath this morning."

"Bath? But Draco is the one who is ill. It would make more sense for him to go to Bath."

"Never," Draco said. "The water is foul there."

"You will be my mother's guest for a few weeks."

"But she's not even—" Amy bit her lip in confusion. Lady Agatha's letter had been mailed two days ago from Bristol. She was not in Bath, but Amy was not about to volunteer that information. She decided to change her tack.

"But what about my breeding program? We missed our chance to buy Covington's stallion."

"Let the mares all rest for a year," Trent said, crossing his arms implacably.

"But Trent. . . ." Amy pleaded. *Why would he not even negotiate?*

"Please Amy, just go and pack. I have enough to deal with."

"Just wait until I come of age."

Trent smiled with satisfaction. "No one looks forward to your coming birthday with more anticipation than I. Mrs. Harris says she can spare Betty from the kitchen, if she does not have to feed the two of us any longer. The girl will act as your maid during your stay. The post chaise will be here in an hour."

"An hour? But when will I see you again, either of you?" Amy looked away. Would Trent notice that her first thought had been of him, not of her farm?

"A week or so," Trent promised. "Can I trust you to deliver this letter?" He tapped it against his cheek. "Or should I give it into the care of Jessup?"

"Jessup is coming? Very well. I will go to Bath," Amy said bitterly as she strode toward the door. "It will cost me a whole year. I hope you are satisfied." Amy spun and wrenched the door open.

"In the extreme. I shall say good-bye to you now. I have to help Draco get ready."

When Amy had closed the door, Draco asked, "Is she going to be all right? I know she is a handful, Trent. But really, sending the poor girl to your mother. You do not want Amy's spirit broken."

"If we are speaking of breaking things, I consider my mother to be the more fragile of the two."

"The other question is, are *you* going to be all right?"

Trent turned and frowned at Draco, wondering if his friend sensed the feelings he was so desperately trying to hide.

"You look like hell," Draco said. "Had you no sleep?"

"Enough to be able to drive. Come, I will help you shave and dress. Shall I hire another coach or will my curricle do?"

"The curricle is better sprung." Draco sat up and held his head as he stood, then sat again. "But what about my horse?"

"Let him pasture here for a few weeks."

"Poor Amy," Draco said as he pulled his boots toward him.

"Why poor Amy?" Trent handed him his riding breeches. "She's the one who caused you to fall."

Draco sent him a confused look. "Are you sure about that? I thought Amy was behind me."

"No, she was ahead of you and faltered at the fence. She told me so herself. You must not be remembering right."

Draco rubbed his eyes and looked about to argue the point.

"Do not worry. It will all come back to you. Now unclench your foot."

A cold rain was falling by the time Amy and Betty left. They both wore hooded cloaks and Trent watched from the window as they got into the hired coach with Jessup holding an umbrella over them. At the last moment when Amy stopped and looked back at the house Trent stepped away from the window. He had to stop thinking about her for a few days. Just until he got the rest of his world straightened out. Perhaps he could find someone respectable to sponsor her in London. That was a laugh. No one he knew who was respectable would take such a request seriously. Jessup waited patiently until they got into the coach.

Betty seemed a responsible girl and would see that Amy got as far as his mother's house. That guinea he had slipped into the girl's hand would assure that she would get them to Bath to shop for dresses and ribbons. Jessup crawled up on the box with the coachman and they pulled away.

Idly he wondered why his mother had never found the time to give Amy a come-out. He would have footed the bill. Had she really meant for them to be married as Amy suggested? He did not think so, for his mother did not care about him. Certainly she did not appear to care about Amy. But it now seemed she had been at some pains to keep Amy isolated from possible suitors, including himself.

His thoughts were interrupted when his team and curricle were brought around and Minton and the footman came upstairs to carry down the luggage. Once Draco had climbed in, Trent took up the reins of his team regretfully, as though he were never coming back, as though this had all been a dream and he had at last awakened.

Draco leaned back in the corner of the curricle and dozed. He had once told Trent that he could sleep anywhere, had even slept while riding. Trent knew what the war must have been like, but Draco spoke of it in daylight as though it were some great lark. Now Trent knew that was not how the man really felt.

Trent would have given anything to have Amy at his side on the ride to London, but it was impossible. He was supposed to be her guardian and even though his reputation was exaggerated, he could do her no good in society except by staying away from her. He had not lived like a monk, but his exploits were nothing compared to what was said of him. And he had never minded that. It kept a great many women away from him, including his mother.

But now that he would have given anything to be respectable, it was beyond his power to change things. And probably it would not have helped. Even the most respectable of English gentlemen could not get away with marrying a ward with a fortune. He would have been sniggered at as a grasping seducer, if he had attempted such a thing.

But in a few months time Amy would be independent of him, his partner in the business. Or she could sell out to him if she liked. Then if they were to marry no one would think that he was cheating her. They might still wink and congratulate him on keeping her close all these years, but he cared nothing for that.

What did he know anyway? He stumbled from one mistake to another, staying at Talltrees alone with her, buying her clothes. She was right. He had treated her with no more regard than he would a kept woman. The only transgression he had not committed was letting everyone see him driving down Oxford Street with her in his curricle.

He had been wrong about other things. He had thought Draco safe, that he had come home whole. And now he knew that was not so.

Before the wheels of the post chaise had gained the main road Amy had formulated a plan. "What are you crying about?" Amy asked Betty.

"I don't think I want to go to Bath."

"We are going to Bath together. And you are going to get your wish."

"What wish, miss?" Betty gave a sniff.

"To be a young lady."

"Whatever do you mean?"

"We are going to trade places, and then Betty, that's me, is going to leave. And you will take my place at Lady Agatha's. Think of it, breakfast in bed with chocolate every morning. Strolling in the pump room, the dances—"

"But miss, won't this Lady Agatha recognize you?" Betty wiped her eyes with her apron.

"She isn't there. I just had a letter from her in Bristol. And she will not be home for two weeks. By then I will come back for you and . . . and then we will return to Talltrees."

"But I do not know how to dance."

"I will teach you."

Betty was a shy girl, but she could remember a good deal. During the day it took the chaise to get to Bath, Amy packed her head with everything she thought would be useful for a lady to know, though she confessed that she was no authority. She even taught her some dance steps in the private parlor at the inn where they had luncheon. By the time they got to Bath, Betty was well rehearsed and Amy had even made some improvements in her accent. But as the carriage pulled up to a door on the Royal Crescent, Betty lost her nerve. Amy almost had to drag her inside. Jessup stayed only to deliver the letter to a grim butler and dump them and their bags in the hall.

This individual informed them that his mistress was not in residence and showed them to a small sitting room until he could figure out what to do with them.

So far as Trent could tell, Draco had slept the whole way to London, as a soldier might who was on campaign and saw a much welcome chance for rest. But Trent could not be easy in his mind about that fall.

That Amy had caused it and had admitted it, surprised him. He had come to trust her skill on a horse and apparently with good reason, since she had managed to ride Flyer herself. And perhaps he had overreacted to Fenwick's threats by shipping her off to Bath. But she was much too alluring, and when he was around her he could not think straight. Sooner or later he would lose control again and do something in public that would ruin her. Until he could plan, it was much better for him to keep Amy at a distance.

If only no permanent harm had been done to Draco. The headache was to be expected, but the dizziness worried him. He drove directly to Lord Marsh's town house and down the alley to the stable entrance. He caught a glimpse of Lord Marsh at his study window on the back corner of the granite edifice and was surprised to find Draco's father home at a time of day when he would normally have been at his club.

"He has had a fall," Trent explained, when Lord

Marsh came out to greet them. Of course, Draco scorned even Trent's aid in getting out of the carriage, but some dizziness overtook him and Trent was there to help him up the several flights of stairs to his room at the back of the house. Trent stayed until Lord Marsh's valet had helped Draco undress and had bullied the protesting soldier into going to bed.

Trent went tiredly downstairs and into the study as Lord Marsh directed. He stood there dumbly and tried to think what to do next.

"Tell me what happened," Lord Marsh said quietly as he entered the masculine room and poured Trent a brandy. The older man's face was more lined than Trent remembered, his brown hair grayer, but he was just as strong and solid as ever, as calm as ever.

Trent swayed a little, feeling for the first time his own exhaustion, now that it did not matter.

"And sit down," Marsh said, "before you fall down."

Trent sat. "It was not his fault. My ward hesitated at a fence. It was either a fall or a collision. Draco hit his head."

"You are sure about this?" Marsh sloshed a small amount of liquor in a glass for himself, but then put it down on the desk without touching it and leaned there to regard Trent.

"Yes, why?" Trent took a swallow of the fiery liquid and coughed.

"Nothing." The older man stared out the window at the alley.

"Do you know about the nightmares?" Trent asked without meeting his eyes.

Marsh turned to him and sighed heavily. Trent could never remember in all the times he had been with the man a spark of anger from him, except that time he had informed Lord Marsh that he had bought Draco a commission. Lord Marsh had come close to hitting him, but had withdrawn his hand at the last moment. Trent wished now that the blow had been dealt and that it had killed him.

"I know, but his mother and sister do not. I have taken the room next to his."

Trent looked up at him. "Every night?"

"No, not as bad as that." The older man paced the small room from window to door and back again. "When he came back from Spain, he scarcely ever slept, at least not at home, so I had no idea. But he took that wound in Belgium and did stay here when he returned. That is when I realized he had a problem."

"Problem? He calls out the name of every soldier he has ever known," Trent said desperately. "He is living in the past and that is the nightmare. He loses them all over again when he wakes up."

"I have heard that litany. But usually he is just restless."

"You mean usually he gets drunk enough to sleep the night through."

"Yes, so it has not been obvious to my wife what state Draco is in. Of course, now Madeline thinks I am having an affair."

Trent ran the back of his hand across his eyes and gave a hoarse cough. "I thought you always had separate rooms."

"Yes, but not in separate corners of the house. She is convinced I am sneaking out at night." Lord Marsh chuckled, then fell silent as he leaned against the desk again.

"When Draco left for the army you told me I had killed your son."

"But he came back to us." Lord Marsh clasped his strong hands together. "I regret how hasty I was. I should have known he could take care of himself."

"But he did not come back the *same*." Trent finally

looked up at the older man. "He drinks far too much. Draco has not come back to us. And for that I must take the blame."

"Nonsense. He is here; he is well, most of the time."

"He is fighting that goddamned war in his sleep every night. That is not well!" Trent stood up and set the glass on the desk.

Marsh stared at the empty glass. "What do you think would have happened to him if he'd had to stay behind?"

"He would have been . . . himself."

"No, he was champing at the bit even before that. He would have joined as a regular, or else fallen in with even more dissolute companions than—"

"Than me, you mean?"

Marsh turned back to the window impatiently. "Do you take me for a fool? I know how you have fought this war with your armaments and your ships, not to mention your money. And I know the other battles you fight with the law."

"Every decision I make seems so right to me at the time." Trent clenched his right fist. "Only afterward do I realize how poor my judgment is."

"Do you think there is a man or woman who does not feel the same? Do not let regret eat you up."

"But I feel so guilty." Trent stared at him, swaying on his feet and not knowing if it was the liquor, the lack of sleep, or both.

"That either. Think of all the times you kept me and Draco from coming to words, or even blows."

"Will it always be that way between you two?"

"Until he has a place of his own. If I could manage to die I am sure he would pull himself together and take control of things admirably."

"Do not say such a thing. Draco may seem bluff but he

cares about you. I am sure of it. And he does not want to step into your shoes."

"It might be healthier if he did take an interest in the estate."

"I had some thought that he might marry . . . but that may not work out. I have decided to ask if he will run the foundry for me."

"He knows nothing about it. That will give it a high appeal for him."

"He needs a challenge, something new, and God knows I am tired of it. But it is *trade*."

"Madeline will find a way to put a genteel spin on it. Do you think you can talk him into it?"

"Depends on how I present it to him."

"Very good of you, Trent, to let him play at ducks and drakes with your fortune rather than mine."

"What do I care about money now that the war is over?"

"I worried almost more about you than Draco when everything ended."

"About me? Why? Oh, that Vox affair."

"It is difficult to settle down to normal life. You may have noticed my son has not sold out. But you, who have so much to occupy you, you too seemed to not care what happened to you."

"I admit to a certain feeling of being lost. There is less to do now, but I wasn't about to put a gun to my head."

"But you did try to put your neck in Diana's noose. She would never do for you. She needs too much tending, like a rose grown under glass." Lord Marsh finally picked up the tumbler, looked at it and took a drink, a sign his lecture was at an end.

"I realize that now. Not an easy woman to satisfy."

"Take my advice and find someone like yourself, perhaps look beyond the ton."

"Oh, you mean a *cit?*" Trent asked with his crooked grin.

Marsh coughed and glared at Trent. "So you saw that, did you?"

"Worse has been said of me. Believe me, sir, the *Morning Post* is the least of my worries."

11

*M*uch to her dismay Amy failed to rise at the crack of dawn, but Lady Agatha's household slept late in the morning, so she decided she would attract less notice if she waited until the doors had been unlocked before she made her escape. She shared a room with Betty, who had snipped off Amy's unruly locks the night before. Amy was giving the girl some last reassurances while watching the traffic out the window, when a familiar whiskey tooled around the circle, looking even shabbier here that it did at Talltrees.

"My God, it's Fenwick. What the devil is he doing here?"

"Your agent?" Betty came to stare out the window.

"Not anymore. Trent fired him. Do you realize what this means? Fenwick must know Lady Agatha."

They waited while Fenwick knocked, conferred with the butler and left again.

"They did not admit him," Betty said.

"That is because she is not at home. He must have been spying on me all these years. Damn. And Trent, without knowing it, sent me straight into his hands. I wonder if the butler let slip that I am here." Amy paced the length of the bedroom, the long cloak flapping about her boots and breeches.

"Oh, miss, I don't want to do this anymore."

"Do not worry, Betty. Fenwick has no reason to harm you, but according to Trent he made some vile threats against me. You have to be brave now to cover my escape." Without giving the girl a chance to disagree Amy pulled up her hood and left.

She slipped out the back door and trudged out of the city, shedding the cloak and the trimmings from her hair at the first bridge on the way to York. She watched as the bundle floated down the Avon, then caught on a snag in the shallows. She shrugged and donned a cap she had secreted and she did indeed look like just what she wanted to be, a stable lad on his way to York for a position. Just to be safe she walked the first stage, intending to catch a coach at Chippenham, rather than at Bath.

She would rather have taken the stage to London and searched out Trent to tell him of Fenwick's villainy, but she could not guess what sort of reception she would receive from her guardian. He might still be too caught up in Draco's condition to worry about her. Draco's accident had caused her to miss her chance at the stud she needed. She'd be safer in York than anywhere, so she would go and bring the horse back herself.

By then Betty's disguise might be revealed by Fenwick and her expedition found out. But that did not matter. She'd show As Ever Trent she did not need his advice or his protection. Most of all she did not need that love he seemed to bestow with such reluctance, then withdraw again when it was inconvenient to be bothered with her. She choked on a sob, for she did need his love and Talltrees would never be the same again without him there.

She did not have to walk all the way to Chippenham,

since a farmer took her up in his wagon. She tried to give him a penny for the ride but he would not hear of it. That meant the clothes she had used for training Flyer were so grubby that they would lead no one to have reason to rob her.

Draco's check and the money she had won at cards were still secreted in several packets about her person. But she had not known what to do with the ring, so she had tied it on a stout leather thong about her neck. If she'd had a chance to cash Draco's check she would probably have enough money to buy the beast outright. If necessary she could pawn Trent's ring and redeem it later. Odd that he had not thought to demand it back from her. Had he been so drunk that he did not remember losing it, or had his concern for Draco pushed every other consideration from his mind?

She conceded that Draco's well-being had pushed such a thing as a stallion into the background for her as well. She had spent an unquiet night worrying over the soldier. But he had seemed so much better the next day she did not see why Trent hustled him off to London. If one of them had thought of it they could have sent word for Lord Covington not to send the colt she wanted. But Trent would have argued against that, not having seen the animal himself. Why could he not understand the importance of what she wanted? As she crawled on top of the mail coach at Chippenham she wondered what he would say if he could see her now. He would explode.

After delivering Draco to his parents' home Trent had gone to bed in his own lonely house, but he slept only fitfully in spite of his exhaustion. He spent the better part of the night worrying the problem of Amy like a dog with a bone, and awoke early, no closer to a solution. Time would take care of his legal obligation soon enough. All he had to do was stay away from her for a few months. That sounded easy enough, but he missed her already. How could she have become such a part of his life in a few short days? It was because she always knew what he was thinking. Even Draco could not do that. She anticipated him, almost as though she were the other half of him, a piece of himself he had been missing all these years.

As he ate an indifferent breakfast the next morning in his empty dining room he pondered his moral obligation, then laughed out loud at the thought of him laying on himself a charge with the word *moral* attached to it. His staid grayhaired butler Fenton eyed him so suspiciously with his watery blue eyes, Trent announced he was going to the office.

Once there he spent the entire day dealing with his considerable stack of mail, to the amazement of Lester. He read each letter and either made a note on it or answered it in his own hand as penance for all the letters of Amy's he had not attended to in the past. If only he had those years to live over again he would not be such a flint-hearted fellow.

Trent laughed again when he realized Lester must be wondering what faux pas he could have committed that would prompt his employer to take on this onerous task himself. It was almost dark when Trent looked up and saw his secretary hesitating in the doorway. He recalled that the man had a wife and two or three children waiting for him at home.

"You should have left by now, Lester. You will miss your dinner."

"Sir, if there is something I have done that does not quite please you—"

"Why? Have I shouted at you without realizing it? I apologize. My mind is occupied."

Lester advanced into the room. "No, not at all. Per-

haps it is something I have omitted to do . . . with regard
to your correspondence." Lester glanced at the pile of
notes ready for mailing.

Trent looked up at him with a challenging expression.
"Did you always sign me *As Ever, Trent?*"

"Why, yes. I saw you use that closing many times. I
thought it was what you preferred."

Trent stared into space as the lamps were being lit in
the street.

"I could change it," Lester volunteered.

"Hmm? No. No matter. It is fine." Trent looked about
his tidy desk. "No mail from Bath, I suppose?"

"Bath? No, you have seen every scrap of mail that has
come into this office this week. Sir, if you wish me to
give notice, you have only to say so."

"Notice?" Trent laughed. "Leave me, you mean?"

"Yes, sir." Lester stood almost at attention.

"Is it something I said? I told you I have been distracted today. Pay me no attention."

"But you have not said *anything*. Forgive my imperti-
nence, but you have not been yourself, sir, since you got
back from Berkshire."

"No, but perhaps I am the man I should have been all
along. You may as well go home, unless there is any unfinished business."

Lester cleared his throat and materialized some fold-
ers from behind his back. "There are one or two
items. . . ."

Trent groaned.

"But they can wait until morning."

"Lester, no one waits for me at home. Trot them out if
you have a mind to."

"Lord Harding's solicitor is looking for someone to
represent him in a crim con suit. There are children, so

there is no question of an annulment." Lester advanced and placed a document before Trent.

"No," Trent said.

"What is that, sir?"

"No, we will not represent him. I know his wife. The veriest mouse. He means to leave her destitute. And it was her fortune that made him. You frequent the coffee-houses for lunch, do you not?"

"I . . . if that displeases—"

"Lester, stop acting as though I have taken leave of my senses. I want you to find out who Lady Harding's solicitor is and approach him about us representing her. Or if she has not engaged a solicitor, make the offer to her."

"But that case will be more difficult. The law is on his side."

"I see no reason to let the law get in the way of justice," Trent said. "Can you get us the case?"

"I shall see what I can do. There is one other matter I wish to lay before you."

"Go on."

"Lord Vair's widow is seeking a new man of business. Her solicitor approached me."

Trent leaned back in his chair. "Vair is the fellow who shot himself last year—gaming debts or something."

"Yes, sir. His affairs are an impossible tangle. There is not much to be salvaged from the estate." Lester placed a bulging portfolio in front of Trent.

Trent leafed through it. "What is your advice, Lester?"

"Well, sanity would prompt us to refuse to represent her, but—"

"But there are children?" Trent guessed, closing the case file up again.

"Yes, sir. All in their minority. I would not have bothered you, but they are about to be put out of their house."

bring her son into possession of a decent income by the time he came of age, when the daughter of the house sailed into the room and stared at him with the innocence of a doe.

"Not now, Crissy. Mr. Severn, this is my daughter, Crissy."

"Pleased to meet you." Trent rose and bowed.

The girl curtsied and fled with a flutter of skirts and Trent sat down again.

"Did you know I have a daughter of marriageable age?" Lady Vair asked suspiciously.

"No, but I can see how we may have to adjust our plans."

"If you are thinking—"

"What? She must have some sort of come-out. How old is she?"

"Seventeen," Lady Vair said icily.

"Oh, that gives us a few years. Just keep her occupied until then. Girls of that age are always into trouble, riding off on horses . . . or . . . what is it?"

Lady Vair ceased looking at him as though he were mad and smiled. "You are a father, then?"

"No, I am unmarried, but my ward is the veriest handful. Well, I have kept you long enough. Lester will call on your solicitor who will explain everything in more detail."

Trent decided to walk home, putting off even further his perusal of Amy's letters. What was there to be gained from that task but more guilt? Yet he had to know the whole of his crimes.

On arriving home he went into the library, still thinking about the relief on Lady Vair's face when she finally realized that he had no designs on either her or her daughter. Probably she would still be suspicious of him for months. Women usually were.

He surprised his butler by requesting a pot of coffee rather than wine or brandy. When he opened the portfolio the top letter was Amy's request for an advance on her allowance and Lester's draft letter refusing her in such formal terms. *As Ever, Trent.* Was he as he ever was, now that he actually knew the enterprising Amy? Fenton brought the coffee and without explanation a selection of fruit and nuts. The man lit an extra branch of candles and left him.

Trent flipped the folder over and started from the back as he munched on an apple. The first notes were directed to his father: thank you's for birthday and other gifts. She must have written to him at the office, and the ever efficient Lester had filed them. This was an unexpected glimpse of a father he had never known. Had Andrew Severn really picked out a new muff for the child Amy? It became apparent that his father had cared about Amy much more than he had cared about Trent, but whose fault was that? He had tried to get close to the man, but Mother was always in the way. "Not a fit occupation for a gentleman," was her condemnation of the foundry. She had even caviled at his spending his holidays in the law office. So when his father always pointedly drove to the city without him, perhaps it had been to placate his mother, not because he did not like Trent.

The next note hit him like a blow to the face; condolences on his father's death. They were the kindest words anyone had ever said to him. He remembered now reading them. And he had not even replied. Lester's formal answer left him chilled. She must have always thought him some cold, unreachable, heartless . . . well, he was. At least that was the image he projected to the rest of the world.

As the years passed, Amy's penmanship improved and she tried a multitude of ploys to interest him in the affairs of Talltrees, or to draw him out about his businesses. Her thank you notes were creative, even when the gift was highly inappropriate, such as the doll he had sent her on a whim when she was seventeen. He shook his head at his own stupidity. And some years there were no gifts, because both he and Lester had forgotten, but there were still letters.

Suddenly when she was eighteen something happened, as though she had grown up overnight. She said something about feeling sure she would be able to handle her new responsibilities. That was when Fenwick had started robbing her in good earnest. He must remember to get Lester to apply for a warrant on the man. He doubted Fenwick really had the money put aside in an account. His explanation that he had been trying to teach Amy to handle her own affairs had almost prompted Trent to heave him out the window. He would be just as happy if Fenwick fled the country, rather than repaying the money he had stolen, but somehow he did not think they were rid of him yet.

The subsequent letters all spoke of a young woman in straitened circumstances, trying to cope with the vagaries of commerce. Lester's constant admonition to consult with the agent in Berkshire must have rankled beyond belief, and he could remember that as his stock answer.

By midnight he had read the lot of them and felt the deepest regret he had ever known. This was worse than sending Draco away for those eight years. This was fifteen years wasted when they could have known each other, could have been friends. Perhaps if he had not ignored her so blatantly she would not now be so contrary and assertive. But was that bad in a woman, no matter what society thought? It was, when she need not have been put through that hell. It said much that she had made a success of her business in spite of him.

140   *Barbara Miller*

He stood up and stared out into the black night relieved only by a lamp at one of the houses across the square. Perhaps it was better he had not interfered all these years. His influence on Amy could hardly have improved her character, and she might have turned out a good deal worse.

On his way to bed he tried to push aside the niggling thought that she might have had some positive effect on his character, but it washed over his mind like a soothing balm. She already had changed him, if only by making him regret his stupidity. He was supposed to be the protector, the mentor, but she was the one teaching him how to go on. And the thought of not seeing her again, even for a week, sawed away at his heart. He had no doubt there were even more painful lessons in store for him from Amy, but he would not deny those chances to be more human for anything.

He had spent too many years locked inside the hard shell that protected him against his mother's bitter words. Just because his own mother did not love him did not make him unlovable. He should have given his father more of a chance. Amy had held out her love to him like a gift and he had walked away empty-handed. Even after he had realized how much he was at fault he continued to blunder. No more. He would check on Draco, then set out for Bath tomorrow and make his apologies yet again. Apologizing was a skill Amy would make him hone to fine art.

12

*A*my arrived in York a day before the sale and found a room at a cheap inn. Plenty of time to inspect the horses and check on their bloodlines just in case there was something better offered than the one she wanted. She would introduce herself as head groom for Talltrees. No, that would not do. Masters might be known. She would claim to be a groom sent to pick out a stallion for Talltrees. The name of the farm would be her entree. As she had swayed along on top of the mail coach she had been thinking about how she would transport a stallion once she found one. She had been intending to ride him back, so she would have to buy a saddle and bridle, but that would only work if the beast had been broken to saddle. Many of them were not.

If she had to buy a steady horse, a stable mate even, to lead him home that would add to her expense. Plus she would have to buy slightly better clothes to even be allowed into the sale. Perhaps she could approach some of the owners privately. She shook her head over that. She did not have the look of a serious buyer. It would have to be the auction and she would have to pawn Trent's ring.

* * *

He dreamed again of the girl on the other side of the grave, but she was not a child anymore. She was Amy, all grown up, and no longer in need of that hug of comfort he had withheld so many years before. There were tears frozen on her lashes but she was quite composed now. She looked at him sadly and turned toward the huge black carriage that engulfed her. He ran toward her and fell down and down to his death. And woke with a start that rocked the bed.

His heart was hammering in his chest as he opened his eyes, but he had been hoping to look out the window on to the stable at Talltrees. All he could see was the back of the house across the alley. He was in London and Amy was a hundred miles away in Bath.

His butler poured shaving water for him and cleared his throat to ask if Trent meant to interview a new valet. Trent sat up on the edge of the bed and blinked away the dregs of the nightmare, only half hearing the man.

"Could you please see to it? I must have enough clothes to last until you find someone."

Fenton raised an eyebrow at this, but nodded and left.

Twenty minutes later Trent had black coffee for breakfast and very little else as he perused again the packet of letters in his vacant dining room, especially the latest ones that seemed so businesslike and adult. He had lost any opportunity to be a real guardian to Amy. And he saw no way to make up for that now. He wanted more than anything to go to her now, to try to explain himself. But would she understand?

Fenton admitted Draco, and Trent looked at his friend in amazement. "I thought you would still be in bed."

"What for? A little knock on the head is no great matter."

Draco seated himself and picked up the coffeepot just as Fenton slid a cup and saucer into place for him. The rest of the table setting appeared by magic and Trent gazed in wonder at his butler's intuitive performance. Why had he never noticed how attentive that man had always been?

"Thank you, Fenton," Trent said.

The man stared at him in surprise, nodded and left.

"Are you going to eat that sirloin or just let it congeal on the plate?" Draco asked.

Trent stared at the meat and lifted the platter. "Help yourself. It is a little bloody to suit me so early in the morning."

Draco accepted the offering and added some biscuits to his plate, leading Trent to conclude he had not breakfasted at home.

"These are good," Draco said, holding up a biscuit, "but not up to Mrs. Harris's standards. What are you reading?"

"Amy's letters. Lester saved them all. She was masterful at disguising her needs with amusing anecdotes, trying to put me in a good humor before asking for what she really wanted, things girls ask their fathers for."

"And are not refused?" Draco asked.

"And are not *ignored*," Trent said with a heavy sigh. "I feel suddenly very old, as though I have been away at sea a long time and a child I left behind has appeared quite suddenly grown up." Trent leafed through them again, smiling. "What I marvel at most is the hours of labor they must have cost her, and her eternal hopefulness, her refusal to accept defeat in the face of my overwhelming . . . indifference." He let the portfolio fall shut. "It cost me something to read them, but it gave me something back, too. I have not missed her entire childhood after all."

"Do you miss Amy?" Draco stared at him intently.

"God, yes. I wish she were breakfasting with us now." Trent shook his head and studied Draco with some concern. There was a bruise on his forehead to be sure, but his eyes were clear. "Considering your condition yesterday I am amazed you are up so early and eating enough to choke a horse," Trent remarked.

"Old habits . . . speaking of habits, I keep expecting Amy to whisk into the room wearing that tattered riding outfit of hers. What do you suppose she is doing right now?"

Trent shook away the image of the black carriage and the courageous face at the window. "Perhaps she is taking an early stroll in the pump room."

"Amy? She never strolls. Your witch of a mother probably has her locked in her room."

"Come now, Draco. Mother may be cold, but she is not so medieval as that." Trent picked up a biscuit, but tossed it aside without taking a bite.

"She fair sets my teeth on edge and I have faced the French guns."

"Amy can get along with anyone. She will smooth things over."

"Perhaps." Draco chewed methodically. "She handled us right enough."

Trent stared at him and pushed the folder away. Since Draco appeared to be fine, all he had to do was speak to Lester about Mrs. Vair, before he drove off to Bath to see Amy. He found himself wishing he did not have to go to the office.

"I have a notion to take a bolt to Bath," Draco said. "Never been there before. You never know. I might like the place. Those nasty waters might do my head some good."

Trent stared at his friend, wondering if Draco were now interested in courting Amy. He didn't know what to say. "Yes, I think you should go. Why not take my carriage?" If Draco meant to romance Amy then Trent would not. Suddenly Trent realized he was weighing a lifelong friendship against the love of his life and Amy was winning. He did not want to concede to Draco, but did not know how to tell him.

"Oh, I thought I might ride," Draco said with a crooked smile.

Trent choked on a sip of coffee. "What are you playing at?"

"I think you should realize I faced far worse than a bump on my head during the war and survived. I'm pretty tough and I don't like the idea of you sending Amy off by herself just to take care of me."

"You were so dizzy you couldn't stand."

"No excuse for you to neglect her. I have to start to come second. Remember that."

"What?" Trent realized he must be staring again.

"In case it has escaped your notice, she is in love with you."

Trent jerked and banged his knee on the table leg. "You must be mistaken. She has every reason to hate me, especially after I shipped her off like a prisoner."

"I know something of love, and Amy has been smitten."

Trent pushed his coffee aside. "What do you know of love?"

"We'll not speak of that, but I have seen the way she looks at you. I have seen that look in a woman's eyes before."

"Next you will be claiming I have fallen head over heels for her."

"I think you would if you would let yourself. You are too tightly controlled by far."

"I should have no thoughts of Amy. I am supposed to be fending off men like me."

"What the hell do you mean by men like you? You may lay claim to a rake's reputation, but I know you, and it is not so."

"So you are not going to Bath to court Amy?"

Draco smiled and arranged his silverware. "I like her fine, but I do not love her, could never stand the competition. It would be torture to meet you and have her eyes caress you the way they do, to have you undressing her in your mind and me with nothing to talk about but the weather."

"We are not like that," Trent choked out.

"I have just spent two days with both of you and you most certainly are. I have never seen such a case of love at first sight."

Trent threw his napkin down. "We fight like ferrets in a sack."

"Exactly. You are meant to be married. Any other woman would be overwhelmed by you and bore you to death in a fortnight."

Trent shook his head. "If you are not going to court her, why are you going to Bath?"

"To apologize."

"For what?"

Before Draco could answer Fenton approached with a considerable stack of mail that Trent riffled through. He pounced on a letter from Bath and slit it open with his butter knife. Fenton raised his eyes heavenward, pushed the letter opener within Trent's reach, and left them.

"A problem?" Draco asked as he reached for the last biscuit.

"Amy's maid has disappeared, and apparently Amy has no idea where Betty is. This note is from the housekeeper. I have an uneasy feeling about this."

"Perhaps the child got homesick and went back to Talltrees."

"Seems odd that Amy would not know that. No matter, I think I had better go and see about this. Apparently my mother is not home at present, so Amy has been taken into the housekeeper's charge."

Draco looked thoughtful at that news. "You should write to Minton and ask him if the girl has turned up there," Draco suggested. "Or, stop at Talltrees on your way to Bath."

"Why so much concern over a kitchen maid?" Trent asked.

"Are you completely without imagination, Trent? Your mother is not at home. Suppose it is not the kitchen maid who has disappeared?"

Trent half rose when he caught Draco's meaning, then sat. "Amy—she would not do that."

"Why not? If I thought of it, I am sure Amy would."

"Because it would make me very angry."

"She told you she caused my fall. That must have made you very angry."

"She was so frightened she let it slip, and I thought I controlled myself admirably."

"Trent, don't be such a fool. Amy didn't make me fall. I misjudged the distance to the fence." He rubbed his forehead. "And the height that horse can jump."

"So she lied because she didn't want me to think less of you. But we both fall all the time."

"She did not want you to feel guilty about . . . any previous injuries that might have contributed to the fall. She chose to take your guilt on herself."

"Oh, no, now I have that to deal with."

"You should have brought her to London with us, instead of sending her away."

"Flaunt her about the ton? There are far too many ugly characters who would be after her. I would never be able to handle them all."

"Well, who is handling them in Bath?" Draco asked.

"She will not meet anyone like that in Bath." Trent folded his arms and then winced at the pull in his still tender shoulder.

"Amy? And you just said your mother is not there to watch her. Where is she, by the way?"

"I have no idea, but I see your point. I should leave immediately."

Draco leaned back in his chair. "You had damned well better do something. I miss her."

"My mother? She terrifies you."

"No. Amy. I miss Amy."

Trent grinned and shook his head. "So do I."

"I tell you again, Trent, if you do not marry Amy you will regret it the rest of your life."

"Show me how to undo my wretched life and I will marry her instantly." Trent's attention was caught by a post chaise and pair that drew up in front of the house. His mother's housekeeper descended from it, leading the maid, Betty. Well, at least he did not have to worry about her whereabouts.

Draco cast his napkin aside impatiently. "But what do you care for—"

The bang of the knocker and whispered voices in the hall distracted Draco. And the door into the dining room was almost immediately opened by Fenton to ask if Trent would see Mrs. Hodge.

"Uh-oh," Draco mouthed.

"Mister Severn," Mrs. Hodge began, then took a breath to begin her tirade.

"Are you not Amy's maid?" Trent interrupted, trying to spare the girl another tongue-lashing.

Betty stood before him in one of Amy's old dresses and burst into tears.

"Foolish girl," Mrs. Hodge said, pinching the child's arm. "Tell Mr. Severn what you told me last night."

"It will be all right, Betty," Trent said patiently. "No one will punish you for telling the truth. Why did you run away?"

"But I didn't."

"She tried to pass herself off as your ward, Miss Conde."

Draco stirred and Trent shot him an accusing look. "Where is Amy now?" he demanded.

"I don't know," Betty wailed. "She—she left the morning after we got to Bath. I was to pretend I was her."

"But where did she go?" Draco demanded.

"She will not tell," Mrs. Hodge complained.

"And it took you an entire day to discover this imposture?" Trent asked, trying again to lever the blame away from the quaking girl in front of them. If she was to remember anything, she must not be terrified.

"How was I to know they exchanged clothes? It is not my job to be taking care of young ladies. And so I shall tell Lady Agatha when she returns from Paris."

"Paris?" Draco asked.

"Betty, think," Trent said. "Amy must have given some clue as to where she was going. Not back to Talltrees, surely."

"No, for she was terrible afraid of Mr. Fenwick, so I don't think she meant to go to Talltrees."

"What do you want me to do?" the matron demanded.

"Leave Betty with Cook," Trent said. "Your expenses will be paid."

"Very good, sir. I shall be returning immediately. And

I will thank you to notify us next time you mean to send us guests."

Draco raised his lip in a sneer as the woman left with the girl. "We could go to Talltrees just to make sure Amy did not return home."

"It's on the way. If she's not there we'll go to Bath and pick up her trail," Trent said as he strode across the hall to the library and reached for a pen. "I must write a note to Lester. If you are coming you had better go home and pack."

Draco got up and came to lean on the doorframe. "I am already packed."

"Then ask my valet to pack for me."

"Uh, Trent, you do not have a valet."

"Stop throwing obstacles in my path, Draco. Tell Fenton to pack my bag and order my curricle harnessed. It is faster than the carriage. I must explain everything to Lester."

13

❧

*T*rent and Draco had passed Mrs. Hodge's post chaise before she left Mayfair. After a stop at Talltrees, a day of hard travel and three changes of horses, Trent drove immediately to the coaching office in Bath. But neither the mail coach office nor stagecoach office had sold a ticket to a red-haired girl, or a young girl wearing a cloak.

"What now?" Trent asked. "The only other way for her to get home would be to rent a horse. I suppose we could check all the inns."

"That stallion she wanted to buy. Where was it being sent?"

"The sale at York."

"We will go to York, then," Draco decided.

Trent got back into the curricle and took the reins from his friend. "I do not suppose you know when these sales are."

"Saturdays."

"Tomorrow. We cannot possibly get there in time."

They drove out of town in the general direction of York and got a change of horses at a coaching inn.

"Do you want some dinner now?" Trent asked. "But

make it quick. Once I set us on the road to York I do not intend to stop."

"No, I'm fine."

The sun was setting as they crossed the bridge over the Avon River that would lead them north. Trent looked down and caught sight of a flash of red in the debris at one of the snags down river. He jerked the horses to a stop so abruptly that Draco protested. Trent took the stone steps down to the river two at a time and stumbled through the flotsam on the muddy band. There was a cloak hooked on the tree root and floating in the dark water.

He felt himself shaking as he waded out in the slow current and the chill that crept cold fingers around his heart had nothing to do with the icy water. His heart thudded relentlessly in his chest as his brain froze. But she had only been gone for a few days. How could this be? He reached for the fabric but it was empty. He reached for the lock of hair and it came away in his hand. He plunged his arms into the river, but there was nothing else there of any substance.

He let the fabric go and it floated away from him. He had the most maddening urge to float after it, anything rather than face what might have happened to Amy. He could hear Draco calling from the end of the bridge and that was all that brought him back to himself. He waded back to the bank and climbed the stone steps. Out of breath, he leaned against the side of the curricle and opened his hand to his friend.

Draco took the wet curl of red hair from him and gave a harsh laugh. Trent stared at him in horror as Draco cast the lock away.

"She has made right fools of both of us. Here we are asking after a red-haired girl when it's a *boy* we should be looking for."

Trent stared at him dumbly until Draco's meaning

came home to him. He nodded, finally taking a shuddering breath. Of course. She had dressed as a boy before.
Why had he not thought of it?

His first fear, that she had been murdered, he pushed
away from him. Amy could not be dead. She was too
smart for that. She would never have tried to get to York
as a girl, traveling alone. What was he thinking? He had
not been thinking, except to get to her, to hold her in his
arms and not let her go again until he could make a safe
place for her.

Amy's secondhand but respectable clothes must have
made her look less like an urchin and more like a groom.
She had still raised brows of surprise when she said she
was to pick out a stud for Talltrees, for the farm was not
unknown even this far north, but as soon as she asked
some knowledgeable questions, the other grooms talked
to her, and even let her have a look at the stock they had
brought for sale the next day.

Now she was undecided. Besides Lord Covington's
colt there was one flashy bay that had some of Tartar's
blood in him, but she decided the connection was too
close even if she had liked the look of the animal. And
there was a gray with good breeding.

In Tartar she had solidness and steadiness from the
Godolphin line. She wanted either Covington's stud descended from the Darly Arab, or the gray with the Byerly
Turk bloodline. Most of the grooms could recite the lin-
eage of their charges back as far as the foundation sires.
But what she was looking at were hotheaded youngsters,
the culls, horses that might tear a mare's neck to pieces
while trying to hang onto her. And the prospect of riding
one of them . . . Amy was daring but she was not stupid.
She knew that she stood no chance at all of getting any of

the three prospects she had seen back to Talltrees with less than a brace of grooms to help her.

And if not for Trent shipping her off to Bath she might have had the horse delivered by Covington's grooms. She still had five hundred pounds left and the ring. But trying to pawn it and hire unknown men looked to be as dangerous as dealing with the unknown stud. For the first time in many years she did not know what to do, and she could have used some advice.

By the time the sale started on Saturday she still had not turned the ring into any sort of cash. Perhaps one of her prospects would be within her reach without the extra money. She could always write to Masters and have him send help.

The highest prices came early in the bidding and two of the colts were gone before she even could lodge a bid. The last came up late, the one who had the most height. The bidding choked at 400 pounds. She was about to raise her hand when the animal scented a mare and put on such a display of ill manners that everything ceased until three grooms could get the animal back under control. One of them had a bitten hand. She thought of Trent and his fears for her handling stallions. The beast might behave better for her than for men, but there were no guarantees. She let the animal go at 450, turned and walked back to her inn.

That was when the enormity of her dilemma hit her. There was no point in going back to Bath, not with Lady Agatha and Fenwick in a conspiracy against her. She decided to go home to Talltrees and wait for Trent there. She would lose a year. He would be angry and disappointed in her. For some reason she dreaded his anger less than his disappointment. His face when she told him she had caused Draco's fall had been so empty, as though there was no emotion strong enough to fill the gap her betrayal had left. But she could not have him thinking Draco incapable of riding. He just needed to watch someone take the jump first so that he could count the horse's strides with his one good eye. It would never have happened if Flyer did not insist on leading.

Trent and Draco arrived by late afternoon on Saturday having had no sleep and only very bad food. To Trent's amazement Draco seemed to thrive on privation. He dropped Draco off at the coaching office, then went to the market to make inquiries. There were only loungers about and one or two drunks at this time on a Saturday. Two of them remembered a lad with red hair, but they would probably have confessed to seeing anything with the promise of a gold coin. None could say if the lad had bought a horse.

"What did you find out?" Trent asked Draco when he returned for him.

Draco rested one booted foot on the step of the curricle. "After I greased the fellow's palm he did confess that a red-haired lad arrived day before yesterday, but he did not sell a return ticket. Of course he was not working this morning. Do we wait?"

"I do not know what to do. She was seen at the sale, but if my sources are reliable, and I doubt that, she did not buy a stallion. Would she try to take such a horse south on her own?"

"Amy?" Draco asked. "She might at this moment be galloping toward Talltrees on some monster of a horse."

"Or she might be lying in a ditch with a broken neck," Trent said in despair. "Where the devil did she get the money for a horse?"

"Don't you remember anything that happens when you are drinking? We both lost money to her at cards;

Wraxton did as well. If she was able to cash my check she had plenty."

Trent squinted as he called to mind Amy's sewing basket. "She had not time to get to her bank. Then she might not have had enough."

"Are you forgetting that diamond you staked?"

Trent moaned. "That damned ring. I had forgotten that."

"May I make a suggestion?"

"Anything. I am nonplussed."

"I shall travel south toward London and try to get word of her at each stop in case she has already left. If she has and I hear something I will leave you word at the coaching office. You can seek out the other fellow who works here and see if he sold her a ticket. If he hasn't you can follow the route she would take back to Talltrees. You might want to make a report to the local magistrate just in case."

"Very well," Trent said as Draco went to get his valise from the back of the curricle. "Draco?"

The soldier came back to look up at Trent. "What?"

"You are not going to ride, are you?"

Draco got a mulish look on his face. "I had planned to take the mail coach to make it easier to trace her. You keep your curricle for mobility."

"You are a true friend, Draco. I will not forget your help."

"Never mind. Just pray that one of us finds her."

The next morning, with ticket in hand, Amy mounted the mail coach. She preferred riding on top since there was room to move and breathe. She thought the man working in the office was looking at her suspiciously but the driver climbed onto the coach and they were off before the agent could do more than stare at her. All things considered, she was glad to be leaving York. It had been a disappointing trip. And she now realized her initial excitement had been less about escaping Fenwick and finding a horse than it had been about defying Trent.

The best she could hope for now was that she had not worried him. There was no possibility of hiding this escapade from him. And she did not think she would anyway. As annoying as he was she did love him. If that was not reciprocated, except when he was in his cups, then so be it. But she would not deceive him about herself.

They had been late leaving so that the driver flogged the horses along at a good pace to the endangerment of the top passengers and oncoming traffic that did not have a care to yield the road. They were only one stage into the journey and had just picked up an energetic team at Wakefield when an oncoming coach failed to yield ground to the much faster mail coach. Amy was glad she was sitting facing forward. Though she was precariously perched at the very back, at least she could see what was coming. The teams missed each other but the coaches sideswiped, flinging all the horses against their traces sideways and causing the other coach to sprawl across the road and land on its side. The mail coach tipped as the tangled team headed for the ditch. Amy leaped for safety and watched from the bank as the equipage toppled to its side.

The other agent had admitted to selling a ticket to just such a lad. And Trent had stayed the night at the coaching inn, hoping to catch Amy in the morning. But he had completely slept through the racket of the coach leaving. No valet, of course. With his fresh team and barring accident he should be able to overtake her within a few hours.

But an accident was the very thing he encountered just past Wakefield. A lumbering stagecoach, woefully overladen, had turned over on a curve dumping its top passengers onto the verge of the road and shaking up those inside. When Trent arrived the team was still stamping and straining at the tangled traces, but the passengers had all been extricated and, to his relief, none looked seriously hurt. The women were harrying the coachman and the men were inspecting the wreckage.

Then he saw the mail coach in the ditch on the other side of the road and the cluster of people around a still form on the bank. He groaned and pulled his team to a halt. Shouting for one of the onlookers to hold his horses, he made his way around the coach and tried to get through the crowd.

"Here, now, sir. Unless you be a doctor, you don't want to look at that sight. The poor fellow's neck is broken." Trent stopped in his tracks, that now familiar thudding replacing his normal heartbeat. Amy was supposed to be on this coach and he did not see her anywhere.

"But—my ward," he gasped. "A runaway. I must see."

"Very well. No one knows who the lad be. Make way for the boy's uncle there."

Trent felt the blood drain to his feet and a strange buzzing in his head. Amy's soft voice came back to him, the way she used to talk to the horses, calming them, cajoling them . . .

They turned the still form over and a strange blank face stared back at him. He thought he must be going mad, for he heard her voice still.

"Easy now, boy," she said. "We'll get you loose in a minute."

Still half paralyzed with dread, Trent turned his head slowly to regard a red-haired lad, now hatless, trying to calm one of the leaders who had a leg over the traces.

"Amy!" he whispered desperately, staggering toward her.

"Trent! What a lucky chance. Help me with these horses, before they bolt again."

Numbly he took the tack of the other beast and said, "Easy," a thousand times until someone came to relieve him of the job Amy, in her managing way, had assigned to him. The two grooms led the team off and Amy looked at him with some concern as they stood alone on the middle of the road.

"Trent, I am sorry. You look awful."

He faltered and almost staggered toward her, crossing that open grave of her supposed death and delivering that long withheld embrace, locking her in his arms as though he would never let her go. He did not know what words of comfort he was saying to her, pouring into her ear as he held her swaying on the York highway. He only knew that she was alive and that he had another chance, a chance to make it all up to her.

"Trent, I am fine, but you look terrible."

His grip on her eased enough for her to see his face and realize that he was breathing hard, as though he had just run a long distance.

"You are angry, and justifiably so," she surmised.

"No, not angry," he gasped out. "Relieved. Just do not ever do that again. Promise me."

He still had an arm around her and she nodded her agreement.

"You were not worried, were you?" she asked as they walked toward his curricle.

"Worried?" he choked out. "I have only thought you dead twice in as many days. Why would that worry me?" He groped in his pocket for a coin for the man holding his team and motioned for her to get into the curricle. Amy ran back to get her valise from the mail coach, stowed it and climbed in. She held the reins as Trent got in and could not help noticing his hands shook a little as he took charge of the horses.

"I suppose you will say this is all my own fault."

"Not unless you were driving," he said with a strangled laugh. He clucked to the horses and drove off from the interested eyes of the other passengers.

"I do not mean the wreck, of course, but getting thrown off the coach. If I had not come looking for a horse, it would never have happened."

"No, it is my fault," he said. "All my fault."

"Yours? But I was the one who went to York."

"And I was the one who made you unhappy enough to run away. What a monster I am."

"You are no such thing." Amy looked at him in some concern. "A little overbearing at times, perhaps."

Trent laughed out loud and Amy was relieved to see some color returning to his face. "Let us argue about this once we get home," Trent said.

"Are you taking me back to Talltrees, then?" Amy asked hopefully.

Trent stared at her. If he did, he had still to worry about Fenwick. "We must go to London first and let Draco know you are not dead."

"Is Draco all right?"

"Well enough to help me look for you. He took the late mail coach yesterday. And I must have missed you by half an hour this morning."

"It was a wasted trip. I did not buy a horse, although there was one I could have afforded. It will cost me a year."

"Why did you hold back from buying the horse?" Trent asked.

"When I started out I thought I could take care of myself, that I did not need anyone, but I was wrong. I realized I could not manage a stallion alone, not safely any-way."

Trent stared at her in amazement. "I give you credit for having that much sense, at any rate."

"But I mostly went to York because I did not know where else to go."

"What do you mean?" he asked blankly.

"I forgot to tell you. Fenwick knows your mother."

"What?"

"He was there in Bath, trying to call on her, but I do not think he realized I was in the house."

Trent gaped at her, dropping the reins so that the job horses slowed to a walk. "But I sent you to Bath to *pro-tect* you from Fenwick. This means . . ."

Amy eyed him, watching him wrestle toward the same conclusion she had. He was not acting much like the de-cisive Trent she knew.

"This means that he has always worked for her, spying on you," he said in despair. "That first day I left a message summoning him to Talltrees, he must have sent her word, or even gone to see her, to warn her that we were together."

"Yes. Of course. Hence her letter to me, but if she did not want us to be together, why did she not simply come to Talltrees?" Amy looked behind to make sure they were not going to get run over.

"And what is the surprise she speaks of?" Trent asked. "I am more wary of that than ever."

"I wonder what Lady Agatha will do when she discov-ers Fenwick has been stealing from both of us, while tak-ing her money, and all the time plotting to marry me if he could. He has managed to betray everyone."

"If I can just once get my hands on him he won't have to worry about Mother. I shall rip his head from his shoul-ders." Trent flicked the reins and started the horses again.

"That's the ticket," Amy said cheerfully. "So glad you are feeling more like yourself."

Other than a brief stop for lunch, Trent was strangely silent and withdrawn the rest of the day. Amy decided not to intrude. She was rather tired herself. Trent booked two rooms at the George in Longborough and ordered dinner for them, which they took in the public parlor. He ordered a brandy and did not eat, in Amy's estimation, enough of the chicken or turbot to counteract that amount of liquor. He kept staring at the cap she had laid on the table. Finally she ran a nervous hand through her curls, and watched his eyes travel to her head.

"You hate my hair, don't you?"

"No, your hair is oddly becoming," he said slowly and carefully, "and almost in the latest fashion. Who cut it for you?"

"Betty, but do not get angry at her."

"It just hit me. She told me you were afraid of Fenwick but it never occurred to me she had seen him in Bath."

"So you talked to her?"

"Yes, Mrs. Hodge brought her to London."

"That's how you knew I had left."

Trent nodded and stared at her clothes until she sighed nervously.

"I know you said you were not angry, but I wish you would shout at me or something. Anything except this freezing silence."

"I am not angry. I am simply trying to figure out what to do next."

"But I thought you were never at a loss for an answer."

Trent looked at her in amusement. "I never had you to deal with before."

"I cannot be unique in your experience. You must have other problems more pressing than I."

"No, I have had other problems, but there was never anything more important than you. I just did not realize it at the time."

"I seem to have managed without you all these years." She ate a few more bites of dinner, then pushed her plate away.

"And how many times have you cheated death by inches because of your daring?"

He was staring at her intensely, those green eyes almost lit from within by some emotion. Hurt? Guilt? Passion? She paused, realizing the absolute truth was necessary in this case. "Only three."

He stared at her as though he had not been expecting an answer. "I thought you would deny it. I should be glad that you were only almost killed three times, and that probably does not even count the coach wreck." He leaned back in his chair.

"You said yourself that was not my fault."

"Or your brush with the Avon River." He looked down into the brandy glass and drained it.

She looked confused. "I never fell in the river. I think you are too drunk to discuss this."

"It would be best if you went to your room and slept. I shall go to mine and think. And if you run off again I will be too tired to come look for you."

Amy walked up the stairs before him and took the key he handed her.

"Lock your door."

"But you will be right down the hall. I hardly think there is anything to worry about here. After all, Wraxton will have no idea where I am."

Trent smiled tiredly, the indentations at the corners of

his mouth making his face look taut and aware. "Of all the things I need to guard you against, I need to guard you from myself the most."

"That is stupid," she scoffed. "You would never hurt me."

He closed his eyes for a moment as though gathering his thoughts. "I do not feel up to arguing with you. Just go to sleep."

He turned to go to his room but her hand on his coat sleeve detained him.

"If you know drinking will make you ill, why do you do it?"

He looked at her in surprise. "The same reason Draco drinks, to kill the pain."

"What pain?"

"*All* the pain," he said desperately. "The pain of being near you, the pain of sending you away, the pain of being alone, of wanting you, but knowing that is the worst possible thing for you." He looked puzzled as though he had just realized how much he had dropped his guard with her, and he tried to pull away.

"Who says so?" she asked, increasing her grip. "Who says it would be the worst thing for me?"

"Some sane part of my mind, a small part, I grant you, but a piece you should be thankful is still working." He laid his large hand on top of her smaller one and looked at them together, then sought her eyes. "It should be enough for me that you are alive."

Amy stepped around in front of him. "Well, it is not enough for me."

"I would be cheating you to take you when you don't even know what you're missing."

"So, you get to decide what is best for me. You have not changed. You talk about giving me my freedom, but you are cutting me off from the one choice I want to make."

"You would be throwing yourself away on me."

"It is *my* life, *my* future, to throw away or live as *I* choose."

He wrenched his arm away and staggered a little, then drew his gaze reluctantly from her. She thought this was almost harder for him than evading her grasp. He walked unsteadily down the hall, and it did not have anything to do with the brandy.

Amy locked herself in as he had said and leaned against the door. So, not only did he want her, but he actually loved her. She remembered that embrace on the highway when he had discovered she was still alive. That had been more than relief. It was a more elemental kind of love that might have nothing to do with her being a woman. It was as though he had been separated from someone dear to him for a long time. It was the sort of embrace that reunited people after war or great disasters. And they had only been apart for a few days. What a chasm he must have in his heart for her to matter so much to him.

He usually dreamed of cold and snow, but tonight it was smoke and flames. Perhaps a portent of hell, in case he should lose his resolve about his ward. When she was apart from him he wanted her, needed her, devised a multitude of ways for them to be together. But when confronted by her innocence and candor, he felt like he was cheating her to love her. He tossed on his pillow and threw off the covers. Then he coughed. Some alarm of warning sounded in his brain. He sat bolt upright and stared. There *was* smoke in his room. He pulled on his breeches and grabbed his boots, hopping on one foot to put them on as he plunged into the even smokier hallway.

He got his bearings and pushed past other guests fleeing in nightshirts to pound on Amy's still-closed door.

When he could get no response he heaved himself against it, pummeling it with his body, time and again, until it gave and he landed on the floor within.

"Amy! Amy, wake up," he yelled as he tried to rouse her. Failing that, he threw the blanket off and picked her up in her nightgown to carry her down the stairs and into the open air. The inn was isolated on the edge of town and still had some grass where he laid her.

"No, no, this cannot happen," he whispered as he shook her, and finally she gave a cough. He chaffed her face and hands and was relieved to see her take a shuddering breath and give another cough. Still, it was some minutes before she opened her eyes and gazed at him.

"Trent, what happened?" she gasped.

"It looks like a chimney fire. Are you all right?"

"I am cold."

"I shall take you . . . to the stable." He picked her up and marveled at what a light burden she made even though his right shoulder was on fire. He walked into the stable and climbed the corner stairs to the hayloft. Here he found enough loose hay to make her a bed. When she shuddered, he stripped off his nightshirt and covered her, then put his arms around her and drew her to him in an embrace that was all protection and had nothing to do with his need. And though he did not think about it coherently, it was a vow to keep her safe from all danger no matter what it cost him. He could not bear to think of her harmed. His heart would not survive another episode like today.

14

Amy snuggled deeper into the warm embrace and ignored the sunbeams that danced across her face. She tried to keep her eyes shut, so that Trent would assume she was still asleep. But the tiny slit of vision she permitted herself showed her motes of dust and bits of hay glittering in the golden light. She was with Trent. Beyond that she did not think or care. She moved enough to glance up at his face. He looked tired and soot rimmed his eyes and streaked his face to which a day's growth of beard added a handsome duskiness. Of course. There had been a fire and he had saved her. His dark lashes rested on his cheeks and she realized she had never seen him like this before, so still and so harmless. Usually those green eyes pushed her away, whether they were sparkling with anger or amusement. If amusement, it was usually at her expense. She wished now she had been able to laugh at herself more, that she had shared more with him.

His jaw was still firm, his chin still determined, but at rest his mouth looked more sensual now that his full lower lip was not drawn into such a tight line. And his disheveled hair was so compelling she wanted to run her hands through it. She contented herself with stroking her fingers lightly on the dark hair running down the middle of his chest. He took a deep breath and stirred, his grip on her tightening. The moment seemed so right. She stretched and kissed him on the lips. He stirred and gave a soft moan. What dreams must he have after the life he had led? She lay as still as she could for she knew this moment would not last. She must look a fright, her hair tousled, with soot on her face and perhaps tears streaking that. But she would not for the world awaken him a moment sooner than need be. She looked at the rise and fall of his broad chest, browned by the sun. Was that from being on his ships, she wondered? His right shoulder bore an angry bruise besides the permanent scar. What had he done now? He stirred and put a hand to his face, rubbing his forehead slowly, as though to erase a bad dream.

Trent smelled hay and horses and imagined himself at Talltrees. But why was he lying in the grass? He finally resolved the blur before him into a face, and when he discovered it was his ward looking curiously at him, he flushed and sat bolt upright. "What the devil? Did I—"

"You fell asleep. Were you hurt in the fire?"

"Fire? Oh, right. Here I was thinking I might have—"

"What?" Amy asked as she stood up, shaking the straw off her nightshirt and handing Trent his. "Is the inn badly damaged?"

Trent was still feeling groggy and was wondering if he might have said or done anything terrible, but Amy spoke like her usual self again and seemed to have every intention of walking across the yard to the inn in her bare feet. "Not at all, I think. It was just smoke. You were watching me sleep," he accused, his green eyes glittering.

"Yes, for a while, and listening to the birds get up. I

never slept outside before—almost outside. Trent, what should we do now?"

"I shall see if our linens are worth salvaging. Stay put."

Trent came back with their valises and a pail of water for washing and turned his back as Amy unashamedly stripped off her nightshirt. He sneaked a peek once at the flimsy camisole and drawers that kept her body from his prying eyes, then went back down the rickety stairs to see if he could find her something to eat.

When he returned she was dressed and determined to share the bread and cheese he had foraged with him as she laid them out on her valise. He quickly washed his face and hands, then put on a clean shirt and his coat. How odd. He had stripped unashamedly for all of his mistresses, but he did not want Amy to see him so, almost as though she could know how much he was hurting if he did not have the refuge of his clothes. He omitted the neck-cloth and sat down to share the meager meal with her.

"I have paid our shot." He tore a bite of bread off with his teeth. "With any luck we may be able to get to London tonight."

"And the adventure will be over."

He stopped chewing as he looked at her bereft face. "Somehow I do not think so."

They were a hour on the road before she said anything to him. "You were dreaming as we slept in the loft. What about?"

He hesitated before asking, "Do you remember getting into our great traveling carriage, alone?"

"After Father's funeral? Yes, I remember it very well. With my mother already dead, Father was all I had. I did not want to leave him there in such bitter cold."

"I remember that I was shivering but you were not. You looked frozen, an ice maiden."

"I was afraid to move. She had already admonished me for crying."

"Where did you go? I mean where did my mother send you? I remember us having to walk home from the churchyard and Father being very angry with her. Did she send you back to your house in Epping?"

"She sent me straight to Talltrees."

"In that thin pelisse?" Trent glanced at her, his sensuous mouth intent with concern. She had the wildest impulse to comfort him, to take away his worry as though what his mother had done was nothing.

"It *was* terribly cold even in the carriage. At the first stop the coachman threw his lap robe over me and got a warm brick for my feet. He was grumbling about the *old harridan*. I suppose he meant your mother."

"She sent you all that way alone? Were you frightened?"

"Yes, because I did not know where she had told the driver to take me and I was afraid to ask him. I thought I was being sent to an orphanage."

"I am so sorry. She said nothing to you? Not even good-bye?"

"She was arguing with your father. Have you no memory of that? It was in an under voice. I think he wanted to keep me. But she grabbed my arm and dragged me to the carriage." Amy could see that Trent was staring into the distance and was glad that the team seemed inclined to trot docilely along the road, for he was not minding them.

"I always remember that day as being completely silent except for the fall of the snow, the sound it made," he said slowly. "It clicked against my hat and settled on my coat sleeves in little hillocks. It beat against the coffin and the roofs of the carriages. They did argue that day. But they did so every day. I must have blocked that out."

"I remember you, so far away from all of us, standing alone, staring down. I wanted to go stand with you, but she would not let me."

"I wanted to come to you and put my arms around you to keep you warm, but I felt frozen to the spot."

Trent turned to her and she could see the regret in his face. It gave her heart a tug to realize there was a point when they could have been friends a long time ago, but that it had been denied them. "She would not have liked that."

"No, I suppose not." Trent sighed and flicked the reins a little to remind the team he was still there.

"Is your shoulder hurting?"

He looked sideways at her, with that slight dent by the left corner of his mouth, what passed for a smile with him. "No more than usual."

"I could drive for a while, if you want."

"I suppose you would know how."

"Of course. Masters taught me." Amy took the reins from his hands and felt the horses mouths through them, one steady, the other pulling for more rein when he could get it, an uneven pair. "Where did you leave your grays?"

"Near Reading. Jessup has gotten them back to London by now."

"So you went back to Bath right away. I thought you were not coming for weeks."

"Draco rumbled your plan, even if Betty hadn't confessed her crime."

"The little fool. After all our rehearsal."

Trent laughed at Amy's outrage. "You must remember that not all women are made of the same stuff as you are. We meant to come to Bath anyway." Trent leaned back in the seat to regard her. "Draco was feeling better and he missed you."

"Missed me? He has no reason even to like me."

"I think you are mistaken there."

Amy risked a glance at him and realized he was baiting her. "And how do you feel about me?"

His lips twitched. "As though I am being punished for all my past sins by having to take care of you."

"Oh, really? No doubt you are my punishment, though what my crime might have been I have no idea."

"Prevarication leaps to mind. You lied to protect Draco's reputation as a horseman."

"I lied to save him from your anger," Amy challenged.

"And as I recall you said you would go to Bath."

"I did not promise to stay there. Not telling you something is not lying to you."

"Do not split hairs, Amy. You probably think it playing fair to deceive me, so long as you get away with it."

"I think it no particular effort," she quipped, "since you generally pay so little attention to me."

"That will change. Until you are wed you will have my undivided attention."

"Or until I am twenty-five," she reminded him.

"No, until you are married. I shall not let some fortune hunter cajole you into an unequal match."

"I do not think I will marry."

"You should be able to find *someone*." He threw up his hands helplessly. "It may be a struggle but surely there will be one man in London willing to put up with you."

"That is more likely than finding a woman for you," she countered.

"I will have you know I am much sought after. I can have any number of women if I want them."

"That was before Diana's rejection." Amy paused then, wondering if that wound still smarted.

Trent chuckled. "If she had accepted me, I never would have known about you until it was too late."

"That is true. If Diana had accepted you, she would still be making preparations for the wedding. And I would still be trying to scrape together enough money for a stallion. I have to admit, as much as I resent your interference, my life has not been dull since you came into it."

"That reminds me. Hand over those winnings from gambling. I will not have you haring off again."

"I cannot. They are hidden in my underthings." She held her chin up.

"Where?" he asked bluntly.

"Safe inside my drawers, held with a pin, if you must know." Amy was teasing him but was unprepared for him to go after them immediately.

Trent pulled out the tail of her shirt and started feeling around inside her breeches.

"Stop it! You will cause us to run off the road."

"Got it," he said triumphantly.

"Ouch, you scraped me with that pin."

"Sorry I grazed you." He dumped into his hand about a hundred pounds in thin gold guineas. "I shall give this back when you are ready to buy your bride clothes."

"I suppose you are proud of yourself, robbing a woman?" Amy taunted even though she was feeling far from outraged at Trent's fumbling with her clothes. Desire writhed inside her, a hunger more compelling than any emotion she had ever felt. She actually began to look forward to London with complacency, and that was not like her. Things could be a good deal worse. Trent was finally paying attention to her. And they had horse sales in

London, as well. Besides, he had found only one packet of money. Trusting soul that he was, he had not even counted it. All things considered she had a lot to be thankful for. Rather than resent Diana she should thank her. But for her refusal, Amy would never have known Trent, not like this anyway.

She wanted him and loved him, but how much was she willing to give up to get him? Her fast approaching freedom from his guardianship was a heady thing. Finally, all the power and money she wanted. And she was determined not to abuse either one. Was she willing to barter that to become his wife? She was not used to having choices to make, all her previous decisions having been made from expediency. And Trent seemed to want to take the most important decision out of her hands. That did not recommend him as a husband.

Before they came to the next posting house Trent took the reins back. The traffic was heavier near the towns and there was more chance of an accident. They pushed as far as they had daylight, but even Trent was ready to call a halt by eight o'clock. When he finally did stop at an inn it was to discover that they could get only one room. Amy thought all through dinner about the prospect of sharing a bed with him and what possibilities that might lead to. He had to keep reminding her to eat.

But when she was almost falling asleep at the table he put the key in her hand and told her to go to bed.

"What do you mean to do?" she asked, afraid he would go to the stable and leave her here alone.

"Sit in the tap room all night."

"Stupid. You will feel like hell in the morning, besides being as disagreeable as an old man."

"It is hard to imagine us disagreeing more than we did today."

Amy went upstairs, undressed, and put on the more wrinkled of her two shirts to use as a night garment rather than wear the smoky nightgown. Then she rolled into the bed, but tired as she was, she could not sleep. Trent did not really want to sit up all night. He was doing it to protect her. And she had no need for his protection in this matter. What she wanted from him was some admission that he loved her as more than a guardian, and that something might come of that. She had not locked the door. Perhaps he would relent and come to the room at least to argue with her.

Amy jerked awake when the tap man and innkeeper delivered Trent to the bedroom too drunk to walk. In front of her astonished eyes they undressed him down to his small clothes and dumped him into bed with her. When they had gone she covered him and curled up beside him, luxuriating in the feel of his hot flesh against hers.

He was drunk and would never know anything about how he had gotten here. He would be angry beyond words in the morning, not to mention embarrassed. She laid her hand against his naked chest, her breasts tightening at the merest contact with him. That feeling of longing, of wanting, was pulsing through her again.

She ran her hungry hands over his chest and arms and identified the scar from the duel. Trent groaned and moved his shoulder, then rolled onto his side and rested his arm across her waist. He seemed to wake a little and she prepared herself to be blasted by him, but he just snuggled into her hair and pulled her closer to him.

His hold on her did not speak of possession but of

comfort and familiarity, of a closeness passing anything she had known. In that moment she decided she would not make him feel any worse than he did already. She would awake before him and he would find her sleeping on the floor. But until then she wished the night would never end.

15

His shoulder hurt like hell, and his head buzzed just on the verge of a headache, but he thought he could ignore the pain if he did not move too much. There was a warm body curled beside him. Lively must have gotten on the bed in the night. He sighed and tried to remember what he was supposed to do today.

Trent opened his blurry eyes to a tousled cap of red hair. He remembered now. There had been a fire. He had carried her to the hayloft. She looked languid and pleased like a sleepy cat. Then the subsequent day slipped into place like a punch in the stomach as his body awoke to the bare touch of her hand against his chest.

He shot backward out of bed with such violence he landed on the floor, banging his shoulder again with a curse.

Amy's face appeared over the edge of the bed, looking almost elfin, with her auburn hair tousled on top.

"Are you badly hurt?" she asked him.

Trent merely shook his head, grabbing a pillow to cover his chest.

"My God! Why did you not stop me?" he asked with a groan.

"If I had known you were going to fall out of bed I would have done my best."

"Not that, idiot. I mean you should have shouted the house down or whatever it would have taken to stop me coming to your bed in my drunken stupor."

"Trent, nothing happened."

Her bare legs appeared over the side of the bed as she hopped out, causing a hitch in the muscles of his groin. "They dumped you here in the middle of the night," she announced.

"I remember no such thing."

"Well, I could hardly tell them to take you away again without revealing the reason for not letting you sleep with me, could I?" Amy asked.

There was a determined knock at the door and a call from without. "Are you all right in there, sir? I thought I heard someone fall."

"He is all right," Amy said with her throaty boy's voice. "Could you send some shaving water?"

"I have it right here."

Amy ran to open the door and take the can of hot water. Trent crawled back into bed and covered himself.

"Will breakfast be served soon?" she asked the man.

"Breakfast will be in a half-hour," the landlord said through the crack in the door.

"Breakfast?" Trent asked as he watched her steal a small portion of the water to wash her face. "I, for one, do not want any," he said. "And you must be mad for taking this so calmly. If anyone ever found out you would be ruined."

"I am no more ruined now than I was the night of the fire."

"That was unavoidable."

"It was no different except in that case you were in control. It's only being taken unawares that has made you irritable."

Amy washed and dried her face and hands, then shamelessly finished dressing in front of him. Why did she always have to be right. He wanted so much to go and hold her, for it to be like it was the previous night. But just holding her was not enough for him. If he could not keep her at arm's length the next few months he *would* ruin her and her reputation would be in tatters.

"You . . . you do this as though it is quite normal to have a man watch you dress," he complained.

"Well, it is not, of course, but I think we should make some haste to get away from here."

"So do I," he said as he threw off the covers and pulled on his breeches. When he reached for his boots Amy came to help him pull them on, for his shoulder was causing him to grunt with pain. Every time she brushed against him he felt a rush of tenderness for her. She was trying so bravely to make light of the situation when she should be frightened.

"Your shoulder is already black and blue. You did not do that falling just now."

Her concern reminded him of the accident with the stallion. "I bruised it breaking into your room at the last inn."

"Oh, I forgot. And now you have hurt it again."

"I am used to having it out of commission."

He sat on the edge of the bed massaging his neck while she poured the water for him and found his shaving gear.

"Do you want me to help you shave?"

"Thank you, but I would as soon cut my own throat as to have you do it for me."

"Perhaps you would like to grow a beard like Draco," she suggested as he walked to the shaving stand and used his shaving brush to work up a lather. He was standing in front of the mirror, still naked to the waist. She never took her eyes from him, so fascinated was she with watching him, his chest, and every swipe of his razor, removing a day's growth of beard.

"Why are you watching me?" he finally asked without looking at her.

"I have never seen a man shave before."

"There is nothing to be learned from it."

She watched Trent wipe lather from the razor. "Are you always this disagreeable when you have been drinking?"

He glanced at her. "Yes."

"And yet you do it deliberately. Why?"

His hands were arrested in their task and he turned to her. "I already told you why."

"Oh, yes, to forget the pain. But at best it's only a temporary solution."

"Amy, please, I feel too foggy for logic today." He turned back to the mirror and nicked himself with the next swipe of the razor. "Damn," he said as he held a cloth to the cut.

"Well, if it is painful no matter whether you are near me or far away, why not keep me with you?" Amy turned away and began to pack her meager clothes as though she had just made the most casual suggestion in the world.

"Yes, so much more convenient to have you nearby to exacerbate the pain."

Amy shrugged and occupied herself by carefully packing his used linen for him.

Her silence made him feel bad about the last remark. He turned to regard her and shook his head at her crudely tied cravat. He took up one of his own neckcloths and fashioned a stylish tie around her throat, hiding her thin neck. His fingers moved deftly until his hand chanced to brush her chin and then his gaze met hers and he felt surprised to be this close to her, to be touching her. He could see a pulse beating in her neck and wanted to kiss her so badly it made his lips hurt. He finally dropped his hands and turned away. "If I keep you for myself people will think the very worst of me. I am your guardian. We should have had a paternal relationship."

"When we are only five years apart? No one would expect that of us. No matter how much they may gossip about you, your money will always make you acceptable. In fact I think your set likes men to be a little bad."

"How would you know that?" he asked, turning to watch her pack her belongings.

"I read the society columns. I know what they say of everyone else. Why should they be harder on you?"

"But sometimes I deserve what they say," Trent said, scowling at her until she shot that hurt look at him.

"I thought the *Post* was silly but my aunt required that I read it, so that I would have some knowledge of the ton, in case—"

"In case I would ever think to present you as you should have been." He picked up his shirt and angled his injured arm into the sleeve. Amy slid it up for him and helped him get it over his other shoulder, never taking her eyes off his chest. He reached to button it and she took over this task. It was such a wifely thing for her to do he could not suppress a smile.

"She did hold out some hope of me going to London, though I never cared."

Each brush of her hand seared him like a hot coal. How in God's name was he going to get through the next few months?

"You are only saying that now because you think it is impossible." Trent took his coat from the back of the chair and tried to get it on himself.

When she went to assist him he complained, "I am not helpless. I can do some things for myself."

"Not get this coat on, by my guess. It is far too tight."

She did have to work his arm through the sleeve and managed it better, he thought, than his valet would have done. But he caviled at her attempts to button it.

"I must think," he said. "As soon as this headache abates."

Trent concentrated on his neckcloth for a full minute and was amazed that she kept her silence all that time. When he had finished she picked up both bags.

"You should have screamed," he said again as he opened the door.

"And had you arrested?"

"If I end by murdering you, I will be arrested anyway."

"Very funny," she tossed at him as they made their way down the stairs. "Do you want to pick out the job horses while I pay the shot?" she asked, using her hearty boy's voice.

"No, I will pay."

"Good, then I shall carry the valises to the curricle and get a team hitched."

"No—yes. Oh, do as you will."

The landlord was staring at them in amusement.

"He is *so* agreeable in the morning," she said to the man, making him grin. "No breakfast, I am afraid. We must be on the road."

She got her pick of the horses, at least, before the other travelers were even out of bed, and had the curricle hitched and waiting by the time Trent strode out of the inn.

"Give me those reins," he said as he climbed into the equipage and then winced.

"I just thought of something," Amy said in a conspirator's voice as they pulled out of the yard. "You did not use our real names, did you?"

"Of course not." He steered the team onto the road with a pained look on his face.

"Oh, good," she said. "There is no problem then."

"No problem?" he almost shouted. "We have slept together. I see that as something of a facer. If anyone guesses we traveled from York to London alone you will have no reputation."

"I do not see that my reputation matters," she said as though bored with the topic. "Why can we not go on as we have for a few more months? You could come to Talltrees and we could ride together—"

"Because you are far too tempting," he whispered and looked across at her. "And I am far too weak." In his distraction he let one wheel drop into a rut and cursed when his shoulder was thrown against the seat.

"You are going to have to let me drive," Amy said. "You may make one stage, but you cannot drive the rest of the way in your condition."

He gave the reins over to her without otherwise acknowledging his need for her help.

"I know why you are so irritable this morning," she said.

"You mean beyond my throbbing shoulder and my aching head?"

"Yes, you are used to being in complete control and these past few days have been out of your control."

"Control? I have just spent ten years in complete chaos, thousands of men dying, ships sinking, cannons falling . . . cannons falling on people. In what way did I have control?"

"Trent, are you all right?"

"Apparently not."

"You will be better when you get back to your normal life."

"How will I be better? I hate my normal life. If I have any control there it is but a veneer."

"Well, none of us do. I know every time a mare foals, I might lose her, but I also know it does not usually happen that way. Life is about taking risks."

"I think I know that better than anyone, but I should only be risking my life, not yours. I should never have confronted Fenwick, just had him arrested."

"So you still feel guilty about that."

"I feel guilty about everything. Every decision I make seems to go awry."

"Because you are trying to control others who have minds of their own. If I do not listen to you how would you expect Fenwick to?"

He stared at her for a long moment, then started to chuckle. "I do not know. That was silly of me."

"Sometimes you have to give up control and give in to your emotions."

"Like handing the reins over to you."

"No, Trent, like falling in love with me."

"That is the worst thing I have ever done."

"Why?"

"Because . . . a hundred reasons."

"Leave reason out of it. Talk emotion."

"I do not know how."

"I shall start. Against all reason I fell in love with you, demanding, autocratic and interfering wretch that you are."

He held his silence as he stared at her flushed cheeks, her intent hazel eyes and those ripe lips of hers. His left arm stole around behind her and he bent to kiss her just as a mail coach passed them and the top passengers hooted and called their encouragement.

Amy laughed and flicked the reins at the team. "You are supposed to say, 'Out of all reason I fell in love with you,' and catalog my faults, if you think you can master them all."

"Beautiful, daring, courageous, resourceful, insightful."

She looked over at him in surprise, her lips parted over those pearly teeth, just on the edge of a smile. "Is that really what you think of me?"

"And dangerous." He pressed her against him with his good arm and she leaned her head back to meet his lips, as desperate for a taste of him as he was for her. They had wasted far too much time in argument. His tongue traced the shape of her mouth before he slipped it inside, pulling a soft moan from her. His hand crept up to cradle her head and he broke the kiss to hug her. He remembered those moments when he had thought her dead and they ripped and tore at his heart. He never wanted to let Amy out of his sight again.

When he finally pulled back to look at her she asked, "Why dangerous?"

He took the reins and guided the horses back onto the road. "Because if these beasts were not such slugs they would have overturned us."

"I do not care if we ever get to London." She took charge of the team.

He stayed close to her whispering in her ear, "I think I know how we can protect your reputation."

"And be together?" She turned her head and he stole another longing kiss from her.

"Perhaps, if you are patient and I can restrain myself."

She cast him an appraising look. "I think I like you better unrestrained. Tell me your idea."

"To present you in London as my ward but under the protection of a respectable matron. If you are still unmarried when you turn twenty-five and are free of me, then I am yours. If you find someone you like better, then I have given you a fair chance."

"I will never find anyone like you. To think I could have been so wrong about you."

"But your original assessment of me was quite correct. . . . at the time. I believe I have changed. I mean to change even more."

She steered the team around a wagon, careful not to jab the horses in the mouth. "I used to have nightmares about you coming to Talltrees, all stiff and disapproving like your letters."

He stared at her in fascination, resting his good shoulder against the seat with his arm around her waist where no passing traffic could see it. He watched her animated face appreciatively as she talked to him, to the horse, or even to herself. She did indeed have the look of a young lad, except for those dimples. Her hazel eyes held all the excitement of youth, the spark of an active intellect. Ideas sprang from her lips as easily as other women might drop idle chatter. Why had no other woman seemed so intelligent to him, so alive with possibilities?

"And what did you think I would do to you?" he asked when she paused.

"Take me away from my castle and throw me into prison."

"What?" He stared at her, fighting the urge to take her in his arms.

"I fancied myself a young Elizabeth. A princess without a friend in the whole world."

"And you were imprisoned," he concluded, remembering that she had said the horses were her only friends.

"Yes, I thought you a harsh, uncaring monarch."

"I had no idea you lived in terror of me. What did you really think would happen to you?"

"That the black coach would come back one day and spirit me away, either to become a real princess, or to my own beheading."

"What?" Trent wrenched his shoulder as he sat up. "You are not serious."

"But instead you came, which was better than that."

He chuckled in spite of the pain. "Amy, you have just compared me favorably to an axeman."

"You know what I mean. The most awful thing would have been for nothing to ever happen."

"Now I am non-plussed. The axeman better than nothing and me better than the axeman."

Her ripple of laughter caught at his heart. She was in love with him and she was putting all her trust in him. He hoped that was not a mistake. Would he break her heart in the end? So few things he tried to do turned out well. Perhaps he tried too hard. Maybe love was simpler than war. Maybe it just happened and you let it, without trying to make it perfect. God, he hoped so, for he was no hand at this.

16

Amy thought her appetite at the inn at Grantham was enough to convince everyone she was a schoolboy. But Trent's rapt gaze was too much like a lover's. People were starting to stare at them.

"Will we get to London before dark?" she asked to distract him.

"Late afternoon if your arms hold out."

"I was wondering if you had decided on a respectable matron."

Trent sighed. "I am going to appeal to Lady Marsh to see if she will take you in hand and present you."

"Draco Melling's mother? Will that not be awkward?"

"You mean because of Diana?"

"Yes, or did you mean never to call or see me?"

"I have not thought beyond a safe place to lodge you. If Lady Marsh accepts you as a houseguest, do you give me your word not to dash off to Talltrees—or any other place—without telling me?"

She paused with a spoonful of stew halfway to her pretty mouth. "Yes, of course. Why are you looking so skeptical?"

"That was too easy. You have never agreed to anything I suggested before without an argument."

Amy looked a challenge at him, her pert lips parted over pearly teeth. It was all Trent could do not to reach across the table and kiss her.

"You should watch the clauses in your verbal contracts." She took another sip of the small beer, and swallowed hard at the unfamiliar bitterness. "You said 'without telling you.' I might leave you a note if something pressing required my attention at Talltrees."

"Ah, now you would think someone such as myself, trained in the law, would have anticipated that interpretation." He tossed off the rest of his tankard of ale in a single long swallow.

She stared at him with a satisfied smile. "I was pretty sure you had not."

"In that respect I underestimated you." He raised his empty tankard to her as a sign that he conceded the point to her.

She smiled at him for she did not like to lose these verbal battles. Half the fun of being with Trent was arguing with him. She had never had anyone to talk to before, no one with the same interests. She wondered if all married couples bantered at each other like this. Her education in that area was nil. But perhaps she did not need a pattern for a marriage. People were all different, so marriages must all play out differently. She could not imagine her relationship to Trent to be anything but unique.

When they got the new team he kept the reins to himself only for a mile, then advised her the nigh horse was so hard-mouthed that she would have to signal any left turn with authority.

Amy had expected that when Trent caught up to her he

would tax her with her many crimes; she had not expected him to sit thoughtfully beside her just looking at
her from time to time as though to assure himself that she
was really there. She was careful to keep away from holes
in the road so as not to jostle his shoulder. In spite of that
she thought he was looking rather feverish as they approached the city.

Trent made light conversation the rest of the way,
pointing out landmarks as they passed the outskirts of
town. He directed her to drive down Oxford Street, then
turn right toward Grosvenor Square. Since they had no
groom with them he ordered Amy to stay in the curricle
till he discovered if Lady Marsh was at home.

As Trent rapped the knocker of the door he realized it
was going on toward five o'clock on a fine spring day and
there was every likelihood Draco's mother was being towed
about Hyde Park in her barouche. He did not even want to
consider the possibility that he might encounter Diana.

The butler, Horton, who was nearing eighty, showed
Trent into the morning room as though he were twelve
years old and went off to find his mistress. Trent wondered
how long this would take, and if Horton would forget his
errand en route and wander about the house for a while,
turning up again in the morning room as though Trent had
just arrived. Trent strode to the window and nearly had a
heart attack when he looked out and the curricle was missing, but he discovered it on the other side of the square.
Amy was walking the horses to cool them. Very sensible.

"Trent, what happened to your shoulder?" Lady
Marsh demanded upon entering the room, her brown eyes
fastened on his arm as though she could see his bruises
through the cloth.

He flinched like a schoolboy, sending a jolt of pain

through his shoulder and causing him to emit an, "Ouch!" that confirmed her guess. He turned to face the fashionable matron who had the same deep compassionate eyes as Draco. "How did you know I had hurt it?"

"You are carrying it the same way you did when you were recovering from that bullet wound."

"I see. Well, it does not signify. I have a matter of importance to discuss with you. My ward . . . has come to town, is waiting outside as a matter of fact."

"Your ward?" She looked startled and peered out the window as though he had mentioned he had a giraffe in the square.

"That is why Draco and I left for Bath so suddenly. But Amy is with me now."

"Amy?" Lady Marsh sent him a penetrating stare and pointed an accusing finger. "Your ward, did you say? Trent, this is not some girl you have taken in and—"

"No, no," he said, capturing her hand. "She is Amy Conde, a respectable young lady, but a trifle . . . odd."

"What do you mean odd? Why have I never met her before?"

"Would you like to?" he asked eagerly.

"Yes, of course, but I do not see—"

"She is outside. I need . . . I need your help quite desperately. I cannot take her to my house—and no—there is no one staying there now. I just need a place for her to stay for a few days until I figure out what to do."

Lady Marsh shook her head. "No, I will not do it, Trent. If she really is your ward, then you and Agatha have been spoiling her all these years, and now that she is unmanageable you want to foist her onto me. It is not fair. I have enough trouble keeping Diana in line and worrying about Draco."

"Worrying about Draco? You forget, I have been doing that," Trent said.

"I am sure I never asked you to," Draco's mother said proudly.

Trent looked out the window in despair, knowing he was losing, but also knowing how much he depended on this help for Amy's sake. He tried to remember how he had looked when he was a boy and had wanted something from this woman, but he had never asked her for anything. She had always just acted like his mother because he was a boy who needed one.

"And I have no right to throw that in your face," Trent said humbly. "Draco is my friend. Sometimes, I think, my only friend. It was unconscionable of me to try to trade on that friendship to get your help. I am sorry I bothered you." He went toward the door, but slowly enough for her to stop him, if she meant to.

"But Trent, I do not even know the child," she protested to his silence.

"Neither did I until a week ago, and believe me, she has not been spoiled." He turned to face her. "Neglected is more like it."

"What on earth do you mean?" Lady Marsh clutched her hands nervously in front of her.

"I had no notion she was almost a prisoner at Talltrees." He raised a hand to rake through his hair, but flinched when it pulled his shoulder. "She has less real experience of the world than one of my servants."

"So she has lived in seclusion?" Lady Marsh raised one finger to her pensive lips.

"She has had such a small life, it would be wonderful if she could have just a few months—even a few weeks— in London to meet people. Without realizing it I made her existence unbearable. That is why she ran away. She might just as easily have been killed, as we feared. I owe her a life and I cannot give it to her," he pleaded. "I need you more now for Amy's sake than I ever did for myself. Will you help me?"

"Trent, I have never seen you like this. You are almost distraught."

"If I were to take her to my house—"

"Oh, no, Trent, you must not." Lady Marsh started forward but hesitated.

"She is something of an heiress," Trent said with a lift of his eyebrows. "So a respectable marriage is not out of the question for her, if I can find the right man."

Lady Marsh arched an eyebrow. "An heiress? Very well, bring her in. I shall do whatever I can for her."

He strode across the room and hugged her. "I knew I could count on you."

Trent went into the hall and ordered a footman to go out and hold the horses, then waved for Amy to come in. It surprised him to realize that he had no difficulty whatever embracing Lady Marsh. Perhaps he had always had a better life than he realized.

Amy came into the morning room uncertainly, turning her cap around in her hands and regarding Lady Marsh with an inquiring look. Then she bowed very skillfully.

"But Trent. I had thought your ward was a girl."

"She is," he said.

Lady Marsh regarded Amy and came to stare into her face.

Amy tried for her most cooperative smile. "The haircut is an unfortunate encounter with my maid and a pair of scissors," Amy said, running a hand through her auburn curls.

"You are very good, but it will not do, masquerading as a boy. As soon as you smile, those dimples give you away. And the hair is not so bad. There is plenty to work with and it curls on its own. It will look better short than long."

"What—what do you mean?" Amy asked uncertainly.

"I shall do it, Trent," Lady Marsh said, turning to him. "I am bored this season with listening to Diana whine. I never sufficiently apologized to you for her behavior."

"I have forgotten it already," Trent said. "I will send Amy's baggage over if it has arrived from Bath. Will you tell Draco, and break the news to Lord Marsh?" Trent started toward the door. "Will he mind very much?"

"Richard will do as he is told, and Draco is out somewhere."

"Thank you, again. Amy, I will see you in the morning to take you shopping."

Amy thought Trent left rather abruptly, perhaps to keep Lady Marsh from changing her mind. She went to the window to watch Trent depart and waved forlornly to him. The green and gold room had seemed so alive a moment ago with Trent's anxious presence. Now it felt dull and empty. Amy smiled at Lady Marsh. "Why does Trent want to take me shopping? I have plenty of clothes."

"I expect he wants me to bring you out, so that you can be married."

"But I do not want to marry anyone else."

"Anyone else? My dear child, surely you do not mean you want to marry Trent."

"Yes, he is thoughtful and kind in an amazing number of ways."

"Trent?"

Amy felt she was not expressing herself well. "Perhaps you have never seen his better side."

"Trent? Forgive me, but he is one of the worst men in London."

Amy lifted her eyebrows in inquiry. "And yet you would have married your daughter to him."

"Richard agreed to the match. I did not, and I was right. Diana would have none of him. Come, I will show you to your room and find you a dress."

"Did she say why? Sorry, I should not be prying." Amy stared about the grand house as she walked with her hostess up the stairs. She had never been in a place so large before.

"No, I think you should know. She said he made her feel like a piece of merchandise, an expensive piece of merchandise, but still—"

"He may have sensed that she does not love him. That would make him cut up stiff."

"It does not matter," Lady Marsh said, leading her up a second flight of stairs. "It will be awkward having Trent call here with Diana still moping, but we will manage."

"I could stay at my house in Epping—that is, if he has not leased it out."

"You have a house of your own?"

"It was my parents' house, and I should be allowed to have the use of it. Now that I think about it, that would be the perfect solution. . . . Why are you staring at me?"

Amy could see a dark-haired gentleman approaching them from the other end of the hall. He had Draco's good looks, though he was leaner and graying at the temples. Draco's father.

"Just how old are you?" Lady Melling asked, as she threw open the door to a bedchamber.

"Twenty-four," Amy said.

"Madeline dear, are you going to introduce me to your young visitor?" Richard asked, his eyes not so soft as Draco's. "Is he a friend of Draco's or one of your protégés?"

The comment had an edge to it as though he did not

approve of her already. Amy could sense that the man was angry and it suddenly occurred to her that since she was still in boys' clothes, he might suspect some romantic connection between her and his wife. She opened her mouth to answer but Lady Marsh interrupted impatiently.

"This is Trent's ward, Amy Conde. This is my husband, Richard Melling, Earl of Marsh."

"Trent's ward?" He said vacantly as he glanced down at her clothes. "Oh, you are the one Draco keeps talking about."

Amy was surprised that he flushed. She was the one who should be embarrassed. She began to wonder what Draco had told his father.

Amy smiled to put him at his ease. "Yes. I run a horse-breeding farm." As an explanation for her appearance it fell rather flat.

"Are you dining with us?" he asked. "You might enliven the table. I am getting tired of women scowling at me."

Lady Marsh sent Richard a vengeful look. "This room will do nicely for you, my dear. I will find you a change of clothing."

Richard raised an inquiring eyebrow. "I would not have thought Trent had anyone staying at his town house just now."

Since Lady Marsh was pointedly holding the door open, Amy went into the pleasant room and was surprised when the door was shut behind her. Lady Marsh was probably going to berate her husband for the reference and she wanted to do it in private. *He had meant one of Trent's mistresses,* Amy thought. *Now why had he let them stay in his London house? Of course, to keep his mother away.* When one analyzed his motives, Trent's actions were really very easy to explain.

17

Amy was determined to get off on the right foot with the Mellings so she proposed to entertain them after dinner with her music. To this end she had asked the aged butler for access to the pianoforte and sheet music and found several pieces she was familiar with. She was toiling away at these, getting the stiffness from driving so much worked out of her fingers when the door to the drawing room opened.

"Amy?" Draco asked, staring at her. "What a relief. How did you get here? You scared Trent half to death with that bundle of hair clippings you threw into the river."

Amy stopped midpiece to stare up at him. "Trent talked your mother into inviting me. How would he have known about what I threw into the river?"

"He found them." Draco leaned on the instrument. "He got soaked to the skin wading out to discover if your cold corpse was attached to them. God, his face looked bereft, as though he were dying himself."

"I . . . I am sorry. I never gave it a thought. He did not look very well when I got thrown off the mail coach, either."

Draco looked confused. "What could you have done that would have gotten you thrown off the mail coach?"

"I did not *do* anything." Amy stood up and closed the keyboard. "It wrecked."

Draco gaped at her and then laughed. "Amy, you are going to be the death of him."

"And when the inn caught fire and he had to break down the door to save me, he was so distraught."

"Brought him to his knees, did you? Good. He does love you, you know." Draco pulled out his cigar case, looked at the clock, then decided against smoking.

Amy frowned at him. "I know. He still feels guilty, but he means to see if by waiting for my birthday it won't look so very bad for us to be married."

"Good idea. You shall be safe here and Mother will teach you the ropes. Guilty about what?"

"Everything to do with me. Will he ever get over it?"

"He has never gotten over sending me to what he came to believe would be my death and I have been safe home for a year. Men like Trent try to take on the problems of the world if you let them. That reminds me. Why did you take the blame for my fall?" Draco paced to the window and back as though he needed some activity to occupy him.

"So that he would not blame himself."

Draco stared at her for a moment and she thought he was going to tell her about his vision problem. But he turned away and strode to the fireplace. How odd that he had seemed so relaxed at Talltrees but in his father's London house he acted like a caged lion.

He spun on his heel. "Somehow we are going to have to make him realize that everything is not his fault."

"Has he always been like this?"

"Oh, yes. On those rare occasions when my parents

had a falling out within his hearing he took it hard, as though it were his fault."

"But, why?"

"Because his parents did disagree about him. Trent would have gotten along fine with his father. But that witch of a mother kept coming between them. Fortunately she was a social climber, so she had no problem with Trent running tame in our household."

"So it is not without precedent for two people who love each other to argue?" Amy asked hopefully.

"No, in fact—" Draco broke off as Lord Marsh entered the room.

"Ah, so you have returned," his father said. "How is our guest?"

Amy underwent Lord Marsh's scrutiny with patience and managed an awkward curtsey. "Thankful to be taken in on such short notice, sir," Amy said cheerfully. "Will you allow me to repay your kindness by playing for you after dinner? That is, if you would like. But perhaps Draco can judge. Would I embarrass myself by playing my music here?"

"Oh no, your playing is first-rate."

"It is as hard to squeeze a compliment out of Draco as getting water from a stone," Lord Marsh said. "So you must be something of a paragon."

"You should try to get Trent to say something nice," Amy countered. "But he did compliment me on my driving, so there is hope, I suppose."

Lord Marsh looked as though he were going to ask her something but Lady Marsh entered then, almost pushing the thunderous Diana ahead of her into the room.

"Well, this is cozy," said Lord Marsh. "Diana, this is Trent's ward, Miss Amy Conde."

"Trent's ward?" Diana asked with a raised eyebrow.

"Only for a few more months," Amy said. "Then I will be on my own."

"He brought you here? Why?"

"Now, Diana," Lady Marsh said. "Trent is like a son to us. It would be very odd if he did not bring his ward for a visit."

"If she *is* his—"

"God, I could use a drink," Draco said.

"Can't you wait until dinner?" His father cast him a mildly accusing look.

"Yes, of course. Who are we waiting for?"

Lord Marsh eyed his petulant daughter. "Trent."

"Trent?" Diana repeated. "I never want to see him again."

Amy thought Diana might be a beauty, but the pout did nothing for her but make lines on her face.

"Then you can go to your room. I am not giving up an acquaintance that I value, because you are taking a pet. You are going to run up against Trent everywhere in London. You may as well get used to coexisting under this roof."

When Trent arrived back at Melling House, with the note almost of command from Lord Marsh folded in his pocket, he found the family and his ward making desultory conversation in the drawing room. His gaze went straight to Amy and she came alive under his regard. He must have realized she was wearing lavender at some point, but she could have been in rags for all he cared. He was so intent at trading looks with her it was some minutes before he realized Diana was glaring at him. He came to sit by Amy out of Diana's direct line of sight.

"How do I look?" Amy taunted with a wry smile.

"I have never seen you with roses in your hair before. Very becoming," he replied.

"It was kind of Lady Marsh to lend me the dress."

"I shall take you shopping in the morning and buy you something more suitable."

When Amy smiled at him, her honey-colored eyes lit up. His longing for her stirred, but it was not centered on his groin or his need. Something about her delight with him made his heart falter as though it could not go on without a touch of her hand. He was about to reach out to her, but remembered who was watching and merely nodded his approval of her attire. He only hoped Diana's nastiness would go no further than staring at her.

"Will you come with us, Lady Marsh?" he asked Draco's mother.

"Of course. It will be amusing to spend some of your vast fortune on a good cause."

"But I have my own money," Amy said.

"Trent can foot the bills," Lady Marsh replied. "No need to worry."

"Amy does have her own money." Trent smiled. "She will come into half of the business in a few months."

"Indeed," Lord Marsh nodded.

Diana sniffed and looked bored.

Trent smiled at Draco, guessing that Lady Marsh had added Amy to her mental list of possible wives for his friend. Draco scowled back at him. If it were possible, Diana scorched Trent with an even more condemning look.

Amy thought the dinner tiresomely long and that all the men drank too much, but she had no frame of reference. As always, Draco arranged his place setting meticulously and emptied his wineglass whenever it was filled. But she understood now, that he did not have to worry about upsetting it.

It might be normal to consume a bottle of wine each during each course of a meal, and then insist on port after dinner. She hoped Trent would decline any brandy since it gave him such a headache. Here she was thinking like a wife already.

While they waited in the drawing room for the men she got the sheet music ready, and then played for a good hour. Everyone seemed absorbed with her efforts except Diana, who kept glancing at the door as though she were expecting someone, giving intentionally visible displays of her impatience.

When the tea tray was finally brought in, Diana excused herself, claiming a headache, from all the *"noise."* Amy thought it unwise of the girl to leave the field, since her retreat, though it might temporarily get her the attention she craved, would do nothing toward putting her in a better mood. The daughter's departure did put everyone at their ease and the talk fell to horses soon enough.

"So you own Tartar," Lord Marsh said. "I thought he must be dead by now."

"He is twenty-six by my count and can still cover two mares a day."

"Cover?" Lady Marsh asked. "What does that mean?"

"Breed, dear," her husband informed her with a conspiratorial glance toward Trent, who flinched at the word.

"That is what I thought it meant." Lady Marsh directed her next remark toward Amy. "My dear, you are going to have to guard your tongue. Women do not typically speak about such things."

"But *cover* is a dignified euphemism for it," Amy argued. "And I cannot fake naïveté about such matters. I have sold far too many horses."

"That reminds me," Draco said. "I must get to Tall-trees and bring back my horses."

"I am having them brought up to town," Trent said, "along with Flyer and Amy's trunk."

"Are you going to keep him?" Amy asked anxiously.

"Yes, but like you, he needs a little town polish."

"I have heard of Talltrees," Lord Marsh said. "I knew Trent went there for horses, but I had no idea it belonged to his ward, and that you ran the place yourself. How did that come about?"

"My neglect—" Trent started to say.

"Trent had far too much to do during the war," Amy replied. "Running the estate was the least I could do. I am at present searching for a new *stud*," Amy said, making Lady Marsh shiver.

"We shall see what Tattersall's has to offer," Lord Marsh suggested, "if Trent does not mind."

"It would be a better use of my money than new dresses," Amy replied.

"Now that solecism I cannot let pass." Lady Marsh clapped her cup onto her saucer. "You must run clothes-mad like the rest of us."

"I've already ordered a new riding habit and evening gown," Amy agreed.

"Horses, again," Lady Marsh admonished. "We must turn your head with some dancing, or the theater. That is what we will do tomorrow. We will go to the theater. Trent and Draco will escort us."

When Lady Marsh declared she would retire for the night, Amy took that as her cue to go up to bed also.

Trent went into the hall, hoping for a word with her, but Draco's exit with the avowed intention of going to his club brought Lord Marsh out of the drawing room as well, and he inclined his head toward his study. Trent felt about twelve years old when Draco's father gave him that look and nod.

Draco glanced at Trent, then the front door, then turned and walked toward the study with them.

"Oh, both of you?" Lord Marsh asked as he waited for his son to close the door. "Sit down, gentlemen. Anyone need a drink?"

"No, thank you, sir," Trent said.

Draco looked longingly at the brandy bottle but shook his head.

"Can either one of you explain why I was left with the impression that your ward was a boy?"

"Why would you think that?" Trent asked.

"The fact that you were both scouring England for her and that she arrived clad as a groom."

"Oh, she went to York to look for a stallion," Trent explained.

"What an enterprising young lady. To York and back all by herself."

"Oh, I was with her on the way back," Trent replied. Then when Draco hissed at him, he realized that was not the best admission to make.

Marsh nodded. "That must be when you complimented her on her driving." He ignored his son as he poured himself a small glass of brandy and sniffed the fumes. "And then you brought her here?"

Trent rubbed his forehead. "It seemed a good idea at the time."

"Madeline seems to have the notion, and I thought I had better get you to confirm this, the notion that you brought Amy here to protect her reputation."

"Yes, that is true," Trent said.

Draco looked worriedly from one man to the other.

"Why not take her back home to Talltrees?" Lord Marsh asked.

"I did not think I should leave her there unchaperoned," Trent countered.

"What happened to her chaperon?"

"She died," Trent said, finally seeing the trap now that it was yawning at his feet. It was a good thing he did not argue court cases.

"Oh, I am so sorry to hear that," Marsh replied theatrically. "But Amy will be in mourning. I do not think the theater is at all—"

"Two years ago," Draco corrected. "Her aunt died two years ago. What else could Trent do under the circumstances?"

"The circumstances?" Lord Marsh paced from the window to the door. "The circumstances are that the two of you stayed in her home with her unchaperoned for several days. Now Trent may not have realized that was dangerous, but you certainly should have, Draco."

"Mrs. Harris, her housekeeper, was there," Draco said, ignoring Trent, who covered his eyes and shook his head.

Lord Marsh glanced from one man to the other. "And Trent must have spent at least one night with her on the way from York. I take it that she is unharmed."

Trent opened his mouth to explain but stopped when Draco stood up.

"She is alive," his friend said. "If you knew the kind of rigs Amy gets up to, you would be surprised Trent did not murder her."

"Draco!" Trent protested.

Lord Marsh held up a restraining hand. "I had a point when I came in here, if you will bear with me. Right now no one knows anything about Amy. It behooves both of you to be discreet in what you say of her, if you do mean

to find her a husband. To that end I will volunteer to prepare a list of suitable candidates." Lord Marsh ignored
Draco's groan.

"You mean to help us?" Trent asked.

"You did the right thing by bringing her here. Of
course I mean to help."

After listening to Lord Marsh's plans to get Amy invi-
tations to several select entertainments, Trent left with his
head spinning. Draco followed him out of the house.

"Are you walking home?" Draco asked, pulling out
his case and lighting a cigar off one of the hall lamps.

"Yes, Draco, what am I to do? I don't want to marry
Amy off to someone on a list."

Draco waited until the house door had shut behind
them. "No need to worry. They have not gotten rid of me
that way."

"But what if someone turns her head?"

"Why not simply marry her now, Trent?" Draco expelled a breath of aromatic smoke as they walked.

Trent shook his head. "No, not while she is in my
power."

"Is that your last word on it?" Draco asked.

"The last you will get from me tonight. If I must dog
their heels on a shopping expedition I will have to get
some sleep. Good night."

Trent had left Draco in the middle of the square, and it
was not until he was entering his own door that it occurred
to him how rude he had been. But Draco would understand.

When he gained his room he remembered with both
relief and weariness that he still had no valet. He looked
about the chamber that had been his father's years ago
and could get no closer to the man. Tiredly he shrugged
off his coat and sat on the bed. Amy's face swam before
his eyes, her new look was even more charming than her

scrubby schoolboy disguise. Her auburn curls had been artistically arranged in what appeared to be charming disorder, showing off her delicate neck to advantage. And she now carried herself with an assurance she had not had before.

He lay back on the bed with a groan. Why had he promised to wait? Perhaps because he had so much power over her it made him hesitate. All women looked at him worshipfully in the beginning. Their eyes always glowed with admiration and . . . what? He hesitated to call it love. Infatuation, perhaps.

Trent rubbed his hand over his eyes. For he could see the end of each affair at its very beginning, could imagine the disenchantment, the pouting, the tears and the eventual ultimatum. He could hear his harsh laughter at the thought that any woman could love him for very long. He always did something incredibly stupid that ended it. Sometimes it was even intentional. Why was that? The answer that came was *boredom*. He did not undress for bed, but lay there thinking over the events of the past week. And he started to laugh.

18

To Amy's surprise Trent kept his promise to go with them on their entire four-hour shopping expedition and was as good as his word when it came to outfitting her. They found two gowns she could wear immediately, and the number of other things they ordered made Amy's head spin. She knew Trent to have the patience for such details, she supposed from accompanying his mistresses shopping. Even though they had argued over it, she found herself liking best in her own mind the ivory gown he had ordered for her in Biddenham.

But the expense of everything was shocking. She could have bought two stallions for the amount Trent must have dropped in a single morning on her wardrobe.

The anticipated visit to the theater came after an unpleasant dinner in which Diana was frosty to the whole family, though whether it was over Trent's return or Amy's presence was hard to determine. When they arrived in the anteroom of the theater, the girl suddenly eyed Amy's light blue gown as though it had a spot on the front. Amy refused to look down at her dress. She was not there to impress anyone. She was not sure why she was here at the Agora, except that Trent had wanted her to come. They decided to use Lord Marsh's theater box since it was closer to the stage.

Trent took her arm going up the narrow stairs. "You did that very well," he whispered.

"Diana sends such speaking looks," Amy whispered. "Does she think people will not notice her rudeness just because she does not verbalize what she is thinking?"

"Yes, she always plays the innocent when called to book, and accuses us of having misread her."

"Let us forget her. I never thought to get to see a play my second night in London," Amy said as Trent seated her and took her wrap.

"I never thought to, either," he replied, as he took a seat slightly behind her, leaving Draco the end seat where there was more room.

"But you have your own box. You must come to the theater all the time."

"Trent frequently has a guest in his theater box," Diana said as she took a chair at the front of the box.

Draco shot his sister a menacing look, taking up the position Trent had left open for him.

"Oh, you mean one of his mistresses?" Amy asked. "But he has given up that way of life. Tell her, Trent."

Trent laughed at the shock on Diana's face. Lord Marsh chuckled, as well, and Lady Marsh sent her daughter a menacing look.

"Since I have had such abysmal luck with mistresses, yes, I suppose I have given them up," Trent agreed.

"Diana, this is no fit subject to be drawing Amy into," Lady Marsh warned severely, completely ignoring the fact that Amy had confronted the innuendo so openly.

"But she was the one who—"

"Shh," her father said, raising his hand. "The play is about to start."

Trent grinned at Draco, drawing another glare from Diana. Trent thought he knew what game Lord Marsh was playing. He was trying to make Diana behave better by holding Amy up as an example to her. It would not work, of course, for Diana Melling was too spoiled to change. He could not think why he had ever offered for her. It may have been to please Draco.

He and Diana would have made an unhappy marriage. She was nothing like Amy. The thought that he could have her to himself if only he was patient sent a thrill through him. She was so close it was good thing he was not seated where he might reach for her on impulse.

It was a delight for Trent to watch Amy study the great chandelier of candles in the center of the theater, giving off a golden glow as it dropped wax into the pit and wafted a rich scent of beeswax toward them. There were more modern oil lamps around the walls and across the front of the stage, but in the semidarkness of the theater box Trent could watch Amy's face without her being aware. She never missed a joke, belying that innocent look. There was so much going on inside her, he wished he could know what she felt every second. It was as though she were participating in the play. She noticed him watching her and smiled at him, as though taking him into her confidence. Her curled russet crop was adorned with white rosebuds again and he thought she looked very much in the mode with that single strand of pearls about her neck. To be sure she was attracting stares from many of the theatergoers.

When the intermission finally came, Draco and his father volunteered to get lemonade for the ladies. Lady Marsh and Diana went to stand in the corridor and talk to their friends, leaving Amy prominently on display in their box. Her chin was up as she looked candidly at the other boxes, her elegant neck looking tempting and kissable.

Trent leaned toward her. "What are you thinking?"

"How odd it is that I should be here, when a month ago I had no such expectation. You make things happen, Trent."

"Not always good things."

"It was good that I was ripped loose from my moorings again."

"Again?"

"When Papa died, and your mother sent me away in the carriage, she never gave me a chance to pack my things, did not even tell me where I was going."

"And I did the same thing to you."

"The point is one should get used to uncertainty. That is all there is in life."

"Your expectations are not high." He brushed his knuckles along the back of her arm, the only skin exposed between the long white gloves and the puffed sleeve of her dress. "That too is my fault. Someday I will fulfill all your expectations."

She smiled at the secret caress. "I give you fair warning, sir, that having to wait will heighten my expectations."

Trent laughed and then glanced around the theater. Wraxton caught his notice since the man was staring at Amy. The fellow had the nerve to smile before turning a shoulder to Trent. Damn his impudence. If he did not think it would upset Amy he would go after the fellow and throttle him now.

Upon further inspection of the occupants of the second tier, Trent was startled to realize that someone was using his theater box. He was even more surprised to discover it was not his latest mistress. He had broken with her before his disastrous encounter with Diana. He must have twitched, for Amy noticed it.

"What is it?" Concern lit her eyes. "Have you seen someone you know?"

"Mother is here. See her in the fifth box from the back, second tier?"

Amy gasped. "She looks exactly as she did fifteen years ago. Her hair is still that frightening black. Her eyes are piercing. How strange. It is as though she has been preserved somewhere, as though nothing has happened to her since that day of the funeral."

Amy shivered a little and Trent laid a reassuring hand on her shoulder.

"Unfortunately it has. That young fellow escorting her must be one of her lovers."

"He looks terribly young," Amy said, her lips no more than inches from his own as he leaned over her shoulder. But the sight of his mother had frozen any romantic impulse Trent might feel.

"She has spotted us and is gesturing," Trent said. "Ignore her."

"They are leaving the box, Trent." Amy gripped his arm when those green eyes had turned on her and Lady Agatha had arisen with a brittle motion.

"She can do nothing to you with me here."

"I think they are coming to see us," she said.

Trent took out his handkerchief to blot his brow. "I feel like a badger trapped in a hedge."

"You are right. She cannot hurt us now." Amy clasped his hand in both of hers.

"No, of course not," he said, patting her hand with his free one.

He was amazed that Amy should show so much courage in the face of what was likely to be an unpleasant, if not dangerous, encounter. Her determination not to be cowed by his mother's approach put some heart into Trent.

"Well, so you are in London," Lady Agatha's throaty voice drawled as she came through the curtain and took a vacant seat. "Your butler kept saying you were out."

Trent thought his mother's voice had the undertones of a large hunting cat. "Where are you staying, Mother?"

"At the Weston. How could I go to the town house? I never know if you have someone *in residence.*"

"You remember Amy Conde?"

"Yes, of course. It was on her behalf that I went to France."

"What?" Trent stared at her. "What are you talking about?"

"Allow me to present René LeMay, le Compte de Crevecoeur."

Amy stared at the blond man who mumbled a greeting with a thick accent and bowed to kiss her hand. He was handsome, she supposed, and there was something disturbingly familiar about him.

"René is your fiancé," Lady Agatha said. "He was trapped in France during the war—"

"Her what?" Trent demanded.

"Amy's father arranged a marriage for her with the Crevecoeur family when she was just an infant."

"Then we have met before?" Amy asked.

René dipped his head and glanced at Lady Agatha as though seeking for words.

Draco must have delivered the lemonade to his mother for he slid into the box to stare speculatively and wait to be introduced. Lady Agatha dismissed him as Lord Marsh's son, setting up his back.

"If we met, it was when we were both children," René said with a nervous laugh. "I fear me that I do not remember of it."

"It would explain why you look familiar," Amy said, staring at him and causing him to smile nervously.

"There was nothing about this in Conde's papers," Trent said. "Such a verbal contract has no legal standing."

"I should think her father's wishes would weigh with you, both of you." She directed a luminous green stare at Amy that would have made a lesser girl shrink.

"If those were my father's wishes," Amy said coldly. "We have only your word that such an arrangement ever existed. And even if it did, I am not constrained to honor it."

Trent's mother showed her surprise at this refusal with no more than a twitch of her eyebrow. "You are perhaps attached to some young man?"

Amy lifted her chin. "Trent is—"

"She is in expectation of an offer," Trent said, laying a warning hand on Amy's shoulder.

Lady Agatha looked from one to the other of them appraisingly. "Well, I have at least done my duty in making you known to each other. Come, René. You may call on Amy tomorrow." Lady Agatha rose to leave but turned on her heel. "Trent, you do not have her at your house, surely."

Draco pushed himself away from the wall. "Miss Conde is a guest of my mother."

"Hmm, yes, I suppose it will serve. Come, René."

"I do not like him," Draco said freely.

"I do not like him, either," Amy agreed.

Trent looked from one to the other in some amusement. "I have more cause to dislike the fellow than either of you, but I am having trouble coming up with a reason. He can never press his claim on you."

"I know that, but he smiles too much," Amy replied.

"He wants you to like him," Trent explained.

"But his smile does not sit well on him, as though he is not used to it."

"Amy is right," Draco agreed. "And his accent seems wrong. I have heard much French spoken this last decade, but no one with that accent."

"And he looks so familiar that it gives me the chills." Amy shivered.

"He gave you your answer," Trent said. "You may have met when you were little."

"No, I would have remembered that," Amy said resolutely. "Why would he lie? He is hiding something."

"Calm down," Trent said. "You do not have to marry him."

"But why did you stop me saying anything about us?"

"No need to tell him anything, not until I find out what his game is." Trent shrugged. "He may be just as he appears, an impoverished nobleman in search of a rich wife."

"That is bad enough," Draco said.

"I wonder how hard it would be to trace le Compte de Crevecoeur," Trent mused. "It should be amusing to try."

Diana and Lady Marsh came back into the box. It was evident that Lord Marsh had abandoned them for his club, and eventually Draco did the same. Amy was glad Trent stayed with them. She could almost pretend they were married. Indeed she wore his ring under her evening gloves, engaging in a harmless fantasy about them attending the theater together as a married couple.

In the carriage Lady Marsh rattled off a list of the men who had noticed Amy and she had remembered exchanging nods with them. They were customers of hers. It did occur to her that telling Lady Marsh she had sold horses to them might not impress her favorably.

Back in her room she stripped off the gloves and opened the package that had arrived while she was out. Another dress ready to wear tomorrow night, this one of yellow silk. She held it in front of her and realized she looked different. Lady Marsh's maid had styled Amy's hair into a puckish delight. The pearls above the faint lemon silk of the dress she held up to herself made her look cherished, spoiled even. She looked much like any other young lady whose parents had cosseted her through her whole life. Except that her hands and arms had been kissed by the sun, and the eyes that looked back at her were not naïve and simpering. She must be careful not to advertise herself as someone she was not. And what was the point anyway? The only man she wanted was Trent.

She spun the ring on her finger so that the cluster of diamonds was visible and held it up to the candlelight to admire the rainbows in it. She had hidden her packets of coins in various places in her room but had been afraid to leave Trent's ring just anywhere. Finally she had slid it on her finger backward so that the set was hidden and it showed only as a simple gold band on her finger. She could enjoy looking at it during secret moments. And she would see him again tomorrow.

She tried to focus on Talltrees, the new crop of foals that looked so promising. But something was missing from the picture. Only when she imagined Trent at her side could she fall back in love with her home. It was a frightening thought that he was absolutely essential to her future happiness, that without him Talltrees might seem as dull and lifeless as one of Lady Marsh's rooms when he had left it. What if some accident were to befall him? She laughed at herself. She had just been lecturing Trent on trusting to luck. What could possibly happen to separate them?

19

———

The next day Trent gave Lester orders to drop all his work and investigate le Compte de Crevecoeur, then ignored his secretary's shocked outrage as he rushed through his pile of letters, consigning half of them to Lester to write and the rest of them to the dustbin.

He arrived at Melling House in the early afternoon only to find his mother and the count in attendance. Amy was being polite and holding her own. Diana seemed absorbed in Crevecoeur's tales from the war. He made it sound as though he were a Loyalist who had gone into exile when Napoleon had risen to power. That might be true. It was a common enough tale.

Since neither Lady Agatha nor Lady Marsh wanted Diana to snare the count, he was cooperating by being coolly polite to her and had seated himself on a sofa next to Amy. Crevecoeur saved the hot point of his devotion for her, upon whom it was totally wasted.

She sent Trent a grimace when no one else was looking that caused him to laugh and then try to cover his omission with an artificial cough. Crevecoeur cast him a measuring look as Trent took a chair on the other side of Amy.

"What did you do during the war years, Monsieur Severn? Were you never tempted to go into the army?"

"Sorely, but my parents prevented it, one by dying, one by threatening to."

"Trent!" Lady Agatha admonished. "That is a flippant way to speak of your father and me."

"Merely stating the facts. I had used to think you in ill health. All that time in Bath must have repaired your frail constitution, for I now discover that you have been junketing about France."

Lady Agatha glared at her son.

Crevecoeur smiled and asked, "How did your father die?"

Trent felt as though a crushing weight had been laid on his heart.

"If it is not too painful to recount," Crevecoeur added.

Trent stared at the man. How could it be other than painful? "He was killed by one of the cannons he was casting at the foundry. He was there alone on a Sunday. It was insane of him to attempt to move that casting on his own. I am not even sure why he wanted to."

"A foundry?" Crevecoeur asked, rolling the *r* such that Trent was sure the man was laughing at him.

Lady Agatha's thin nostrils flared at the word. "I thought we agreed not to speak of the—that place or any of the other businesses."

"You are eager enough to speak of the money they provide," Trent said glibly, causing Lady Marsh to cast him a warning look. It was the sort of look a mother gave her son when he was misbehaving.

Amy heard Trent out and turned a cold eye on Crevecoeur. "I think Trent and his father did as much to win the war as Draco and the other soldiers. You could not have spent the entire time in prison, René? You look far too brown and well-nourished to have been locked up so long."

"He went back to France after Napoleon's first defeat," Lady Agatha said for him. "Then was arrested when the emperor returned to power. He has been out of prison nearly a year."

"I am surprised then that you waited so long to come to England," Amy countered.

"I had affairs to settle, the recouping of my estates, for one."

"And have you?" Trent asked. "Gotten back your lands? Where are they exactly?"

"Alas, no. It is useless. Even if the claim were to be answered, I have discovered my brother still lives. So it is left up to me to make my own way in the world."

Crevecoeur had said this with such regret, the fact that his brother lived, that Trent found his mild irritation with the man growing to a positive dislike, especially because he unnecessarily rolled the *r* in *world*."

"And how have you managed that so far?" Amy asked. "You must have done some work when you were in exile."

"In America and lately in France I have been an instructor of dance, fencing and dressage. I propose to take up the same occupations in this country."

Amy arched her eyebrow at that announcement but did not inquire further. This amazed Trent, for Amy should have been interested in a man who knew something of horses and how to train them.

"Ready for our drive?" Trent asked, hoping his ward would take the hint.

Amy showed no surprise at the invitation, though this was certainly the first she had heard about a drive.

"Yes, I was not even thinking about your horses'

standing. Let me run upstairs for my shawl. Lady Agatha, Count," she said as she nodded slightly. "I am sure we will see you again."

Trent waited for her in the hall and took her hand to lead her out to the curricle as though they were escaping some prison.

As they turned the corner and drove into the crowded park, Trent chuckled. "I was half afraid you would say, 'What drive?' "

Amy laughed. "And lose a chance to be rescued? I was racking my brain for a way to get rid of them. I do not feel right having people coming to see only me at Melling House."

"Lady Marsh would never care."

"What about Diana? She hates me."

"You exaggerate."

"No, I overheard her asking her mother why I had to stay there, especially now that Lady Agatha has returned. And she complained I will hold them back and not be invited anywhere."

"And what did Lady Marsh reply?"

"That I would certainly be invited every place they were, that I deserved a chance to marry since I would not throw it away as Diana had, and that she wanted to see at least one marriage in the house."

"Upon which Diana burst into tears and ran to her room," Trent guessed.

Amy turned to stare at him, cocking her head to one side. "How did you know that?"

"She always does. It is her only defense." Trent steered around a carriage and avoided a pedestrian by checking the team for a moment.

"It will seem odd to people though, me staying with the Mellings, when my godmother is in town."

"I thought you never regarded what people thought of you."

"I never thought I had to worry about it in Berkshire, but as I glanced about the theater last night I realized many of my customers are members of the ton."

"What?" Trent turned to gape at her.

"Mind the dog, Trent."

Amy grabbed for the reins, but Trent pulled the team up before they trampled the terrier that had escaped his mistress.

"You nearly ran over him," Amy complained.

"It had not occurred to me that you might know some of those men," Trent said. "How many?"

"I have sold horses to at least a half-dozen men who were at the theater last night. Some of them recognized me and nodded. That is good, is it not?"

She turned to look up at him so hopefully he could not bear to convey his fears to her. "Of course, who else would your customers be? Then you will certainly be invited places, but it would have been better if you had become acquainted with them some other way, perhaps met their wives."

"They did not bring their wives unless the horse was for her. Besides, I do not think I have much of an understanding of women."

"Meaning you do understand men?" Trent glanced at her but kept most of his attention on the horses, since the tracks through the park were becoming unbearably crowded at this time of day.

"Most of them are rather simple."

"Oh, thank you very much."

"Except you. I cannot fathom what you are thinking. But generally men like a good horse, some amusement, some comfort, and no worries. Women on the other hand . . . They seem to have such small lives. Much smaller than mine. Is it necessary that I go into raptures over a dress or piece of jewelry? For I have a good deal of trouble faking my enthusiasm when we go on these shopping expeditions."

"So I have noticed. The yawning gives you away, my dear."

Amy tweaked her shawl about her shoulders more securely. "I keep thinking what a waste of time and money it is."

"Do not worry. It is my money we are wasting, not yours."

"But it is my time. And to what point?"

"Am I wasting your time now?" he asked, fishing for the insult he knew she was more than capable of delivering.

"No, for we are having a useful discussion. But why must we delay?"

"To save some shred of my reputation, not yours. I shall never live down my past, but if I marry you without ever giving you your freedom I will be looked on as a blackguard. And that might affect the way people treat you."

"Very well." She sighed and looked down at his hands.

"I thought you were going to complain again about losing a whole year."

She smiled at him. "You are assuming I have stopped looking for a stallion. Even if there is nothing to be had at Tattersall's I might discover some gentleman who knows of one. So I can see some advantage to staying."

"And a disadvantage."

"The count? His clumsy advances are easy to repel."

"When you are being chaperoned. I warn you to always be in the company of Lady Marsh or one of the Mellings."

"Are you that worried about René?"

"René, is it now?"

"It is easier to spit out than 'Crevecoeur.' There is something you are not telling me."

He thought for a moment and much as he liked to protect her, she needed to know. "I saw Wraxton last night."

"Where? At the theater?"

"Yes. He does not seem at all cowed by my promise to murder him. I think I must be getting soft."

"That may be due to your association with me."

"That would be likely to make me more menacing."

Amy shrugged. "We may have exaggerated the danger from him."

"Nevertheless, make sure you do not go about with only a maid for protection. As for Crevecoeur, I do not even believe he is a count."

"Neither do I. Nothing he says rings true and he thinks that because he sugarcoats it with that accent he can get away with it. If I ask him any really piercing questions, he pretends he does not understand me, when I am quite sure he does."

"Try to steer clear of him and Mother, then."

"Of all the women I have met I understand your mother the least. If René is ineligible, why would she be sponsoring him or throwing him at my head? It is almost as though she wants me to make a misalliance."

"Good question. What is in it for her?" He studied the back of his grays.

"You do not understand her either, then."

"No, I am afraid not, but I see I must try, rather than dodge the problem as I have been doing all my life."

"Trent?"

He saw that hopeful look again and knew that she could ask him for anything at this moment and he would grant it. "Yes?"

"Wouldn't you rather just drive away from here and not worry about what anyone thinks of us?"

He drove for the space of a hundred yards before he could form an answer. "God, yes, but that would ruin your life as mine has been ruined and I want something better for you. I want you to have all the things I have not had, a home, children, friends, someone to love you . . ."

"Now that you have reformed we will have all those things together."

"Hard to believe my life could change so radically in a week."

"But it was time," Amy said simply. "Things come to you when you are ready for them. Something ends. Something else begins. That is the way of it."

"What is between us will never end."

He delivered her to Melling House in good time for them both to get changed for dinner. He was not sure who had been invited tonight but he hoped that it was not Crevecoeur and his mother, though he had his fears. And he hoped it was none of the men who were Amy's customers.

As Amy changed into the lemon yellow evening gown with the help of her new maid, Molly, she was all the more determined to make Trent proud of her. If she could run a whole stud farm she could certainly handle social engagements without getting into trouble. Dealing with her customers had actually been good training for London. The pearls Trent had bought for her were at her throat and Lady Marsh's dresser had twined some extra strings of pearls through her hair. She smiled at herself once in the mirror, hoping Trent would be pleased with her. As she went down the stairs it surprised her to realize that she had not thought of her mares and their need for a stallion more than twice today.

There were already several couples in the withdrawing room. They were older, like the Mellings, and much inclined to smile fondly upon her. She knew Lord Grey from when he purchased a hack three years ago, but thought she had better not mention it, in case his wife did not know. It was always better to be vague or say nothing when in doubt.

Trent came into the room then and she felt herself suddenly safe. His eyes roved over her appearance and he smiled.

"I like your hair that way," he said, taking her hand. He looked puzzled at the band of gold on her ring finger, and she was about to whisper to him why she wore his ring backward, to keep it safe. But Lady Agatha and René appeared and Lady Marsh introduced them as though it would be a high treat to spend the evening with them. She would have to get Trent alone later and find out if he wanted the ring back. She did not want to give it back but fair was fair. He had been foxed when he had lost it to her. She conjured in her mind a romantic setting, perhaps in the garden after dinner. She would present Trent with the long lost ring and he would kneel and say something unique and poetic. He would ask her to marry him immediately, not because she was pushing him, but because he loved her, because he could not live without her—

"Amy?" René asked. "I offered a penny for your thoughts. Was that not enough?"

"I was woolgathering. How do you like London?" she asked vaguely.

"I have not seen much of it yet. But tomorrow we go to Lady Wakefield's assembly. Will you be there?"

"I think we shall."

"Good. It will be convenable to know someone."

Amy cocked her head at his sudden slip. "Yes, I am quite sure it will."

Trent could tell by the snap of Diana's fan that she was angry, but he could see no reason for it, except that Amy was the center of attention in the drawing room and she was not. Knowing how she could cut up everyone's peace when she was in a foul mood he strolled across the room to engage her in conversation, hoping to redirect the brunt of her wrath toward himself rather than his ward.

"Your mother need not have invited mine to her dinner just because Amy is staying with you."

"She need not have invited Amy, as far as I am concerned."

Her dark eyes looked almost black as she directed a wounding gaze toward Amy.

"Oh, yes, a tray in her room would suffice, I am sure," Trent said.

"Well, why did you bring her here?" Diana treated him to a spoiled pout.

"Because taking her to my house would have ruined her, and my mother was nowhere to be found."

"You mother is here now." Diana flapped her fan impatiently.

"Staying at a hotel with that . . . count. That is hardly a safe place for Amy."

"Your mother could stay at your house now."

"She will not. We had a falling out about that a few years ago."

"Well, if you mean to find a husband for the girl, I wish you would do so and relieve us of the necessity of entertaining her."

Trent stared at her. He thought he wore his love for Amy on his sleeve, that the most casual of acquaintances must have guessed it. But he had forgotten how self-focused Diana was. "That is my aim. Look, everyone is here. Will you walk in to dinner with me to show there are no hard feelings?"

"I will take your arm, but not because I have forgiven you."

She said this last lightly as though she were flirting with Trent, and it set off an alarm bell of warning in his head.

"I do not expect you to forgive me for proposing to you."

"It was the manner in which it was done."

He hesitated as he pulled out her chair and studied Diana's self-possessed profile. The hairs on the back of his neck rose, signaling flight would be advisable. She had changed her mind about him and was trying to trap him. He saw his name card, sat beside her, and smiled uneasily. "You will have to tell me someday, where I erred."

She stared at him. "Someday? I will tell you now."

"Forgive me, but the dinner table is neither the time nor place for such confidences."

Amy watched from across the table as Trent quietly blotted the slight sheen of sweat from his brow and upper lip. So Diana was after him again. She had been proud and foolish to have turned him down when she had no better prospect. She had probably done it because of Trent's clumsy proposal. Now she was realizing the error of it and wanted him to come crawling back to her.

Well, he did not have to crawl to anyone. He was the focus of attention of all the women at the table. His cold green-eyed stare dazzled them and left them tongue-tied, all but his mother and Lady Marsh . . . and her. She was learning to see beyond the proud gaze, the flaring nostrils. Trent was lonely, desperately so. Now he was a hunted man as well.

Amy nodded automatically when the footmen started to serve the first course and tried to focus on the green peas and pilchards that were put on her plate. But she was not at all hungry, at least not for food.

Draco laid a hand on her arm from his position beside her. "I asked if you were enjoying yourself."

"Well enough. Diana means to have Trent, after all."

"I hardly noticed how he is faring. I am too busy staying a jump ahead of Lucy Manchester."

"The towheaded girl?" she asked, taking a sip of water so that she could look across at the woman.

"You demolish with an adjective. Yes, she is the one. Her mother has been after me for her daughter this whole past year."

"Do you like her?"

"She is far too predatory for my taste. I know she seems merely sweet and insipid, but underneath lurks a lioness. I shall be lucky to come through the evening a free man." Draco bumped his wineglass, but managed to grab the stem before it spilled. Once he had grasped it safely he emptied it at one draught, calling a rather scathing look upon him from his father.

"Poor Draco. No wonder you are more at ease in the country."

"Yes, good food, amusing company, horses to ride and no one pursuing me."

"I prefer to have no one pursuing me, as well." Amy glanced in the direction of René Crevecoeur.

"Mother does not approve of your count or she would have seated you next to him instead of me."

Amy thought about this for a moment before she asked. "What is the significance of her seating us together?"

He hesitated. "That she does approve of you."

"That is very sweet of her, but she must know I mean to marry Trent."

Draco gave a bark of laughter. "Even if she knows it she may still hope. Trent should not have told her you are an heiress. When I first came to Talltrees he blurted it out as though that would make a difference to me."

Amy stared at him. "Why did Trent tell you that?"

Draco's eyes looked a little glassy from the sudden influx of wine.

"He wanted me to marry you, thought it would be the perfect way to get you off his hands."

She felt a hot embarrassment beating in her brain. Trent had tried to marry her to Draco? What did that mean? Was Trent taking her now only out of duty? Because Draco was so clearly not interested in her? All those words of love she had tutored Trent to say, were those from his heart or had he merely given up and was marrying her because he felt he owed her something?

She opened her hand to gaze at the diamond ring cradled inside it. She noticed Draco twitch with shock when he saw it and turned to him. "I wear it this way to keep it safe. I suppose I should just give it back to him."

Draco cleared his throat. "Have a care no one else sees it. They might leap to conclusions."

When Draco turned his attention to the lady on his left, Amy studied Lucy and decided the girl was as selfish and dangerous as Diana. Poor Draco had learned what to avoid by sitting across from it at the breakfast table. At least he had never felt hunted when he had stayed at Talltrees. That was because she treated men as equals.

Later in the drawing room she was called upon to play a few pieces for the company. She chose the ones Trent liked the best and traded looks with him. He seemed jumpy, as though he would rather not be there. The music did not have its soothing effect upon him. But that might have been because of Diana's proximity.

René must have been thinking she would not notice he was trading occasional comments with Lady Agatha. Amy had the sudden feeling she was being treated by them as some prize mare whose merits were being discussed. Whatever she did she would make sure she stayed out of René's grasp.

Lady Agatha leaned forward, her green eyes glittering, and whispered in the count's ear. Amy hated that Trent's mother had the same green eyes as him and the same smile. But surely that was all they shared; the hardness that Trent copied from the brittle Lady Agatha had to be a sham. He was passionate and loving inside, just too tightly controlled. Control. Was he controlled enough to pretend a love he did not really feel, to fake what she had taught him?

René tilted his head and smiled wickedly at Lady Agatha, his sensual lips never revealing his teeth. His mouth seemed too self-assured to Amy, too self-indulgent. Amy did not like to be talked about. She ended the piece with a definite flourish and rose to go back to her chair. René came forward with effusive, insincere protestations of *admeeration*. Trent looked as though he would like to toss the man out the window.

Lady Marsh was unsuccessful in persuading Diana to play for them, so several gentlemen, including Draco, made an excuse to leave the room, patting pockets in search of cigars, Amy thought. She tried to get to Trent but Diana grabbed his arm before Amy could manage it, and when René persisted in following her, she informed him she needed to go to her room for something, almost running up the stairs.

* * *

Trent had been raptly admiring Draco's escape, and thinking that he should take up smoking, or at least pretend to, when Diana snapped him up and suggested they push back the furniture and have an impromptu dance.

"Rather late for that," Trent said, more interested in making sure Crevecoeur did not follow Amy than in moving furniture. "Besides, who would play for you?"

"Amy will," Diana said. "She may as well make herself useful."

Trent removed her hand from his arm. "I do not think she knows any dance music."

He gained the hallway to see Draco trapped between Lucy Manchester and her mother. Poor fellow had never even gotten to smoke. And Trent had never seen such a desperate look on his face. Trent threw himself into the breach and asked Lucy if she wished to take a turn around the small garden at the back of the house, causing her mother to have palpitations and to almost snatch her daughter back to her side. Draco started backing toward the stairs, but bumped into Lady Agatha and sidestepped with such alacrity he trod on Crevecoeur's toes.

As the count hopped on one foot Lady Marsh came into the hall to ask what everyone was doing in the hall. Diana latched onto Trent's arm again, the injured one, and he bent to take her weight off that shoulder.

"Draco and Lucy wanted a moment alone," Mrs. Manchester said accusingly, "but we seem to have too much of an audience for him to make any serious declaration."

Trent saw Amy come tripping down the stairs at the point where Draco had finally gained the bottom step. She stopped and glared in Trent's direction just as Diana kissed his cheek. He was so busy extricating himself he missed Amy taking Draco's arm.

"I was looking for you," Amy said to Draco.

"Me, what for?"

"We can no longer keep it a secret," Amy said.

Trent saw Draco stare at Amy in utter stupefaction before a flutter of suspicion jumped into his gaze. Now what the devil were these two playing at?

"Why not?" he asked vaguely.

"Because it would cause others pain to withhold the news." Amy twisted the hardly noticeable ring on her finger to reveal the magnificent diamond that was to have been Diana's engagement ring.

Draco staggered and stuttered. "Ah, um, Amy has consented to become my wife."

Amid shocked gasps and exclamations of surprise Trent felt himself stagger. He had a squeezing sensation in his chest as though a serpent had curled about his heart. He closed his eyes and swallowed, taking a shallow breath or two until the worst of the pounding had passed. Was this some sort of joke, some rescue mission to save the beleaguered Draco from the Manchester girl? Or were they serious?

Trent opened his eyes and looked up to see Draco holding Amy's hand up to the throng gathered at the foot of the stairs, more like a referee would declare a prize-fighter the winner than like a young man showing off his affianced's ring.

Amy glared accusingly at Trent.

Into the dead silence that followed the gasps of the Manchester woman, Trent felt the need to do . . . something. Diana's shrieks when she beheld the ring, her ring, on Amy's finger, seemed to split the tension in the hall. Trent pulled his arm away and backed toward the door.

Lord Marsh returned from his walk outside, looked at his daughter, who was pushing past Draco and running up the stairs as though she behaved in such a manner all the time. In fact, she did. When he saw the tableau at the foot of the stairs and heard the gasped words, *engaged,* he smiled and went to Amy.

"Welcome to the family, my dear. I am well pleased with this turn of events."

Lady Marsh, too, came forward, smiling, to kiss Amy on the cheek and embrace her.

Trent backed to the door and let himself out, filled with a leaden weight that he was trying to call justice. This is what always happened to him. He should be glad that it had all turned out well for Amy and Draco. There was something awful stirring inside him, however, twisting any joy he might have felt for them into a hideous resentment. But he was stupid to be jealous of them, the two people he cared most about in the world.

As he walked home he thought about how he would be shut out of their lives now except for holidays. He would be alone again. But that was what he was used to, what he deserved.

Still, he felt as though he had been shot through and had simply not fallen yet. He staggered a little as he crossed the street. Then he recognized the feeling. It was an old pain and one he had felt many times. It was regret, but it had never hurt so very much before. This was the biggest regret he would ever have, to lose Amy.

When he finally got to his house on Bedford Square he was out of breath, as though he had been running. He closed the door behind him and took up the single candle that remained on the hall table. He heard Fenton's brusque footstep coming from the back hall and waited patiently.

"Good evening, sir. I did not hear the carriage."

"I walked."

Fenton hesitated, looking at him closely, checking to

see if he were drunk, Trent supposed. "Very good. I engaged a valet for you as you requested."

"Thank you, Fenton. I trust he is not sitting up waiting for me, too."

"No, he does not arrive until the morrow."

"Again, I thank you. I will be in the library for a while. You may go to bed."

"Very good, sir."

Trent lit a branch of candles from the single one and surveyed the liquor arrayed on the side table. He could not drink any of it, he realized, without feeling terrible tomorrow, but he would feel awful tomorrow no matter if he drank tonight or not. He might as well kill the pain for a few hours. He took the brandy decanter to his desk, put his feet up and poured a glass. Even though he told himself he should not, he unlocked the drawer that held Amy's letters.

20

***

"*T*rent! Trent!" Lady Agatha shrieked from a distance. "Where the devil is that boy?"

Trent stirred and mumbled. "I shall get up soon, Mother."

"I assure you he came home last night, my lady," Fenton said, also remotely. "But his bed has not been slept in."

Trent opened one eye. What was Fenton talking about? He was sleeping in it now. Trent reached for a pillow to drown out the clatter of the voices and fell. He looked dazedly at the chair, the floor, and his library. Without getting up, and without being able to see very well, he tried to pull the stack of letters back into some kind of order.

"So there you are," his mother said acidly as she threw open the door and stalked in.

"Must you?" he asked from the floor. "This is my house. I thought we agreed you would not set foot in it again."

"But you have allowed your ward to throw herself away on that soldier, a dragoon of all things. Not even a general. You must have come unhinged, to whistle half our fortune away by handing it over to the Mellings. They do not need it."

"*Our* fortune?" Trent asked, forcing the other eye open, but regretting it when he saw two of his mother. He managed to get to his feet and secure the letters in the desk before noticing that the brandy decanter was empty.

"Did you really give your permission for that match?"

She paced back and forth in front of him, making him feel queasy with the constant motion. He sat and rested his head in his hands.

"If you did you cannot have considered what this means to you," his mother continued. "She takes with her half of everything, not just the money and her estate, but the law firm, shipping firm, and your precious foundry as well."

"I trust Draco," Trent said, rousing himself to stand.

"But can you trust Amy Conde? For she is the one who will run the show unless I miss my guess. Before you know it, you will have lost everything."

"I have already lost everything; my father, my friend, the war."

"The war was not lost."

"But it was my work; it was all I had to do that mattered. Father felt the same way about the war and you ridiculed him for it."

"He could have made a fortune selling arms." She stopped in front of Trent. "Instead he almost gave them away to the government. He was a great fool, like you."

"What future would you design for Amy, marriage to your pretty count? How much did he promise you to secure Amy for his bride?"

For a small woman his mother's slap hurt beyond what he was expecting. But it did serve to sober him.

"I want what is best for the girl. With René she will have a title and someone who will adore her."

"Is he really a count or just some pretty face you picked out?"

"Do not be absurd. In France the title is inherited by all the sons, just not the lands. And René will know how to manage her as well as her fortune, which you do not seem able to do."

"And what does Mummy get out of all this?" Trent demanded. "There must be something in it for you. Is René your lover?"

He caught her arm before she was able to strike him again. He was always amazed at the strength in her fragile frame. He stared into her green eyes and could not fathom what she was thinking beyond some primordial hatred for him. That was the only thing he had ever seen there, and after the flash of hurt it caused him, he always faced the question: Why? After knowing the forgiving motherliness of Lady Marsh, Trent had come to regard his own parent as some sort of abnormality, like a bitch that kills and eats its own young.

"Let go of me," she said through the long clenched teeth that showed her ugliness. Trent did back away from her and release her, but he never lifted his gaze from her eyes. If he did she might strike at him again like a poisonous snake.

"You are just like your father. That is why I have such contempt for you."

"How ironic. He always accused me of being like you."

"You are an unnatural son. You care more about your trollops than about me."

"Well, I have come along as you taught me. Do not pretend you were faithful to Father. I knew about all your lovers, but I kept quiet."

She sent him a smile that was a leer. "I suppose you did not want to hurt him, as though he could be hurt by anything. He was as dense as a doorpost."

"He was a good man. I would have done better to be more like him than like you."

"For your information, René is not my lover. He is my protégé, an orphan of the war."

Trent saw something unusual then, a softening in his mother's face that made him curious. "Where did you meet him?"

"Paris. He has lived by his wits all these years, but just barely. The poor boy nearly starved a dozen times over."

She said this last with such a desperate rush she did betray one thing to Trent: she who had never cared about anyone, did for some reason care about Crevecoeur.

"Just how long have you known him?"

"A long time, a very long time. He has given me the adoration I never got from you."

"Then he has very bad taste." Trent locked his desk as though he could keep Amy safe that way.

"I want him to marry Amy."

"And I am supposed to do what?" Trent leaned on the edge of the desk. "To fulfill your whim I am to tear her from Draco, who cares about her, and give her to a penniless émigré, moreover a man she does not even like?"

"She has never been given a chance to get to know him. What would I have to give you to make it happen, a marriage between René and your precious Amy?" She leaned on the desk, her thin hands corded with the strain of her desperation.

Trent stared at her in fascination. "Why is that so important to you? You who have never loved anyone before in your whole life. Why would you care about a man with a pretty face, unless he is more manipulative than you? The question that I want answered is, what has René promised you if you marry him to Amy?"

"A family. At least one household where I will be a welcome visitor in my old age."

Trent stared at her for a moment in horror, then

laughed harshly. "A family? You never wanted the one you had. You cannot now convince me you want your goddaughter's children to drool all over you."

The door opened and a stranger, a young man, stood apologetically in the opening, with Fenton in the background. The brown-haired lad cleared his throat and said, "Your shaving water is hot, sir. Mr. Fenton bade me tell you."

"Thank you, uh . . ."

"Reeves, sir."

"Thank you, Reeves. Will you ask Mr. Fenton to show Lady Agatha out?"

"You will regret not helping me," she warned under her breath, as her sharp tread bit into the wooden floor.

"I will regret it, no matter what happens. You will see to that."

By the time Trent had shaved and dressed with Reeves's help, Fenton had delivered a tray of coffee to his bedroom and Trent was beginning to feel almost human. He looked on Reeves with smiling approval. Not only did the lad take orders and refrain from fussing, but he had bearded Lady Agatha's wrath to help lever her out of the house. So the boy had courage, too.

Fenton cleared his throat. "I forgot to mention that the horses arrived yesterday along with a trunk."

"Good, have them saddle Flyer for me. Flyer is the tall black horse."

"Very good, sir."

"And have Jessup take the other horses and the trunk around to Melling House." Trent swallowed hard when he thought of Draco and Amy riding together. As he downed the coffee and ate a bit of the toast that came with it his tired brain still grasped at the straw that maybe the engagement had been a ruse. Just yesterday she had suggested they run away and marry clandestinely. But if Amy had been planning any such jest with Draco she would have warned Trent. She would never be spitefully cruel.

Then he remembered that last glare she had cast at him and felt again the weight of Diana on his arm. Revenge? He did not think women played such games.

By the time he walked out to his small stable, the grooms had gotten a saddle on Flyer, but he was in danger of escaping three of them. And Jessup knew his tricks.

Trent took the reins and calmed the horse, which waggled its head up and down, jiggling the bit in its mouth.

"Any other animal would be glad of a day's rest," Jessup said. "This brute wants to run."

"Then I shall let him run," Trent said as he mounted. Flyer launched himself from the yard and almost into the side of a carriage before Trent managed to curb his exuberance. He kept him on a tight rein until they reached Hyde Park, then let him gallop across the open green, waiting for the small buck Flyer usually gave when coming to the end of a good gallop, but the horse was distracted by a mare on the south bridle path. What was worse, she was distracted by him, and even though Trent had charge of Flyer, the young stud's trumpeting caused the mare to disobey her rider so persistently Trent was afraid they might have a runaway on their hands, not to mention a display of breeding right in the middle of the park. He rode the colt away from this distraction, only to find another in a barking lap dog. Flyer pranced up to it, possibly with the notion of making friends, but the dog rushed at him and once again flight seemed the best alternative. When they gained the tree-lined drive Trent brought Flyer to a controlled canter and began to wonder if it was the best idea to bring such a horse to London. At least managing the beast kept his thoughts off of Amy.

One thing was certain. He had to get him out of the park. He turned the horse in the direction of the city, hoping he would be able to find someone at the docks competent to hold the animal for him. He usually ran his ships out of Portsmouth but he had a ship being outfitted at the London docks for a voyage to South America for tin and coffee. It suddenly struck him that he had never been to South America and this might be a good time to go. He toyed with the idea the whole way to the docks where the *Tigress* was waiting. She had been pulled in close to the pier to winch aboard the masts and sails she would need. Trent stared up at the top gallant yards and felt the sudden urge to climb. Anything to get away from thoughts of losing Amy.

Flyer was content to be left in the charge of a cabin boy who fed the horse bites of biscuit. Trent stripped off his coat and went aloft to see how the work progressed. He had spent many an hour up here as he learned the craft. He had made himself as much a nuisance on the first ship he had boarded as he had at the foundry.

It would be best if he could escape this way and avoid the wedding. Amy and Draco would be happily pregnant by the time he returned. The image caught him like a knife in the chest. Then he realized he grieved for Amy more when he was separated from her than when she was in sight. But at least she and Draco would not see his envious looks, his resentment of their happiness.

The wind was fresh and clean up here, billowing his shirt, but there was no joy in it. What else could he do then? Bury himself in work? He was just climbing down when a carriage approached along the quay. Trent recognized the team as Lord Marsh's and his heart gave a jerk when he realized it was Draco and Amy. She stood up and waved to him. She looked distressed. His return wave and shout, "I'm coming down," caught Flyer's attention and the horse began dancing nervously when it realized he was so far off the ground.

He climbed down carelessly, swinging from mast to ratlines as though he did it every day. He could see Amy taking the reins as Draco came to help the cabin boy with the nervous Flyer. At the top of the mast with the wind whipping his hair he had tried to find his freedom. He might have known Amy would bring him back to earth and remind him of his responsibilities.

The closer he got to the deck, the more he dreaded the meeting. He grabbed his coat and crossed the gangway to the pier, putting it on as he trod along the narrow plank.

"Did you happen to ride Flyer in the park this morning?" Draco asked. "They were still coaxing a mare out of the Serpentine when we arrived."

"Yes, retreat seemed the only honorable option." Trent forced a smile and plunged ahead. "How is the engaged couple this fine morning? And by the way, when is the wedding? I must find a proper gift for you."

Amy opened her mouth to object in some way but Draco interrupted.

"When the stars fall down," Draco said. "When life becomes insupportable—"

"Do not joke, Draco," Amy said. "We are in the devil of a fix, Trent, and trying to figure a way out of it. When Draco told me at dinner that you had offered me to him, I doubted you. I thought you were only intending to marry me out of duty."

"What do you mean?" Trent asked as he paid off the cabin boy and mounted Flyer to suppress the colt's urge to bolt.

Amy sent him a pleading look. "I only displayed the

The Guardian 243

ring to keep Draco out of the clutches of Lucy Machester. And, I admit, because I was angry with you."

"You did know it was an act, surely," Draco said, looking at Trent with some concern, but then getting into the phaeton before Trent could reply. "I would never use your own ring to steal Amy from you."

Trent felt a loosening of the serpent that had entangled his heart and a sudden rush of blood to his extremities that made him feel giddy. But he could breathe again. "Yes, of course. Did I carry it off well enough?"

"You were perfect," Amy said. "But it turns out Lord and Lady Marsh are delighted with the match. They are pressing Draco for a date."

"And how is Diana coping?" Trent asked numbly.

"As you might expect," Draco replied. "A deal of weeping, heel-kicking and breakage, mostly confined to her room for the moment. Because of the ring, you see."

"And I think because she is no longer the center of attention," Amy added.

Draco glanced at Trent. "I am not entirely sure it is safe for Amy to stay with us."

"Ah, that aspect of it had not occurred to me," Trent said. "I may have to make other arrangements." He could not help picturing him and Amy together at his town house, even though he knew it was an impossibility.

"What other arrangements?" Amy asked.

"Do you think that Lady Marsh is the only respectable matron I know in London? I shall see what I can contrive."

"But what will we tell Draco's parents when we do not get married?" Amy wailed. "I like them and I hate to disappoint them."

Trent shrugged as he watched Draco back the team and turn it. "I council delay. They hardly know you.

When they become aware how headstrong, managing and deceitful you are, they will be glad at the end of a fortnight to hear that you two have decided you will not suit."

"Trent!" Draco protested.

"Thank you very much," Amy said. "That aspect of the situation had not even occurred to me. You set my mind completely at rest."

Draco laughed. "And I gain a short respite from being hunted."

"Maybe even until my birthday," Amy said. "What will you do then, Trent?"

"Why, take you to the office with me. The work has been just piling up since I have become entangled with you. And the foundry is positively crying for a woman's touch."

"Stop joking," Amy ordered.

"But I am not. If ever there was woman who could run a law office, a shipping business, or even a foundry, it is you."

"But Trent," Amy protested.

"Sorry, but I must run this beast to tire him out or he will bring the stable block down." As Trent rode off he called back over his shoulder. "The theater tonight. Be ready."

"What do you make of that?" Draco asked as he steered the team past the warehouses and toward Ratcliffe Highway.

"I do not know, except he seems to need to regroup."

"From the look on his face yesterday when you sprang the engagement on everyone, I thought he was about to keel over."

Amy shook her head. "Why did I ever doubt him?"

"Do not worry. Every relationship has these little difficulties."

"I am engaged to you now. I see that as more than a passing bar to my marriage to Trent."

Draco was silent for a time, appearing to focus on his driving. But suddenly he smiled.

"You have a plan?" Amy asked.

"I am a soldier. I always have a plan."

It was a new play and the theater was packed. Though she, Draco and Trent had come to the Agora with Lord and Lady Marsh, they sat in Trent's box this time so they could speak freely. This was Draco's idea, but Amy wondered if it was wise to give his parents the opportunity to puff off the engagement with them not around.

This time, when men looked her way she had the courage to acknowledge with a smile those who nodded at her. Even Wraxton, who leered at her from across the way, received a tolerant look from Amy. She smoothed her ivory silk dress, the one that had just arrived with her trunk. Of all her new clothes, this was the dress she liked the best because it was the first thing Trent had bought for her. She could imagine being married in it. Yet if she were to spill something on it, it would not worry her overmuch, except for the expense.

She could be said to be enjoying herself. She had the man she loved and her best friend both beside her tonight. Unfortunately, she was engaged to the wrong one, but according to Draco, that was a small matter.

The soldier asserted that with him as escort, she and Trent could spend all the time together they wanted. And Amy was now perfectly safe from any other offers of marriage. However the same did not hold true for Trent. So Draco took Amy to stroll the corridors during the intermission while Trent fought off the advances of a forward young matron. When Trent finally got away and came upon them, Draco excused himself to go outside to smoke.

"So people do not come to the theater to see the play, but to visit and trade gossip," Amy concluded as she walked at his side.

"And to hunt," Trent said as he led her back to the box.

She sat and looked up at him, her beautiful mouth pensive, her eyes sad. "I am sorry I doubted you. But why did you offer me to Draco?"

"That was an age ago."

"That was less than two weeks ago."

Trent looked out over the glittering audience. "Because I did not feel worthy of you."

"And now you do?"

He grinned sheepishly. "No, I am still not worthy, but in my own grasping way I have decided I cannot live without you. I want you in spite of all my flaws."

"I think I love you because of them. I have come to expect every pompous little quirk."

He chuckled, then looked around the theater. "People are staring at us."

"Benignly, most of them. Draco will be back in a moment to lend us propriety."

"I think Draco is more a slave to his tobacco than to his drink."

"Pompous of you to say anything when you drink to excess yourself."

"I told you why I drink, and far from helping the situation, you make it worse." He shut his eyes and looked away.

"But you—So you did think I had betrayed you. God, Trent, I am so sorry." She grasped his hand and held onto it as though someone were trying to tear them apart.

"Yes, I thought I had lost you for an entire night and an entire bottle of brandy. It was hell."

"Nothing like that will ever happen again."

"I have never felt such despair before, not even when Draco was wounded. Well, maybe when I thought you had drowned in the Avon, or broken your neck, or suffocated during the fire. I feel lost without you. Nothing seems to matter."

She had seldom seen his face so thoughtful, his mouth so tempting.

She tightened her grasp on his hand. "I am delighted to be your new obsession."

"What do you mean?" he finally asked.

"It used to be winning the war."

"You should be proud to know that taking care of you is more work than everything I did this past decade. That may sound absurd coming from someone who spent the war behind a desk."

"You did not get to be the man you are by sitting behind a desk. You helped cast those cannon, and put them on the ships, if I mistake not. You sailed those ships to Spain and Portugal, and when the need arose, loaded and fired those cannon to protect the ships."

"Who told you all this?" Trent asked accusingly.

"I figured it out for myself."

"Do not admire me. Your love is enough."

"But it is true. You are just as much a hero as Draco. Only no one knows it except me." She almost raised her hand to caress his face but remembered in time where they were.

The curtain rose on the next act, and Amy tried to focus on the play, but what was going on in her heart and Trent's was of more concern. He had thought she had betrayed him, but had been too proud to storm at her. He had just left and that was probably the way he always dealt with betrayal. She must never do anything like that to him again.

"Did I miss much?" Draco asked as he slid into the box out of breath as though he had been running.

"What's the matter with you?" Trent asked.

Trent's accusation caused hissing from those actually trying to hear the actors.

"Can you imagine? Someone tried to rob me right in front of the theater," Draco whispered.

"Are you hurt?" Amy asked.

"I avoided his knife but got a kick in the ribs. No great matter. And I almost ran him to earth. If it had not been for that curb I missed—"

"You listen to me, Draco Melling," Trent warned. "I want you to stand up at our wedding, so do not get yourself mangled again."

"I shall do my best to stay intact for your sake."

21

⚜

*I*t was after midnight when they returned to Melling House. Lord and Lady Marsh stopped their discussion of the play and parted in the hallway, going to their separate rooms. Draco handed Amy a candle but did not bother to pick up one for himself. Draco saw her to her door, then followed his father to the end of the hall where his own room overlooked the stables.

Amy entered the darkened room and froze, for someone was sobbing quietly, not what she had expected to encounter. Her silly maid must be tired and wanting her bed. Amy lit the candelabra and turned to find the room a disaster. Every piece of clothing was tossed about, some of it rent and ruined, and all her new ribbons and fine things thrown on the floor. Even the bed hangings and draperies had been pulled down. *Diana,* she thought.

She located Molly crouched beside the bed and wedged in against the night stand, then spent the next ten minutes coaxing her out and convincing her she was not angry that the girl had been unable to stem the tide of Diana's wrath. Amy examined the girl's face and once she assured herself that the child had not been beaten sent her to her room.

When she assessed the damage more carefully, she was glad Diana had not found the scissors. Most of the destruction was superficial and could be mended with a needle and thread, but the anger and despair that had wrought it could not. Diana would never accept her or like her. To insist on staying here could drive a wedge between the girl and her parents. Well, she did have another option.

She went to the wardrobe and pulled out the valise that held her boy's clothes. To her delight nothing in here was harmed at all. She wrote a note designed to ease Lady Marsh's concerns, packed a few things, and donning her best boy's clothes, let herself out of the house.

"What do you mean she is gone?" Trent demanded of Draco the next morning. Trent had just ridden into the stable yard at Melling House on Flyer to find Draco was waiting for Hannibal to be saddled.

"She took Cullen and left in the middle of the night," Draco said as he mounted Han. Trent was trying to control Flyer in the small cobbled yard, forcing the grooms to keep dancing out of the way so as not to be trod upon.

"But why? She seemed perfectly fine when I left her with you. Draco, what did you do to her?"

"Nothing, but Trent, if you could see her room, you would realize why she has run away. Diana ripped up all her things. It set me back on my heels, and I am used to destruction."

"Did she hurt Amy? If she did—"

"No, Amy's note says she must not stay where she is causing so much trouble. She will return Cullen later. She does not sound frightened, just determined."

Draco passed the note to Trent, who tried to focus on it as his horse fidgeted under him.

"You think she has gone back to Talltrees?" Trent asked in despair. He did not believe Amy was not frightened.

"Where else?" Draco asked.

"But she promised me she would not do this sort of thing again without giving me fair warning."

"Are you coming or not?" Draco demanded as he swung up onto Han.

Before Trent could answer him Lord Marsh came out of the house. "Trent, I am so sorry. I knew Diana was jealous of her, but I had no idea. So spiteful. It was worse than any tantrum she ever threw as a child. Please find Amy and apologize for us."

"Oh, we shall find her, all right," Draco said. "Just like old times, eh Trent?"

"What does he mean by that?" Lord Marsh asked with a puzzled frown.

"Nothing," Trent replied. "His head is addled by love." He released Flyer, and Draco followed as they raced through the quiet neighborhood and toward the edge of town.

Amy woke up and knew that she was home, not Talltrees, but the house in Epping. How often had she dreamed of her room here and all the things she had left behind. But she had never once been allowed to come back here while it still would have mattered to her. Once she was on her own she had lost the desire. What could be here but bitterness? She climbed out of her childhood bed the better to examine the shelves of toys and books. Things had been kept well dusted. She opened the closet but it was empty.

The caretakers, the elderly Rowlings, had been surprised to see her, but they had recognized her. They had

brought her into the kitchen and given her warm milk and
gingerbread as though she were still ten years old. Lady
Agatha had robbed her of many things—her childhood,
for one. But she had exiled her to Talltrees where she had
thrived. If there was one thing she had no time for, it was
regret. She must get to Trent's house in London before he
was told she was gone. She did not want to worry him
again.

After sharing biscuits and tea with the Rowlings she
went to the small stable and saddled Cullen, then rode
back toward Mayfair. It had taken her hours to find her
way to Epping in the dark. Now she made the trip in less
than an hour, only to be told by a stiff butler that Trent
was out riding. He would not admit her, but when she
begged to leave a note he stood at the library door while
she wrote a few lines to let Trent know where she was, or
at least, where she would be tonight. She had work to do.

"Where could she be?" Draco demanded, pushing
aside the cold luncheon Minton had Mrs. Harris throw together for them. "I wonder if we overrode her."

"Amy?" Trent drank a swallow of coffee and stared
somberly at the bread tray. "There is only one road that
makes any sense. And she had a lead on us. If this was her
destination she would be here by now, unless some accident has befallen her."

"She might have stopped at an inn or to rest Cullen.
What a mad girl. It is a good thing I am not marrying her.
She would worry me to an early grave. In her own way
Amy is just as bad as Diana."

"That she is not." Trent glared at him. "She is neither
insane nor irresponsible. She does not do dangerous
things except out of necessity. I begin to think she never
left London."

"But she had nothing to wear but a ball gown. Oh, no. Trent, do you think she ran out of the house and tried to get to you?" Draco's eyes were dark with despair. "She might have been murdered and be lying in a gutter somewhere."

"You used to be the calm one. Who kept me from drowning myself at that bridge in Bath?" Trent leaned tiredly back in his chair, running a hand over his eyes.

"But that was before I realized how dangerous London had become. Imagine that, I was attacked outside the Agora, and in the presence of two other men."

Trent shook his head. "I had forgotten about that. You should not be riding about the country."

"It was just a bruise. Besides, I feel responsible. Why didn't she come to me for help? I was right down the hall."

Trent squinted at him. "That is not her way, to ask for help."

"I keep racking my brains to think where else she may have gone."

"My God!" Trent stood up and pounded the table with one fist. "I am the stupidest fellow in Christendom."

"We are agreed on that, at any rate." Draco pulled a chunk of bread off the tray and began to gnaw on it.

"She has gone to Epping."

"Epping?" Draco swallowed the dry bite. "To the races?"

"No, her parents' London house is at Epping. The one we use when we go to the races there."

"Well, I think you might have mentioned this place before."

"I'm going to start. Flyer will be rested by now."

"I will wait a few hours to rest Han and take him by easy stages back to London. I mean to stop often to inquire at the coaching houses."

"Just in case I am wrong?" Trent turned at the door to send Draco a wry grin.

"It has been known to happen."

Trent would have reached Epping well before dark had Flyer not thrown a shoe. It took some time to find a blacksmith courageous enough to attempt to shoe such a fidgeting beast. Trent held his breath as he trotted the horse into the stable yard of the tall house, but a whinny from one of the stalls and an answering call from Flyer convinced him he would find Cullen within. He let out a sigh of relief and wondered how he could have been so stupid as to have overlooked this place.

An upstairs window rasped open. "Trent, you got my letter," Amy said.

"Actually, no."

"Then how did you find me?" Amy whispered fiercely.

"Process of elimination. I am embarrassed that it took me so long."

"Put Flyer away. I shall let you in."

Ten minutes later Amy was waiting for him at the back door with a candle.

"Where are the caretakers?"

"Asleep. I knocked them out of bed in the wee hours last night. I had rather not wake them again. They must be in their eighties. Besides, your presence might be hard to explain."

Trent followed her up the stairs to a room at the back of the house and looked about him. "This was your room?"

"Yes, when I was a child. It was the only place I could think to go. I wanted to come to you, but I remembered what you said about not entering your town house."

He went to her and hugged her, not as long and as hard as he had after the coaching accident, but he had to know in his heart she was safe. He had to have the feel of her in his mind freshened, like a comfortable memory. It was a mistake, of course, for he felt a tug of need that distracted him from comforting her. He closed his eyes and tried to separate himself from the man he was, tried for just an hour to play the hero for her.

"What is it, Trent? I know I have worried you again."

"No more than usual. Just tired."

"Lie down while I tell you what I have found out."

"Oh, no, that would be a grave mistake. What have you been up to?"

"Well sit down then—not on that chair." Amy jumped to remove the article of furniture from his reach. "It will fall to flinders under you."

He compromised finally by sitting on the bed.

"I went to see Mister Lester."

"In those clothes?"

"Yes, oh, I explained all that to him."

She spun the small chair around and sat on it backward, causing Trent agonies of desire as he watched her shapely thighs.

"I had thought there was something familiar about René's name. Mr. Lester had found some information, but only for the past few years. He had not thought to check the firm's accounts. I could remember hearing the name when I was a child. But I could not remember where."

"So there was a Count Crevecoeur?"

"Yes, he is dead, of course, but Lester discovered that ten years ago there was a thousand pounds sent to René Crevecoeur in America."

"Mother said she had known him a long time."

"And before the war an amount was paid each quarter into a banking house in Boston for a Louise de Fornais."

"What is the significance of that?"

"Louise Forney was the governess your mother inflicted upon me. Don't you see? As soon as René was old enough not to need a nurse anymore your mother brought her here to look after me. When I saw her name in the records I realized it was René that had sounded familiar, not Crevecoeur. She must have said the name when she was drunk."

"I knew nothing of her. Or if I saw the record I must have thought it some rent or retired servant."

"It was not my money or your money, but your mother's. The firm handled her affairs, too, in those days."

"But she found another man of business when Father died. What a slap in the face. This Louise, if we could find her, might be able to shed some light on the connection."

"It gives me chills to think that your mother has always had me spied on," Amy said as she came to sit beside him. "I always thought I was so free at Talltrees."

He put his arms around her and pulled her against him. "None of them can hurt you. But why would my mother be sending money to either of those people?"

"There Lester could not help us. Perhaps René is some orphaned distant relative, but why hide him? Especially considering the war. He would have been far safer and far better off in England. And he was not in prison."

"What does this tell us?" Trent asked tiredly, stroking her head with one hand and feeling it lean against his shoulder.

"Very little." Amy snuggled against him. "And nothing useful in my present predicament. Why can't I stay here for the next few months? At least I have some fond memories of this place, and I won't have to be forever avoiding Diana."

"But what about about Lord and Lady Marsh?" Trent asked. "They are very upset over what has happened."

She looked up at him. "I know now why you like

them so much. I have made them miserable without meaning to."

"It is not your fault. One thing is certain. You cannot stay here alone." He looked about the room as she cuddled against him and realized how easy it would be to make love to her now. They would be married soon enough to cover an early child. But he resisted cheating her out of a wedding with all the proper trimmings.

"When I left here after Papa's death, it was as though I had died myself, stopped living one life and took up another. I feel like a stranger to myself."

"You might have stayed here and been happy," Trent said. "Instead you were uprooted and lost . . . everything."

"It was not your fault. You knew nothing about it." She turned to face him and he saw the slow slide of tears on her cheeks as the persistent moonlight shone through the shutters. Without thinking he followed his heart and took her into his arms, enfolding her and encircling her in a protective hug that he wished could keep her safe from the past as well as the present. "I cannot claim ignorance as my defense for that whole time. I should have made it my business to find you."

After a shuddering sigh, she dried her eyes, and looked up at him. "How did you know I would come here?"

"Just a guess. When I get wounded I always try for home, though I am a little confused about where I belong. What did she say to you?"

"Who?"

"Diana. She is the one who sent you off in a panic."

"Nothing. I never saw her. I think she has changed her mind about you."

"Yes, but if she wants me now, the emotion is not mutual. I find it hard to believe that a good man such as Draco could have such a witch for a sister."

Amy sniffed. "I cannot go back there."

"I will think of something. Lie down and get some sleep. We will ride out in the morning before anyone is about."

Amy clung to him. "Lie down with me."

"That I must not do," he whispered desperately.

"I am not asking you to love me. Just hold me like at the inn after the fire."

When she lay back against the pillow, he covered her, and against his better judgment lay down against her back, placing one protective arm across her. And though he was wearier than he had ever been, he held sleep at bay so he could savor holding Amy. He was trying to hold her not as a lover but as a guardian. It was the role he should have filled long ago, but it was too late for him to think of her in that way. She was not a child, but a being dearer to him even than Draco. He did not want to wait, but he did not think she wanted anything from him tonight but protection. He had to think of a way to keep her safe.

He could not plan when he was this tired and she was so close. He nuzzled the back of her neck, drinking in the fresh-washed scent of her. She wriggled in his arms and turned to him, stroking his jaw, running two fingers along his lips to the corner of his mouth. He kissed her fingertips and knew he was lost. She raised her face and met him in a desperate kiss that became a silken duel of tongues. Where in the devil had she learned this? He was about to ask when she broke the kiss to stand up and begin to strip off her clothes, all but her large shirt.

He rolled onto his back to watch her, but he felt too tired to argue with her. He merely smiled at her optimism. "No, Amy. I have ridden eighty miles today. Do not ask it of me."

"Too tired, As Ever Trent?" she chided. "You should take better care of yourself."

She knelt and began to undo his coat and shirt front,

running a tentative hand over the new scar Tartar had left on his ribs. When she tugged at the buttons of his breeches he gripped her hand.

"Do not do this. It is wrong in every possible way."

"If that were true my heart would tell me so. You are not as the world thinks you, some hardened rake. For one thing, you do not have the time. But why lead people to suppose that?"

"To avoid aggressive women," he said with a chuckle as he held her hands.

"But we are meant for each other. We love the same things. We mean to be married anyway."

"And we come to verbal blows at every meeting, this being a good example." He watched as her hands evaded his to undo the buttons one by one. He closed his eyes with a groan.

Her agile hands worked their way into his small-clothes and caused him to gasp with his need and bang his head on the headboard of the small bed.

"Will it work this way, with no gravity?" she asked as she straddled him. The kiss of her warm flesh against his made his temptation complete. He could not—would not—stop her now to save his soul.

"Gravity has nothing to do with it." His voice sounded raspy even in his own ears. He slid his hands along the fine sleek muscles of her thighs, then grasped her bare hips to guide her and drew a gasp from her.

"What is happening, Trent. I feel so . . . so hungry, I think."

"Your need is as great as mine. Just remember that you started this."

When his engorged member slid into her moist entrance it jolted him as though he had discovered some new land. She moved experimentally and made him groan.

"You have no barrier." He ran his hands upward to tease at her breasts, then threw the shirt over her head, so that he could finally see all of her.

"After all my falls off of horses, it would be extraordinary if that were intact."

"Lean forward," he begged. He raised his head to suckle first one, then the other breast suspended over his mouth.

Amy whimpered when she sat up again. He moved and gripped her arms at the elbow. She did likewise and he began the slow rhythmic dance that would take them away from all their cares. At least this eliminated the uncertainty. He would have to marry her now. Even as he thought about how he had acquiesced to her, how he had let this happen, he was amazed that he had given up control to her. He had never let anyone else control him, had never trusted anyone that much.

Amy was amazed, too. Nothing in her experience had prepared her for how much she wanted Trent, how keen every nerve ending perceived the give and take of his flesh inside hers. She wanted it never to stop, this sweet sliding of flesh against flesh, and wondered how she would ever be satisfied. Just when she thought she would cry out with sheer joy, Trent picked up the pace and she had to hold tight to him to keep herself centered. His lips were clenched into a tight smile and his breath came in short gasps.

The shudder of a muscle spasm inside jolted her into a rapid series of gasps and shook her with a wonderful warm tiredness that left her hungry for more. When his bouncing was so fast that she did not think she could stand any more he groaned aloud and held her. She felt a wonderful slippery wetness that soothed all her inside muscles. She slid off him to rest in the crook of his arm.

"I love you," she whispered.

"I love you," he said brokenly. "I never thought it would be possible for me to say those words to a woman."

She stroked a stray lock of hair away from his brow. "You are a quick study once you admit a deficiency."

"I hope my deficiency was only on the poetic side," he said as he pulled the blanket up around her.

"You were perfect." Amy snuggled into his warm, safe embrace. "I told you we belong together."

22

❧

"My God, Trent, what are you about?"

Draco's desperate whisper jolted him out of a pleasant dream, he and Amy making love under an oak tree. He rubbed his hand across his face and squinted at the candle Draco held. "I did not hear you come in."

"Obviously. Sleeping with Amy. I think you had better forget about reputations and marry her as soon as may be arranged."

Trent eased himself off the bed, careful not to tug the blanket away from Amy.

"You should have just taken her home," Draco said, leaning against the desk.

"To my house?"

"No, to mine." Draco put the candle down and sighed.

"It took you all this time to get to Epping?"

"No, idiot. I got held up by a couple of highwaymen. I shot one and rode over the other. Then I had to find this place in the dark, and then break in. Do you think that was easy? I am amazed I have not landed either in gaol or the asylum because of you two."

Trent laughed. "I am rather amazed myself. I have

thought of someone who may be able to help us," Trent said as he buttoned his disordered clothes. "But not until morning."

"Well, it is almost dawn." Draco gave a grunt of pain and slid slowly down against the desk in spite of his obvious efforts to stay erect.

"Draco, what is it? Have you fallen again?" Trent felt his friend's chest and his hand came away bloody.

"What is wrong with Draco?" Amy asked, grabbing her shirt and sliding it on over her head, her tousled curls popping out through the neck hole.

"I think he has been shot. Light more candles."

Amy quickly complied and Trent found a bullet slice high on the muscle on Draco's shoulder near his neck. It was bleeding only sluggishly now.

"I shall go for water and bandages," Amy said, throwing on her clothes haphazardly.

"Do you think you might find any brandy?" Trent asked.

Draco grunted and opened his eyes. "What happened?"

"You fainted," Trent said.

"Nonsense. Help me up."

"Not until we learn the extent of your injuries."

"Just a scratch."

"Which you failed to mention. One of the highwaymen?"

"Yes, damn him," Draco said, glancing sideways at his shoulder, trying to see the wound, and when he could not, reaching a hand tentatively toward the spot.

Amy came back with a pitcher and basin, some linen and a bottle.

"Cooking sherry?" Trent asked, holding it up to the candlelight.

"I shall try it," Draco said.

Trent poured some into a tumbler for him. "If you can stomach that, my good burgundy is wasted on you."

Amy snipped the tattered layers of uniform coat and shirt away. "I think there are some shreds of cloth embedded."

They had Draco lean forward in her arms as Trent cleaned the wound.

"Must you be poking about forever?" Draco grumbled.

"Unless I miss my guess you will neglect also to see a surgeon about this," Trent said, "so I am doing the best job I can."

"Cannot let my mother know. Lucky I have clean clothes with me. Amy, can you get my valise from the stable?"

"You should rest," she argued.

"We must be gone from here before morning. I think Trent should get a marriage license and then he will not have to worry about where to lodge you."

"We have no choice now," Trent agreed.

"What do you mean, no choice?" Amy asked. "There is always a choice."

"But I thought you wanted to marry me."

"Of course, I do. But first I have to break off my engagement to Draco."

"But there *is* no engagement," Trent persisted.

"But the rest of the world does not know that. Consider Draco's position." Amy gathered up the debris from Draco's wound and left them.

"What am I supposed to make of that?" Trent demanded as he got a pillow to prop Draco up. "Doesn't she want to marry me now that the suspense is over?"

Draco laughed and reached for the bottle of sherry sitting on the floor.

"Making love was her idea." Trent raised Draco and

tucked the pillow behind his head. "What does she want from me?"

"Not to be ordered about, apparently." Draco took a long swallow from the bottle and coughed.

"But what am I supposed to do?"

"You idiot. What will people think of her if she turns up married to you a day after our engagement is announced? She needs time."

"Well, I suppose that would look like you could not hang onto her."

"Or like you seduced her," Draco insisted.

"Very well, I concede the point. We will have to wait."

"Mostly because it would look very ill for Amy to be leaping from one man to another."

"She never used to care about any of that."

"She has realized that you care, so now she does, too."

"But I do not."

"Examine your conscience, my friend. I think you care more for public opinion than I do."

Amy pushed the door open and dumped the valise on the floor. In her boys' clothes she looked to Trent like a young stable lad.

"Is Draco going to be able to ride?" she asked.

"Yes, of course," Draco replied.

She strode to the window and bent to look out, the muscles of her thighs wonderfully revealed in the leather riding breeches. "It is getting light. I will go saddle the horses."

After she left, Trent felt Draco's gaze bend upon him and turned to assess his friend's fitness.

"Do not worry about me," Draco said. "I have been in far worse circumstances."

When the butler at the modest town house showed them into the morning room, Lady Vair was just about to sit down to tea and toast. Trent saw the look of surprise on her face turn to one of pleasure as she rose to greet him. And it was genuine pleasure, though not perhaps because of him, only that he was not an early bill collector.

"This is my ward, Amy Conde, and my friend, Captain Melling. I have a favor to ask of you, a big favor."

"You have only to name it," she said, releasing his hand to indicate a chair for Amy and one for Draco. "Let us have some breakfast and then we can talk."

Trent was glad that Lady Vair did no more than raise an eyebrow at Amy's attire. Truth to tell he was glad for the tea, though Draco pulled a face over it. Amy was looking at him in that indescribable way she had, half-amused, half-admiring. It encouraged him to plunge forward with his request.

"Amy needs a chaperon until I can arrange for our marriage."

"You are to be married?" Lady Vair smiled at him.

"For the moment Amy is engaged to Draco," Trent explained.

Lady Vair digested this as her butler entered with another tray of toast and two pots of jam.

"If you have time they can make you something more substantial," she said.

"This will do very well," Draco said, as he helped himself.

"I have heard about Diana, if that will save you the pain of explaining it," Lady Vair said. "It is all over town that she cut up your clothes."

"Yes, hence my strange garb," Amy said, holding out her cup for more tea. "She did not take the news of our engagement well."

Draco paused in his meal to add his mite. "Diana expected to be married first. Center of attention and all that."

"I see. Well, of course, Amy can stay with me."

"I shall have the rest of her things sent over today," Trent said. "I think we should all go to the theater tomorrow night, to try to cast some semblance of normalcy over events."

"Would you like my daughter Crissy to come, too?" Lady Vair asked. "That might lend even more credence to your situation."

Trent nodded. "If you think it would do her no harm. Let me leave a sum of money with you so that you can supply any deficiency in Amy's wardrobe." He stood up and took some bills from his wallet to lay them on the table, fully aware that Draco's eyes followed his every move.

"I will be ready, Trent," Amy said. "Are you taking Draco home now?"

Draco heaved himself out of the chair and went to the door as Trent took his leave.

"Yes, I will see you tonight, then." Trent looked back once before he left the room.

Amy went to the window and looked out to make sure Draco was not swaying in the saddle. But he rode as though nothing at all had happened to him.

"When did he fall in love with you?" Lady Vair asked.

Amy turned and smiled at her. "Trent, you mean?"

The older woman nodded with a smile.

"It seems an age."

"Will it not be an impediment to your marriage, being engaged to his best friend?"

"Oh, that was just a ruse to help Draco escape his many pursuers." Amy returned to the table and poured herself more tea.

"Trent is a much maligned young man. He saved me and my children from utter ruin."

"He is amazing, is he not?"

"Does anyone know your engagement is a sham?"

"Only Trent."

"Then it will all work out. An announcement after a time that you do not suit, a few assemblies, a ball, and then your sudden engagement to Trent, your childhood sweetheart."

"People will think he married me for pity, to save me from falling into a decline."

"Do you mind so much?"

"Not a whit. I care more about what they think of him."

"Then you will do well together. And you will be happy, for he is not a gamester."

"No, I am the one who takes all the risks."

"What is it, Draco?" Trent asked. He did not like Draco's bowed head, nor the way he fumbled with his reins. He tied Cullen's reins to a ring on his saddle and angled Flyer up to Han in case Draco fell. "You are not going to faint again, are you?"

"I did not faint. I was resting my eyes. I do not think it will answer, Trent, leaving Amy with one of your mistresses, even if she is long past being your mistress."

Trent laughed. "Marissa Vair would cut your liver out if she heard you say that about her. She is not one of my women. She is simply one of my clients. I handle her financial affairs."

"There must be more to it than that. She was so happy to see you. I think she would have done anything for you."

"I rescued her, financially speaking. When her husband shot himself her affairs were in sad disarray. I helped get them in order and secured her children's future—What is the matter?"

Draco shook his head with a sad smile as they made their way back to Mayfair.

"You do not believe me?"

"Yes, of course I do. It is exactly the sort of Galahadish thing you would do, but are you aware your name is romantically linked with hers?"

"Is it?"

"As it is with Mrs. Fisk and with Lady Connault. Did you also rescue them?"

"Yes. If the world wants to gossip, I do not see what I can do about it. In fact, I think being seen with my ward will help a great deal to put down any gossip about Lady Vair, though that had not been my original intent."

When they rode into the stable yard the door at the back of the house flew open and Lord Marsh stood there, his arms folded as he stared at them. "Drunk again?" he asked.

"I am perfectly sober," Draco protested.

"He just got shot by a highwayman," Trent added.

Lord Marsh sprang down the steps and stared at Draco as he dismounted.

"Why did you say it like that, Trent?" Draco swayed a little. "Just a nick, but I lost a deal of claret."

Trent thrust his shoulder under Draco's good arm and walked him to the door.

Lord Marsh proceeded them into the house and signaled for a servant. When he caught up to them in Draco's room he said. "I have discreetly sent for the doctor. Try, if you can, not to wake your mother again. Did you find Amy?"

"Yes, she is with Lady Vair," Trent answered for Draco.

"Odd place to go," Lord Marsh said. "I did not even know they were acquainted."

As Trent helped Draco to the bed, Lord Marsh set down the candelabra. "Come to the study before you leave the house, Trent."

"Why did you tell him I'd been shot?" Draco asked. "Just help me off with my coat and boots."

"Why are you never willing to show any weakness in front of your father?" Trent eased Draco out of the red coat and was pleased that the bandages had held. He pulled off both boots and set them aside.

"None of your business, Trent." Draco brought his legs up onto the bed and lay back. "When shall I meet you tomorrow night?"

"Seven. Will you be able?" Trent tossed a coverlet over his friend.

"If I sleep all day today and tonight."

Since Draco said no more but lapsed into a regular breathing pattern after a tired sigh, Trent left him. He had the cowardly impulse to slip away without the interview with Lord Marsh, but the stair creaked just where it always had and the man came out of his study to motion to him.

"Brandy?" Marsh offered.

Trent glanced at the bottle. "No, thank you. A bit early for me."

"I am still working on yesterday's quota. Is Amy frightened?"

"No, not at all. She was more upset that the maid had been terrorized. And she is feeling guilty for imposing on you."

"That sounds like her. Well, she must come back before the gossip runs rampant."

"Do you ask that to save Amy's reputation or Diana's?"

"My daughter's. There has been so much talk about her that I see nothing for it but to send her home for the rest of the season."

"She will not go."

"I suppose I could tie and gag her."

Trent chuckled at the prospect and ran a hand over his

eyes, realizing for the first time how very tired he was. "I will leave Amy to visit with Lady Vair for a few weeks. If your good wife will give it out that she was an acquaintance of Amy's mother that will help. As for bringing her back here, we shall have to see."

"Is . . . is, uh, Draco all right? Really?"

Trent came to attention. "He says he is and the wound seems slight. Why do you ask?"

"I know he is your friend but he is my son, still."

"Two highwaymen. He took a wound high on his shoulder, here." Trent put his hand over Lord Marsh's shoulder and felt as though he had wounded the older man who swayed and shook his head.

"Has he only survived the war to die by mischance in England? Why is he forever getting hurt?"

"The fall off Flyer will not happen again," Trent said. "I am buying that brute. But it does seem odd that Draco should be attacked twice in as many days."

"Twice?"

"Footpad tried to rob him outside the Agora."

"When?"

"The day after the engagement," Trent said. He felt a shiver of awareness set up the hairs on his neck and arms. "Just since he announced he was going to marry Amy."

"What is it?" Lord Marsh asked.

"She is an heiress, but really, why would anyone . . . ?" Trent got up and paced to the door.

"Surely you don't think there's a connection."

"I have to go now. Do not let Draco leave the house."

"Trent? Trent, get back here."

Trent ignored the order, feeling badly about that, but needing the few hours of quiet reflection before he could resolve whether Draco's refuge in the engagement, though it made him safe from women, was not putting his life in danger from someone who wanted Amy enough to kill for her. It was either Wraxton or Crevecoeur. Unless there was someone Trent did not know about.

Trent hailed a hackney and ordered the driver to take him to Severn House. Flyer was more than tired, and caused less confusion in the commodious Melling stable than in the smaller one behind his house. It did not seem possible that anyone could feel sure enough of winning Amy to think he could have her merely by disposing of Draco. Both incidents might just be accidents.

Then Trent thought of his mother's visit.

23

*I*f he had wanted some time for quiet reflection the office was probably not his best choice. Lester brought another stack of letters to Trent's already crowded desk. "By the way, your former agent stopped in and left a check for over 3,000 pounds. It seems in line with the lists of variances you gave me."

"What the devil?" Trent demanded. "You mean Fenwick?"

"Yes, so I stopped action on the lawsuit. I hope that was the right thing to do."

Trent leaned back in his chair with a heavy sigh. "Damn. I had rather have him arrested."

"We could try to pursue that, but since you have been made whole I'm not sure we have much of a case. I assume Mr. Fenwick is still discharged?"

"Certainly, after the threats he made. Now why would he not just flee the country? Why would he actually pay the money back?" Unless there was much more to be made another way. Not from marrying Amy. He must clearly know he is out of the running.

"I have no idea," Lester said. "Unless it might be our reputation for successful suits."

Trent shook his head, knowing speculation was useless. "Yes, that must be it. Did you find out any more about Crevecoeur?"

Lester pulled out a slip of paper. "Younger son of Count Crevecoeur. Yes, there is such a person and he might be him. No advantage to that. Lands are gone. No money."

"Any crimes in his past?"

"Served with Napoleon's forces, then a Royalist again, then an emperor's man again. He was not alone in that."

"I suspected some such history."

"Turned his coat more often than I beat my carpet." Lester laid the paper on the only clear spot on the desk and went back to work.

Trent rubbed his throbbing temples. His mind went back to his friend's recent spate of accidents. If it was Fenwick, he had hired London thugs to do his dirty work. But not on his own behalf. Neither Crevecoeur nor his mother would have such connections in London. They needed Fenwick to get rid of Draco, hence the bailout.

There was one other possibility. Trent ruminated for only a moment before he launched himself at the door and yelled for Lester.

"If it is about the shipment of china—"

"No, who gives a damn about that?"

Lester was turning away with a careworn expression when Trent added, "I need you to see if you can get wind of how Lord Wraxton is doing financially. I want to know how desperate he is for a rich wife." Lester opened his mouth to protest but Trent went back to his desk and applied himself to the piles of paperwork, not doing much more than sorting and jotting cryptic notes to Lester on the more pressing matters. It did not help that an adoring face kept swimming in front of his gaze. He could almost see those mischievous honey eyes, almost feel that determined mouth working over the skin on his collarbone, those firm thighs and talented hands. . . . He threw the quill across the room and left the office, ignoring Lester's protests just as he had Lord Marsh's.

"We have seen this performance already," Amy said to Lady Vair. "I wonder why Trent wanted to come again."

"My dear, one does not go to the theater to see the play, not entirely anyway. One goes to be seen. Crissy, sit back a little. People will think you forward."

"But, Mother, you said we want to be seen." The slight blond girl was trying to act grown up by pursing her lips and nodding to people she could not possibly know.

"There is a fine line between establishing a presence and being pushy."

"And Trent sent his coach for us rather than coming himself. That is very odd. It makes me wonder what he and Draco are up to."

"Well, he said to be here and here we are."

"You trust him implicitly," Amy said.

"As you should. Of all the men in London, he is the only one I would say could be trusted implicitly."

"I know that."

Lady Vair fanned herself as she glanced at Amy. "Captain Melling was not feeling very well yesterday morning."

"Not feeling well? Of course not. He'd been shot. That must be it. Trent went to check on Draco and sent the carriage to us because he did not want us to be late."

"Shot? Where?"

"In the shoulder. He did not seem to think it was serious."

"I meant—I'm sure Trent took care of him." Lady Vair waved to an acquaintance across the way.

"They are the best of friends."

"We shall have to be careful how we explain you dumping one of them and marrying the other." Lady Vair continued to smile and nod at people as these words left her lips.

Amy glanced at her, almost by now used to these facers that she slipped in as though she had just asked if you wanted one lump or two. "That is my reason for refusing to marry Trent immediately. How long do you reckon I need to leave between engagements?"

"Till the end of the season would be best, if you are not to be the talk of the town."

"Months?" Amy said in despair.

"You are already the talk of the town," Crissy said helpfully.

The curtain at the back of the box parted and Crevecoeur stood regarding Amy so long that she let her eyes slip to her dress thinking something was amiss. That had been a mistake. She should never let anyone make her doubt herself like that.

"I see no rents or tears," he said, smiling at her confusion.

"What do you mean?" she asked frostily.

"Miss Melling was reported to have taken a knife to your wardrobe."

Lady Vair cleared her throat. "I do not know you, sir."

"Not even a pair of scissors," Amy said, "and I am surprised you listen to servants' gossip, René."

"I am le Compte de Crevecoeur," he said, snapping to

attention and clicking his heels together, "but I wish you would call me René."

"This is Lady Vair and her daughter Crissy."

"Mon plaisir," he said as he bowed over each of their hands in turn and kissed them.

Amy watched Crissy's eyes grow round in admiration and shrugged.

"Are you perhaps neglecting Lady Agatha?" Amy asked as she glanced at the proud matron across the room. Even from here she could see the green of the woman's eyes glittering speculatively.

"She will be content to wait for me."

"She does not look at all content. I do not think she likes me."

"Your mind has been poisoned by her son. Lady Agatha holds you in the highest regard."

Amy avoided looking at her godmother again, but noticed the flutter of a fan from the Melling box. Lady Marsh waved to her and after a deal of prodding Diana acknowledged her with a nod. From the pit Wraxton sent her his crooked smile, as usual. Amy waved at the Mellings and sent Wraxton a bored glance.

Booted feet in the hall broke the tension of the moment as Trent and Draco appeared. Suddenly the box seemed crowded and Amy could breathe a sigh of relief as Draco sat on the other side of her. Did René's eyes stray to his shoulder?

"Crevecoeur, I did not look to find you here," Trent said brusquely.

"Someone has to look after Amy."

"Draco is well able to do it."

René bowed stiffly and left. Trent sat down. "Did we miss much?"

"The play has not even started," Amy said.

Lady Vair whispered behind her fan to Trent. "Your mother sent the Frenchman over, and the Mellings have acknowledged us."

"Good, things are going well."

Amy got the feeling the entire play was not happening on the stage. Trent seemed oddly formal, as though he were not himself. She turned to Draco and whispered. "Are you well enough to be here?"

"Oh, if we were at the front I would have rejoined the fighting by now."

"Something has been bothering me," Amy said.

"What?" Draco asked.

"Am I much of an heiress?"

Draco avoided her eyes and looked at Trent, but he only shrugged. "You are possibly among the wealthiest women in London. Why?"

"Did anyone try to kill you before you became engaged to me?"

Lady Vair's indrawn gasp and the dead silence that ensued told Amy she had hit some nail on the head.

Draco laughed. "All the time. London is crawling with footpads and cutpurses."

Crissy looked like a fawn about to bolt.

"It is his size," Trent said. "Draco makes such a big attractive target."

How like them both, Amy thought, to try to pass it off as a joke. But if Draco were killed she would never be able to forgive herself. She would simply have to think of a way to end the engagement quickly.

During the intermission Trent took her to the Melling box and she chatted to Diana about Lady Vair and her daughter. No one watching them would have guessed there had been any rift between them. People would assume that the tongue-waggers had got it wrong again. Amy thought it was kind of Trent to do this for the Mellings. If he did it mostly for Draco and the parents it was still a kindness.

When Trent finally escorted them home, Draco stayed in the carriage and Lady Vair shepherded her daughter upstairs, leaving Amy alone with Trent in the small sitting room. He merely commented, "That did not go so very ill."

"Did it work?" Amy asked.

"It may have gone some way toward putting down the speculation. Your name was being tossed around at the clubs. I do not know who started the gossip, but—"

"More so than Diana's?"

"In a different light. They all know about her foibles—high-strung and selfish. But they will talk about you more because you are an unknown quantity . . . and an heiress."

"And because I am an outsider and engaged to Draco they will not like me."

"The women will not like you. You stole him out from under a lot of aristocratic noses." Trent stood uncertainly as though he meant to say more, then turned to go, but stopped at the door. "I think I should tell you they know about the ring."

"What could they possibly know?"

"That I offered it to Diana and that it now graces your finger. We have to make up a story about that."

"Why can I not tell them the truth?"

Trent chuckled. "That you won it playing silver loo with three drunken gentlemen? I hardly think that will do you credit."

"But Wraxton knows the truth of it."

"No doubt he is the one who set it about that it was Diana's ring. It would have been easy enough for him to guess what was in that box I staked."

"Then tell them that you were so distraught over her refusal, you threw the ring at Draco and told him to find himself a wife since you would never marry."

"Hmm, that is good. That might wash. But what will they think then when I do marry you?"

She could see his green eyes glitter, but was that amusement or derision?

"Trent, I was joking. Why do we have to set anything about? I do not care what anyone thinks of me, except you." She came toward him and he opened his arms to enfold her.

"This is very unwise," he mumbled as he kissed her neck, her cheek, her eager lips.

"Lady Vair says we should wait till the end of the season," she whispered in despair.

Trent grave a crack of laughter. "Impossible. Even a day seems like an age without you."

"The days are impossibly long. I am used to working or else arguing with you. I never thought I would miss that."

"My secretary thinks I have run mad, always sending him off on some fool's errand."

"What must he think of me showing up there at your office like a stable boy?"

"He likes your spirit." Trent put up a hand to stroke her curls and she sighed against his chest.

"What are we to do, Trent? Whether I break the engagement or Draco does, it will not reflect well on him."

"Believe me, he can take the blow better than you. Much as he dislikes it, as soon as you free him he will be fair game again. At least you have given him a short respite from the pursuit of women."

"But I have endangered his life, I fear. I know he denied it, but I am right. Trent?"

She pushed back to look at him and see regret in his eyes.

"As it happens I am having that investigated. Mr. Lester has connections in the coffeehouses and gin parlors. You can get some amazing information if you are willing to pay for it."

"The truth?"

"There is a certain honor about that in the lower orders that does not exist in high society. You get what you pay for there, but not always here."

"And some aristocrats are shams, like me. A horsewoman dressed up like a princess. But I do not want to be a princess anymore."

"What do you want?"

"To be back at Talltrees with you."

"That is something we can agree on. I will find the quickest route to it, but first we must make all safe in London." He kissed her again as though he would not see her for a long time and tore himself away.

Amy dragged herself up the stairs to pick out her clothes for tomorrow. How different it was here. She was used to wearing her riding habit the better part of the day. Here she rarely got through the day without at least three changes. She, Lady Vair and Crissy were invited to tea at the Mellings'. She should be able to wear gloves to cover up the ring. But Amy thought they were pushing their luck to compel Diana to be civil to her again. And Amy was only engaged to the woman's brother. Diana had no inkling it was Trent Amy would eventually marry. She did not even want to imagine Diana's reaction to that news. Surely the Mellings would have taken her back to the country by then.

The next time Amy would see Trent would be Wednesday night at Lady Holt's party. That would make everything that happened in between doubly boring.

When she thought of Talltrees and her waiting mares the urgency seemed to have gone out of the issue. So there would be no foals next year. More sleep. She and Trent would both appreciate that. Talltrees was not so far from London that they could not live there and come into town a few times a week to handle business. She was looking forward to being a great help to Trent.

24

Even though Lady Vair's house was out of the way, Amy was beginning to feel trapped and exposed there, that it was not a safe refuge. She had several times noticed someone loitering across the street and pointed him out to Lady Vair. The man was there again when they left for the tea. Amy thought she had better tell Trent.

The tea actually went quite well, with Crissy latching onto Diana and bombarding her with questions about what to expect during her come-out. To Amy's surprise Diana not only tolerated this attention but warmed to the girl. Amy made a mental note not to draw any attention away from Diana. There were mostly ladies present, so there was no danger of Amy being drawn into any discussions about horses unless Draco initiated them, and he must have had marching orders from his mother. He moved about the room like a diplomat spreading compliments and joking with the ladies, who all looked at him worshipfully. Some of them then turned an envious gaze toward Amy, but the most she had to fend off were inquiries about the date. She fell back on the difficulty of getting her bride clothes in order and they clucked sympathetically.

Lady Agatha appeared late, as though she were only discharging a duty visit. Amy was relieved that René was not with her, but the withering green glare was bad enough. She almost felt that the woman could see through her, through the sham engagement. When she actually sat next to her Amy screwed her courage up and met her eyes.

"So you are still in town. We had expected you to go back to Bath by now."

"René is to take up residence in London. We are looking for lodgings for him, someplace large enough for him to pursue his occupation."

"Yes, the fencing lessons."

"Too bad you two did not make a match of it," the older lady said in a coaxing voice. "René could have been a great help to you, schooling your horses."

"You know about my business?"

"I made it possible. Do you really think that Trent would have let you engage in horse-trading if he had known what you were up to? It was only because I took responsibility for you that you had as much freedom as you have enjoyed all these years."

"Freedom? With Louise there? Did she write you every week what I was doing?"

It was the first time she had ever seen Lady Agatha hesitate. But the woman's teacup continued its path to her mouth and after taking a sip she finally said. "Louise is a trusted employee. It is a mark of my regard for you that I was willing to give her up all those years."

"Why didn't you tell me she worked for you?"

"What difference does it make? She came to care for you as much as I did and you dismissed her as though she were a clumsy kitchen maid."

"You can blame Mr. Fenwick for that. He suddenly decided to make me pay her wages, along with everyone else's. You paid Fenwick to spy on me, too."

"To look out for you. I never expected he would feather his own nest with your money."

"When did you find out about him?"

"When René started looking into things for me. My association with Mr. Fenwick has been as unfortunate as yours. And to think I recommended him to my husband for the position. Now I find he has been cheating everyone."

"And importuning me to marry him."

That drew a snap of fire from the green eyes. Lady Agatha clapped her cup into her saucer. "That I did not know. We shall see about this."

Gratified that she had not only revenged herself on Fenwick, but had made Lady Agatha uncomfortable, Amy followed up with, "And when Trent rumbled his lay the man threatened me."

"You poor child. You should have written about him years ago."

"I did, but Trent ignored me."

"I mean you should have written to me. I would have done something. I do not know why you see me as your enemy. I have always been on your side."

"That view of it had never occurred to me. Why did you separate me and Trent when we were children?"

Lady Agatha sighed theatrically. "I had thought of the possibility of a match between you two, but Trent has turned into such a rake, and a cold man. He discards women as though they were soiled clothes. No, you would be far better off with someone like René, who would worship you."

Amy was not even tempted to tell Lady Agatha about her and Trent. This last speech had seemed too rehearsed and there was no warmth in those green eyes of hers. They glittered like ice. If Trent had been a cold man, Amy knew where to lay the blame. But he had never been as his mother described him and now he was in love with her.

After going to chat with Lady Marsh and Diana for a moment, Lady Agatha left and Amy felt herself relax, almost as though she were thawing after being out in a snowstorm.

"Are you all right?" Draco asked. "What did the witch say to you?"

"Nothing I believed." Amy just hoped she had not given away to Lady Agatha anything that could give her an advantage. Going back over their conversation, she thought not. And she had managed to make her point about Fenwick. Her godmother would never trust him again.

The next evening Amy realized that whatever her reception had been at the theater or the tea, among picked company, things were quite different here at Lady Holt's. She bit her lip as she glanced around the crowded ballroom, reluctant for the first time to make eye contact with anyone. Her dress was the ivory one she had been wearing the night of Diana's attack. But it had been decorated with a ruffle of silk at the bottom and a knot of flowers at the bosom. No one should even recognize it.

Since Crissy was not out yet Amy had come under the escort of Lord and Lady Marsh, who had procured her the invitation. But her presentation to such ladies and gentlemen as the Mellings were acquainted with produced raised eyebrows and no very encouraging words of acceptance. Diana had abandoned her as soon as they entered the room and gone off with two other young ladies. Was that thoughtlessness or deliberate rudeness?

She looked desperately around for Trent and when she could not find him began to hope for a mercifully short evening, since no one seemed inclined to ask her to dance anyway. She was approached by Mr. Whiting, who wanted her to sell him one of her mares. They talked for some minutes before his wife got his attention and recalled him to her side.

After Whiting had broken the ice several more men approached her about horses and she joked with them as she would have at home, even though she knew this was not the sort of thing most young ladies discussed with gentlemen. She was beginning to find herself the center of a raucous crowd, and even though she knew it was bad for her reputation, it was so much better than standing about alone.

She was wrestling over what Trent would say about her discussing business deals at such an event when René approached.

"You are looking very pensive," he said, taking her hand.

"I am trying to manage a stud farm in Berkshire from London. And it is not an easy job at the best of times."

"It seems not to be an occupation for a lady." He drew her hand through his arm and encouraged her to stroll with him.

"Why not?"

"For one thing you have to deal with men like that. Lady Agatha sent me to rescue you."

Amy was not sure why this made her feel more wary than ever. "That was kind of her."

"Also horses are so big, so dangerous." He slurred the last word as though it contained an *x*.

"But René, they weigh over half a ton each. They would not squash me any flatter than you if one fell on me. So there is little difference between a woman managing them as opposed to a man."

He cocked his head at her, then smiled slightly, with that fullness of lip that reminded her of someone. It was a mixed association, both pleasant and dark. Or else her memory, however fuzzy, was tainted by her dislike for René.

"What is it?" he asked. "You seemed on the point of saying something."

"Nothing. It is only that you remind me of someone."

"Vraiment?" he said with his too-ready smile that dispelled the lingering familiarity. "Who do I put you in mind of?"

"I do not know. It must be a chance resemblance."

"You are not dancing?"

"I have not been asked."

"Dancing is stupid. Continue to walk with me and we will ridicule the turbans and feathers of the dowagers together."

Amy laughed and relaxed her arm in his, seeing no harm in this mild diversion. He was actually quite amusing when he likened one egret-ridden head to a bird throwing a fit, and a severe bejeweled headdress to that of a desert sheik. She wondered if this silly man could be guilty of the attacks on Draco. And if not René, then who was it? Perhaps Lady Agatha on his behalf, and without his knowledge? Perhaps she had even hired Fenwick to do it. It was possible.

The thought that Fenwick might be in town rather than in Berkshire cast a gloom over her even before she saw Trent approaching across the floor. René must have read the expectation in her eyes, for he turned toward her guardian, the smile bleeding away as though the life were being drained from him. At that moment, and for no other reason than the thunderous look on Trent's brow, Amy had to admit that her sympathies were with René.

"What do you mean by making a spectacle of yourself?"

"We were strolling," Amy said. "We never left the room or any of the dozen things you warned me about."

"You should have danced with several men instead of spending all your time with one."

"No one asked me," Amy complained.

"You should—you should have contrived better," Trent sputtered.

"That is absurd, Trent."

René laughed and bent to salute her hand before walking back to Lady Agatha.

"You will dance with me now," Trent ordered.

"Since you asked so pleasantly, yes, I would like to dance."

"Where the devil is Draco?" Trent asked.

"The card room. He does not like to dance and he was sorely tried yesterday at his mother's tea. He deserves a respite from me."

Trent found that a country dance, though it gives one time to think of retorts when flirting or trading pleasantries, was unsatisfying when all he wanted to do was chide Amy for undoing their careful handiwork. They had been trying to play her off as a respectable country-bred girl, but according to the few remarks he had heard on his way in she had spent all her attention on horse buyers and the Frenchman.

"But I did not go up to men and offer to sell them horses. They seek me out," Amy remarked when they came together.

"You might put them off," Trent countered.

"That would be rude indeed. Some of them are already my customers."

"Then you should have avoided them."

"And you should have been here earlier. I do not see why you are so angry with me."

"I am not angry with you!"

Since this was spit out with such force he caused the lady next to Amy to jump, Trent pressed his lips firmly together and refused to speak at all after that. When the dance was over he took her elbow in an unbreakable grip and guided her off the floor.

"Where are you taking me?"

"To Lady Marsh. And you are to stay with her. No more strolling with René."

"I do not see what harm it does. He can do nothing to me in a ballroom."

"Because you make him think he has a chance with you."

He left her wordlessly by Lady Marsh, with Diana scowling nearby, and went off to get control of his temper. Only then did it occur to him that his scene with her might have been worse than what she had been doing, that his anger was not just at the one or two remarks he had overheard about Amy's attentions to the Frenchman, but about his lack of credentials as a guardian. If people talked about her as a wild girl, it was his fault more than hers. He had brought her here and, moreover, he had ruined her.

By the time he made his way to the refreshment room Trent was feeling very guilty, and he was so tired of that, it made him feel ill-used. He found a tray of filled champagne glasses and tossed one off, wondering what effect it would have.

Why had she insisted on falling in love with him and idolizing him when he was, of all the men here tonight, the one most a danger to her. That night at Epping had proved it. That night! He picked up another glass of champagne and downed it, starting to feel a slight buzz in his head.

He played the love scene over in his mind as the sweetest thing that had ever happened to him in his life. And he could recall almost all their wonderful talks on the way back from York. He loved Amy more than life itself, yet he had just ripped up at her for something that was not her fault. What was the matter with him? He had never felt this way before. And then he recalled that he had, those few times when it seemed that Draco was interested in her. If he could be jealous of his best friend, of course he would have a stiff-legged dog-in-manger reaction when Crevecoeur laid hands on her.

A familiar wicked laugh assaulted his hearing at that moment, and he turned to see Wraxton joking with young Wainwright. The man turned and almost bumped into Trent. Wainwright looked from one to the other and left.

"Wraxton, I should throttle you. I told you what would happen if you gossiped about Amy."

Wraxton's head came up and his eyes narrowed. "Stop baring your teeth at me, boy. Is it likely I would malign a woman I would admire to make my wife?"

Trent snorted his scorn. "You mean you have some notion of applying for her hand?"

"I have a title and estates. . . . I shall say it for you, heavily encumbered estates. You did not need to go checking on that. I would have told you. But I am hardly a rarity. And I have a fondness for Amy."

"You tried to—"

"Tut, tut, that was before I knew she was an heiress. I thought she was one of your light skirts, and truth to tell, I had a notion to take her away from you if I could."

"And one way you could do that would be to ruin her chances with anyone else, hence the salacious gossip."

"If you imagine I am the only one in London with a

reason to gossip about your ward, you are more naïve than she is."

"If it was not you, who was it?"

"I do not know, but I can probably find out."

"Indeed? And why would you do anything to help me?"

"You mean because Lord Marsh preferred your suit for Diana's hand to mine? Fortunes of war." Wraxton shrugged his thin shoulders.

"Much good it did me."

"Why would I go out of my way to harm Amy?"

Trent regarded him. The man's eyes seemed a little fogged with drink, but sincere. "That is why I hate this society. Mischief is not done for any particular reason. They chew at someone just because he is different, hard-working, or . . ."

Trent became aware that Wraxton was staring at him as though he had run mad. The man shrugged and went in the direction of the ballroom. Trent had been thinking of his father never being accepted into these circles since he was in trade and made no excuses about it. Trent's own acceptance among these people had been bought with his mother's position.

Feeling a certain numbness behind his eyes, and liking it, he had yet another glass of wine.

He jumped when he discovered Diana was at his elbow and stared at her as though she had appeared out of a fog. "I suppose you want to dance, too," he demanded.

"I prefer to walk and see the gardens." She pouted behind her fan.

"It is dark. That would be most imprudent."

"If I were to go with you?" She took his arm, but he did not cooperate.

"With any man, but your father or brother."

"Oh, I think my reputation could stand a moonlit walk with you. After all, you are almost one of the family."

"But would mine?" Trent asked wickedly.

"My refusal of you had more to do with being forced into marriage than with any objection to you. Father said I must make up my mind and I was not ready."

Trent hesitated as he saw the trap yawning again. "That is not how I remember it, and you were absolutely right in your assessment of my character. I am a rake and we would not suit."

"No one minds a rake, not if he means to reform."

"I mean to have consistency in my life."

"Then I would consent to be your wife."

"I hate to point this out, and I do so with all delicacy, but I have not asked you to marry me, and as for a woman proposing to a man, why it simply is not done."

Diana glared at him. "You were eager enough to propose to me two weeks ago. Why now do you object to a renewal of our engagement?"

"Ah, if I may point out, we were never engaged. I offered once, you refused. That was the end of the transaction."

"Transaction?" She took a step back from him. "Just because I would not let you buy me—"

"What I got for my pains was a very expensive lesson. And I had thought I knew all there was to know about women. I find you more practiced in flirtation than any creature I have ever seen."

"Are you comparing me to your mistresses?" Her eyes narrowed, making the irises look black.

"If the shoe fits—"

The crack of her slap rang throughout the salon, and indeed Trent swayed a little from the blow. He just wished she had not hit him the same place his mother had.

"I think my case is proven. We would not suit." He bowed and turned his back on her, leaving her alone and trembling with rage. It was while he was walking away that he realized he should have been more conciliatory. Diana herself might be the source of the gossip about Amy. Would he never get any wiser, but keep blundering from one mistake to another?

Amy spent the next hour making strained conversation to Lady Marsh who was trying to see where Diana had gone. Amy was approached by young Lord Tarrdale for a dance and consented to take the floor with him, expecting that his excitement bespoke some bet or request to do with her horses.

Instead, as they swung through the steps of the open waltz, he confided, "Do you know that Captain Melling meets Wraxton on your account?"

"What do you mean?"

"They have argued and a challenge was given. Honor can only be satisfied with a duel. Is it not exciting above anything?"

"But this is terrible!" She stopped in the middle of the floor. "Draco could be killed."

Tarrdale stopped too. "But I have laid my money on Melling, him being a soldier. In fact, I have put fifty pounds on him, to kill his man or back Wraxton down before the day."

"How can you bet on men's lives?"

"They will be shooting at each other if I make fifty pounds out of it or not."

"Oh, I am out of all patience with you." Amy spun on her heel and left him alone on the middle of the floor.

She went in search of Draco to have the truth of it and found him coming out of the card room with a set of worshipful young men on his heels like a pack of hounds. She grabbed his arm and walked with him.

"Is it true you are engaged to fight Wraxton on my behalf? For if it is I wish you would not."

"I am not fighting him for your sake. Well, not entirely." Draco took her arm and gently drew her aside. "He was asking questions, asking who was talking about you, who knew aught against you. He is obviously the one behind the attacks on me as well as the gossip about you."

"What do you mean? Why would he?"

"By what I hear he is done up, in debt to his eyebrows. He needs your fortune. He tried gossip to get me to dump you. When that did not work he instigated those attempts to put me out of the way. He has a grudge against me anyway for roughing him up at Talltrees."

Amy stared at Draco, trying to determine just how drunk he was. "But is it not playing right into his hands to stand up and let him shoot at you?"

"It will be a fight out in the open. That is something I can handle. I hate subterfuge."

Amy stared at him in amazement and whispered desperately, "But we are not even engaged, not really. Why are you doing this?"

"Because Wraxton has it coming, and because Crevecoeur gets on my nerves, always slinking around trying to make trouble, the French mouse."

"What does René have to do with this? Did he provoke your quarrel with Wraxton?"

"I would have quarreled with Wraxton anyway. It does not matter who is responsible. I meet Wraxton day after tomorrow in the woods by Epping Forest."

"But there must be some way out of this," Amy said numbly.

"You are not worried, are you? My mother is giving a

ball the Monday after. Anyone who comes will have to accept you since it is mostly for you. It is frosting Diana, but there is no help for that. So put on your prettiest dress."

"But, Draco, where are you going now?"

"My club. I have to lodge a bet."

"But Draco—" Amy objected as she tried to follow him. She stopped herself when she realized she was the object of much curious attention. There probably were women who would have liked to have duels fought over their honor but she was not one of them. She needed to stop this. Trent could probably manage it, but she would have to tell him of Draco's vision problem and she doubted the soldier would like that.

When she finally found Trent he reported that Lord Marsh had already taken Diana home and that Lady Marsh would ride in his carriage to take her back to Lady Vair's house. Lady Marsh was strangely silent and Amy wondered if she knew her son's life was in danger again. When they arrived she stayed in the carriage while Trent walked Amy to the door. As soon as he saw that it was unlocked he turned on the top step to go.

"We must do something to stop this duel," Amy whispered to him.

"How did you find out about it?"

"You were not going to tell me, were you?"

"I will be with him in case anything happens. But Draco is an excellent shot and Wraxton would be a fool to make it a killing matter."

"But if Wraxton is indeed done up, will he care whether he has to flee the country or not? Cannot you barter a resolution without weapons?"

"If Wraxton is willing to apologize. Yes, of course."

"Trent, please!"

"I can only do that with Draco's permission."

"And he would say no. I hate these stupid conventions."

Trent's shuttered look was answer enough.

"You must talk Draco out of this," she pleaded.

"You refine too much upon this meeting. No harm will come to Draco."

There was no comforting embrace this time. Trent turned on his heel and walked to the carriage. Why should he comfort her? She was the cause of every bad thing that had happened to Draco these past weeks. She might not be able to get the implacable Trent to help, but she was not going to do nothing.

25

⊶⊰⊱⊷

*I*f Draco and Trent were immovable on this matter, Amy thought of trying to talk to Wraxton. But she had no idea where to find him or how to arrange a meeting. And even if she could manage to talk to him she could think of no way to dissuade him.

There was one other person she might turn to. After pacing about the house the next day and reluctantly receiving callers, mostly ineligible young men who were hunting-mad, Amy came to a decision. Late in the afternoon, under the guise of visiting Lady Marsh, she took her new maid and hired a hackney to take them to Melling House. The loiterer pointedly ignored her. Perhaps he had been hired by Lady Agatha. What a bother.

When Horton informed her that her ladyship was driving in the park Amy said, "It does not matter. I have come to see Lord Marsh." She sent her maid to visit in the kitchen until she had finished.

Horton stared as Amy deliberately removed her gloves a finger at a time.

"I do not think his lordship is home to company."

"This touches on the welfare of his son. He will see me or I will wait until he leaves his study."

Lord Marsh opened the door with a worried frown on his face. "Amy, please come in."

Horton showed her to a chair in the mannish room, but left the door ajar.

"What is it, Amy?" Lord Marsh asked. "Shall I send for some tea?"

"I would not have come to you if the situation were not extreme. Draco goes to duel with Wraxton at dawn tomorrow near Epping Forest. I have mined the young men who have called today for information. The assignation is to take place in the woods behind the Hedgebird Inn. You must stop it."

He had stared at her all through this speech with absolute attention. When she finished he sat down and shook his head. "I have just been getting on a better footing with Draco. If I interfere in any way, he will never forgive me."

"You are as bad as Trent," Amy said. "If someone does not do something Draco may be dead by tomorrow morning, and all over my honor, as though I even care. Why do men have to be so stupid?"

"If you put it to Draco that way, might he see reason?"

"Draco is far too proud to admit he is in danger."

"Wraxton," Lord Marsh mused. "I would not have taken him as one to pick a fight."

"It surprised me as well. But it was at Lady Holt's in the card room. There is no telling but what the others may have set them on each other just for the sport of it."

Lord Marsh poured some amber liquid into a tumbler, but only pushed it about on his desk. "Wraxton may be reputed to be an excellent shot, but Draco is better."

"Was better," Amy corrected, watching him for signs of relenting.

"What do you mean?" His eyes met hers, finally, in a penetrating stare.

"Draco is blind in one eye, or nearly so. I am almost sure of it. He cannot judge distance anymore. He cannot possibly win. And he is so big Wraxton cannot possibly miss him."

Lord Marsh leaned back in his chair with a heavy sigh. "Now why would he confide that to you and not to me?"

"He did not confide in me. I guessed it from the way he rides. Plenty of skill if he is following someone, but has no idea where the fence is if he leads. And he always arranges his silverware precisely so that he will know where it is. He drains his wineglass immediately for fear of knocking it over. Are you listening to me?"

Lord Marsh nodded as though he was recalling seeing each of these things. "You sound as though you really do love Draco."

Amy flushed and dipped her head. "I care about him."

"If I try to intervene, Draco will resent me worse than ever."

"He is going to die unless we do something. And I am not going to stand by and let it happen." Amy jumped up and put on her gloves.

Lord Marsh stood up abruptly. "What are you going to do?"

"I do not know yet but I will think of something."

"I have an idea." He came around the desk to take her frantic hands.

"Well?" She tapped her foot impatiently.

"I know where Wraxton will be drinking tonight. Leave everything to me."

"My experience with men to date has not led me to place much trust in any of you."

Lord Marsh laughed. "Go home. I will send you word tomorrow."

"I must know what you are planning. Will you take me with you?"

"No, that I shall not do, but I will escort you home."

Though she resisted his aid, Lord Marsh had his team harnessed to his phaeton and drove her and her maid home himself, waiting until they entered Lady Vair's house before he drove away. Amy was relieved they were not engaged to go anywhere tonight. Lady Vair took it as a bad omen, but Amy was glad, for she could never have enjoyed herself knowing what the next day might bring. She went to bed early and woke automatically at three in the morning. She took this as an omen that she was supposed to attend the duel.

Donning her boy's clothes she slipped out through the kitchen, secreting a knife in her boot, just in case the man who had been spying on her followed. She walked through Mayfair in full realization of the danger, and frequently looked over her shoulder when she thought she heard footsteps. No matter. Once she got a horse she could evade anyone.

She knew her way into the stable at Melling House and had no trouble keeping Cullen quiet enough to saddle him without waking the grooms. Indeed, one of the grooms must be gone since Lord Marsh's phaeton and team were not present and neither was Hannibal.

Trent watched Draco leaning against a tree. If he mistook not, his friend was fast asleep. It should be him waiting to meet Wraxton, him defending Amy. But if he insisted, he would insult Draco. Since he had heard about the meeting he had felt powerless to fight the code that brought these two men here. Amy had been terrified and she did not frighten easily. But she had no experience of such matters. And he had to admit that he had only his own unfortunate meeting to fall back upon.

He remembered it well. His mouth had been dry, for he had known that he must fire into the air. He had been in the wrong, had bedded the man's wife, even though it was she who had sought refuge in his house. So he had set himself up as a target for Lord Vox, who had neatly caught him in the shoulder. He had expected the pain. He had not expected that he would never get over it. And of all his mistakes that was the one he felt the least guilt over. A stiff breeze rattled the young leaves on the trees. It had been a year ago on a spring morning much like this one, with the crickets still chirping and no morning birds yet singing.

A tilbury rattled down the lane and three men got out of it—Wraxton's surgeon and seconds. Draco opened one eye but was not about to rouse himself. Finally Wraxton's phaeton came into view and Draco stood up and stretched, working his shoulders.

"Good," Draco said. "He is early."

"It is Wraxton," Trent confirmed, "but look at his face. Seems to have been in a fight or something. Shall I let him cry off if he wishes?"

"No, I wish to proceed, with the understanding I don't want to make it a killing matter."

"I have already apprised his second of that." Trent walked toward Wraxton's friends and asked, "Would Lord Wraxton apologize for insulting Amy Conde?"

Wraxton stepped forward on his own behalf. "It was never my intention to insult her. And I will not apologize for desiring to make her my wife."

"Very well, then," Draco said. "Ten paces."

"What?" Wraxton asked. "Ten paces is too close. You might kill me."

"You do not look as though you could walk a step more."

"Oh, very well."

After a careful inspection and loading of the pistols, during which two other vehicles and several horsemen came into the clearing, the principles chose their weapons. They strode apart, turned and fired. When the smoke cleared they were both still standing, but Trent could see the white of Draco's shirt through his coat sleeve, so knew he might be nicked.

"What say you, gentlemen?" Wraxton's second asked. "Has honor been satisfied?"

"Again," Draco commanded, handing his pistol to Trent for reloading.

"We never agreed to a second shot," Wraxton complained.

"Draco," Trent whispered. "If you kill him, even by accident, you will have to leave the country."

Draco laughed. "That's true. It could be my big chance to get away from my family."

"*Draco,*" Trent pleaded, still not reloading the gun.

"You are using me," Wraxton protested.

"Reload the pistols," Draco ordered.

A horse and rider pushed forward from the crowd. Trent thought for a moment he recognized the horse, and then he realized why. It was Cullen. And Amy sat atop him in her boy's garb.

"What the devil?" Wraxton said as the beast shouldered him out of the way.

"You idiot," Draco yelled at Amy. "What are you doing here?"

Amy looked coldly down at them. "I say to you,

Draco. If there was any honor in this meeting, it has been satisfied. If you mean to fire again it will be through me."

"Oh, the devil take it. Very well, Wraxton, I am satisfied. Trent, get this idiot away from here."

"Miss Conde!" Wraxton whispered under his breath.

Trent watched as Amy rode out of the clearing and up to a carriage in the woods. Once he saw Draco safely mounted on Han, and that the soldier meant to ride to the inn for breakfast with a few others of the men present, Trent mounted Flyer and followed her.

He did not know what to expect, but he had not expected to see Lord Marsh here.

"It was wonderful, sir," Amy said. "Wraxton could hardly see. Someone had—"

"I know," Lord Marsh said, turning a blackened eye toward the early morning light.

"Sir, what happened to your eye?" Trent asked involuntarily.

"I had a bad night at Boodle's, a bit too much to drink."

"Can I assume that Wraxton fell in your path?" Amy asked.

"And insulted me," Marsh said proudly.

"And you sought immediate redress," Trent guessed.

"You know how impetuous I am. I did not give him time for a formal challenge."

"Impetuous?" Trent said in confusion.

"Don't ever tell Draco," Lord Marsh requested.

"Then you had best have walked into a door," Trent advised.

"A door? Nothing so tame. My new colt bumped heads with me."

"Ah, yes, of course." Amy smiled and heaved a sigh.

"I am for bed," Lord Marsh said. "Draco will drink

with that lot until midday. Hop in, Amy. I will take you home."

"I will take her," Trent said coldly, not succeeding in keeping the disapproval out of his voice.

"Unchaperoned?" Lord Marsh asked. "Are you sure?"

"I may beat her, but nothing more severe than that."

Lord Marsh drove away with a laugh and Amy rode up the lane beside Trent, but turned left rather than right toward town.

"Where are you going?" Trent demanded as he kneed Flyer into following her.

"Back to my house at Epping."

"No, you don't. You mean to seduce me again."

"You have vowed to beat me, sir. You can scarcely do so in front of Lady Vair. Besides, I left my riding habit at Epping."

Trent expelled an impatient breath. "Do the caretakers not think it odd that you show up there in the middle of the night and sometimes not alone?"

"They are mostly deaf and do not question my comings and goings."

"You ruined yourself tonight, you know. Wraxton most certainly recognized you."

"I had to stop it. If men are stupid enough to shoot at each other I will not let it be over me."

"If you had waited at Lady Vair's as I told you to do—"

"The next shot might have killed Draco and you would have been powerless to stop it."

"You never listen to me," Trent complained as he cantered beside her.

"This was important," she argued. "This was Draco's life."

"But a man, a soldier, gets called out to defend your honor and you show up and *threaten* him?"

"I did not mean to, but when it looked like he meant to kill Wraxton, I could not allow that either."

"What do you care for Wraxton?"

"I do not want anyone to die for me. If Draco had been killed I could not have lived with myself and you could not have lived with me."

Trent realized it was more difficult to conduct an argument on horseback than on a dance floor, but still he persisted. "You do not understand about Draco."

"I understand him all too well, better than you. He has his pride and his own sort of pain, just as you have."

"Yes, I know about it, but he will get over it in time."

"He will not get over it," Amy shouted. "If you knew about it why did you let him fight half-blind? He can't even see the distance to a fence. He could not have hit Wraxton without several tries at it. And that would have given Wraxton several shots at Draco."

"Half-blind? What are you talking about?"

"Trent, you said you knew," Amy accused.

"I know about his nightmares."

"And I had been so careful. He did not want anyone to know about his eye, not even his father."

"You must be mistaken."

"If you were not so blind yourself you would have realized he cannot see out of one eye, not well anyway. Why do you think he has taken so many falls? Why do you think he arranges his silverware so carefully and keeps his wineglass empty?" She turned unerringly down the street that led to her house.

Trent followed her numbly into the small stable yard, thinking over all she had said and realizing that she was right. He had been blind to Draco's problem.

He dismounted and took her reins as she threw her lithe leg over the saddle and slid to the ground. Trent almost asked why she was unsaddling her mount and leading it to a stall, but he knew why. He did the same for Flyer and followed her to the back door. She stooped to retrieve a key from a crack in the bricks. Then she led the way up the back stairs to her small room on the second floor. She did not even strike a light but swept the curtains aside to let some daylight in and began to strip off her clothes.

"I know what you are doing and it will not work," Trent said.

"Then why did you come with me?"

"To talk some sense into you." Trent turned away from her naked form, biting his lip against the ache rising in his chest. This was not simply need, the way he thought of need. This was desperate desire. He wondered if he would die without Amy.

She came to put her arms around his waist and leaned against his back.

"You are trying to make me spend my anger by making love to me," he said.

"No, I am trying to convince you that prolonging this ruse is madness. You must want me just as much as I want you. And if we end this false engagement immediately and get married Draco will be safe."

"But that does not make me lose my reason as you do."

She crept around in front of him and he tried to hide the fact that he was shaking with the effort to control himself.

"You and Lord Marsh betrayed Draco tonight. I suppose you want me to keep your secret." He would not look at her.

She stared up at him, studying his face. "Lord Marsh did not act dishonorably. He was only trying to even the odds by blacking one of Wraxton's eyes."

He grasped her arms and held her away from him, knowing he was safe so long as her skin did not brush his, as long as he did not bend to kiss those lips that trembled so temptingly.

"So I go on making mistake after mistake. I told you to wait at Lady Vair's and trust me. That all would be well. And I was wrong."

"But you did not know how much danger Draco was in."

Trent turned away from her and went to sit on the small bed with his head in his hands. "Why did he never tell me?"

"You know why." She came and sat beside him. "The same reason you never speak of your hurts."

He stared at her, those few inches away from him, hearing what she was saying with half his mind while the other part of him took in her beauty, the ripeness of her breasts, the slender grace of her limbs.

"Arrogance, pride?" he asked.

"Vulnerability," she corrected. "And a reluctance to worry his parents more than they have been worried."

Trent thought over all Draco's latest instances of clumsiness and wondered how he had been so blind as to not see it. And Draco did try to hide things from his parents. When he looked at Amy again he was amazed that she had worked his coat off of him. She was kneeling on the bed now, her tempting breasts no more than inches away.

"He *could* have been killed," Trent said as though in a trance. He watched her unbutton his shirt but nothing was registering with him for the moment except that he had very nearly lost his best friend.

"But he was not, and you will take better care of him from now on, without letting him know that you know." Amy pushed his shirt down and pressed her body against his chest.

He groaned. "So, I have blundered again. If I ever had a notion of competence you have cured me of the misconception."

"There is only one area in which I require you to be competent," she countered.

"I cannot help myself," he said as he rolled her in his arms and threw her back on the bed, lowering himself over her. He kissed her sweet mouth and invaded it, knowing she would meet him in a daring challenge. His right hand kneaded her breasts, pulling small sighs and moans from her.

He stood up only long enough to get rid of his boots and strip off the rest of his clothes. He knelt over her again and was about to slip his hand between her thighs when she locked her legs about his waist as though she were hanging from a tree limb.

"You are too eager," he said. "I should stop myself from loving you to teach you a lesson."

"Punish yourself to control someone else. That is the old Trent."

"I thought we came here to punish you. That would be one way of doing it," he said, posing himself at her entrance, pressing only the tip of his manhood inside.

"Trent, I swear if you hold back now I shall never forgive you."

"I can, you know. I have will power where you have none."

"Is that something to be proud of?"

He pushed himself up with a wicked light in his eyes but Amy clung to him, locking her ankles and using her calf muscles to try to pull him into her.

"You have the most incredible legs, but you cannot get me inside you if I do not choose to be there."

"I suppose you are right," she said. "A woman cannot force a man."

He chuckled and rested his manhood at her entrance again to taunt her.

She stroked his knee with one hand and reaching behind, pinched his hamstring tendon at the back of the knee, causing him to pitch into her with a gasp.

He laughed at her shriek of pleasure. "Serves you right, you little vixen. Where did you learn that trick?"

She groaned as he moved inside her. But when she saw he did not mean to retreat she loosened her grip enough for him to maneuver and set up that slow rhythmic motion that drove her mad.

"With the right pressure," she whispered between gasps of pleasure, "in the right spot you can always get a recalcitrant stallion to do what you want."

Trent laughed and caused her even more euphoria as he shook inside of her. "I am a villain, and should be locked up for doing this."

"I do not think so. I think you are the best of men, or you will be with a little more work."

He stopped moving but lay, throbbing inside her. "That does not say much for the rest of them."

"They all think they are better than they are. You think yourself so much worse that you stand out for your modesty."

"Modesty?" He started to withdraw from her, but she whimpered with regret and he lay back down, pushing his manhood more fully inside her, keeping at least as much control as to decide when exactly he would disgrace himself.

"I never mean to argue with you." She stroked his cheek and kissed him in small places; his jaw, his cheek, the corner of his mouth.

"Nor I with you, but you do such unsafe things, and I cannot control you."

"Of course you cannot. No more than I can control you."

"But I *need* control."

"Does that make you strong?"

"It makes me what I have to be to deal in my world."

"Then come into my world, where love makes you strong, where you would be capable of anything." She ran her warm hands along the muscles of his back, causing him to jostle her inside.

"I am trying, trying to let things just happen, witness tonight. But where will it end?"

"At the altar, of course, happily and like any good tale, with us together."

"But I am not used to being happy. If I ever saw happiness I was only an observer, an outsider looking in. The Mellings taught me what I was missing, but not how to enjoy it."

"No one can teach you that. You have to let go of everything, money, possessions, even those ensnaring businesses of yours. You have to understand what is important."

He looked at her, with her boy's hair tousled about the pillow. "But how can we be happy if I cannot know you are safe?"

"By trusting me to take care of myself."

"But I want to do that."

She sighed as he throbbed inside her, amazed that he could be so dense. Patiently she took his right hand, intertwining her fingers with his, as she gazed into his eyes. "I feel one with you," she whispered. "I think of nothing else when we are apart." She used her other arm to draw his head closer, their lips no more than a whisper away from each other. "Part of me goes with you on all your dangerous adventures. I am not satisfied unless I can touch you." She ran a finger along his cheek. "To be without you is to be only half a person, only half alive. I do not control you either, but I do trust you. I trust you to come back to me. You must learn to do the same."

Her lips met his and he groaned, then moved inside her, slowly at first, then with increased rhythm as though he were running. There was a sheen of sweat upon his brow and his eyes looked wild as though he had found an answer where he thought there was none. She gasped and moaned, thrashing with the delight of his hot pursuit of her. As she sighed and flailed wildly he released his seed with a groan of relief. "At last," she whispered, "you understand."

He pulled her inside his embrace. "I understand your love, I understand our oneness, but not how to let go." He locked his arms around her in a hug so desperate with emotion that she could only melt into him as his heart slowed its beat to a more normal rhythm.

Amy lay quietly for a long moment, committed to marrying Trent in his imperfect state, and mending the rest of him later. He had come such a long way. He was caring now, almost obsessively so. He was going to have to learn trust next, to give up control to her when she knew best.

"You trust Draco," she said. "You trusted him not to die today, trusted him through a whole war. That must have been hard."

"I never knew it would come to that. When I bought him the commission it was to keep him from enlisting as a regular. First Royal Dragoons. Initially there seemed little likelihood they would ever see action if the thing could have been resolved quickly. How could I know it would go on for so long?"

"But Trent, you had no more right to try to control Draco, than me. And as you saw it did not work."

"I have every right to control you. You are still my ward. If I can find a way to get you away from here and lock you safely in a tower, I will."

"Your prisoner now, just as I was your mother's all those years?"

"No, my wife."

"There is more to marriage than love, more to a relationship than dominance and concession. There has to be sharing."

"We do share in everything equally, all the businesses will be half yours."

"Trent, that is not what I meant at all."

"What do you want from me?" he asked desperately.

"I want to share all that pain you were talking about. I want to know the truth of you. If you cannot share that, we will never have a marriage."

26

~~~~~

Trent had silently taken her back to Lady Vair's in the morning and she had not heard from him for an entire day. A note had arrived late Saturday warning her to be ready to drive with him the next day.

"So, this is where it began?" Amy asked, staring about at the foundry ground floor, at the great base of the furnace that reached up through to the second story, and at the openings through which the molten metal was poured into the molds. Even on Sunday there was heat from the banked furnace and the smell of metal in the air, plus lingering wisps of smoke. A huge anchor lay in the forging area with one hook on and the other laying ready for work on Monday. The heavy-linked chain had already been attached and she stared at the worked links, thinking of the sweat and toil it took to make such a huge thing. She had never before felt such respect for men's work.

From the great rafters hung numerous sets of ropes and chains with blocks and tackles for winching heavy castings about. Everything was so oversized it looked like a giant's workshop. "It is Sunday," she said. "That is why there is no one about."

"I want to explain why I hurt so much all the time, why I need control." Trent closed his eyes and swallowed. "I found him here with a twelve–pounder on top of him. It was the biggest gun we had ever made."

"Your father," Amy said reverently, looking at the place on the floor where Trent stood.

"It was a Sunday." Trent's voice echoed hoarsely in the great area. He turned his face up and a sunbeam stole through the floor above to burnish his dark hair. "His legs and pelvis had been crushed." Trent looked down at the spot on the floor. "I winched the cannon away from him but that just seemed to make his pain worse. I do not know who he thought I was, but . . . someone other than me. He told me to be careful. And talked about *her son. Be careful of her son.*" Trent looked at her, his green eyes glittering with remembered pain. "Do you understand, Amy? My father thought I had killed him."

Amy started toward him, wanting only to comfort him, but that was not what Trent wanted. He turned his back on her.

"He never brought me here, where I so much wanted to be. I had to sneak down here and learn the work when he was not around. I always wanted to be wherever he was, but Mother would not allow it. I hated that he conceded to her. I wanted him to confront her and take me away to train me himself."

"Did he know what you wanted?" Amy came to take Trent's hand timidly in hers.

"No, because I never told him. There never seemed to be a chance."

"Why was he here alone on a Sunday?" she asked.

"Someone had sent him word and he said he had to go to the foundry. When he did not come home I came to look for him."

"Against your mother's wishes?"

"Very much so. If I had been with him more, perhaps I could have prevented the accident."

"Accident? But who was he meeting?"

"No one would ever admit to it. Afraid of me, I suppose."

"You are assuming it was one of the workmen."

"Who else would it have been?"

Amy did not answer him but climbed a ladder to look at a block and tackle setup and the expert way it was tied off. And the chain rigging had latch and pin fasteners that could not have come loose by accident. She came back down.

"Do you understand? He never liked me and in the end my neglect as good as killed him."

"Trent, he might have said anything in those last moments. It need not have meant anything. Why would he have been trying to move a cannon himself?"

"I can think of no reason. I did not know that then, but after learning the business, I can see no reason for what happened to him."

"He would not have, could not have, loosened one of those fastenings and gotten under it at the same time."

"So someone else loosened it. Are you thinking it was deliberate?"

She chewed her lip. "I do not like to think so."

"It is what the magistrate suspected," Trent whispered.

"And who did he think did it?"

Trent hesitated and swallowed hard. "Me."

"Oh, Trent! How terrible for you." She came to embrace him. "You are braver than I ever thought, to be able to come here and take up his work, knowing this is where your father had met his end."

*   *   *

"It was needful." He swayed in her arms. Why had he brought her here? What had this to do with her, anyway? Yet Amy seemed to understand.

She lifted her head and looked up at him with the tears sparkling on her lashes.

"This is what you mean when you talk about killing *all* the pain."

"Yes. Drinking does not help, of course. I cannot even forget his death anymore."

"I had no idea. You dare not give up control or you will be overrun."

"He did not say my name that day. He did not know me, but kept talking about *her son*. And when I went home and told Mother, she only looked surprised and then began making funeral preparations as though she had been waiting for it to happen. I wanted to strangle her. I wanted—but then I remembered I never get anything I want. I cannot afford these feelings you splash about. They hurt too much."

"Of course they do. You did love your father to have felt his pain so."

"But love makes me weak."

"It makes you vulnerable. It takes courage to love. You have plenty of that."

She shivered in his arms and he was sorry he had forced her to listen to this.

"Your mother w-was not shocked? she asked.

"Yes, but she accepted it so readily," Trent said in a choked voice. "You might have thought I said the cat died."

He felt her arms grip him and he caressed her hair. When he was with her he believed her, that it was not his job to make everything right, but when he went back to his work he felt that if he did not keep all the reins in his hands the world would fly apart.

"Let us go now," Amy said.

"Do you understand?"

"Yes, I understand what happened, but not why. Do you still believe it was an accident?"

He took a breath and looked down at her. "I have worked with these men for nearly a decade, trusted my life to them on occasion. There is not one of them who would have left him here like that."

"Then whoever he was meeting had nothing to do with the foundry, except that it was a good place to create an accident. You say your mother seemed unsettled but not surprised. Could she have hired someone?"

"Someone like Fenwick? I suppose it's possible."

"It does not seem like his kind of crime. But he was working for her then. She got your father to hire him."

"How did you find that out?" Trent asked with a puzzled frown.

"I asked her at the tea. She is quite an actress in her own way, all concern for me."

"Yes, she used to be like that with me until we descended to open warfare. She could not control my father, could not make him knuckle under to her except where I was concerned. At that point in my life she must have thought she could still control me."

"I do not like to think she had anything to do with it. I would rather it had been an accident."

"Either way, if I had come with him, I might have saved him."

"Or died yourself."

He nodded. Some part of him had died, still pinned to the floor of the foundry. The part that believed in justice, goodness and happy endings. Whatever change Amy had wrought in him, she had not managed to revive that ghost.

* * *

Amy paced Lady Vair's small sitting room, now empty of company. They had no callers yesterday afternoon, the day of the visit to the foundry, or today, not even gentlemen. And soon it would be time to have dinner and change for the Mellings' ball. She had small appetite for it. The loiterer was across the street again, not the same man always. She wondered if they were the same ones who had attacked Draco. She had decided not to burden Trent with them.

Except for those nights in the house in Epping, she would never think of London as a pleasant interlude. She had come here against her will, become entangled in the affairs of the Mellings, and had her character assassinated by someone. But that was the least of her worries. Draco had almost died several times because of his association with her.

And worse almost than that danger was what she had found out about Trent's father. She was almost sure his mother had something to do with that. Andrew Severn had died in 1808 at the beginning of the war. That was why Trent had not gone into the army. If his father had lived would Trent have sailed off to Portugal with Draco?

And who would go to that length to keep him in England? If his mother had hired someone, of course, she might have acted surprised at her husband's death. But even if that were true, she had not been cold-blooded enough to willingly let Trent go to find the body. He said she had tried to stop him.

Perhaps this penchant for controlling things was a trait Trent inherited from his mother. She could not control her husband and him selling armaments cheaply to the government. With him out of the way, she might have thought she could milk the businesses and that Trent would let her do it.

But if she had planned the murder for profit or to keep Trent in her world, she had not taken into account the mettle of her son. For it had the opposite effect of opening the businesses up to him. She would not have counted on that, on his supreme competence, on his ability to grasp control of a disaster and bring it right.

Lady Vair came in with some parcels and sent Amy a sympathetic look. "You will wear that carpet out."

"What are they saying of me today?" Amy went to look out the window toward the grassy square and the man leaning on the railing.

"Do you really want to know?" She sat down tiredly.

"Of course I want to know. I have to face these people tonight."

"That you entertained men at your country estate unchaperoned." She looked at Amy to see how she would take this.

Amy shrugged. "That, at least, is true. Spill the worst of it, for I will hear it whispered behind my back tonight."

"That you sell more than horses at Talltrees. That you use it as a convenient place to entertain your lovers."

Amy laughed. "If that were true, surely I could have found a cover that was less bother and less expensive."

"Most of these people are not strong on logic."

"But none of them have said that I cantered about the country with two men, dining at inns, or that I dressed as a boy to break up a duel in the woods at Epping?"

Lady Vair raised an eyebrow. "You have been busy. Trent will berate me for letting you have so much freedom."

"It was Draco's life at stake. How does my reputation compare to that?"

"No one says either of those things. Is that significant?"

"It means the person spreading the gossip is not Wraxton, as Draco supposed. And now that I think about it, Wraxton knew nothing about this ring being the one Trent offered to Diana." She held it up to gaze at it in the candlelight.

"Who did know, who would wish you harm?" Lady Vair asked, but Amy could see she knew the answer.

"Diana. But she is the least of my worries. I think now that it is not Wraxton trying to kill Draco. He met him honorably in a duel. He would not have hired thugs to assassinate him."

"Those attacks may have been coincidence." Lady Vair calmly shook out a length of silk and held it up to Amy as though they were not discussing attempted murder.

"I cannot take that risk. I shall have to break off the engagement . . . tonight."

Lady Vair stared at her and blinked. "Well, that should set the cap on a delightful evening."

Trent came for them in the carriage, looking more withdrawn and distant than ever. Even though he was handsome in his black evening clothes Amy could tell he would have been more at ease in his riding breeches and boots. She was wearing amber silk tonight. She thought it became her, but made her look less innocent. That was fitting.

They were not late by any means, but enough guests had preceded them to provide Amy with an entrance, if that was what she wanted. Lord and Lady Marsh greeted her warmly, but Diana turned away at that moment to pointedly confer with someone else. So that was what they meant by the *cut direct.* Amy smiled at the artificiality of it, and was determined to stand there and make the woman recognize her, but Draco came out of another room and took her by the arm.

"How goes it with you?" he asked.

"I am fine. And you?"

"I feel like bolting and they are not even talking about me. It is not Wraxton," Draco said.

"How did you arrive at that conclusion?"

"I remembered he never saw the ring."

"I am going to give it back to you quite publicly tonight and tell you we shall not suit."

"I shall have to bolt then, to stay ahead of the harpies. Do you care if I go to Talltrees?"

"I might turn up there, myself," Amy said with a smile. "Will Trent think to look for us there or should I warn him?"

"Yes, what a plan. He will be as mad as fire even if you do prepare him. And when he is angry you can get the better of him."

"He will not like the situation being out of his control," Amy warned.

"Was there ever a man so obsessed with making things right?"

"I knew he tried to keep me on a tight rein. I did not know he felt he was driving the rest of the world as well."

"Yes, he is a strange fellow and hard to get to know. I should say he is closer to me than to anyone, and he confounds my understanding."

"He is watching us with something like suspicion on his face. Will it hurt you much if I slap you and throw this ring at you?"

"Oh, not yet, the evening is young," Draco said jovially. "Let me give you a reason first."

"What reason do we need but a lover's quarrel?"

"We need another woman. Flirt with Wraxton a moment while I go find one."

Amy did wander in Wraxton's direction. She was amazed that the crush of people parted so easily for her, each of them afraid that she would stop and strike up a conversation. In truth she rather liked people being afraid of her. It gave her a strange sense of power.

Wraxton, on the other hand, did not move, but crossed his ankles as he leaned against one of the pillars that held up the room, and grinned at her, his right eye still black and blue.

They both ignored the press of people that moved toward the center of the ballroom as the musicians started playing.

"So you have got the courage to face them all, after what is being said of you."

"Approval is no carrot to me. If the women all disdain me and the men think I am a great gun, that can only be good for business."

"Be careful who you say that in front of. I have heard some nasty references to your business."

"And you are not gloating. After I gave you that scar on your hand."

He glanced at the still red area and smiled as though it brought back a fond memory. "I am willing to play by the rules once I know what they are. But whoever is doing this to you—"

"Does not know I do not care."

"Then you do not think I have a hand in it. I promise you I took Severn's warning quite seriously."

"I am surprised that you challenged Draco, who is just as dangerous."

Wraxton blew out an impatient breath. "I was goaded into that when I'd had too much to drink."

"But not by Draco."

"If you must know it was your mousy French cousin. The man has a nasty tongue in his head when he chooses to use it. As for being French . . ."

"Yes, there is something about his accent."

"Crevecoeur told Draco I had insulted you. I do not think that calling you a game pullet is insulting, do you?"

Amy laughed. "No, I must regard that in the light of a compliment, after my interference in the duel."

"But no one knows about that," he protested.

"And I am surprised that exploit is not the talk of the town."

Wraxton grinned. "Ah, but you have exceeded gossip with that one. If I were to tell of it, I would not even be believed."

Amy laughed. "So you have given up your pursuit of me?"

"Yes, but not because of Severn or Melling. It is you I do not think I could handle."

"I am in the habit of pushing about thousand-pound horses. Is it so odd I would try the same thing with men?"

"Hence my decision to find a lesser quarry and one with a better reputation, besides her wealth. I do not want to give up this life, you see, and they will never accept you in London society after this."

"I want to spend all my time at Talltrees anyway."

"I thought you would take that view of it. I will leave you now, for Severn is glaring at me and having escaped one duel with my life, I want to avoid another encounter, at least until my vision has cleared."

She watched Trent walk stiffly in her direction, trying not to call attention to himself and failing. "What do you mean by talking to Wraxton while I am busy trying to undo this latest pack of lies?"

"They are not his lies," Amy said. "Even Draco realizes that."

Trent was quiet for a moment. "Who then? He might have tried to destroy your reputation to get Draco to dump you, and when that did not work he planned to disable or kill Draco, so he would have a better chance at you."

"Trent, look at him. He would not do that much plotting in a whole year. I do not think it was Wraxton who hired the men who attacked Draco."

He curled an eyebrow in surprise. "I suppose it could have been Fenwick."

"But how would he hurt my reputation? He does not go about in society."

"But he can frequent the coffeehouses and inns where the servants go for their pleasure. Because he is from Berkshire he would be believed on that head."

"I could see Fenwick hiring thugs, but not thinking of something as elaborate as character assassination."

"Do not forget the connection to my mother. If he can blacken your reputation so that Draco throws you over and no one else will have you, you may turn to Crevecoeur as Mother wishes."

"Never. What you say may be true, but I still think it was Diana."

"She would not dare. Her father has threatened to shut her up in the country."

"But gossip is something that can never be brought home to her. She is perfectly safe in saying anything she wants of me."

"We shall see about that."

"Trent, no. The Mellings have faced enough unpleasantness on my account. Besides, she is dancing with Wraxton now, and if you go over there you are sure to start a fight with him."

"Where the devil is Draco, anyway? *He* is supposed to be guarding you, not me."

"Looking for a woman to make me jealous so that I can break the engagement."

"What?" Trent stared at her with that helpless look he had when events were beginning to spin out of his control.

"Trent, it is the only way I feel he will be safe, until we find out who has been trying to kill him."

"And you were complaining about me heaping shame on the Mellings. This is absurd."

"Then we thought to escape to Talltrees. Would you like to go with us?"

"You are insane, both of you. Stay right here. I am going to find him and put a stop to this. I have to do everything myself," Trent grumbled as he strode away.

"Trent, wait."

Amy jumped at a hand on her shoulder and the sound of René's voice in her ear.

"Forgive me. I did not mean to startle you. Severn does not seem happy with you."

"He is not a happy person most of the time. Unlike you, he smiles very little."

"So I have noticed. But he is more distant tonight than usual."

"When he is acting cold Trent looks too much like his mother," Amy observed. "It must be the green eyes."

"Actually he favors his father more, except for the eyes and the mouth."

Amy turned and stared at him, at the sensual mouth with the distinctive indentations in the corners. It gave her a chill, like being in the presence of a ghost. "How would you know? You never met Trent's father."

René's eyebrows scowled at her and his mouth turned down. "Lady Agatha told me."

27

❦

Trent had scoured the ballroom and refreshment salon and had not turned up Draco. Now Amy was conversing with Crevecoeur and Trent realized he was jealous of the man, which made no sense. Amy detested Crevecoeur. There was nothing to be jealous of. But everyone, including Lady Marsh, fell for his *pauvre* French émigré act. And Trent's own mother was sponsoring the man.

Trent forced himself to calm down and walk back into the refreshment salon. He was about to reach for champagne when he remembered he needed to keep a clear head tonight. He ladled himself a cup of lemonade from the punch bowl, causing Lady Marsh to stare at him as though he were twelve and perhaps running a fever. He turned and walked back into the ballroom, sipping the tart-sweet liquid. His gaze sought out his mother and he could see her across the room, the glint of her green eyes visible even at this distance. She was watching Amy and Crevecoeur.

When had he started caring about what his mother did? It suddenly occurred to him that he was jealous of Crevecoeur for his mother's sake, not Amy's. How could he still want his mother's approval after all she had done, or not done? It was as though, having been denied her love, his emotional life had been arrested when he was much younger. And that was why he had decided control was more important than feelings. It was not his father, whom he had loved, who made him an emotional cripple, but his mother, who had rejected him.

She had tried when he was younger to get him on her side. But the more he became like his father the more she pushed him away. Why had she ever married his father if she had always hated him?

He saw her clearly now, an aging, brittle woman who dyed her hair and never smiled unless to sneer, never said anything that was not a cut. He had thought he had eliminated her power to wound him by walling himself up. But seeing someone else make her laugh, make her flirt girlishly, abraided the old wound. Crevecoeur was more than a protégé to her.

They occupied the same suite of apartments at the hotel and people had begun to talk. What was there about the man to call forth her regard—he hesitated to call it love. But it was obvious she did care about Crevecoeur, where she had never cared about her own son. Trent thought it might be only to taunt him. And it was working. He closed his eyes and mentally let go of the hurt and felt a flutter of freedom in his chest. Let her have Crevecoeur, however she wanted him. She was just an old woman who looked foolish to the world.

Trent opened his eyes again, but too late. He saw Draco approaching Amy with Clair Kimble on his arm. She had been his last mistress but one. He groaned, but slipped through the crowd in an effort to reach them in time. Just as he broke through the throng of people he heard a resounding slap and saw Draco visibly flinch. Amy thrust something at him and left the room.

There was dead silence for a moment, then the murmur of the gossip mill starting again, grinding this bit of news into grist for tomorrow's visits. Trent tried to push past Draco to go after Amy, but the soldier detained him long enough to place the large ring in his hand.

"She's all yours now."

"Idiot," Trent hissed.

"Don't mention it."

Trent stared at him in amazement, wondering if Draco had lost part of his hearing as well as his sight.

Amy had gotten as far as the hallway when she realized it was not so easy to walk away from an evening entertainment when you were a woman rather than a man. She made for the back stairs with some notion of taking refuge in the stable when Diana came into the hall looking victorious.

"I knew it would only be a matter of time before you did something to give my brother a disgust of you."

"He is not disgusted with me. I am the one who decided to break the engagement."

"And where is the ring?" Diana demanded, backing Amy into a corner between a table and chair. Amy saw René come out of the ballroom. Even though she hated him, she sent him a desperate look.

"I gave it to Draco."

"It should have been mine," Diana said.

"Then you should have accepted it when it was within your grasp," Amy said.

Diana glared at the approaching Frenchman. Amy could see a sneer on René's face as though he were about to break up a cat fight.

"Your tendre for Severn will come to nothing," René said. "Believe me. I know all about lost causes."

"Why did you change your mind about Trent?" Amy asked.

"None of your business," Diana said with her usual pout.

"Have you not heard?" René asked. "All her other prospects have run away."

Amy shook her head. "I do not listen to gossip."

René smiled. "You probably do not spread any, either."

"What do you mean by that?" Diana asked.

"I think you know. You got away with it when Amy was engaged to your brother. People hesitated to attach your name to such lies. But now . . . now if you say such things, I will do something about it."

"What?" Diana sneered at him.

His hand moved so swiftly Amy never saw him grasp the woman's chin, but he had Diana's neck craned back with the edge of his palm pressing into her delicate throat and her head against the wall.

"No, René. Let her go." Amy grasped one of his arms with both her hands, but it was like holding onto a piece of iron.

He looked at Amy, then back at Diana and smiled. "If you ask it, little one."

Diana massaged her throat, the color flooding into her face. "You are mad," she choked out and ran back into the ballroom.

"She is the one who is mad," René said, looking possessively at Amy.

"Then it was not Fenwick," Amy said.

"What about Fenwick? That little worm. I do not know why Lady Agatha—" René smiled. "Come, we will walk together."

Amy took a step back. "You do not know why she employs him? Originally it was to spy on me, I think, to give her fair warning if I left Talltrees or were in danger of marrying."

"*Non,* Louise . . ." He looked uncertainly at her.

"Yes, your nurse in America, when you were young, but when you were older Lady Agatha sent her to me as a governess." Amy kept her voice neutral.

"To watch over you, to teach you French."

"So Lady Agatha always intended that we would marry."

René smiled, she guessed, at her quick understanding.

"As she said." He took Amy's hand and drew it through his arm. "Your father wished it. And now that you are unattached, so do I."

"Wait." Amy snatched her hand back. "Did she tell you about Fenwick's self-interest in this matter? He has been trying to get me to marry him. He has betrayed both of you over and over. He stole from me, from Trent, and no doubt from Lady Agatha. Then he planned to get everything in the end if he could."

René's nostrils flared. "*Vraiment.* I told her she could not trust the man."

"You had better warn her," Amy said as she backed away.

"Later." He grabbed her wrist and tugged her after him down the hall toward the back stairs. "We must talk in private."

Amy thought of screaming as René ran down the steps, tugging her after him. She thought of fainting, but that would play right into his hands. If only Trent had followed her from the ballroom instead of René.

"Melling is a fool to flaunt that Kimble woman in front of you, and in public."

"We would never have suited anyway. But he did not have to do that to get rid of me."

"Marry me. I will never treat you so."

"I do not think I would like to be married, after all." Suddenly she stopped at the back door, dreading going out into the garden with René.

"Not even to Trent?"

"Trent is my guardian. It would be unconscionable for him to have feelings for me."

"But he does. I have seen the way he looks at you, the way you look at him."

"You are mistaken. He only wants to control me."

"Come, we will walk." He pushed the door open and compelled her to follow him into the small courtyard. She quickly traversed this, deciding to make for the stable, where there might be a groom about, than stay in this confined area alone with him.

He still had hold of her arm and he pulled her to him in a hurtful embrace. She got her forearm and fist in the way of a kiss, but he captured that hand too in a grip more implacable than Trent's ever was.

"I can teach you a thing or two about love."

"But René, this makes you no better than Fenwick," she said as she wrestled one arm away only to have the other captured.

When he thought he had her contained he laughed and bent to kiss her. She thought it was stupid of him not to take into account her legs. She was wearing only dancing slippers, but so was he. She trampled on his left foot as hard as she could, making him curse. Then, with a little distance gained between them she kicked him in the knee. He yelped and went stiff-legged as though he might fall over. But his grip on her wrist was ruining her aim.

Trent had searched the entire floor again before he decided Amy must have left the house. He leaned out the open window on the back stair landing and thought he caught the tone of Amy's voice raised in anger. Running down the next two flights Trent burst out the back door and saw Crevecoeur wrestling with Amy as he cursed in French. Trent hurtled across the yard and was on Crevecoeur like a hornet, thrusting him away from the struggling Amy and knocking him into the short box hedge.

The Frenchman fell backward but rolled and recoiled like a snake, coming up to hit Trent in the stomach at full tilt. As he gasped and bent over, he was vaguely aware of Amy running toward the stable calling for the grooms to come and help.

Trent locked with Crevecoeur, grappling for some advantage, for there would be no help. The grooms were all in front of the house holding teams. Besides, he had been looking forward to this.

The Frenchman deliberately threw them both to the ground, rolling back into the hedge and out of it. At some point Trent saw Amy approaching with the handle of a carriage jack. That was not good.

"Amy, find Draco."

They broke apart and Trent went down at her feet, hoping she would leap back. Before he could roll out of the way Crevecoeur grabbed Trent's right arm and kicked him in the shoulder twice. Trent felt each blow as though he had been shot again, going limp after the second.

Amy swung the jack handle and connected with Crevecour somewhere, for he let go of Trent and looked at Amy in shock, as though it was unthinkable for her to hit a man. He did not know Amy very well.

Trent struggled to his feet and lunged for René again, but by then some of the grooms came running back. Though the first two hesitated to intervene, Jessup plunged in and grabbed Crevecoeur, so that gave the others the nerve to get between them.

Trent's shoulder had gone numb for the moment. If not for that he would have continued the fight.

"You will meet me for this night's work, sir," René said, nursing his arm, and wiping blood from his chin.

"Yes, and kill you for it," Trent threatened. "Send your friends to me, if you have any." Trent stood straight, not willing to let the Frenchman know how much he had hurt him.

Draco came running down the steps in time to see René turn and walk unsteadily out into the alley. "What the devil was that all about?" the soldier asked.

"Me again," Amy said bitterly. "Now we are worse off than before."

Trent turned to her, his left hand nursing his right arm. "Do not say so. It was only a matter of time before I had it out with that man."

"So we are not escaping to Talltrees?" Draco asked.

Trent turned to his friend. "No, and you must act for me."

Draco groaned. "Not another duel."

Amy hugged Trent. "He knew you had a bad shoulder and kicked you where it would hurt the most. How can you possibly fight him now? You can barely move your arm."

"Do not concern yourself. I will take care of Crevecoeur. And this time you had better not interfere. Promise me." He stroked her cheek with his left hand.

"How can you ask it, Trent?"

"I know, interfering is what you do best. If you will examine your actions over the past few weeks you will realize that you have more of an obsession for control than I have. Promise you will not appear to throw yourself between Crevecoeur and me. This has a bearing on my trust in you."

Amy took a breath to argue but Trent raised her chin with one hand and she reluctantly said, "Very well, I promise, but we must talk."

"No, Draco, take her home for me. I have things to attend to."

28

❧

She had not slept all night. She dressed and went downstairs but could not even stomach tea. Should she tell Trent about her suspicion? She thought there was a connection between René and his family. It might make him hesitate to deliver a blow that could save his life. And if she told him what she suspected René was guilty of, Trent could become so enraged it might stack the odds against him even worse.

Trent had asked her for several promises. But she had only promised not to appear at the duel; she had made no promises about trying to stop it. She ignored the lounger in the street and made a special trip to Melling House to discover the time and place from Draco. He received her in the morning room and would not tell her, but did let slip the fight was to be with swords.

"But Trent will never be able to wield a weapon, not in his condition." She clenched her small hands.

"What was I to do? Trent challenged Crevecoeur. That gives the Frenchman the choice of weapons." Draco was pacing again, the length of the morning room.

"And René is a fencing instructor," she reminded him.

"Do not worry. If things go awry I will stop it."

"How will you stop it?" she demanded.

"I do not know, but I will think of something."

She gritted her teeth the whole way back to Lady Vair's. Now she had two of them to worry about again. Why were men so quarrelsome and stupid about honor. If only women were in charge—but there *was* a woman in charge of this mess, so to speak.

As soon as she entered the house she sat at the desk in the morning room and wrote a letter to Lady Agatha. If she cared about René as much as Amy suspected, then she would not want him risking his life even if she no longer cared about Trent. The footman who carried the letter did not return with a reply. Amy threw herself down on the sofa to wait but spent the next hour pacing the room. Without knowing the hour of the meeting she had no idea when she would run out of time. She must *do* something.

Finally she went to change her clothes. As Amy Conde she could do nothing, discover nothing that would help her. But as a groom, she might pick up some news. If she went to Trent's stable pretending to look for work she might get an inkling when his curricle would be called for, or when Flyer was to be saddled. She would have to avoid Jessup, of course.

She walked toward Mayfair turning over and discarding one plan after another in her mind. She was almost abreast of Green Park when she caught a familiar figure out of the tail of her vision. Fenwick. She dived into the press of traffic to avoid him, hoping to gain the park where she could perhaps evade him in the undergrowth. But she had to stop in the middle of the street or be run down.

"Got you!" he said as he latched onto her arm.

"Let me go or I'll scream."

"Go right ahead," he said, dragging her toward a hackney. "I shall tell them I am a thief taker and you a cutpurse."

"Why would they believe you over me?" she demanded, then looked down at her clothes.

"You shouldn't have told them about me. Made a load of trouble for me, you did. I told Severn what I would do to you." Fenwick held her at arm's length to avoid a well-aimed kick. "Had men watching the house for days."

"What do you want with me?"

"You know what I want. A quick marriage. And then I get everything."

"Never. There is no way you can compel me," she argued as he dragged her along the walk.

"Then I've got nothing to lose, have I?"

They were almost to the hackney when a carriage pulled up. Amy was about to call out for help when she realized it was Lady Agatha's. René leaped out and grabbed Fenwick by an arm and his coat collar.

"Get into the carriage, Amy. I will deal with him."

Lady Agatha leaned out. "You wretched girl. What do you mean by walking the streets like that? You might be recognized."

"I do not care," she said as she watched René frog march a protesting Fenwick into the park.

"Well, get in. We must talk. Tell the driver to take us around the park."

Amy did as she was bid, though it went against the grain to take orders from her godmother. If they became allies in stopping this thing it would be an uneasy peace. At least she knew where René was now, so Trent would be safe for the moment.

"Now that I have inquired at Lady Vair's for you, and she has missed you, she is also worried about you. What is this nonsense about a duel?"

Amy took off her cap. "Does René deny it?"

"Of course he denies it. A duel would be the stupidest thing imaginable."

"But he is lying. I know you are ruthless, that you would do anything to get your hands on my fortune, but do you mean to do it at the expense of Trent's life?"

"Stop being melodramatic. René has no designs on Trent."

"René is an expert swordsman and Trent has a badly injured shoulder. There can be only one outcome."

"You are wrong," Lady Agatha said with her polished certainty showing a slight crack.

"Confront him again. I tell you René is committed to meeting Trent. You will be able to tell by his face that he is lying. You will see it in his smile."

Lady Agatha stared at her for a moment. "You are mistaken. René would not do something so foolish, something expressly against my orders."

"You always meant for René to have me, to have my fortune. That was why you left me at Talltrees all this time."

"René is a good boy. He deserves to marry well."

"But I tell you he means to have Trent's money, as well. When the last partner dies the business goes to the remaining one, me. René means to kill Trent, besides marrying me."

"You are insane," Lady Agatha said. "René needs only to marry you. He does not need Trent's money."

"If you will not stop this to save Trent, consider the possibility that René might be wounded or killed. Anything can happen—"

There was a report, a shot, muffled and ominous. Nothing out of the ordinary, since soldiers from the Horse Guards exercised their mounts here and they were all armed. But it felt like a clap of thunder to Amy's soul. She had a feeling she finally had her revenge on Fenwick.

She swallowed hard. So this was what it felt like to kill a man, even indirectly. It was not a good feeling, but a queasy emptiness.

She shuddered, then reached for the door to leap out, but without the coach even stopping, the door was yanked open and René jumped in. "Well, this is cozy." He stared at her breeches, his sensuous mouth pouting in concentration.

"Did you settle with Wraxton?" Lady Agatha asked.

"Wraxton will not give us away."

Lady Agatha studied René's face intently.

"I think we had better keep Amy with us until arrangements can be made for our marriage," he said in a languid drawl that had so much of the intonation of Lady Agatha that Amy now knew why he pushed his French accent.

"You cannot force me to marry you," she said, standing her ground.

"Without Trent to protect you, you will have to do as Lady Agatha says."

Lady Agatha looked from one to the other of them, with the first look of alarm Amy had ever seen on her face. "René, you are talking nonsense. We will go back to Paris and take her with us. You will not meet Trent again, do you understand?"

René stared uneasily at her. "I challenged him to fight me. I must appear at noon."

"Why?" Amy asked. "After all you have done, honor cannot mean that much to you."

Lady Agatha stared at her, then turned to René. "You will be governed by me, and I say you shall not fight."

Amy shrank back into the corner and glanced at the door as René turned to Lady Agatha and began to argue the point. But he saw that Amy planned to bolt and he grabbed for her, pinning her arms against her sides in a viselike grip and clapping a hand over her mouth.

"What are we going to do now?" Lady Agatha asked.

"I think you may be right. We will carry her out of the country."

"And if she still refuses to marry you?"

"I will persuade her."

Trent strode about the clearing, bare-chested, testing the heft of Draco's sword. "Why did you make it for noon? That is a ridiculous time to meet someone. The authorities are sure to get wind of it."

"I thought you might need the light. And why are you fighting half-naked?"

"Many wounds come from getting someone's blade caught in your clothing. A jacket or shirt offers no real protection anyway."

"How would you know that?"

"One of my ships was boarded by the French off Coruna."

"I did not know you sailed with your ships."

"Sometimes. By the way, if anything should go amiss I left papers with Lester to put Amy's trust in your hands for the next few months."

"She would be mad as fire if she found out about that."

Trent shrugged. "I had to do something."

"Nothing will go wrong," Draco said. "You are better with a sword left-handed than many a man is with his right."

"Let's hope that is a surprise for Crevecoeur. Where the devil is he?" Trent thrust the sword into the scabbard he still wore and went to his discarded shirt and coat to pull out his watch. "It is getting on toward one o'clock. Something must have gone wrong. You do not suppose Amy managed to intervene in some way that delayed him."

"She promised not to interfere," Draco said. "She is safe at Lady Vair's where I took her last night."

"But if Crevecoeur is not here, where is he?" Trent raised his hand to his head and flinched at the pain that shot through his bruised right shoulder.

Trent had a sudden waking vision of the open grave, and snow on the ground. But instead of a child shivering on the other side, or even Amy grown up, there was Amy in boy's clothes. She looked longingly at Trent and he managed to sidestep the grave. Just as he was almost to her she was pulled into the carriage and this time his mother was there looking vindictively out the window.

"Hmm. You may be right," Draco said. "I will ride a little way down the road to see if he is coming."

"No, go to Lady Vair's to check on her. I am convinced she is not there." Trent wrestled with his shirt for a moment before he tossed it aside and plunged his arms into his coat.

"Where do you go?" Draco asked.

Trent untied Flyer and mounted. "To see my mother."

"Like that? Draco demanded, picking up the discarded shirt. "Are you mad?"

"Coward," Amy said as she wrestled her bound hands into a more comfortable position behind her in the carriage seat.

"Do you think I care what you call me?" René asked.

"So you *can* be made angry."

"And it took you to do it, you little fiend." René raised the back of his hand as a threat.

"I hope you are not anticipating wedded bliss with me."

Lady Agatha grabbed his arm and gave it a pinch that made him wince. "Stop it, both of you. Amy, you are far too intelligent and too observant for your own good," Lady Agatha accused.

"Whatever you are planning, it will not work," Amy warned.

René reached across the seat to cup her chin in one hand. "Once I ruin you, I think all objections to our marriage will cease."

Amy stared daggers at him, but realized it was probably not the best moment to reveal her relationship with Trent. She turned to her godmother. "You would let him do this?"

Lady Agatha shifted her gaze from René to Amy. "You could marry him quietly, rather than struggle against the inevitable. It is not as though there is anyone else. You broke off the engagement with Melling."

René smiled wickedly. "And I can bribe enough witnesses to say we are man and wife that you cannot gainsay them. Then it will be the asylum for you."

Amy bit her lip thoughtfully. "That still will not put my fortune in your hands."

"I think Trent will pay handsomely to know you are not chained in a dungeon somewhere." René pulled his sword scabbard out of the way and lounged back in the seat.

"It will be a little inconvenient trying to conduct such a scheme from a continent away," Amy argued.

"We will find an intermediary," Lady Agatha replied.

Amy cocked her head to one side. "Fenwick?"

"We will have to find someone else," René said, causing Lady Agatha's eyes to bulge.

"What is the matter, *ma petite?* No more objections?"

"There is something in what you say," Amy agreed. "If I agree to marry you, can the wedding be as I wish?"

"It is too late for negotiations," René said.

"Too late for a wedding in England, but we could be married in France with no fuss," Amy offered.

"And what do you want?" Lady Agatha asked, her green eyes glittering suspiciously.

"Only that Trent and Draco should be safe. I have caused them both enough pain."

René and Lady Agatha looked at each other, but she answered, "Agreed."

"And I want my mother's jewels and her wedding dress."

"Fripperies can come later," René said, pulling the curtain aside and looking down the road the way they had come.

"No, I want them now. We have to change horses before we get to Portsmouth anyway. We may as well stop at Talltrees for my things. We can get a fresh team there and take the horses with us, have something decent to ride in France. Remind me to have them put my sidesaddle in the carriage. And Cook can feed you while I pack my things."

Lady Agatha looked at her as though she were mad. "You are a managing little thing."

"Well, I have had to be to handle Talltrees all these years."

"If you try anything . . ." the older woman warned.

René lounged back in his seat and pulled a pistol out of his coat pocket. It smelled of spent powder. He proceeded to clean and reload it and Amy managed not to shudder, thinking of Fenwick's fate.

"If she tries anything, I'll start shooting her horses," René said. "Believe me, she will become extremely cooperative."

"Very well," Lady Agatha said. "Have them drive to Talltrees, but do not let her out of your sight while we are there, René."

After finding out from his mother's maid that she had been instructed to have all the trunks packed and transported to Portsmouth, Trent had galloped to Melling

House to meet Draco as agreed. When he got there, Lord Marsh was having Cullen saddled.

Draco shrugged helplessly and said, "Amy is gone and Lady Vair has no idea where. All she could say was that Lady Agatha came looking for her."

"We are headed for Portsmouth," Trent shouted.

"We shall have to change horses somewhere," Lord Marsh warned.

"So will they. If I know my Amy, she will convince them to stop at Talltrees. I trust her to delay them long enough for us to catch up."

They launched from the yard and though Han and Cullen were equally matched, Trent on Flyer outrode them. "See you at Talltrees," he called back as he left them in the dust.

29

❧☙❧

"*M*asters," Amy said, alighting from the carriage with René at her elbow. She rubbed her newly released wrists. "We need fresh horses. Hitch up Talus and Brutus together."

"But, miss," Masters protested as he took in her boy's clothes.

"Do not just stand there," Amy said with a wink. "We are in a hurry. You heard me. I have to get something from the house."

Lady Agatha got out and looked about her. "I would dismiss him if he argues with you." She preceded René and Amy up the walk to the house, inspecting the flower borders critically on her way as though she were going to do something about them.

"I shall have Cook put together a quick luncheon for you," Amy advised. "It will save time if you eat while I get my things."

"See that you do not cost us time," René said. "We only need two horses to get us to Portsmouth."

"Nonsense, René," Lady Agatha chided. "We have to stop somewhere. If not here, then at an inn. Let us go in and have something to eat."

When they got to the house the unflappable Minton gaped at Amy's guests.

"Coffee and tea, Minton, and whatever else that may be got to the table quickly."

Amy scampered up the stairs, fearing for a moment that René meant to follow her. Instead he remained downstairs to berate Minton for being a slow top.

She had engineered the stop with some thought of escaping, perhaps down the trellis. But she had no doubt that René would do exactly as he said. Brutus and Talus were her least favorite horses and they detested each other so much there was no possibility of them pulling a carriage in tandem. But she did not want them shot either. She would just have to comply and ride to Portsmouth with Lady Agatha and René.

Surely Trent would realize what had happened when René did not meet him. He must have discovered their destination and left London no later than three o'clock. It was just getting on toward sunset, the mists starting to rise from the stream and the pond. Nothing had to be resolved now. She would go with them and carry the danger away from Talltrees. If René had disposed of Fenwick as she suspected he would not cavil at shooting Minton, Masters, or even Cook.

Fifteen minutes later Amy came down with a valise and a leather box. René jumped up from the table and came through the open door of the dining room to take the valise.

Lady Agatha rose and strode into the hall. "I will hold that," she said.

"No," Amy said as she struggled for possession of the leather box.

René stepped between them and knocked the box from their hands. What fell out was not jewels, but a pistol and loading kit.

"You little demon," René said, snatching up the pistol. "It is loaded, no doubt. Well, you will get into the carriage now or I will shoot your incompetent serving man."

He snatched up the pistol and handed it to Lady Agatha, then drew his own. "Shoot anyone who tries to stop us. This bullet will be for her if we fail to get away."

"I will go," Amy conceded, ignoring the discarded valise as René grabbed her arm and marched her out the door.

Amy could see the chaos in the stable yard from the garden. Brutus was in the traces but fidgeting, and Talus was baring his teeth and refusing to get anywhere near the other horse.

"What the devil?" René asked.

"They will settle down in a moment," Amy promised.

The thud of hooves on the drive tore their attention away from the incompatible team to a rider on a lathered black horse who looked as though he would career into them.

"Trent!" Lady Agatha wailed.

René raised his pistol, but Amy bucked into him and the shot went wild.

"If I did not need you, I would strangle you where you stand," he whispered viciously in her ear. He drew his sword and laid it across her throat, backing out of the yard and past the exercise fields, dragging her with him.

Amy could see Trent dismount and send the stable boys scattering to cut off René's retreat down the drive and toward the house. Masters released his hold on Talus, who charged Lady Agatha and knocked her down.

"Let Amy go!" Trent shouted to René. "We will let you both leave. Just let her go."

"You little bitch," René said in her ear. "You are coming now or I will throttle you."

Lady Agatha got to her feet, still holding the pistol. "Not that way, you fool. You will be cut off."

"This is all your fault, you witch," René shouted at her.

"I have warned you about losing your head," she said, trailing after them.

When Draco and Lord Marsh rode into the stable yard, as well, René dragged Amy backward through the gate toward the bridgehead, his sword at her throat. She was vaguely aware of the chill in the air, the light fog that would frost the grass by morning. And she wondered if she would live to see it.

"You wanted to meet me," Trent taunted, drawing his sword. "I am here to fight you."

"I mean to kill you, but not until I get you alone."

"Do not fight him, Trent," Amy warned. "He killed your father."

"Stupid girl, you do not know what you are talking about," Lady Agatha said desperately as she struggled after them.

"René was there in the foundry the day your father died, probably trying to get money from him. He is the one who released the chain that brought the cannon down on your father."

Lady Agatha stared, her mouth gaping. "René, is this . . . ?"

"You never loved him," René shouted, dragging Amy backward across the bridge. "You were glad when he died. More money for you, and your freedom."

"Is that what you thought I wanted?"

"You loved me, not your husband. And you love me still, not *his* son."

Suddenly Trent saw it, where the familiarity Amy kept talking about came from. René had not inherited his mother's eyes, but he had her mouth. "So that is what Father meant when he gave me the warning."

"Yes, " Amy said. "He was trying to warn you about *her* son, the one she had in secret with Crevecoeur before her marriage, the one your father would never recognize. René is your half-brother. If not for the similarity of the mouth I would never have suspected."

Lord Marsh said, "That is why her family made her marry your father so quickly."

"I shall kill you!" Crevecoeur screamed as he pushed Amy aside. His first blow was parried by Trent, but bit into the wooden handrail on the bridge, nearly cleaving it in two.

To Amy's surprise Trent wielded his sword in his left hand, parrying René's angry assault as though he did this sort of thing every day.

Lady Agatha still clutched the pistol and was pointing it, though it wavered, as the fight moved from side to side of the bridge. Amy looked about for some weapon in case she might have to intervene. When she could find nothing else she picked up René's discarded scabbard and backed up as the conflict moved across the bridge. Flyer was still dripping sweat and evading the groom, who was trying to catch him. He followed after Trent like a great black dog, holding his head up to keep from stepping on his trailing reins. She hoped he was not going to add his confusion to the tangle. But confusion might be what was needed.

The grooms, previously not knowing whether or not to interfere, were emboldened by the Mellings to draw closer. René must have seen them, for he renewed his attack savagely, like a cornered animal.

Trent backed away from the onslaught, but lost his footing near the edge of the bank and hit his right shoulder on a fall to the ground. Amy gasped as from a prone position he blocked the next attack. She heard the rattle of feet on the bridge as she was about to dive in to deflect René's next blow.

When she gasped and dropped back, René darted a glance around and saw Flyer, teeth barred, charge him. The animal champed down on René's shoulder with his teeth and shook him.

"No!" Lady Agatha screamed. Amy heard a report and saw René go limp in Flyer's teeth. When the horse let go of him, René's weight snapped the wooden rail, dropping him into the rocky stream.

Amy could hear Lady Agatha screaming "No!" over and over as the old woman waded through the icy water to get to her son. Trent scrambled to his feet as Flyer pushed forward to nuzzle him.

"Good boy," Trent said, reaching up to pat the horse's great head. "But I think you and Amy both might have trusted me to take care of Crevecoeur on my own."

Draco and his father were wading out to stop the distraught woman from drowning over René's body.

"I think you might have told me you could fight with your left hand," Amy said, turning her face away from the scene in the stream. She was not sure if the mist that swam before her eyes was from the stream or if she were near to fainting with relief.

"Why did she never tell me about Crevecoeur?" Trent asked as he gazed down at his half-brother. "I would have helped him. I would have been happy to have a brother, even a half-brother."

"I do not think he would have appreciated that," Amy said, throwing an arm around his waist. He felt warm against her, and alive. It might so easily have been otherwise.

"And why did you not tell me all this before?"

"I did not know if it would make you hesitate at the wrong moment or fly into a dangerous rage."

352   *Barbara Miller*

"Always trying to protect me, even from myself, when I am supposed to be your guardian."

"I do not want you for a guardian. I want you for a husband."

He crushed her to him and kissed the top of her head.

She looked at Lord Marsh. "Sorry for all the scandal, but it is Trent for me or no one."

Lord Marsh came to kiss her cheek as Draco carried Lady Agatha to the house. "I am happy to welcome you into my family again, for you must know Trent is as much a son to me as Draco."

They were walking back to the house when an express rider pulled a sweating horse into the stable yard. Amy wondered what new calamity was to befall them.

She cowered against Trent as the groom brought the messenger, but the man handed the letter to Lord Marsh, who broke the seal and scanned the contents with a tired sigh.

"What does it mean?" Trent asked.

"It means we have beaten an express rider here when he has had two changes of horse. Amy's beasts are tireless."

Trent chuckled.

"Oh, you mean the letter?" Lord Marsh scanned it again. "We had thought my daughter sleeping late. As it turns out she has been gone all night. Left a note that she has eloped with Wraxton."

Amy gasped and Trent groaned. "You will need fresh horses, after all."

"I am not going anywhere." Lord Marsh folded the paper and put it into his coat.

"You may yet overtake them before they reach the border."

"No, she has made her bed. Let her lie in it."

* * *

Trent lay on the bed in his room watching Amy disrobe. It seemed an odd thing for her to be doing with the rays of the setting sun breaking through the draperies. The red light shone on her hair. She was wrong. In this light it was most definitely red.

When she got down to her shirt she came to undress him. As she stripped off his rent and bloody coat she said, "I know your mother deserves little consideration from you, but it was unkind to send her on to Bath in her wet clothes. She was shivering with the cold."

"She sent you shivering here all those years ago. If I could have arranged for a blizzard today I would have."

"What will happen to her?"

"Nothing if the magistrate really believes she was trying to shoot the horse."

"Was she, or was she trying to save you from René?"

"Or René from me? I do not think I want to know." He put up a hand to cradle her cheek.

"It was kind of Draco and his father to see to the body and get it to Bath."

"Perhaps they merely wanted us to have some time alone." He stilled her hands as they washed the slight cut on his right arm.

"Yes," Amy agreed. "They have much to discuss. This will give them time."

"I do not think that your assertion that you meant to dress my wound fooled anybody."

"I do not think so, either. Do you mean to hold off from me now just because we are not married yet?"

"No, for we soon will be, that is, unless you mean to be tiresome about the settlements."

"I shall have to consider them, of course," she joked. "Do you think you have shaken your need for control and gotten in touch with your emotions enough to propose like a properly bemused swain?"

Trent hesitated as though trying to remember something. "Yes, I have . . . loved you for an age, but feel unworthy. I cannot live without you and if you refuse me I do not know what I will do. Why, I might put a period to my existence unless I can have you—"

"Enough," she said, stopping his protestations with a kiss. "I believe you."

"And high time. As it is we may already have a child in the works."

Amy laid a hand over her taut stomach with an amused grin.

He got up with no more than a slight groan and stripped off his boots and breeches, then his small clothes. Amy tied a token bandage around the scratch on his arm, then fastened her complete attention on his arousal. As he walked toward her she pulled her boy's shirt over her head and sat on the edge of the high bed.

"You are being very passive all of a sudden," Trent said as he laid her back and bent to nuzzle her breasts, resting his hand between her thighs.

"Why should I not be content?" she asked and gasped at the tricks his tongue was playing with her aroused breasts. "I have everything I want now."

"Everything but your stallion." He kissed her and begged entrance to her sweet mouth with his tongue, but she almost bit him when his fingers excited her other entrance.

"Must we talk of horses now?" she asked, kissing him hungrily and running her hands along his thighs.

"I only meant that now I seem to be more important than a horse to you."

"But I have my stallion."

"What a compliment."

"I did not mean you. Masters informs me that the mares are all refusing Tartar, that they have already been bred."

"How is that possible?"

"Flyer must have done it when he leaped the fence at night. He caught every mare that had already foaled."

"Good Lord. What a rapacious beast."

"And I strongly suspect he has Byerly Turk blood in him, besides the Darly strain from his mother."

"That gives you all three lines; Byerly, Darly and Godolphin."

"I know. So except to go to church, we need never leave this room again."

He poised himself at her entrance. "It is not about possession or control, is it?"

"No," she said as he slid into place with a sigh. Her gasp of pleasure was almost more than he could bear. He wanted to make children with her and raise them, to be with her every waking moment. As he moved in and out, patiently teasing her arousal to the full, he thought for the first time of a future with her as a certainty.

"What is it about, Trent?" she whispered, then gave a whimper of pleasure.

"It is about trust and sharing." He twined his fingers with hers and was silent but for his hard breathing as his rhythmic give and take, his stroking of her keen arousal, occupied all his concentration for a moment. But when she gasped and trembled with pleasure, he relented and released his seed, sighing with the effort. His muscles all felt wonderfully alive and hot. He rolled over onto the bed and gathered her to him.

"You have learned your lessons well."

"You have been a cruel headmistress, to make me seek the truth without telling me the secret."

"Those feelings were always inside you. Even without the Mellings for example, you would have found the capacity to love me."

"But to confess my love is not to admit a weakness, but a strength."

"Yes, together, we are capable of anything."

She nuzzled against his chest as he drew the coverlet over them.

"Sleep," he said. To his amazement nothing hurt anymore, not his flesh nor his heart. All was healed as Amy buoyed him up and joined him in a rest well-deserved and a dream that strummed the chords of his memory like her fingers played over his flesh; Amy in her boys' clothes, Amy at the pianoforte, Amy smiling impishly at him with her tousled mop of auburn hair, Amy riding side by side with him, forever.

Sparkling Regency romance from

BARBARA MILLER

Dearest Max

My Phillipe

Sonnet Books
Published by Pocket Books

3038-01